THE BOOK OF CAIN

HERB CHAPMAN

THE
BOOK OF
CAIN

CARROLL & GRAF PUBLISHERS, INC.
NEW YORK

First Carroll & Graf edition 2001

Carroll & Graf Publishers, Inc.
A Division of Avalon Publishing Group
19 West 21st Street
New York, NY 10010-6805

Library of Congress Cataloging-in-Publication Data is available.
ISBN: 0-7867-0849-2

Manufactured in the United States of America

For Jeanne

acknowledgments

I WISH to thank my friends and sage readers Clay and Kerry Drummond for their generous comments and even more generous support. Stephanie von Hirschberg provided unfailing encouragement, wisdom, patience, and so much more. Stephanie, I'm lucky to have you as my agent and friend. Philip Turner's vision and enthusiasm helped find a much richer and darker heart for this novel, and his thoughtful editing greatly improved its final shape.

I especially want to thank my wife, Jeanne, whose support and sacrifice enabled me to complete this work. I have never received a greater gift.

Finally, I owe a tremendous debt to the extraordinary work and dedication of the pioneers of the Behavioral Sciences Unit. Among the sources to which I am greatly indebted: Ann W. Burgess and John Douglas's *Sexual Homicides: Patterns and Motives,* John Douglas and Mark Olshaker's *Mindhunter* and *The Anatomy of Motive,* and Stephen Michaud and Roy Hazelwood's *The Evil that Men Do.* I am also indebted to Stephen Michaud and Hugh Aynesworth's *Ted Bundy: Conversations with a Killer* and to Wilton Earle for *Final Truth: The Autobiography of Mass Murderer/Serial Killer Donald 'Pee Wee' Gaskins.* All were insightful and disturbing in what they reveal about the darkest manifestations of our nature.

CONTENTS

When God prepares evil for man,
He first damages his mind.
> —Anonymous

He who fights monsters might take care lest he
thereby become a monster. And if you gaze for long
into an abyss, the abyss gazes also into you.
> —Friedrich Nietzsche

THE BOOK OF CAIN

PART ONE

ALICIA OWENS thought it lucky that she was driving through the town of Jeffcoat, rather than on some dark road, when steam began rising from the grill of her red Camaro. To avoid the heavy Saturday night traffic around the strip malls and fast food joints of Jeffcoat's main drag, Alicia had cut through an older part of town, along narrow streets lined by mature trees with sparse traffic, so she felt doubly lucky when she saw a convenience store scarcely a hundred yards ahead. It was an older store, its front crowded with a rack of fat butane tanks, paper machines, and—lucky again—a pay phone near one corner. The only car parked in front was an older station wagon. As Alicia slowed to make the turn, she glanced through the plate glass windows and saw a heavy woman with curly gray hair sitting on a stool behind the counter and figured the wagon belonged to her.

Alicia swung the Camaro into the corner space closest to the phone, her headlights briefly shining along the store's brick sidewall, and Alicia blinked as she thought she saw something move at the back corner. She looked more closely and there was nothing there; it probably had been just some weird reflection caused by her headlights.

Switching off the ignition, Alicia twisted and checked on Jennifer in the backseat; she still slept soundly. Leaning between the bucket seats, Alicia plucked a soft cloth from where she had tucked it in the side of the car seat and wiped some drool from her daughter's mouth. It seemed impossible that Jennifer would soon be a year old. Changing now almost daily, a distinct face had begun to emerge out of her baby fat and her hair was definitely going to be blond, like Alicia's—and Alicia hoped that, unlike her, Jennifer would not have to tease and generously apply hair spray to give her hair body. One thing about Jennifer did not change: she remained an incredibly easy child—just like Alicia's mother said she had been. Soon, she and Alvin planned to start trying for a second child, and Alicia hoped that he or she would be half as easy as Jennifer.

Alicia pushed open the Camaro's door and climbed out into a warm May night, alive with the trilling of cicadas and moths batting around the convenience store's lights. She smoothed the lap of her tan skirt and walked around the front of her car, the plume of steam rising from the grill now barely visible. At the pay phone, Alicia fished in her small purse for a quarter, hoping that her luck held and the phone worked— if so, she might still get to bed at a decent hour. She had stayed at Betty Powell's baby shower later than she had intended. Tomorrow was Mother's Day and after church she and Alvin were having dinner at her parents' and then going to Alvin's parents' for supper, and Alicia wanted to bake cakes tonight to take to each. Oh well, she'd just have to catch up on her sleep tomorrow night.

Thinking of Alvin at home, Alicia again felt a little hurt that he had not gone with her tonight. He had accompanied her to showers when they were dating and during their first year of marriage, for a while any-way. Now, married two years, she thought Alvin watched too much sports on weekends. Alicia kept telling herself that this was one of the adjustments to marriage, and that Alvin was a good and gentle man, and that she really shouldn't complain. But she didn't want them to drift apart; she wanted them to stay close and keep being true best friends like they had been in high school. For a while now, Alicia had thought that they should talk about these things, but she certainly didn't want to start nagging Alvin, she didn't want to become that kind of wife.

Oh well, Alicia told herself, at least this way they weren't stranded together. Alvin could be here in ten minutes—if the pay phone worked. Alicia held her breath, dropped in a quarter, and got a dial tone. On the second ring Alvin picked up. "Alvin, it's Alicia. The damned car's overheating. Will you come and get me? I'm at the Quick Stop on Martin Street."

"Sit tight and I'll be there in just a bit," Alvin said.

"Thanks. See you in a few," she said, and hung up. Alicia started walking back to her car, again feeling a little hurt because before hanging up Alvin hadn't said he loved her, like he had always done when they were dating.

Suddenly, Alicia was startled by a loud thump, like a metal door slamming, which came from somewhere behind the store and was followed by cries of pain. "Oh! My hand! I've crushed my hand! Someone, please help me! Oh, please! Someone, please! Oh, it hurts! Please, help me!"

Alicia stopped and stood frozen, listening to these pleas for help and trying to peer into the dark beyond the store's far corner. The pain in these cries touched her, and the pleas threw her into conflict between feeling uneasy about the dark back there and the indecency of not helping someone who might be badly injured.

Drawn by the pitiful sobbing and moaning and begging, Alicia cautiously eased down a narrow sidewalk toward the back. When she reached the corner, she put her one hand on the rough brick edge and peeked around. Behind the store was an empty parking lot with a large church on the far side, its prominent steeple appearing pale blue in the weak quarter moon's light. Dim streetlights from around the church reflected darkly on the shadowy contours of a large van parked a few feet from where she stood, its rear doors flung open. The injured man's cries drew her attention to a couple of feet behind the van, where she saw his dark hump as he kneeled on the ground. "Oh, God, my hand," he said, and Alicia could tell from the tilt of his shadowed head that he was looking at her. "I've broken my hand. I stayed late to set up the church for tomorrow . . ." He paused, breathing hard like a badly wounded animal, then said in a gush, ". . . and then my van wouldn't start and I was looking for a flashlight and got so frustrated that I slammed the door on my hand. Oh, God it hurts . . . oh, it hurts."

Alicia stepped even with the corner, her hand still touching the brick as if it were a safe base where she could not be tagged, could not be made *it*. But . . . the church, what this man said had happened . . . it all made sense. Yet, she remained unsure what she should do.

"Please, there's a flashlight near the van's door," he pleaded. "Please . . . get it, so I can see how bad it's hurt."

Still, Alicia hesitated.

"Please help, please? Oh, God, I can't move my fingers!"

More on impulse than conscious decision, Alicia hurried to the back of the van, squeezing between the man and the van's opened doors. She felt his shoulder pressed against the back of one leg as she leaned into the van, set down her purse, and began patting the hard metal floor looking for a flashlight. The man's shoulder moved away from her legs, and Alicia sensed a shadow rising up behind her. Surprised, she hesitated before reacting, and in that barest moment a hand roughly slapped something sticky over her mouth and the man's other hand thrust something inches from her face, the weak light darkly glinting off a large knife that he showed her for a half second before pressing it under her chin.

"If you don't do exactly what I say, I'll slice up your face," he hissed in her ear. "Go along and you won't get hurt."

His lips then brushed her earlobe and Alicia stiffened, trying to think, but unable to get beyond a repeated thought that this could not be happening, that it had to be a joke, that at any minute he was going to say ha, ha, I fooled you. Sorry that I scared you.

In the same breath, rival thoughts began to take half-shape: she needed to get away or scream or do something to stop this, because it wasn't a joke, it was really happening. But the hand over her mouth was pushing something sticky onto her skin and suddenly the knife was shifted and the side of its cool blade pressed against her cheek.

"It's razor sharp," he whispered, so close the tiny hair follicles in her ear tingled.

Panic rose, Alicia tensed. Then she realized that there was nothing she could do, and she felt herself go limp and small sobs shook her body. The man lewdly pushed his hips against hers and buried his face in her hair, and she heard him breathe in. With sudden violence, he pushed her hard into the van, driving her further and further inside, then shoving her against the metal floor, bruising her and climbing onto her, his knees straddling her and the weight of him sitting on her ribs and chest making it hard to breathe. He grabbed first one wrist and then the other, snapping something cold and metallic around each.

He then climbed off her and was gone and Alicia briefly felt tremendous relief. Even as he wrapped tape around her ankles, she felt relief and told herself that if she went along and endured the inevitable and didn't anger this man, then it would soon be over and she could go home and be with Alvin and Jennifer and that she would eventually get back her life by being around people she loved.

The rear doors slammed shut, causing Alicia to jump and feel panicked anew. Lying now on the cold metal floor in almost total darkness, she again thought that this could not be happening, that it just couldn't. The man climbed into the front seat and started the engine. Alicia twisted so that she could see the back of his head, a dark outline against the weak light beyond the windshield. It seemed impossible that any human could so willfully cause another person to suffer. How could he bear to do something like this, Alicia wondered. What kind of man could do such a horrible thing?

1

silhouette

I

AT THE Communications Center, John Keenan collected the case materials that had arrived overnight, then hurried down the stairwell to the basement warrens that housed Behavioral Science. He liked the focused quiet of Saturday mornings—a few minutes past seven A.M. to be exact—when the FBI Academy Building's halls were empty and the telephones mute.

As was his way, Keenan exited the stairwell walking as if he were about to burst into someone's office to make demands. The straight-ahead energy of his walk was one of the first things others noted about him. Another was his size. He was somewhat over six foot three, and appeared to be as broad and solid as a park statue. He usually wore traditional G-man dark suits of gray, black, or navy blue with a good cut and of durable fabric, though he eschewed the status brands. Today, he had on black slacks, a white shirt, and, his only concession to it being the weekend, a navy blue windbreaker rather than a coat and tie. Coarse dark hair framed a broad face that was undistinguished except for eyes that seemed recessed a bit too far and whose eagle-like fierceness often made others uneasy when Keenan turned his full attention on them. Nothing in his demeanor invited others to tell jokes or chitchat before getting to the point.

Keenan unlocked his office and a wave of cold air engulfed him— long ago, he had jimmied the protective cover and reset the thermostat to its coldest setting. Rather than use the overhead lights, Keenan switched on the halogen lamp on his desk, dimly illuminating the disarray of his office. Files, journals, and technical manuals were jammed in bookshelves, stacked on cabinets, or piled on the floor. A methodical man, Keenan could retrieve any given material within moments. Always racing too many deadlines, he had found it more efficient to pile than file.

He tossed the case file onto his oversized desk, then shut the door and dropped his windbreaker across files stacked in a chair beside his desk. Years ago, he had commandeered this office because it was roomy and had it's own closet-sized bathroom, where he now drew water for a pot of coffee, brewing it this morning for extra jolt. He had awakened before seven as he did every morning, surging with restless energy as if someone had shot amphetamines directly into a vein, and this vigor generally stayed with him at least through midday. Today, though, he felt charged as usual, but not particularly sharp. It had been a demanding week.

Keenan had spent Monday through Thursday in Huntsville, Texas, meeting during afternoons and evenings with Elgin Cordell prior to Cordell's scheduled Thursday night execution. The condemned man had opened up to Keenan about his life and crimes and said he felt a rare bond with Keenan. Cordell had asked Keenan to attend his execution, said it would give him some comfort. But Keenan's work was done, so he flew home instead, arriving at his residence in an Alexandria, Virginia, suburb at a little past midnight. Yesterday, he had put in twelve hours reviewing tapes of his interviews with Cordell and completing his profiling report on the recently deceased man.

Then, before he could get way from the office last night, Keenan fielded a call for assistance from South Carolina. Yesterday, the bodies of three women in varying stages of decay had been discovered hidden in a ravine. A task force hunting what had been dubbed the Saluda Woods Killer would convene tomorrow. Keenan had come in early this morning because he planned to be at that meeting, ready to present a profile of the killer.

As Senior Profiler, Keenan could have assigned this case to someone else. His department had added two positions a couple of years ago and another this spring. He no longer needed to work seven days a week and could have let this tough deadline swallow a younger agent's weekend. But most of the other agents had families, while he lived alone, and Susan Chen, whom Keenan had been seeing regularly now for several months, was at a conference in Chicago. Plus, Keenan still held on to the tougher cases, and this one looked tough—they had very little to go on and a killer who, in all likelihood, would not stop.

Before the coffee finished brewing, Keenan poured a cup, settled at his desk, and took a deep breath, as if readying himself to plunge into icy water. He then opened the case file.

First, he ordered the material chronologically and, after doing this, lay aside everything except the two Missing Persons Reports—there were only two because the skeletal remains of the initial victim had yet to be identified. Keenan always began by studying the victims. Where were they and what were they doing when they disappeared? What was their personality? How might they react to a threat? The more he knew of the victims, the more he would know about why they were targeted and what the killer had done to take possession of them.

Attached to the Missing Persons Report of the second victim was a professionally done photograph of a thin-faced woman with short, light brown hair and frugally applied makeup. Her blouse was buttoned at the collar and she wore a cameo brooch on her jacket lapel. Keenan thought she looked like a cautious woman. The information at the top of the report identified her as thirty-eight-year-old Cindy Mahoney. She had worked as a secretary for a realty company, was recently divorced, and her sixteen-year-old son, Danny, lived with her.

At a little past midnight on Saturday, April 11, Cindy Mahoney was last seen leaving a company party at Marlene's, a nightclub in northeast Columbia. According to a friend, she turned down a co-worker's offer to escort her to her car because he had had too much to drink and she did not want a married man coming on to her—like her ex-husband had done so often with other women. The next morning, Cindy Mahoney's son reported her missing, insisting that she would never stay out all night. Told he would have to wait twenty-four hours to file a report, he and an uncle conducted their own search and found her white Taurus parked near the rear exit of Marlene's overflow parking area. The keys were in the door.

Keenan thought it highly unlikely that Cindy Mahoney would willingly get into a car with a stranger. She sounded like a vigilant woman who would not be easily approached for a blitz-type assault. If she did not know her killer prior to this evening, which being the second victim he thought most likely the case, then the killer probably had lured her into a vulnerable position—and the most common ploy for doing that was by feigning injury or disability.

In a city of Columbia's size, her disappearance would have gotten fair media coverage. People would become more cautious, more wary of strangers. How the killer adapted to the added vigilance would say a lot about his character—how bold is he, how resourceful, how determined.

The other victim thus far identified was twenty-one-year-old Alicia Owens. Her photo showed a smiling, fair-complexioned, girl-next-door type with teased blonde hair. She had been married and had an eleven-month-old daughter, Jennifer. On Saturday, May 9, Alicia Owens had gone to a baby shower while her husband, Alvin, stayed home to watch a Braves game. At approximately ten P.M., she called her husband from a convenience store in Jeffcoat because her car had overheated.

Keenan scanned several pictures of an older Quick Stop, its front crowded with newspaper machines, an ice machine, a rack of butane tanks, a yellow air pump, and a red Camaro parked near a pay phone on the store's far left. A yellow ribbon cordoned car, phone, and the side of the building.

When Alvin Owens had arrived at this store, he found Jennifer asleep in the car seat and Alicia gone. Behind the store was a church parking lot that exited onto the next street. In this lot, about eight feet from the store's corner, police found a custom-made gold earring belonging to Alicia that was in the shape of a dolphin and matched a pendant of the same design. The killer had definitely lured her to him. And he had slipped under the increased vigilance by taking a low-risk victim—someone unlikely to become a victim of such a crime, as opposed to a high-risk victim such as a prostitute—and he had abducted his victim in a setting that posed high risk for him.

On a yellow legal pad, Keenan wrote South Carolina and today's date, May 16, at the top. Then, in bold, block letters, he wrote "Organized" and underlined it twice. The abductions were well planned and the killer transported and hid the bodies, which classified him as an Organized Type Serial Killer. Organized Killers were usually average or above intellectually, and socially competent enough to make a good impression during casual contact. They were the Ted Bundy's and John Wayne Gacy's who live and work among us hidden by a *mask of normalcy*.

On the legal pad, Keenan also wrote:

> —bold but not reckless
> —shows a lot of self-control > probably late twenties to early thirties
> —lures victim to him > uses deception
>   > probably feigns injury or disability
> —shrewd choice of setting > had canvassed prior to abduction
>   >question those in area for earlier suspicious
>   sightings
> —probably used weapon to subdue victim
> —drives late model car that keeps in good condition > possibly van or RV

When Keenan had studied all the detailed background information collected during the Missing Persons Investigations, he turned his attention to the statement of Andrew Scalaro, the man who discovered the bodies. A community college psychology instructor, Scalaro said that he was taking a Friday afternoon walk in the Saluda Woods with his dog, who, attracted by the rancid odor, led him into the ravine, where he saw the bodies hidden in a cavity formed by three boulders wedged together. Scalaro's story sounded plausible and there was evidence that he had puked, as he said he had, after seeing the victims' remains. Yet, Keenan could name a half dozen cases where a predator had thrust himself into the middle of an investigation by using such ploys as reporting the discovery of bodies—Scalaro should be quietly checked out.

. . .

At a quarter of eleven, the first forensic report arrived from the lab of the South Carolina Law Enforcement Division, SLED for short, and Keenan's mood became even grimmer. Cindy Mahoney's remains had been too decomposed for forensics to find much, but Alicia Owens had not been dead very long. The report indicated that her body had been cleaned with a weak bleach solution, including her lower intestines, which were otherwise empty. There was a conspicuous absence of fiber or other tissue matter on her body and Dr. Goldstein, the head of SLED's forensic lab, believed this could only have been achieved by cleaning the bodies while wearing protective apparel such as hair nets and rubber gloves, and then wrapping the body in plastic for transport to the dumping site.

Toxicology found measurable amounts of strychnine, diazepam, and charcoal emulsion in Alicia Owens's stomach. As a result of finding strychnine, further analysis revealed multiple small fiber tears, depleted levels of adenosine triphosphate, and elevated lactic acid. There were also multiple tears in the tendons, ligaments, and fascia. Alicia Owens had been critically poisoned with strychnine and then given the standard treatment of diazepam and charcoal emulsion.

Keenan added details to the silhouette taking shape on his pad:

> —methodically cleans the bodies > knows how evidence is collected
> > possibly some law enforcement background
> > neat in dress and appearance
> —knows strychnine treatment > possible EMT or other medical training
> —has secure place he takes victims > probably lives alone
> —use of poison to create muscle spasms for ritualized sexual assault???

By noon, a crick had formed in Keenan's neck that felt as unyielding as knotted tungsten. He pushed back from his desk, stood, and slowly rotated his head as far as he could against the grabbing tightness. Minutes earlier, a clerk had brought down the faxed autopsy report on Alicia Owens.

When Keenan had done as much as he could for his neck, he sat and began reading the autopsy and immediately saw this killer's signature. The things a criminal does in order to carry out a crime constitute his modus operandi, or MO. An Organized Killer's MO is intended to enable him to take control of a victim while avoiding detection and arrest, and his methods will change to accommodate differing circumstances and as the criminal learns from experience. The *signature* refers to what the criminal does to satisfy himself. The signature comes directly out of his motives for committing a specific crime and does not change from victim to victim. Keenan wrote "Sadist" on his pad and put a check in front of his guess about ritualized sexual assault.

Before he could add more notes, the communications officer buzzed through a call from the Sheriff of Jeffcoat County, where the Saluda Woods victims had been found.

"Mr. Keenan, this is Arnold Inabinet. Anything for us yet?" said the sheriff, who had a pronounced drawl.

"When you get an ID on the first victim you may want to carefully rework her abduction. It's iffy, but sometimes there's a connection between the killer and his initial victim. Also, this guy Scalaro should be checked out."

"Scalaro's wife says he was definitely home on the night the Owens girl was abducted, so he doesn't look too promising. And we made an ID on the initial victim from dental records a little while ago. A prostitute. We'll get the information to you soon." Inabinet briefly paused. "Mr. Keenan, if my information is correct, I understand you know a SLED officer named Will Paxton fairly well. I'm calling because I'd like your opinion of his capabilities."

The question, though unexpected, was easy to answer. Will Paxton was a young officer with SLED, and the opportunity actually to work a case with Will had been an added incentive for Keenan to take this case. Keenan had first met Will two years ago while on an instructional rotation for the FBI's National Academy Police Training, and Will came to Quantico as one of the younger officers accepted for this demanding training. Afterward, Keenan served as consultant when Will revised SLED's protocols for hunting a serial predator, and they jointly published these new guidelines in the FBI *Law Enforcement Bulletin*. Impressed by Will's initiative and skills, Keenan had written SLED's Chief, Carl Jones, to recommend that Will become SLED's liaison with Keenan's department, which Will had been for the past year.

"Paxton's competent, methodical, honest, communicates well," Keenan told Inabinet. "He's a good man."

"What about toughness?" Inabinet asked and without waiting for a reply elaborated. "Here's my dilemma. As you know, the bodies were found in my jurisdiction, so I'm primary. But there were abductions in two other jurisdictions, so this is going to be a multi-jurisdictional investigation. The other chiefs and I are going to head this thing, but we need somebody running the day-to-day investigation. You know, someone to turn our priorities into daily assignments, make sure everyone gets all the information as it comes in, and to coordinate with agencies like yours, that sort of thing. The legislature has determined that coordinating across jurisdictions is to be done by SLED."

"And you're considering Will," Keenan said.

"That's right. I think young Paxton did a hell of a job developing guidelines for this type of investigation. He came over and reviewed them with my senior investigators last winter. I like the way he thinks this kind of investigation should be run. And like you said, he communicates well. But he's what . . . in his late twenties and never been through anything like this, so I don't know if he can stand the heat.

"Now, there's another fellow at SLED named Martin Stith, who was in my department the last time we had a case like this. He's also gone through Academy Training. He has a take charge temperament and he's tough; no doubt he could handle the pressure. And he has rank over Paxton. But he's . . . not very diplomatic, tends to rub people the wrong way.

"Of the people I know at SLED, they're the two most qualified. I'm sure there are others, and Chief Jones may have someone else in mind, but I'd rather not have an unknown. So of the two, I think Paxton more likely to run things the way I want them run, if he can take it. I'd like your opinion."

Keenan thought Will had more than earned a chance to prove himself. "I completely agree with your assessment of Paxton's qualifications," Keenan answered. "He's prepared himself to do this job, emotionally as well as technically. I think he can handle it."

"Better know he can handle it."

"He can," Keenan answered, though he knew that it would take a little more chaffing for Will's skin to sufficiently thicken. But he believed Will had the intelligence and determination to handle the pressure. And, since Keenan had already assigned himself this case, he could remain in close enough contact to coach Will through the rough places.

II

Later that evening, Keenan was still in his office, dog-tired and pushing to complete the profile before flying to South Carolina tomorrow morning. At a little past eight, Will called to get Keenan's itinerary so he could have someone meet him at the airport, then said that he had been selected as Task Force Coordinator. Keenan did not mention Inabinet's call, but they talked for almost thirty minutes about how Will should approach his new duties.

2
_____

a b o m i n a t i o n

I

THE LARGE meeting room of the South Carolina Law Enforcement Division Headquarters could comfortably accommodate forty persons. Keenan had never before been in this room, yet everything about it seemed familiar. Small clusters of mostly men dressed in off-the-rack suits stood in back near the coffee urns and doughnuts. Thick case folders lay on the tables, a slide projector squatted on a tall roll cart behind the last row, and a narrow podium stood in front beside a lowered screen.

As three o'clock neared, everyone began drifting to their seats. Keenan settled in the first row on the far left with a Styrofoam cup of burnt-tasting coffee. Beside him sat SLED's amiable medical examiner, Orin Hatcher, a pudgy, red-faced man with thinning silver hair and dressed in a pale blue seersucker suit. Three years earlier, Hatcher had been in one of Keenan's classes when he had attended the National Academy Police Training at Quantico.

"At the risk of sounding rude," Hatcher said, in a voice reminiscent of old South aristocracy, "your classes on psychological profiling were highly disturbing. I have examined mangled bodies with utter detachment, Mr. Keenan, but I wish you had not shown us the video made by those two thugs in Colorado."

"You mean Nunez and Van Owen?" Keenan said. Charles Nunez and Fletcher Van Owen were a pair of serial killers who had lured victims to their wilderness cabin with ads for cheap electronic equipment. Once there, the victims were tortured and raped over several days, and when couples were involved each was forced to watch his or her partner's suffering. The killers videotaped everything and sold the copies on the shadowy snuff-film market. Van Owen died resisting arrest, but Nunez escaped and remained at large. "I believe every time I've used that tape, I've only shown a few seconds," Keenan said.

"A few seconds too many," Hatcher replied. "For weeks afterwards, those images appeared in my dreams, as you predicted they would. Now, it seems we have something just as bad here."

Keenan thought it important to confront law officers with the unwatchable savagery of the men they hunted. He wanted them to leave his class haunted and driven. Though he kept the exposure short, never more than a brief segment or two, he knew most would have nightmares, just as he had nightmares when he first joined Ben Lockhart's Behavioral Science Unit. For a while after going to work for Lockhart, Keenan thought he had made a terrible mistake, thought he could never purge images of torment and assault from his every waking and sleeping moment. In time his distress subsided, not because he had gotten used to these images or learned to purge them, but because his outrage became greater than his revulsion. He channeled his outrage into single-minded determination to solve each crime's puzzle, his emotions walled behind a discipline so tight that any strong feelings felt as dangerous as a crack in an overburdened levee.

. . .

At exactly three o'clock, Sheriff Inabinet walked slowly to the front of the room, frowned at the forty or so persons crowded inside, and drawled, "Y'all know why we're here." Inabinet carried at least thirty pounds more than even a lenient weight chart would advise and his face bore the weathered creases of someone who had come up through the patrol ranks. He was bald, and there was a sharp contrast between the seasoned tan of Inabinet's face and the white scalp above his cap line.

"We're going over everything today," Inabinet said. "At eight tomorrow morning, the core members of this task force are going to meet and go over everything again. And every Monday until we stop this son of a bitch, we'll meet and go over everything again." Frowning, Inabinet's eyes swept the room. "We've asked division leaders from each jurisdiction to be here today because they're going to be providing extensive support. Now, if any of my men fail to give less than one hundred percent cooperation to anyone on this task force, regardless of jurisdiction, they'll be walking the hot cement writing parking tickets when the temperature hits a hundred in August. And I think Chief Wolcott and Sheriff Barnett feel the same way. Is that clear?" Inabinet again frowned and slowly surveyed the room.

"Awright," Inabinet drawled. "Will Paxton will be coordinating the day-to-day details of this investigation. He's going to start the review and later we'll bring up some technical experts."

With a slight nod, Inabinet moved to the back of the room and Will walked to the small podium, the shirt of his dark blue uniform riding up in back the way Keenan had noticed it tended to do. Will's tanned face was round, which caused him to appear pudgy—though he was not—and to look younger than twenty-eight. A pencil-thin mustache matched the black color of his short hair.

Will signaled for the lights to be lowered and activated the slide projector. On the screen appeared a police mug shot, front and profile, of a moderately obese woman with stringy hair and pocked skin. Will did not seem hurried and this pleased Keenan.

"As far as we know," Will began, "there have been three abductions. Betty Reeves was the first victim. Though Betty Reeves is the name on her driver's license, she also used several street names including Betty Reed, Angel Reed, and recently Angel Rivera. Her police jacket lists her age as thirty-five and details six arrests—four for prostitution, one disorderly conduct, and a bust for possession of crack for which she served eight months of a two-year sentence at the Women's Correctional Institute.

"At around nine P.M., Saturday, February 8th, Reeves was last seen soliciting on Two Notch Road near the Hilltop Motel, where she rented a room for one hundred dollars a week." In rapid succession, Will flipped through several slides of a broad street crowded by wooden electrical poles and the worn facades of businesses that were already third tier when built four decades earlier. Among the seediest was the eighteen-unit Hilltop Motel, its sign badly faded, the driveway steep, the parking area narrow, and its nearest neighbor an adult bookstore.

"Eight days after Betty Reeves disappeared the motel manager, Kyle Stedge, filed a Missing Persons Report. Stedge said he thought she had left town on a whim because her kind do that all the time, and he was only filing the report so he could legally clear out her belongings and re-rent the room. There was no follow-up investigation."

Orin Hatcher leaned close and whispered, "She was probably forgotten before the ink dried on the report."

Keenan nodded and breathed out, suddenly aware that he had tightened a little. He had boosted Will into the coordinator's position and, therefore, felt a greater than normal investment in how well the young officer did, sort of like a parent whose child stands alone before an audience. It pleased him that Will had started well, focusing on the facts of the case without conjecture. Considering that most of these officers had years more experience than Will, it was the smart play—and exactly what Keenan had advised during Will's call to him last night.

As Will continued moving competently through his presentation, Keenan noted only one small tic in his composure. When the smiling picture of Alicia Owens lit the screen, Will paused briefly. Keenan would not have noticed except that last night Will told him that Alicia's husband, Alvin, had been in his high school class. Will said that he and Alvin weren't buddies or anything, but that he liked Alvin and thought him a decent guy. He also told Keenan that Alvin was torn up with guilt because he was watching a Braves game that had reached the bottom of the ninth when Alicia called to tell him she had car trouble, and Alvin had watched the rest of the inning before leaving to get her.

After Will reviewed the victims and what was known of their abductions, he ended his presentation with the location of the bodies. First came an aerial photo of a wooded area, bordered on the east by sprawling residential communities and the west by the Saluda River. "The area of the Saluda Woods where the victims were found is away from commonly traveled paths," Will said. "The bodies were extremely well hidden in a cavity formed by boulders wedged together at the bottom of a steep ravine."

Then, the only sound came from the clicking of the slide tray as half-second images of the victim's bodies, from every imaginable angle, flashed on the screen. Betty Reeves' skeleton lay with its back on the ground, the bones of her legs fallen to either side from where she had initially been posed, probably with her legs spread. Cindy Mahoney's raggedly decomposed remains lay on top of Reeves with her head positioned in the prior victim's crotch. The body of Alicia

Owens lay atop the others, her back down, legs spread, her pale skin almost translucent except for her left side, which had turned purple.

When the screen went blank, Will simply said, "Later, Special Agent Keenan will comment on the positioning of the bodies."

II

Orin Hatcher's turn to present came and he walked unhurriedly to the podium, laid a manila folder upon it, then paused to scan the dimly lit faces. "Because the first two victims were so badly decomposed," Hatcher began, his enunciation precise, "identification was made from dental records, and these bodies could only tell us a few things, the most notable being that each had an index finger cut off prior to death but not long enough for substantial healing to occur. The first victim also had her nose and left jaw broken. We found tears in the tendons connecting muscle to bone in the second victim, but the first was too decomposed to ascertain if she experienced similar trauma." Hatcher paused, and even in the dimmed light his face looked red and slightly moist.

"Time of death can only be estimated to have occurred within two to three weeks of their disappearance. It is probable, however, that their fate was similar to the last victim and death occurred within a few hours to a few days after abduction. I cannot definitively determine cause of death, but considering the connective tissue tears, my opinion is strychnine poisoning.

"The last victim was well preserved and able to tell us quite a bit." The screen filled with a close-up of a pale bruised wrist; a picture that seemed strangely drained of color. "As you can see from the slides, she had severe bruising on both wrists . . . and ankles." The image on the screen changed. "This bruising is consistent with prolonged use of hard restraints. And in this blowup . . . you can see the expected double indentations caused by handcuffs. She also had bruises on the left side of her face . . . two on her back . . . and a bite mark on her buttocks. Unlike the first two victims, all appendages were intact.

"There were tears of the anal sphincter consistent with anal sexual assault prior to death. We did not find any vaginal tearing. From Dr. Goldstein's findings of depleted ATP and elevated lactic acid, I am fairly certain that rigor mortis occurred immediately upon death, which is consistent with strychnine poisoning. It is my opinion that strychnine poisoning was the primary cause of death. Acute symptoms of strychnine poisoning are convulsions followed by progressively severe spasms, often with the victim violently jackknifing. These spasms often cause tears in the muscles, fasciae, and tendons. Given the anal tearing, I believe he assaulted that poor girl while she was in spasm," Hatcher said. Anger was in his voice.

Hatcher took a deep breath before continuing. "Dr. Goldstein also found diazepam and charcoal in her stomach. Along with pure oxygen, these are used in the standard treatment for strychnine poisoning. Based on the varied stages of healing in the muscle tears, it is my opinion that, over a period of three or four days, he poisoned her to full tonus, then revived her at least twice prior to the fatal incident.

"I want you men and women to know what that young girl went through," Hatcher said, his face now bright red. "Each of you know how much a single cramp can hurt. At times, that girl's whole body was in spasm. Her suffering must have been unbearable."

. . .

Orin Hatcher seemed aged as he returned to his seat beside Keenan. The lights came up and from the back of the room, Inabinet said, "We've been going at it for a while. Let's take a fifteen-minute break, then Mr. Keenan is going to tell us what kind of man did these things and why. Fifteen minutes, no longer."

Before Keenan could head for the bathroom, Hatcher looked at him, his eyes red-rimmed, and said, "It is most peculiar, Mr. Keenan. I did the autopsy, dictated my report, and somehow managed to block out the full horror of what happened to that young woman until I had to describe it publicly. My God, she was three years younger than my baby girl." Hatcher shook his head, then said quietly, "Years ago, a friend who was at the liberation of Dachau posed a question to me, which at the time I dismissed because I believed that the experience had left him so distraught. He asked how a loving God could allow such abominations. Well, Mr. Keenan, I would also like that question answered."

III

The lights remained up as Keenan, the last to present, walked unhurriedly to the front of the room. He wore a dark blue suit with a maroon, striped tie, and carried a folded list of one-word prompts that he would consult at the end of his presentation to make sure that he had not omitted some key detail. Keenan stepped away from the podium, moving closer to where the seasoned detectives watched with hard faces. When he spoke, his voice carried easily, yet sounded conversational.

"If you answer a homicide call, and find a male sprawled atop broken dishes with a butcher knife in his gut and no other wounds, you know what happened because the crime scene tells you the whole story," Keenan said, beginning his usual introduction to profiling. "One look at that kitchen and you have a clear image of the argument starting and escalating. You know the victim probably used his size to intimidate his wife or girlfriend and, as he closed in, she stabbed him. You also know that if you come across as understanding and question her while she's emotional, she'll probably tell you exactly how it happened. You know these things because you've seen this crime scene again and again.

"Fortunately, you don't often see the type of crime we're dealing with today. But the psychological profile is developed in the same way. The crime scene and evidence tell us specific things this killer did and we compare his actions to others who have committed similar crimes. We've now conducted detailed studies on well over a hundred and fifty incarcerated serial killers. These studies are the experience from which we draw our conclusions.

"But I want you to keep in mind that the characteristics we identify in a profile are only probabilities. For example," Keenan said, "we are probably looking for a white male because, with ritualized sexual assaults, victim and perpetrator are usually of the same race. We are probably looking for a right-handed man because the left side of the first victim's jaw was broken. We are probably looking for someone who is fit and strong because there are no signs that he dragged or carted the bodies to the ravine, he carried them." With each point he made a small slashing gesture. "Based on his careful attention to detail, we are probably looking for someone who is neat in both grooming and dress. But these are only probabilities. Each killer will be unique in some ways, so some items will not fit him. If someone does not exactly match the profile but the evidence looks good, go with it; good investigative work is what will catch this guy."

Keenan paused to allow the commonsense basis of what he had said thus far to sink in. He always began with things that the good detectives had already figured out, because he most wanted to reach the good detectives, who are by nature both skeptical and curious. Keenan was an outsider from a slightly different orientation. For these investigators to seriously consider the psychological profile, he had to earn credibility. To this end, he kept his body language open and emphatic, and based every proposed attribute on solid evidence—if questioned on any point, he could give concrete reasons.

When no one commented, or challenged him, Keenan continued. "There are no matching crimes in the VICAP database, so it is likely that this guy is just beginning to hunt and kill. He shows a lot of control, so he is probably in his late twenties to early thirties. But he has been thinking about killing for years and probably worked up his courage by doing things like voyeurism, rape, or arson. Keep checking files of sex offenders and red flag any that contain reports of anal assault or cruelty to animals.

"The abductions are well planned. He transported and hid the bodies after death. These traits make him what we call an Organized Type. He will have average or above intelligence and be socially competent enough to make a good impression during casual contact. When you investigate him, acquaintances aren't going to point fingers and say, 'This guy is weird.' And when you arrest him, those who know him will not believe it at first.

"Organized offenders are usually employed, often in skilled jobs, though they have a history of underachievement. His understanding of strychnine treatment may have come from EMT training, military medical corps, or hospital employment. And he was able to eliminate so much forensic evidence not because he's lucky, but because he knows what we look for and how we go about getting it. This guy has studied the same books on forensic recovery that you have, so he could also have some type of law enforcement background."

As he expected, murmurs and rustling movement swelled and Keenan waited for the noise to subside before continuing. "While Organized offenders are often involved in relatively stable relationships, this guy keeps his victims for several days, so he probably lives alone. If he is living with a partner, he'll have a weekend house, rental property, or some other place that affords absolute privacy."

A black man in a gray pinstripe suit casually raised his hand, index finger extended. "I've read about cases where these guys somehow hook up with a partner," the officer said. "Could we be looking for two people?"

"I don't think that's very likely," Keenan answered, moving a couple steps to his right to stand in front of the questioner. "When two killers are involved, each has things he wants to do, so we usually see more than one type of assault. In this case, we see only one very specific type of assault. It's unlikely that two killers would be driven by such a singular desire. Also, the killer possesses his victims over several days and probably believes he's creating some type of intimacy, so a second person would be an unwanted intrusion."

"All right," the officer nodded, then gestured with a finger extended, "but what about this? Considering how he assaults them, what about a passive homosexual partner?"

"I think that's even less likely," Keenan answered. "True, he only assaults the victims anally, but what's he after?" Keenan paused. "Basically, he hates women and wants to make them pay by doing the worst thing he can imagine being done to anyone, including himself. We've identified childhood sexual abuse in approximately a third of the serial killers we've studied, but I promise you the true incidence is much higher. I've seen studies of adolescent sex offenders that report as many as 70 to 80 percent of them have been sexually victimized. I believe this figure is an underestimate because so much shame surrounds their own abuse that perpetrators usually find it much easier to tell us about the horrible things that they have done to others, than to admit their own traumas. That's why I think the anal assaults are significant and why our man is more likely to be a gay basher than gay."

The officer again nodded. "That makes sense."

Keenan paused to see if anyone else had questions or comments. A light sheen of sweat had formed on his forehead. In a smaller, less formal group he would shed his jacket. When no one else spoke up, he resumed his presentation. "To prolong the murder high, the killer keeps a memento of each kill. This will be something he can look at or touch to boost the potency of his memories, like underwear, a snippet of hair, or jewelry. Cindy Mahoney was wearing a herringbone necklace and bracelet. Alicia Owens a dolphin-shaped gold pendant with a diamond for an eye. He may have kept these or given them to someone—such gifts are often used to indirectly express anger. The pendant was custom-made, so you may want to make this public and ask anyone seeing it to contact you immediately.

"He possesses the victims for several days so it is highly probable that he is photographing or, more likely, videotaping what he does to them. Be sure to specify these things in your search warrants and take every tape regardless of how it's labeled or what's on the first few minutes. He also may have kept the fingers of the first two victims, so specify this in your warrant and take everything in the freezer, even if it looks like prepackaged collard greens."

As Keenan paused to allow this to register, an officer who sat slouched in the second row with his arms crossed over his chest asked in a gravelly voice, "Do you think the killer knew Betty Reeves?"

The man had the chest of a linebacker and hair the color of dark honey that he combed straight back. Keenan had noticed him earlier, partly because of a red welt of a scar that ran from below his left eye to the bottom of his chin. He had also noticed him because of his posture and facial expression, and figured he was either one of those cops who thought profilers no better than shamans and psychics, or one bitten by resentment at how the media showered golden attention onto Behavioral Sciences. To a cop who had just spent eighteen hours checking and rechecking dead-end leads, the attention paid Fed glamour boys, who waltz in and then go have dinner with their families, rubbed like a raw deal. And most detectives thought Fed hotshots took more credit than they deserved while dodging the failures. On this issue, Keenan sided with the detectives, who he believed carried a much heavier front-line burden than technical experts like him.

As he had done earlier, Keenan shifted to stand in front of the questioner. "No, I don't think the killer knew Reeves," he answered and waited, figuring the man had more he wanted to say.

"Then why did you recommend we commit so many men to reworking the Reeves abduction? We have half a dozen detectives talking to every employee of every seedy business on Two Notch Road. Next, we're going to question every john picked up in the past nine months. All because you said there was a chance the perp knew Reeves. So what exactly are you saying?"

"Think about it," Keenan said evenly. "If you wanted to begin abducting and killing, where would you start?"

"Probably with someone who wasted my goddamned time," the officer said, drawing muffled laughter.

"So would I," Keenan agreed. Long ago, he had disciplined himself to stay calm when challenged; few things can undermine credibility as quickly as getting defensive. "But if you had a general desire to kill," Keenan said, "and you were a little nervous about it, you'd probably start in a place where you had seen someone and thought 'I could take her.' This guy has sat in the dark somewhere on Two Notch and saw how easy it could be. Maybe he went there as a john, or maybe, just maybe, something else connects him. Betty Reeves was his first victim because she was a prostitute and prostitutes make easy victims, but she was also his first victim because of where she hustled. After her, he felt bolder, expanded his hunting ground, and went after the women he really wanted. So far, Two Notch is our best shot at finding some link to this guy, and I know that's not great news."

For a moment the two men stared at each other. When it became apparent the man had nothing more to say, at least for now, Keenan looked away and continued.

"I want to wrap up by addressing the killer's mental state. The man you're looking for is a loser who believes he has gotten the shaft his whole life, and grew up fantasizing about all the things he could do to get even. As a kid, he was sneaky; he damaged property, hurt animals, and maybe set fires. Who he hurt didn't matter because he thought everyone deserved to be taught a lesson, and harming others made him feel superior. With puberty, sexual content became mixed with his fantasies of revenge and he repeatedly masturbated to these fantasies until sexual sadism became the only thing that turns him on. Added to this mix is an inability to feel empathy for any but his own needs, and a belief that women look down on him and, even when women treat him nice, that they are using him or mocking him."

Keenan stepped forward until he almost brushed the first row of tables. "The first two victims each had a finger cut off, but not the last victim. If cutting off a finger was part of the fantasy he was trying to bring to life, he would have done it to all three. The first two women have been described as strong willed; the last was said to avoid conflict.

He cut off the first two women's fingers because they would not do something he wanted them to do—probably, they refused to take the poison after the first time. He could have force-fed it to them; but making them drink it reduced them to his puppets and made him feel superior, just as harming others makes him feel superior, and that's what this guy is really after. He wants to dominate and control others by any means he can. To deceive, to manipulate, to overpower, to take others against their will—all of these things make him feel superior, and everything he does, he does for this reason."

Keenan paused. There was no rustling of paper, no shifting or coughing. He softened his voice and spoke more intimately. "Most of the Organized offenders I've interviewed say that once they abduct someone, the control they have over their victim makes them feel God-like, and taking the victim's life is the ultimate power rush. But that rush never lasts very long. So, all these men think about is hunting and killing. This man will not quit. Look at how he positioned the bodies. This guy is so angry that torture and murder is not enough, he wants to degrade these women even after they're dead. And as angry as he is, he's probably going to escalate, and quickly. He is both bold and cunning. You should consider him very dangerous, and when you go to talk to a suspect, never go alone.

"One last thing. I don't think he's going to cool it because the bodies have been found. So far, all of his abductions have occurred on weekends, separated by four or eight weeks. I think this is because he works weekends with one weekend off a month, and that's when he hunts." Keenan paused and scanned the frowning faces. "If this pattern holds, we've less than three weeks before he takes his next victim."

3

metamorphosis

I

GOLD-TINTED sunlight bathed the Paxtons' modest brick home, adorned by low boxwoods at the corners and beds of multicolored flowers in front of the windows. The neatly edged lawn had withered somewhat from the summer's harsh sun, as had most of the lawns in the young subdivision.

"Another proactive technique you might try," Keenan said, as Will looped his dirt-worn Bronco into the driveway beside a rusting yellow Tercel, "would be to hold a vigil, say . . . for Alicia Owens, and have the family put something unique on her grave . . . like a cross with her name on it, and then watch the grave in case he tries to take it as a souvenir."

"All right," Will said. He left the engine running so that cool air would continue to hiss through the plastic vents, and turned to face Keenan. "Oh, by the way, the guy at the meeting with the scar is a SLED investigator named Martin Stith. I'm sure he thinks he should be coordinating the investigation and tried to give you a hard time because he knows that you and I have worked closely in the past."

"Will he work with you?" Keenan asked.

"Yeah. He's aggressive as hell, but dedicated," Will replied, and switched off the engine.

Keenan swung open the Bronco's door and a surge of heat swept over him.

"Looks like hot weather has come early this year," Will explained as he came around the front of the vehicle and they started up the short sidewalk to the front door. "It usually doesn't get this hot for another month."

Keenan wondered if Will had shifted topics to avoid carrying their grisly discussion into his home. He had known several officers who tried to draw that line, and this was the first thing Will had said that did not pertain to the case since he insisted that Keenan come to dinner, that his wife, Marianne was expecting him. Typically, Keenan's schedule left little time for social gatherings, which suited him fine. Recently, at the urging of Susan Chen, he was trying to be a little more social. And his flight back to Alexandria did not leave until ten, so he really didn't have a good reason for declining.

Before they reached the front door, Will's five-year-old son, Zack, charged from the house to greet them. Will hoisted the brown-haired boy above his head, while playfully warning him that he needed to come down from there right this minute, which drew a stream of giggles from Zack. Distracted as he watched the boy's laughing face, a nudge in the crotch startled Keenan, as a yellow lab, tail vigorously wagging, unabashedly sniffed his most private area.

"Don't worry, she doesn't bite . . . usually," said a slender woman, dressed in jeans and beige knit top, as she came out the door. "Hi, John, I'm Marianne. I see you've met the rest of the family." Simultaneously, she shook Keenan's hand and pulled the dog back by its choke collar, then ordered, "Molly, sit." Brown hair hung in loose waves on Marianne's shoulders. She had a button nose, smiled easily, and hazel eyes that shined with genuine interest as she looked at Keenan.

"I'm certainly glad her intentions are friendly," Keenan said gesturing toward the dog and returning Marianne's smile. His fellow profilers would have been pleasantly surprised to see that his face didn't crack when he loosened up a bit.

"John, it's so good to finally meet you," Marianne said as they followed Will and Zack inside. From a small, marble landing they stepped down into the living room, where Keenan detected a faint odor of Endust. "Let me take your coat," Marianne offered. "As hot as it is, I can't believe you're wearing a jacket and tie. How about a cold beer?"

"I'm so dry, I'd prefer a large glass of water," Keenan said, sidestepping the awkwardness of explaining that he never drank alcohol.

"Then water it will be," Marianne said. "John, if you want to freshen up, there's a bathroom through that door." Marianne pointed to a door on the right side of the room. "I've just a few things to do in the kitchen and we'll be ready to eat."

In the half-bath, Keenan splashed cold water on his face. When he came out, there was no one in the living room; he started toward the door that Marianne had indicated was the kitchen, then noticed a newspaper lying on the coffee table. Curious as to what the local paper was reporting, Keenan bent and picked up the paper. A banner headline read, "SALUDA WOODS KILLER BAFFLES POLICE." This certainly might feed into the killer's arrogance and possibly make him careless. It also lessened the chance that he would lay low and not seek victims for a while. Keenan then thought of Will and what a tough thing it must be to have one's family read headlines like this. If more murders occurred, these headlines would become far more scathing. And, too often, Keenan had seen self-doubt's corrosive effects in the stooped shoulders and averted eyes of proud detectives.

II

Keenan sat with his sleeves rolled to his elbows and one arm resting on the oak table in the breakfast nook of the Paxtons' bright and roomy kitchen. The aroma of brewing coffee had replaced that of lasagna. A ragtag assortment of photos and kids' art was splattered on the refrigerator, stained glass hummingbirds hung in each of the nook's three windows, and a two-foot corn plant grew crookedly in one corner. Keenan had turned his chair toward the sink where Will, now wearing jeans and a blue polo shirt, ran a hot spray over a pasta-smeared plate before placing it into the dishwasher. Marianne sat across from Keenan. Zack, excused as soon as he finished eating, now played in his room.

It had been a pleasant evening, for which Keenan gave Marianne much of the credit. She had kept things casual, dining in the breakfast nook rather than the formal dining room. And by tacit agreement, no one mentioned the murders. Yet, they remained on everyone's mind, as evidenced by Will's preoccupation early in the evening, when Marianne had carried the conversation by comparing notes with Keenan on what each thought made a good instructor. Gradually, Will relaxed, joined the conversation, and Keenan took this as another sign of Will's ability to balance the pressures.

Will put the last of the plates in the dishwasher, then turned and leaned against the sink, drying his hands with a dish towel. "When

Marianne graduates in August," he said, "with math as her specialty area and a 3.7 GPA, the teaching jobs will come looking for her. She's already had some inquiries. Then we can really start saving."

"Shows how hard up they are for teachers," Marianne replied and shrugged. "And besides, we might have another baby before we start all that big savings."

"Very possible," Will said and smiled at her. "Either way, we already have the property. It's land my father bought before he died. A house on the lake was his dream too, but he kept putting it off."

"You told me your father died young," Keenan said. He was only eight years older than Will, yet Keenan suspected the early death of Will's father accounted for some of Will's eagerness to seek his advice. "You and your father were close?"

Will tossed the dish towel across his shoulder. "We were close when I was a child. Once I started junior high, I became convinced my father didn't know anything, and we mostly argued." Will shook his head. "I remember that after this one argument, I went to my room to sulk because my father wouldn't let me do something. I can't for the life of me remember what it was I wanted to do, though at the time it seemed like the most important thing in the world. Anyway, I could hear my father in the living room telling my mother how he was so frustrated that he could barely control himself. Then, he said he'd read somewhere that a father's love is like a raindrop fallen to earth, and said, 'damned if that ain't true.' Well, I thought it was the dumbest thing I'd ever heard, and the next day made jokes about it with my friends and then forgot about it until the night Zack was born. Then, when I held Zack for the first time, I remembered what my father had said and understood exactly what he meant." Will paused. "So, I've tried to be as good a father as my old man, because, sooner or later, Zack will be on his own. But if I can . . ."

The telephone rang and Marianne picked up the wall phone near the table. "It's Carl Jones," she told Will. Jones was chief of SLED.

"I'll take it in the living room. Excuse me a minute, John."

The coffee had brewed and Marianne went to the counter and began filling two mugs. "John, we've been doing all the talking and hardly given you a chance. I'm curious about how you became a profiler, it doesn't seem like the kind of work a boy dreams of growing up to do!"

"I was lucky," Keenan said. "After earning a master's in psych, my first job was at a mental health center, where I probably set a world's record for becoming disillusioned. I had no tolerance for people who made excuses rather than making the changes that would clearly help them. Looking back and knowing how results oriented I am, it's not surprising I was so unhappy. But at the time, I didn't know myself that well."

"So what changes did you make to improve your life?" she asked as she placed a steaming mug before him and sat, her eyes shining as she studied Keenan.

"Thank you," said Keenan and fingered the mug's handle. "My first change was to find a job in a mental health unit with the Virginia Department of Corrections, where I had no illusions about changing anyone."

"Sounds like you still had some changes to make," Marianne said and arched her eyebrows.

"I guess, because not long after moving to Corrections I went to a seminar on criminal personality patterns and Ben Lockhart, who had recently been appointed chief of Behavioral Sciences, was the after- noon speaker. As I listened, I realized that Lockhart was doing things that really made a difference, and the way he actually studied criminals made more sense than anything I'd ever encountered in the field of human behavior. So, I began an extensive application process and a year later went to work for Lockhart. I was his first experiment in recruiting someone with a behavioral rather than strictly law enforce- ment background. He hasn't done that again, so . . ." Keenan shrugged and smiled.

"And are you satisfied now?" Marianne asked and cocked her head to one side as if skeptical.

"I wake up early every morning eager to get to work and lose vaca- tion days every year because I refuse to take time off."

"That sounds to me like you're more driven that satisfied," she said, studying him closely.

. "I'm both," Keenan admitted, then smiled. "Whenever I do some- thing that's not work related, I usually can't wait to get back to what- ever case, or article, or training preparation I'm working on."

Marianne frowned. "What about marriage, friends, recreation? Where do they fit in your life?"

Keenan leaned back and did not answer immediately. He was typically reticent to say much about himself, yet Marianne's warmth and intense interest had plucked a surprising openness from him all evening. More surprising, he enjoyed it. Still, his professional life was one thing, while his personal life seemed so relatively unimportant. But he liked Marianne, thought her open with no agenda beyond getting to know him. Plus, Susan Chen was always goading him to talk about these same areas.

Keenan breathed out, almost a sigh, then said, "Before going to work for Lockhart, I was married, had barbecues with friends, watched sports on weekends, and I think was scared to death that this was all there would ever be. I guess I'm one of those people who need a cause." He shrugged and half-smiled. "My marriage didn't survive. Ruth, my wife, tried hard to accommodate, but I didn't have room back then for anything but my work. When I'd been with the Bureau eleven months, she called it quits, said she couldn't cope with the guilt of being so angry at me when children were disappearing in Terre Haute—that was the case I was working on at the time. She did the right thing. She's remarried and has two children. I think she's happy."

Marianne looked concerned. "Surely, John, you must have someone you're at least dating?"

"I've been seeing someone casually," Keenan said and glanced away, reluctant to admit that maybe it was a little more than casual. "She's a forensic psychologist at Georgetown. And so far, I'm avoiding my usual pattern."

"And what pattern is that?"

Keenan winced, wondering why he had mentioned that. Every interrogator knows that suspects usually trip themselves up by answering more than they are asked. Keenan looked down, shook his head at this slip, then answered truthfully, "All right. My pattern is that whenever I become involved with someone I get busy, go on the road, and two or three weeks go by before I call. For some reason, women get annoyed at that."

"I can't imagine why that would upset any woman," Marianne said, shaking her head. "Make sure you call her tonight, okay?" A furrow formed between Marianne's eyebrows. "May I ask you something a little more personal?"

"Shoot," Keenan said, wondering what could be more personal than his social life.

Marianne cradled both hands around her coffee mug. "Doesn't all the tragedy of what you deal with get to you?"

"I stay focused on my job and don't think about it."

"You can really do that?" Marianne asked, tilting her head and looking a little skeptical.

"In my department, you have to or you don't make it."

"I know that's what Will's trying to do, but he's so . . . compassionate. If we're running late for something and come across someone broken down on the side of the road, we're going to be even later. He can't ignore someone in trouble; it goes against his grain. This thing that's going on . . ." Marianne hesitated and Keenan thought her eyes looked moist. She glanced down, then back at Keenan. "More women are going to die before this thing ends, aren't they?"

"When these cases break it usually happens fast. One solid lead and it unravels in a day." Keenan gave his usual pat answer.

"Do you think more women are going to die?" Marianne pressed, staring at Keenan with surprising intensity. "I'm not asking out of morbid curiosity. Will hasn't slept well since this thing started, and you saw how preoccupied he was earlier. I want to know what my husband is facing."

Slowly, Keenan nodded. "I think there will be at least one more murder. And unless our guy makes a mistake or somebody notices something, there will be more."

"So this thing could go on for months?"

Keenan nodded. "There's a chance it might."

"I thought so. Do you know what scares me most? Knowing that something like this has to change Will. My worst fear is that he might become bitter, like my father. At some point, John, my father just quit trying and began blaming everyone and everything for whatever was wrong in his life. Will's the opposite; what most attracts me to him is that he's so positive. I don't know if I could handle it if he became bitter."

Keenan reached across the table and touched the back of Marianne's hand. He felt unusually at ease with her, and because even this level of intimacy was rare for Keenan, it affected him more deeply than it might those with richer social lives. "Will's character is solid," Keenan said. "He'll have a tough time, but he'll come through it okay."

"I'm going to hold you to that," Marianne said and forced a smile.

"How are you holding up?" Keenan asked, and drew back his hand.

"I'm not sure. This is embarrassing, but I was paying for gas today and this guy came in and stood fairly close behind me and I got the willies, for no reason other than that I didn't know him. And when I left the filling station my heart was racing and I just kept checking my rearview mirror. All the way home, I kept checking it. John, I consider myself a levelheaded person, but I was scared. And I don't like looking at people with so much distrust. I don't know if these violent creeps have made strangers of us all or just shown us how much we are strangers."

Light reflected on the nook's windows as a car drove slowly down the street. Keenan watched it for a moment, then said, "Some of both, I think."

The door from the living room opened and Will returned. "Sorry I took so long," he said. "Nothing new. Jones just wanted to talk about tomorrow morning's meeting."

"That reminds me," Keenan said, and stood. "I hate to cut this evening short, but I need to call a cab and get to the airport."

"Absolutely not," Will said. "I'll drive you. I need to go by headquarters anyway and get things ready for tomorrow."

Rising, Marianne took Keenan's large hand between her much smaller ones and squeezed tightly. "John, I'm so glad to have finally met you. You're always welcome here."

"Thank you for an enjoyable evening," Keenan said, and meant it. When on-site, he usually had dinner in restaurants with belching cops and talked about nothing but law enforcement. By inches, his life was becoming a bit more rounded. He was dating Susan Chen, more or less mentoring Will, and he had stopped marking himself off the teaching rotations as often as he had in the past. Sure, his department had added new positions so he finally had a little breathing room. But he also knew that every few years we all need to realign our lives to accommodate changes in ourselves. Or maybe he was reading too much into simply enjoying himself this evening.

Before Keenan left the Paxtons' bright kitchen, he glanced around again and for the first time saw such a setting as something other than merely an anchor.

4

dead-ends

I

WILL PAXTON drove slowly along the dark road leading to the Family Shores Campground, gravel crunching beneath his tires and light dust trailing behind. A patrol car flashed at the campground's entrance and Will held his shield against the window as he drove past. Ahead, patrol units and unmarked cars crowded both sides of the road and a small group of onlookers stood in the reflected glare of portable floodlights set up inside a yellow-ribbon perimeter.

Will parked his Bronco in a grassy area between two unmarked Caprices, got out, and immediately began swatting away mosquitoes. Overhead a dark canopy of hardwoods allowed only brief glimpses of a waxing quarter moon. He pushed a stick of Juicy Fruit into his mouth to cover the smell of beer on his breath and walked toward the bright lights.

When the call came, Will had been slouched on his couch trying to think through the fatigue and find some hidden pattern in the growing heap of maps, reports, summaries, and the five-inch-thick computer list of suspect names called in by nervous citizens. Sitting up and rehashing everything was marginally better than tossing in bed. Exactly two weeks had passed since the task force first met. Two weeks of sixteen-hour days, and nothing to show for it but dead-end leads and a growing sense of dread—if the phone rang late at night, Will felt like puking. And tonight, the call he most dreaded had come.

Bugs looped in crazed circles around the floodlights that shone on the campground's bathhouse and surrounded the adjacent field. A half dozen technicians, wearing rubber gloves and carrying cases of various sizes, worked inside this perimeter.

Will asked for Sheriff Inabinet and a uniformed officer pointed to a stand of trees where the white-gas glow of a camping lantern hung from a branch and harshly illuminated a small group that stood clustered around a picnic table. On the ground near the table, five buckets of mosquito-repelling tallow flickered. Will slapped a mosquito from his neck and started that way.

Inabinet stood at one end of the table, listening to a wiry man with curly hair who gestured angrily. Will guessed that the man was Marvin Carmichael. Two girls, each with long, red-tinted auburn hair, sat on one of the table's benches. Will already knew their names. The smaller, who had a blanket wrapped around her shoulders even though the night was muggy, was eleven-year-old Cookie Carmichael. Her fourteen-year-old sister, Caroline, sat with her arm around Cookie's shoulders. Caroline turned and nodded mutely at whatever a gray-haired woman sitting beside her said, and light reflected in the tears streaming down her face.

Will reached the group, as Marvin Carmichael, who had a face like Popeye with deep smoker's crease, told Inabinet, "We didn't do anything stupid. Shelly just took the girls to the bathhouse to do their nightly stuff. That's all. Then the girls wanted to walk back alone so they could talk. Maybe they shouldn't have done that," he said, oblivious to what his daughters heard. "But we've been coming here for years and we're not from here and nobody told us that you had this kind of problem."

Noticing Will, Carmichael turned toward him and again pleaded his case. "She's just lost, I tell you. That's all. This sort of thing can't happen to us. Goddamn it, we didn't do anything stupid."

Will saw the anguish in Carmichael's face and the huddled fear of those two girls, and for the first time in his life knew passionate hate. How could any human so gleefully cause such devastating suffering? And goddamn it, for what?

In the face of this terrible wrong, Will felt utterly helpless. His frustration was such that had he been alone he might have gone on a rampage by kicking over benches and slamming the table against the tree, then stomping the boards until they cracked—there was simply no other adequate way to express how he felt. But Will was not alone, and not bent to pointless tantrums, so the only thing he could do—inadequate as it might be—was to say, "I'm so sorry."

Carmichael glared at Will. "Listen buddy, sorry don't cut it. Why haven't you caught this son of a bitch?"

Two weeks of failure had drained Will. And now, for the second time this week, he had offered impotent comfort to a stricken man. Two days ago, on Friday evening, he had become so ravenous to do something positive that he had visited Alvin Owens, resolved to offer whatever support he could.

Alvin lived in a modest ranch-style house that was located in a sub-division so new that most houses still had straw holding grass sprigs in place. An aunt staying with Alvin had shown Will into the dining room, which was separated from the kitchen by a bar-like counter. Alvin sat at an oval table feeding his daughter from a small jar of baby food—just as Will had once fed his son. Behind Alvin, slatted blinds were drawn tight across sliding doors.

"Hey, Will," Alvin said as Will entered. Slightly overweight, Alvin had reddish-blond hair and a wispy mustache of the same color. His face looked tired and puffy.

Dressed in his uniform, Will held his wide-rimmed hat at his waist with both hands. "Alvin, I wanted to stop by and see if there's anything I can do."

"I appreciate that, Will," Alvin said and tried to coax a spoonful of pulpy food into the infant's mouth, but she spit it out. For a moment, Alvin froze, holding the empty spoon a few inches from her face and seeming unsure what to do. "Alicia mostly took care of her," he said, then used the spoon to rake some of the mess from his daughter's chin. "I helped some, but it was just when I felt like it. I should have done more."

Will laid his hat on the table and moved around it to put a hand on Alvin's shoulder. "I do the same with Marianne, you know, mostly play with Zack while she does the real work."

Alvin nodded as he wiped his daughter's face with a soft cloth. When finished, he looked at Will and said, "Will, since you asked, there is something that maybe you could help me with, something I can't get out of my mind." Alvin hesitated, then said haltingly, "When Sheriff Inabinet took me in to show me Alicia's body, he . . . he just showed me her head and . . . the left side of her face was all purple." Alvin's mouth quivered. "I asked Inabinet if she'd been beaten and he told me the discoloration—that was his word, discoloration—was from blood settling because she'd been laid on her side after she died. Now don't get me wrong, Will, because I appreciate everything Sheriff Inabinet's done, but I can't help but think that he just told me that to make me feel better. And nobody else will tell me anything. Will, was she beaten?"

"No, Alvin. What Sheriff Inabinet told you is true."

"What all did he do to her?"

"Alvin, it won't do you any good to get into things like that. You're better off to remember her like she was and leave it at that."

"That's what the other cops said. But it's going to come out sooner or later. And I want to know. I have to know. Not knowing is driving me crazy. I just keep imagining the worst." Alvin looked at Will, pleading, and his mouth quivered again. "I thought maybe since we know each other that you'd help me. Will, it's worse not knowing. Please, believe me it is."

Will believed that what had happened to Alicia was probably worse than anything Alvin could imagine. Will doubted that he could handle knowing that something like that had happened to Marianne. He had come here determined to do something for this man, no matter how small, but he could never tell Alvin about the brutality preceding Alicia's death. Never.

"Alvin, I'm sorry, but we can't release any details until we arrest the bastard."

Alvin's eyes were red and wet, and his mouth tightened as he fought tears. "Will, I won't tell anybody. I promise."

"I can't Alvin. Not until we get this guy. And no matter what it takes, I promise you that we'll get the bastard. Until then, there's not a lot I can talk about."

Alvin looked away and mumbled, "Sure. I guess I understand."

. . .

But Will had not stopped the bastard before Shelly Carmichael disappeared. Now, as investigators swarmed the Family Shores Campground, they officially said they could not be sure that this was the work of the Saluda Woods Killer. But Will knew, they all knew.

"I ask you why you haven't caught this guy?" Marvin Carmichael repeated.

His face burning, Will said, "We're doing everything we can, but . . ."

"Bullshit!" Carmichael interrupted. "If you were really doing your job this wouldn't have happened."

Will looked away and Inabinet said something that Will didn't pay attention to because he noticed that the two girls were staring at him. Probably, they blamed him too. After all, their father had just said that it was his fault their mother had been taken. Hoarsely, Will said, "I'm going to check on the evidence team," and walked away with his head down.

Will had always believed his compassion a strength. Then he had watched confiscated tapes at Quantico and studied the case histories, and left those sessions dazed like a disaster survivor. John Keenan had said focus on the facts of the case, focus on solving the puzzle, focus on what you need to do. So Will had focused on those things because, intuitively, he knew that, like the sun, you can't look directly at such horror for very long without being damaged.

Now, after two weeks of grinding, his inner blinders had been splintered and Will could not stop the vivid images of what would soon be done to Shelly Carmichael. She might cry and beg, but nothing she did would make any difference. Painful spasms would tear her muscles as she was brutally raped. It was very likely happening now. And there was not a goddamned thing he could do to stop it.

5
———
doubts

I

"LIKE I told you before," Alfonso Reese said testily, "the bitches was following me. Not just spying on me, but thinkin' that 'I got this stuff you can't have,'" he said in an exaggerated falsetto. A sheen of sweat covered his brown skin as he leaned over the table toward Wynton Carlisle. Reese's hair was long and hacked unevenly because he didn't trust anyone near his head with scissors. "They always acted like they was better'n me. But I showed 'em, I showed 'em good," he added, then glanced at Keenan who sat at the end of the table, and like Carlisle, wore a sports shirt. Reese had labeled Keenan a white devil and watched him warily. To Carlisle, a black man, he looked for understanding.

"I can see how you think that," Carlisle said.

"What? What are you saying? 'That I think that.' You tryin' to fuck with my head. Well, fuck with this," Reese said and swept the notepad and aluminum ashtray from the table, then stood.

Keenan surged to his feet and held out a hand, not close enough to invade Reese's space, but pressing that invisible border and forcing Reese to consider if he really wanted to tangle with this big devil. "He wants to understand, you just have to help him," Keenan said.

"I don't have to do nothin'."

"No, you don't. But he wants to understand. He just needs your help."

"He's too stupid."

"Maybe."

"Now, you tryin' to get in my head. I want to go. You don't know who you fuckin' with." Then he screamed toward the door, "I want to go."

.   .   .

A few minutes later, Keenan and Carlisle sat in the conference room made available by the warden of Florida State Prison. "Did you see it coming?" Keenan asked.

"No," Carlisle said, shaking his head. Carlisle was movie-star-handsome with the build of a running back, which he had been at Davidson. He had spent eight years as a field agent before being accepted into Keenan's unit. In two prior training interviews, Carlisle acquitted himself well with men who were stone-cold psychopaths. But so far, things were going badly with Reese, who was serving consecutive life sentences for killing three women near the Miami housing project where he had lived. Reese left the bodies at the site of the murder and had a history of mental illness, traits that classified him as a Disorganized Type offender. Thus far, Reese's disjointed logic, rapidly shifting affect, and overall inappropriateness were throwing

Carlisle curves that Keenan thought he gracelessly missed because of an unwillingness to go inside Reese's world.

"Instead of reviewing tonight's tape," Keenan said, "we're going to listen to one I had Ben Lockhart ship overnight. It's with a pedophile named Russell Grough who was convicted of killing a four-year-old boy." Keenan then played a segment. On the tape, as Grough described the repulsive things he had done to this child, Keenan displayed an eager fascination and a lackey's admiration for Grough. During the first few minutes of the tape Carlisle once smiled weakly at Keenan, grimaced a few times, and shifted restlessly in his seat. Then he settled into looking only at the recorder, though a couple of times he sneaked uncertain glances at Keenan that were, perhaps, tinged with disgust. Keenan let the tape run on a few minutes longer, just enough to let Carlisle see where he was going:

Keenan: "Well, Russ, what choice did you have. I mean, the way society refuses to accept the love between an adult and a child."

Grough: (His voice pleasing, like that of a radio announcer) "It's natural, really. If they left us alone there'd be no need to hurt the kids. It'd be best for us all."

Keenan: "Yeah, it's really those sanctimonious pricks' fault. They don't give you any choice"

Grough: "Yeah, it really is John. So I did what I had to."

Keenan: "That takes courage. Especially the first time. It had to be tough."

Grough: "Actually, the first time was an accident."

Keenan: "I can't imagine a man like you having an accident."

Grough: "What can I say, I'm a passionate guy."

Keenan: "What happened?"

Grough: "I went to Wheaton . . . No, I can't talk about that, John. Only what I've been convicted of."

Keenan: "I understand. You can't trust anybody, not really. And I know that must be tough."

Keenan switched off the tape. Carlisle, who had two sons, looked like he had tasted something sour and avoided looking at Keenan.

Keenan let Carlisle struggle with these feelings for a few seconds, then said, "Grough, like every man, wanted to feel respected. I spent four nights becoming the best buddy he ever had. By the fifth night I had him convinced that I was like him, and he told me enough that we were able to end two families' uncertainty about what happened to their child. I also showed Grough a couple of the rougher child porn photos that the Bureau had confiscated and told him I'd share any others that I came across. His appetite whetted, he told me about a shop I should try and code words that would put me in touch with someone who catered to what he believed were my special interests. I passed the information to Cook County investigators and it led them to Craig Brierholt."

Keenan watched recognition come into Carlisle's face. "We didn't want to foul up our chances of pulling off something like this in the future, so we never made public Behavioral Science's role in capturing him. You know the rest. Brierholt will probably be executed sometime next year."

Standing, Keenan said, "I want you to listen to the Grough tape again tonight. Then I want you to review your interview with Reese and come up with a strategy. Let's meet for breakfast at eight."

.   .   .

In his sports shirt, Keenan probably looked more like a man on vacation than a working FBI agent as he returned to his motel at quarter of ten. During the day, the maid had restored the air conditioning to its usual level, so Keenan turned it back to its coldest setting, then checked his messages. Will Paxton wanted Keenan to call him at home. He had talked to Will during both of the weeks since the task force convened. Sitting on the bed beside the nightstand, Keenan dialed and Will picked up on the third ring.

"Will, it's John Keenan."

"There's been another one," Will said. He sounded tired.

"Lockhart sent me the Carmichael Missing Persons Report on Monday. But he wasn't sure it was our guy because he hit earlier than expected."

"A trucker spotted the body this morning. It was caught on some rocks in the Saluda River," Will said. "Autopsy found the identical signature."

"Anything more on the vehicle?" Keenan asked. In his statement, the campground owner said that at around eleven he was in his kitchen getting a snack when he heard a car leaving and looked out his window and glimpsed the rear of a dark colored van or RV.

"We had a hypnotist work with him yesterday and he's now pretty sure that it was a van with an external spare tire and the color might have been dark brown or dark red. We made this public tonight and have already gotten over thirty calls from people who know someone creepy that drives a dark van. Otherwise, no one saw anything, so I guess he'll go on rubbing our noses in it."

"Rubbing our noses in it?"

"Yeah," Will said. "An unweighted body dumped in a river in a highly populated area — you know what that means. The bastard thinks we can't catch him and he's flaunting it."

"Maybe," Keenan said. It was true. When Organized Type killers leave the bodies where they are easily discovered, it's a sign of contempt, the killer's way of showing the police that he is in control. "But think about it, Will, there are other possible reasons," Keenan added. "You've found the first bodies and know what he's doing, so there's less need to hide Carmichael. And even though this guy cleans the bodies, water might wash away any fibers or hair that he missed, and if he weighted her down, he would have had to use rope or strips that might catch fibers. Plus, what he did was easy; he drove to a secluded bridge and dumped her. Quick in, quick out."

"Yeah, I know . . . I know," Will said wearily. "It's just that we keep running into the same dead ends, and there's not a goddamned thing I can do about it except wait for him to kill someone else." Will sighed and then Keenan heard him take a drink of something and wondered if it was alcohol.

If Will unwound with a beer or cocktail, so what? A lot of people did that. Keenan, however, never drank alcohol under any circumstances and was especially sensitive, perhaps unreasonably so, to its use. He'd known too many investigators who numbed themselves with booze when the hunt stalled. Despite his effort to be fair-minded, Keenan felt disappointed and annoyed with Will.

"I've never in my life been this frustrated," Will said. "You know, lately it seems that even when I try to help someone, nothing comes of it." Again came the sound of Will swallowing. "I told you I know Alicia Owens' husband, Alvin?"

"Yeah," Keenan said, frowning.

"Well, I went to see Alvin to pay my respects. The guy's driving himself nuts obsessing about what all was done to Alicia and begged me to tell him. I told him I couldn't but he just kept begging me. And do you know what my gut reaction was? I wanted to shake him and tell him to get over it. Can you believe that?"

"Will, it's not a good idea to get so close to a victim's family, even if you know them. This kind of investigation is hard enough as it is."

"I want to help Alvin, and I'm going to. I've found out that on Monday nights there's a group that meets called Parents of Murdered Children, and anyone's welcome who's had someone they love murdered. I'm going to take Alvin to that meeting, even if I have to drag him."

"Will, I don't think . . ."

"No, you listen for a change, because you're wrong about staying away from victims' families. I'm not going to turn my back on Alvin. I can do my job and try to help him. It's the least I can do," Will said, followed by the sound of him taking another drink and then a tin can being crushed—a beer can, Keenan thought.

"Will, what you're trying to do for Owens is admirable," Keenan said more tartly than he intended. "But it's a lousy idea because it's distracting you from what you need to be doing. The way you can best help Owens is to stay focused on the case and do everything you know how to do, then do it again and again until the case is solved. That's what he most needs from you. Maybe later you can help him in some other way, but now is not the time."

"John, I don't care what you think. I have an obligation and I'm going to do everything I can."

Keenan sat upright and his face flared red. "Then you better remember that this thing could go on for another six months, a year, maybe longer. If you keep going like you are, you're not going to make it."

"So I need to suck it up, stop whining, and get tougher, is that what you're saying?'

"It's not a question of toughness but of taking care of yourself so you can do your job."

"I do my job sixteen hours a day. I'll be in touch if there's anything new," Will said and hung up.

Keenan slammed down the phone. Briefly, he considered calling

Inabinet and telling the sheriff he had doubts about Will's . . . what? His toughness? A call like that would cut Will's legs from under him before he had a fair chance to prove himself. It would be disloyal. Besides the locals worked with Will every day. Surely, they were in a better position to gauge how well he handled the pressure. After all, it was their call, not his.

6

trip wire

I

DURING THE following week, Keenan spent three days at the Lincoln County Jail in Davenport, Washington, observing and offering suggestions as local police interrogated a farmer named Robert Reynolds. Five bodies had been discovered on Reynolds' farm near Odessa, three in a disused well and two in shallow graves behind a toolshed—and they were still digging. All of the dead men had their skulls crushed and were believed to be migrants or drifters who had worked for Reynolds. Apparently, Reynolds did not like to pay his help.

On Saturday morning, Keenan had a final breakfast meeting with the Lincoln County prosecutor, then drove to Spokane and from there flew to Seattle for the coast-to-coast flight home to Virginia. During the long flight, he was pinched into a seat designed for someone half his size, which gave his accumulated fatigue a ragged edge.

He finally arrived home at a little past nine. Keenan owned a single-level, brick house in an older Alexandria suburb. The house smelled faintly of Pine-Sol from Thursday's maid service and seemed strikingly quiet. Keenan deposited his bag in the foyer, turned up the AC, then returned to his car for the supplies he had picked up at the supermarket.

After unpacking the groceries, Keenan poured a large glass of iced tea from a gallon container and went to the bedroom he had converted into a study. Keenan was a tidy housekeeper, not a great feat considering how little time he spent at home. His study, though, was a miniature of his office at the Academy Building, with smaller piles of books and folders. He switched on the green-shaded desk lamp, then raised the blinds of a window that overlooked his patio, where a sparse patchwork of moonlight slipped through ancient maples. Keenan stood looking out for a moment. Maybe after he made his two calls, he would unwind by sitting outside for a while.

One of the calls would be social, a pleasure actually. He wanted to let Susan Chen know that he had made it back and could keep their date for tomorrow afternoon. They planned to hit some museums, have dinner, then go back to Susan's house in Georgetown. If he had had to cancel again, as he had the past two weeks, there would be no undercurrents; Susan's work ethic matched his own and, being a forensic psychologist, she understood what was at stake. It was her passion for forensics that had initially attracted him. But as Keenan got to know her better, he admired her keen intellect and wry sense of humor. Lately, he had also discovered that she could be very sensual. If he were not so exhausted, he might drive up tonight and really unwind. Keenan smiled at the thought and had no qualms about tomorrow being a "work-free day."

Turning from the window, Keenan thought about the other call he needed to make and stopped smiling. Over a week had passed since he and Will had argued. He needed to put their relationship firmly back onto a professional plane. He had let things get too personal with Will, let it distract him in the same way that he believed Will was distracted by his involvement with Alvin Owens. Keenan had underestimated the potential of Will's compassion to swamp him—and he had overestimated his ability to coach Will through the rougher spots. He especially regretted blowing off Inabinet's concerns about Will's inexperience. As a result of wearing blinders, he had boosted Will into a leadership position for which Will was apparently not yet ready, and therefore he had an inescapable obligation to help Will get through this manhunt.

Before making the calls, Keenan checked his messages. Ben Lockhart wanted him to call ASAP. Keenan dialed Lockhart's home number.

"There's been another murder in South Carolina," Lockhart said without preamble. "And we might have a break with this one."

A small surge of adrenaline bought Keenan fully alert. "What do you have?"

"The victim's name was Mary Williams, age thirty-six," Lockhart told him in his methodical way. Keenan always thought Lockhart would have made a good accountant. He also thought Ben would be a formidable poker player, because he was the shrewdest and most inscrutable man Keenan knew. "Williams was divorced and lived with her seventeen-year-old son, Gary. Thursday morning, an employee of the jeans store she managed, Slack Happy, called her home at around ten to find out why she hadn't shown to open. The son works nights, and says the call woke him. He checked, saw that his mother's car was in the carport, then found signs of struggle in the bedroom, and called the police."

"Our guy's not a stalker," Keenan said, "he's a spider."

"That's what the locals thought. We might still think that if a couple of kids hadn't gone parking Thursday night on an old logging road that runs parallel with a railroad track. Our guy had left her body spread-eagle on the rails. She'd been beaten while alive with post-mortem mutilation of her face and genitals. And the killer hacked off most of her hair," Lockhart said, then paused.

Keenan leaned back in his chair and with his free hand absently rubbed the back of his neck. Mary Williams was definitely not a random target; she had clearly been the victim of a rage attack. In the hundreds of cases Keenan had studied, he had never seen a victim's hair cut off by a stranger—it was too personal a humiliation.

"This sounds more like a domestic homicide that someone is trying to make look like the Saluda Woods Killer," Keenan said.

"That's why I didn't call you until we got the autopsy today. He only had anal intercourse, poisoned her with strychnine, and cleaned the body identical to the others. None of that is public knowledge, so it can't be a copycat. Official cause of death was manual strangulation, but that's consistent with a rage attack. It looks like he tried to bring his fantasy into it with the poison, but was too pissed to pull it off."

"And when he calmed down," Keenan picked up the line of reasoning, "he realized he'd screwed up. So he cleaned the body and left her on the tracks, hoping a train would mangle her so badly that we wouldn't find out that he'd treated her differently, because somewhere there's a connection."

"We know the connection," Lockhart said. "It's Andrew Scalaro, the man who found the first bodies. Scalaro held his first class of the summer session Wednesday night. Not only did Mary Williams attend that class, but angrily told the class she thought the Saluda Woods Killer was too pathetic for any woman to ever be with him willingly."

"I'll be damned," said Keenan. It was not that unusual for a man who found a body or, in this case, bodies, to be the killer. Some predators loved playing such bold and arrogant games.

"The police detained Scalaro yesterday afternoon," Lockhart said. "John, I want you to go back to South Carolina and see what you think of Scalaro. He looks like a damned good suspect. But if it's not him, we have to worry about how agitated the killer has become because of Williams's remarks and his loss of control with her. We know damned well what the son of a bitch will probably do to make himself feel like he's back in control."

"I'll go tomorrow," Keenan said.

After hanging up, Keenan leaned back in his chair and rubbed his forehead. The scent of the chase would sustain the adrenaline surge for a little while before fatigue finally drained him. He leaned forward and dialed Will's home number.

"Will, this is John Keenan," he said when Will picked up. "Lockhart gave me a rundown. How are things going?"

"Like shit," Will said. "We released Scalaro a couple of hours ago. We don't have one concrete thing to link him. All we found at his house even remotely related were a few books and articles on crime and a few girlie magazines, but nothing with bondage or the rough stuff that would appeal to our guy. He also had a small quantity of rat poison in the crawl space beneath the house. That's it. So he's back out there."

"Alibi?" Keenan asked and sipped his tea.

"Consistent, but shaky. He claims he was home Wednesday night by nine-forty and his wife confirms it, but it's not airtight. She said she's usually in bed by ten and takes a sedative called Restoril three or four nights a week. She says she's never awakened and had Scalaro not be there, but hell, he could be slipping her extra. Anyway, she's so upset by all the uproar that she's gone to stay with her parents until everything gets resolved."

Keenan's eyes felt dry and he rubbed them. Something seemed to be stirring in the back of his mind that he couldn't quite pin down. Despite the brief arousal, fatigue and jet lag made it hard to think clearly. "How is Scalaro handling himself?" he asked.

"Like a pro. He acted exactly the way you'd expect an innocent person to act—got angry, cried, pleaded with us to believe him. At first, he said he didn't need an attorney, but got one this morning. With his psychology background, he has to know something about interview dynamics. It has to be him. There's no other explanation for the killer being in that class. And it's obvious why he targeted Mary Williams. Did Lockhart tell you what she said?"

"Yeah," Keenan said. Again, something stirred in his mental fog, but whatever it was stayed just beyond his reach.

"Well, at least the asshole won't be parading as an expert for a while."

Suddenly alert, Keenan sat up and planted his feet on either side of the chair. "That's right, you told me a while back that Scalaro had been doing commentary on television." Will had told him that after he discovered the bodies, the media had sought interviews with Scalaro, made him something of a local hero, and Scalaro had played up his master's in psychology to present himself as a self-styled expert on serial killers. Will had said that one local television station had even started using him for expert commentary whenever there was a development in the case.

"Yeah, he's still playing the expert. We've taped them all. The asshole's been eating it up."

"Think about it, Will," Keenan prompted. "It was too much to be mere coincidence, yet the killer was there. Let's say for the moment that it's not Scalaro. If so, the killer could have been drawn to the class because he had seen Scalaro on television and knew there was a very good chance that Scalaro would show off by talking about serial killers. Our guy probably didn't give a rat's ass what Scalaro thought; he wanted to watch the students' reactions. Will, you need to look very closely at the students in Scalaro's class. It also might be a good idea to talk to Scalaro again, but with the focus on the students."

"I'll do it in the morning," Will said, though not with the enthusiasm Keenan expected given that a promising lead had just opened.

Not only did Keenan think the investigation at a crucial point, but he shared Lockhart's fear that, if the killer felt things slipping out of his control, he would try to reassure himself by killing again, maybe even doing something more dramatic. That's what Ted Bundy did in Florida. Frustrations kept heaping on and, in an attempt to restore his faltering control, he had gone to Chi Omega sorority house in a blood-frenzy and savagely bludgeoned four young women as they slept, killing two. One of the dead bore deep bite marks on her buttocks and around her nipple, as well as signs of brutal sexual battery with rough objects. Keenan thought the killer they now hunted capable of something that extreme.

"Ben suggested I do another on-site to look at the interviews," he said. "I should have no problem getting a flight in the morning . . . if you're agreeable."

With only the barest of hesitation, Will said, "We'd welcome the help. I'll make sure I talk to Scalaro before you get here. See you tomorrow."

Keenan hit the disconnect button and breathed out slowly. The immediate threat in South Carolina had put everything back into perspective.

"Like it or not," Keenan said aloud, "we are going to work together."

Keenan then called Susan and canceled their date for tomorrow. She said she understood.

7

suspect

I

WILL PAXTON trudged up the steep sidewalk, a manila folder in his hand. A creeping wet spot spread between the shoulder blades of his dark blue uniform. It was scarcely ten o'clock and already the heat had soared into the mid-nineties. Where the walkway split, Will chose the fork leading to the side of the slate-gray, two-story house and entered a screened porch. He removed his flat-brimmed hat and mopped sweat from his forehead, then took a deep breath and rang the bell. Switching his hat to the hand with the folder, Will gently flapped both folder and hat against his leg as he stared through the door's panes into a dimly lit kitchen. He had come unannounced, hoping that face-to- face it would be harder for Andrew Scalaro to refuse to talk to him.

When Scalaro entered the kitchen and saw yet another cop on his porch he hesitated, then slowly approached the door. "Get out of here, you bastard," he yelled through the glass. "My attorney says I don't have to talk to you unless he's present, so go, get out of here."

"Please, give me one minute?" Will asked and held up his index finger. "I'm here because I need your help."

"I said go away."

"Damn it, I might be able to clear you," Will shouted, louder than he intended. Knowing he had to keep his edginess in check, he said more evenly, "Please, at least let me explain."

Scalaro stared through the glass for what seemed to Will a long time. Finally, he eased the door open a few inches and said, "Don't play me for a fool. What do you really want?"

"May I come in and explain. I promise, I'm not here to trick you. I really do need your help."

"I'm through helping people," Scalaro said.

"Then do it for yourself."

Scalaro hesitated, then said, "Oh, what the hell. You've already ruined my life and there's nothing else you can do to me, so I'll listen to your lies." Flipping a switch, Scalaro stepped back from the door as a fluorescent light flickered on.

"Thanks," Will said and, following Scalaro's gesture, crossed to a small oak table in the kitchen's breakfast nook. This spot suited Will because it was in plain view of the uniformed officer who sat beneath a festive beach umbrella, knee deep in kudzu, atop the bank behind Scalaro's house. Another Jeffcoat County patrolman was parked on the street in front, along with two news vans to keep him company.

Looking at Scalaro across the table, Will felt revulsion. A thin man with a short beard and hawk-beak nose, Scalaro had close-set eyes beneath a thatch of dark hair. For the past forty-eight hours, Will had hated that face, believed it evil incarnate, believed it the face of a sadist and a coward who had murdered five women. Will wanted Scalaro to be the man they hunted so bad that he had fervently prayed for new evidence to prove his guilt. The possibility that Scalaro might not be their man left Will as empty as if he had lost his faith. Will again studied Scalaro's eyes, hoping to find the reptilian flatness that John Keenan had said he often saw in serial killers' eyes. This flatness, Keenan believed, occurred because a void existed where the human should be. Scalaro's eyes were wide and dilated—scared eyes, Will thought.

"My name is Will Paxton and as you can see I'm with SLED. With your consent, I'm going to record what we talk about. You see this right here." Will pointed to his shirt pocket above his badge. "It looks like a ballpoint pen clicker but it's actually a small microphone attached to a microrecorder. I want you to know this, and that this session is not about you."

"So you say," Scalaro said. He leaned back in his chair and watched Will the way a cornered animal might.

"Do you mind if I tape?"

"Only if I can get a copy to show how you lie."

"We haven't lied to you," Will said.

"But you've lied about me. After you people handled all my stuff, you told the media a pack of lies, calling *Playboy* pornography. You've done everything you can to make me look like a pervert, just so you can clear your books. You people have no conscience."

"You know we had to investigate you." Trying to put his revulsion aside, Will leaned forward and gestured with his palm up. "Think about it, you discovered the bodies of the first victims and then a woman who attends your initial class of the summer session becomes the latest victim. That's too much to be a coincidence."

"Goddamn it, it was a coincidence."

"I don't think so. But you might be able to help me prove that you're not guilty."

"Yeah. Right. Just like the cops outside are here for my protection. I know what you're doing. You're playing good cop. Well don't . . . just don't," Scalaro said and waved his hands in front of him as if swatting away a gnat.

Rather than argue, Will waited to allow Scalaro a chance to vent. After a couple of seconds, Scalaro asked, "Did you see the news last night? Did you see how they showed me pulling into my driveway and walking into my own goddamn house, and how they made me look guilty as hell? The same goddamn people that were so glad I was doing commentary for them not three days ago, and they loved saying that I'm the primary suspect, that even though I was released I'm still under twenty-four-hour surveillance. And with them lurking out there, I can't walk to the bottom of my driveway to get my Sunday paper without ending up on the news again tonight looking like some goddamn sneaky criminal. Even the lady next door . . . I've been her neighbor for two years, a good neighbor, and when I got home yesterday from the hell you put me through, she was weeding her goddamn flowers and you should have seen how she looked at me. She didn't wave, she hurried inside. She was repulsed by me . . . by me." Scalaro's eyes were red and wet. "So tell me, Paxton, how do I put that behind me and go on being a neighbor like nothing ever happened? And how do I do that with the people at work? And my students, if I have any after this? How could these people think that I'm some kind of monster? How could they think that about me?" Scalaro asked, and stared at Will, his expression pleading.

"I'm sure it's hard to put something like this behind you," Will said. "But what you're going through can't compare to what happened to the victims and their families. You should understand that. You saw what he did to those women."

Taking a napkin from its holder, Scalaro rubbed it hard across both eyes, then blew his nose into another napkin. "On top of everything else, I still have nightmares about what I found in the woods that day." Sniffling, he asked, "Okay, what do you want to know?"

"I want to know about the students in your class. What you remember about each one. If there was anything at all peculiar."

"What? You want me to point out someone so you can put him through what you put me through? What if I'm wrong? I won't do that to anyone."

"With or without your help, everyone in that class is going to get a hard look. If you can remember something, maybe it will spare some decent kids the kind of trauma you went through."

"No," Scalaro said, shaking his head. "I'll not put anyone in that situation. No. And why are you so hung up on my class? The odds are a million to one against him being there."

"He was in the class and you're why he was there."

"Bullshit! You really are desperate, aren't you?"

Will bit back what he wanted to say. He had disliked Scalaro even before he became a suspect. Maybe it was an accident that Scalaro had discovered the bodies, but it was no accident the way he had parlayed this tragedy into gain, and this galled Will.

"The killer was in your class," Will said, "because he had seen you on the news and knew you would talk about the murders. By being there he could watch the students' reactions and feel smug about how scared and angry he had made everyone. He was there because you attracted him."

"To hell with you. I'm not responsible for what happened to Mary Williams."

"I didn't say you were."

Defiantly, Scalaro tried to stare down Will, but couldn't do it and looked away. For several seconds, he rubbed the back of his neck while staring at the floor, then stopped rubbing his neck and looked at Will. "She was so outraged by the killings," he said quietly. "I remember her exact words. She said that 'whoever killed those women was a pathetic coward who was too inept and too afraid of women for any woman to ever willingly spend time with him.' She kicked the killer's trip wire." Scalaro sighed. "All right. What do you want to know?"

Will opened the manila folder and pushed it across the table. "Look at the class roster and tell me what you remember about each male."

Scalaro ran his fingers through his hair and slouched over the roster like a schoolboy being tested on material he hadn't studied. Moments later he raised his hands in supplication. "This is no good. I can't remember. The class only met once. I don't even know which face goes with which name."

"Okay. I want you to run through everything that happened. Start at the beginning."

"Ah, let's see. It was an Intro Psych class and I began the way I always do. I went over the syllabus, my expectations on attendance, how I test, a little about the midterm paper, and I showed them how I thought they should use the text. It's pretty dry stuff and after I get it out of the way I like to do something interesting, so I told them we'd take a break and afterwards, because of the murders, we were going to talk about the dynamics of serial killers."

"Did anyone ask or do anything that was unusual during that part of the class?"

"Nothing that I recall."

"Go on."

"So I did add/drop during our break, and when we started back, I . . ."

"Wait a minute," Will interrupted. "Tell me about add/drop?"

"Oh, some students on the official roster want to drop the class and there are always a couple who are not registered that want to be added."

"Were there any drops or adds that night?"

Scalaro rubbed his forehead. "I think there were three adds. Yeah, one woman and two men. And one of the men didn't want to be added."

Leaning forward, Will said, "Tell me about the guy who didn't want to be added."

"When I call the roll, I always pay attention to students who don't answer and make sure I add them. You see, I had an incident last year, so I'm now a zealot about procedures. Anyway, the other two came up but this one guy didn't, so I signaled for him to approach and asked him if he was registered. He said he wasn't sure about the course and wanted to check it out first. I told him that to stay in the class, I needed to add his name to the roster and see an ID—that's a school requirement. Later, if he decided not to take the class, I'd erase his name. He thought about it, then took out his driver's license and handed it to me, when actually I was asking for his school ID."

"Did that strike you as peculiar?"

"Not really. Sometimes, if a student has outstanding parking tickets or bounced a check at the bookstore, they hold the ID until he or she pays up. I try not to embarrass students by making a big deal out of it, so I accepted his license and if the registrar bounced him, so be it."

"What else do you remember about him?"

"He sat in the back. I don't remember him participating. And when the class was over, he literally pushed ahead of a couple of students who had come up to talk to me and told me to erase his name because he wasn't taking my class. I said I would, and he left in a hurry."

"So his name is not on this roster?"

"No. That's a list of preregistered students. I won't . . . I wouldn't have turned in add/drops until next Wednesday. I can't believe they didn't tell you that when you picked up the list."

"Did you erase his name?" Will asked more forcefully than he intended.

"I know what you're thinking. This guy could be . . . but we don't know that. I . . ."

"Did you erase his name?"

"No, I didn't. Erase is only a figure of speech. I drew a line through it. It's in my briefcase upstairs. I'll get it."

"I'll go with you," Will said. It was standard practice when questioning a murder suspect in his home to keep him in sight at all times, and Scalaro officially remained the primary suspect.

Scalaro stared at Will, hurt and anger replacing his brief flirtation with excitement. Scalaro knew all about standard procedure from two days earlier when three policemen had watched him change clothes. "So you lied," he said. "You still think I'm a suspect."

There were officers outside. If Scalaro had told the truth, then at the very least Will owed him a little dignity. But he couldn't do it. "Others will ask, so I need to make sure you don't doctor the roster. It's in your best interest, too."

Looking like a hurt lover, Scalaro pushed out his chair and said, "Sure."

As Will followed Scalaro up the stairs, he quietly unsnapped the guard over his .38 Smith and Wesson, just in case.

Scalaro led him into his study and placed a leather carrying case on his desk. "It's in the side pocket. I'm not going to touch it," he said and stepped back, so that Will had to turn sideways to keep him in view. The roster contained thirty-two printed names with social security numbers. Pointing at the bottom of the second page, Scalaro said, "Down here are the add-ons. This one is a young kid named Lenwood Trammel, and the man I told you about is Isaac Drum. See, here's his name with a line through it. You satisfied?"

Will picked up the roster and stared at the name. "May I take this?"

"What the hell," Scalaro said. "You'd just take it with a warrant if I refused."

"I would. But thank you. You've been very helpful."

II

Back in his vehicle, Will radioed the dispatcher, an easygoing woman named Margaret Sherer, and asked her to get the addresses of Lenwood Trammel and Isaac Drum from DMV records. He also asked her to initiate background checks. While waiting, he removed the recorder from his pocket and replaced the tape with a fresh one. This done, Will tried to relax and strummed his fingers on the steering wheel, looking no place in particular. The sunlight seemed extra harsh and Will thought this a sensory distortion from having gotten practically no sleep last night. Then he noticed Scalaro's newspaper in the delivery box. Leaving his hat on the seat, Will got out of the patrol car and retrieved the newspaper. A reporter shouted, "Is Scalaro under house arrest?" Will ignored him and once again trudged up the steep walk, this time to Scalaro's front door, which was clearly visible to the whirring news cameras. When Scalaro answered, Will handed him the paper and then, knowing that if he was wrong the images now being recorded would haunt him with years of humiliation, he shook Scalaro's hand.

. . .

When Will returned to his car, Sherer had the requested information. Eighteen-year-old Lenwood Trammel was listed at the same address as when he obtained his learner's permit two years earlier—probably still living at home. Isaac Drum, age twenty-two, lived at 51 Old Market Road in Jeffcoat County. This past November he had turned in a military permit when applying for his South Carolina license. Neither man was listed in SLED's sex offender data bank and Sherer had initiated a search of the FBI's offender files.

Will asked for directions to Old Market Road and started that way. Ten minutes later, Sherer let him know that neither Trammel nor Drum showed up in the FBI's bank. "You want backup?" she asked.

"Nah. All I'm going to do is take a quick look, so let's treat it as just another routine student check. If I see anything suspicious, we can go back with a warrant and numbers."

"10-4. You're the boss, so I guess you know what you're doing," Sherer replied.

Will, though, knew only two things for certain. He had failed to prevent more women from dying, and he now knew better than to put too much hope into any one lead. He had done that with Scalaro, only to watch in mute rage as he and his attorney had walked out of the Jeffcoat Detention Center. This seething anger stayed with Will last evening after he went home. It had been growing dark when Marianne started next door to bring home Zack. "What are you doing? Are you crazy?" Will had yelled. "Will, I'm only going to get Zack," Marianne said. "I've done this hundreds of times." "Things have changed," he told her, "and you can't take stupid risks. I'll go." It was the most he said to Marianne all night. They had known each other since high school and he had never treated her this way. But he didn't seem able to help himself.

Even after Keenan had called and suggested that Scalaro's local fame may have attracted the killer to his class . . . even after Keenan offered this hope—and an olive branch for the breach between them—even after all this, Will could not bring himself to apologize to Marianne. Too frustrated to sleep, too mentally ragged to think, Will had sat in the dark sipping beer until the beer ran out. Then he just sat in the dark.

III

Old Market Road was two lanes of potholes and crumbling asphalt lined by sagging, vine-covered fences. Beyond the fences were the jury-rigged outfits of men who farmed after they got home from their day jobs. More fields had been given back to brush and tinder-dry scrub-grass than were cultivated.

Will drove slowly, checking mailbox numbers until he found the box marked 51. One side of the mailbox was caved in, probably from redneck polo, played with a pickup truck and baseball bat. Will pulled into the gravel driveway in front of a wooden, one-car garage.

The rest of the house had a brick exterior painted white. Other than a picture window, with its green drapes drawn tight, the house's windows were small and high. Hedges of unruly redtips grew along both sides. The nearest neighbor was at least three hundred yards away and trees obscured their view.

Will radioed the dispatcher. "10-25 51 Old Market Road. I'm expecting an FBI agent from Quantico named John Keenan to be at Headquarters soon. Would you have the duty officer send him to the communications room and put him in touch with me? After I talk to Drum, I may go see Lenwood Trammel before I come in."

As Will crossed the threadbare yard, he reached into his pocket and switched on the miniature recorder. "Sunday, June 14th, 11:23 A.M.," he said. "Checking out at 51 Old Market Road to interview Isaac Drum, who was present in Andrew Scalaro's class on the night Mary Williams was abducted. This place sure affords a lot of privacy."

8

crisis

I

WHEN KEENAN stepped through the open door of SLED headquarters' Communications Room, a pear-shaped woman sat at a wide counter with her back to him, and spoke urgently into a radio microphone. "Agent 11-332, please respond." The woman had light brown hair and wore a white sweater over her uniform because the spacious room was cooled to the preferred tolerance of the banks of electronic equipment, rather than the warm-blooded operators. She waited a couple of seconds, then repeated, "Agent 11-332, please respond."

Close beside her, a telephone pressed to one ear, stood Martin Stith, the man with the large scar who had challenged Keenan during his presentation to the task force weeks earlier.

"Goddamn it, no answer," Stith said and slammed the receiver back into its cradle. "Contact Jeffcoat's dispatcher and get someone over there ASAP."

The dispatcher swiveled to her right, switched on a different radio, then pulled a blue manual from a shelf crammed with similar manuals and began running her finger down the page. Keenan thought he should stay out of the way until they resolved their problem, so he waited just inside the door. Absorbed by the crisis, neither agent noticed Keenan.

With one hand on the back of the dispatcher's chair and the other on the desk, Stith hovered over her as she keyed a setting into the radio and said, "SLED HQ to Jeffcoat dispatch."

"This is Jeffcoat. What's up?"

"We need assistance. One of our officers checked out at a Jeffcoat residence at 11:23 and we can't raise him. We'd like someone to check and make sure he's okay."

"Sure, we'll have someone drift that way."

With a rough jerk, Stith pulled the microphone from the dispatcher. "This is SLED lieutenant Martin Stith. We don't want any drifting, we want somebody's ass there ASAP. The officer was investigating the serial murders and might be in trouble. The address is 51 Old Market Road. The officer's name is Will Paxton."

"What?" said Keenan, stunned.

Stith jerked his head around and stared at Keenan, then turned back to the radio as it crackled, "This is Unit 7. I'm on my way. Current 10-20 on Highway 125 seven miles south of Jeffcoat. ETA Old Market Road four, maybe five minutes."

"McGrady, this is Blanchard," another voice said. "I'm three or four minutes behind you. Sit tight until I get there, all right?"

"10-4," McGrady responded, his voice barely audible through a siren's wail.

Keenan crossed the room and stood beside Stith, both men expectantly watching the radio. He tried to remember if Old Market Road was Scalaro's home address, but wasn't able to think with his usual clarity. Keenan knew this had to be a temporary breakdown in communication, that Will was fine, that Will would never recklessly put himself in harm's way. Or would he?

"What's Jeffcoat dispatch's number," Stith demanded. The dispatcher consulted the manual and gave him the number. As Stith reached for the telephone, he bumped hard against Keenan. "Stay out of the way," he ordered, then punched in the number. "This is Stith. I know Dan Blanchard; he's a good cop. What about McGrady? . . . Uh-huh . . . Fuck, only six months. Any other experience? . . . Goddamn it . . . No . . . We don't know what they might be walking into . . . Yeah, that's a good idea. ASAP. And tell the kid to lay off the siren. No use alerting the bastard. And leave this line open . . . Then get someone to help you . . . I don't care who, just do it," Stith said and lay the receiver beside the phone.

Seconds later, Jeffcoat's dispatcher called for a third unit. "This is Unit 23," a woman's voice said. "I'm already en route, but at least fifteen minutes away. Anybody closer?"

"Negative."

"All right. I'm kicking it."

"10-4. Also Unit 7 and Unit 9, SLED advises the first units approach quietly, so Code 2. Unit 23, you've so far to travel, go Code 3 for now."

"This is Blanchard. Will SLED HQ please tell us what they know?"

Stith again commandeered the radio. "Paxton went to interview a man named Isaac Drum in connection with Mary Williams's murder. He went without backup. He signed out at 11:23. When he hadn't signed back in by 11:45, the dispatcher tried to raise him on his portable unit, couldn't get a response, and called me in. We've tried Drum's phone, but no answer. All we know about Drum is that he turned in a military permit when obtaining his South Carolina license this past November. He's a white male, with dark hair, blue eyes, and is listed as five-ten, one hundred and eighty pounds. He owns a maroon Chevy van, license number RJM 629."

This information shook Keenan out of his daze. He stepped around Stith and asked the dispatcher if he could borrow the DMV report. At an unoccupied space on the counter, he called the Communications Center at the Academy Building in Quantico. "This is Keenan, badge SA 10-9872. I want a complete background check run on Isaac Abraham Drum, including military records. I want it top priority. Fax it to me at South Carolina's SLED Headquarters."

When Keenan hung up, all he could do was listen helplessly to the low static of the radio, damning its silence, dreading its next words.

9

cry uncle

I

FENCE POSTS blurred past and small bumps threatened to send the patrol car airborne. Usually, the big engine's surge was pure visceral pleasure for Dan Blanchard—but not on this call. Blanchard loved driving fast, always had. As a kid, he first knew envy from watching cop cars jackrabbit up the road. This was not the main reason, though, that he became a cop. Blanchard became a cop because of Uncle Frank, his mother's brother. Frank had been a North Carolina state trooper, and he was without a doubt the most decent man Blanchard had ever known. Every year on Dan's birthday, the present from Uncle Frank always arrived on time and his call was never a day late. When his family visited, Frank would use a couple of vacation days to take the boys fishing, shoot pool, target practice, and do the one thing Dan thought more special than even the state fair—he would take Dan and his little brother Matt for a ride in his patrol car, and Frank would fly. Dan's friends got tired of his bragging that Uncle Frank was the fastest cop on the road. And when Blanchard first joined the force, Ma Bell's stockholders must have reaped big bonuses from the calls to Uncle Frank, who gave Dan more practical how-to tips than the sergeant that he rode with for the first six weeks.

So it was not surprising that Dan Blanchard thought of Uncle Frank as he thundered down Route 7. The call said an officer might need assistance, that they couldn't raise him on the radio. Probably a wild-goose chase, a lot of guys turn off their handset so the constant chatter won't squirrel an interview. But things just kept getting rougher out here; it got you thinking. An officer was killed up in Greenwood last fall. Another in Orangeburg not three months later. And could it really have been a year since Uncle Frank made a routine traffic stop on I-95 and was gunned down by a fifteen-year-old in a stolen car. No damn wonder that, as Dan Blanchard responded to this call, he drove like an angry man.

The radio crackled, "Unit 7 is 10-20 at 51 Old Market Road."

"Billy this is Blanchard, stay put until I get there."

"10-4."

Already driving near his limits, Blanchard pushed a little harder.

"There's a marked SLED unit out front," Billy McGrady reported. "No other vehicles visible, but there's a garage with the door closed. No signs of activity. Shades drawn on all windows. Huh. Dan, there's smoke coming out the chimney."

"He's burning evidence," a voice growled, that Blanchard now recognized as Martin Stith.

"10-4," Blanchard said. "ETA two minutes."

As he approached Old Market Road, Blanchard barely slowed. Just before the junction, he twisted the steering wheel sharply, putting the vehicle into a controlled slide. His hands were sweaty and the wheel slipped a fraction, which he immediately corrected, but the car fishtailed and kept sliding sideways toward a huge water oak. Gripping the wheel to allow no play, Blanchard stomped the accelerator, spewing a hard stream of gravel that sounded like shotgun pellets as they cracked into trees and fence posts. The right front wheel slipped off the pavement before the tires, smoking and spinning faster than the eye could track, caught and the patrol unit shot forward, then, like a pendulum, fishtailed the other way. Blanchard kept accelerating and the car straightened. The road was rough, though, and Blanchard had to slow to a jolting sixty-five. He was breathing hard and sweat beaded on his forehead. He knew he was driving recklessly, and that after this rutted road the car would need a front-end alignment before it again rode true. Right now, that didn't matter.

.   .   .

Blanchard braked hard and came to a stop just past McGrady's unit and behind a SLED squad car pulled into the gravel driveway. Dust drifted in the still air as Blanchard got out and surveyed the small house through the dark lens of his aviator's sunglasses. The sun, directly overhead, was searing hot. Sweat beaded on Blanchard's ruddy neck and dampened his frizzy, rust-colored hair.

McGrady, lean and baby faced with a dark mustache, walked over to join him. "This don't feel right," the younger man said. "Two police cars pull into the front yard and nobody even looks out the windows. And in weather like this, why the hell would anybody build a fire except to get rid of something. And you know Dan, if that SLED agent was able, he'd be out here by now."

"Yeah," Blanchard replied without taking his eyes from the house. "I don't think it would be too smart to just walk up and knock on the door. Cover your ears." Blanchard leaned into his patrol car and gave the siren a three-second blast. There was not even a ripple of drape movement. He hit the siren again. Still nothing.

Jerking the lever to pop the trunk, Blanchard walked behind the car and lifted a bullhorn from among his jumbled gear. "Will Paxton, please acknowledge or come out," he electronically bellowed, waited thirty seconds, and repeated, "Will Paxton or Isaac Drum or whoever is inside, please acknowledge. We only want to know that Officer Paxton is okay." Sweat dripped down Blanchard's forehead and a wet patch swelled across the back of his uniform fast enough to track its progress. Blanchard waited about a minute, as Billy McGrady stood beside him and smoked a cigarette in quick drags.

Sliding back into his car, Blanchard picked up the transmitter and gave a rundown of the situation, while McGrady leaned over the open door, taking nervous hits on the cigarette.

". . . so we need to secure that house right away," Blanchard ended his report.

"Dan, this is Dee Tucker. I'll be there in another eight or nine minutes; wait for me."

"Can't afford to, Dee," Blanchard answered.

"This is Inabinet," a gruff voice cut in. "What's going on out there?"

Before Blanchard could answer, Stith took over, "Sheriff, this is Martin Stith. The fucker that's been committing these murders may be holding Will Paxton hostage."

"Boy, you watch your mouth or get off my frequency. I'm leaving church and my wife is in the car. You understand."

"Yes sir," Stith replied. Stith's sudden meekness surprised Blanchard. So far, this guy Stith had come across as a bona fide asshole. He figured Stith was probably like most bullies, either trying to walk on you or kissing your ass.

Refraining from further vulgarity, Stith described the situation. He also reported that a couple of state troopers were fifteen minutes away and that an ambulance had been dispatched and would wait at the entrance to Old Market Road until the area was secure.

"You said Paxton is in uniform?" Inabinet asked.

"Yes."

"All right. Blanchard I want you in charge," Inabinet drawled. "You have probable cause to enter that house. Come up with a plan to secure it, but wait for Tucker. This fellow Drum may have Paxton's radio, so don't broadcast what you're gonna do. And if there's any resistance at all, you wait for more backup. Got it?"

"10-4. I'll radio as soon as it's secure." Blanchard returned the transmitter to its cradle, then used a hand towel that he kept on the front seat to wipe the sweat from his face. He slipped on his sunglasses, got out of the car, and walked to the trunk. "If you have a vest with you, put it on," he told McGrady.

"Right," McGrady replied, dropped his cigarette, and crushed it out with his toe before walking to his own patrol car.

Lifting a Kevlar vest from the trunk, Blanchard slipped it on and began methodically tightening the straps, becoming more focused with each hard tug. He next took his Browning .12 gauge from the trunk rack, checked the magazine, and pumped a round into the chamber. Walking over to where McGrady was still cinching his vest, Blanchard said, "I'm going to check the back of the house."

"I'll go with you," McGrady offered. The kid lifted his own Browning from the trunk and leaned it against the car's back panel while adjusting his vest's straps.

"No, you watch the front," Blanchard instructed. "Make sure you keep your vehicle between you and the house. And you may want to lay your shotgun across the seat where direct sunlight won't heat the metal and make it hard to handle. Be back soon."

Blanchard surveyed the house again, then with quick steps moved past the vehicles and ran to the edge of the garage. His body armor held heat like a down jacket.

At the corner of the garage, he readied himself, then spun around it, the shotgun pressed to his shoulder as he looked intently over the blue-steel barrel at the back corner. With one hand, Blanchard tried the gate. Rusted, it required a hard push to open and squeaked loudly. So much for surprise, he thought. Gripping the heavy shotgun with both hands, he squeezed through the gate and hurried along the side of the garage, acutely aware that its plywood walls did little to muffle noise and offered only a fatal illusion of cover.

At the back corner, Blanchard turned his back toward the garage, careful not to brush against it because he knew how loud even the scratching of mice in an attic sounded. Sweat stung his eyes and dotted his sunglasses. He was breathing hard. Inhaling deeply, Blanchard swung around the corner and went into a crouch with the shotgun ready against his shoulder. The backyard was clear, though it had not been mowed in weeks. He squinted into the shadows of the trees beyond the yard's perimeter. Clear.

The house extended about ten feet beyond the garage, with firewood stacked against the wall facing Blanchard. The woodpile's plastic cover had been carelessly tossed a few feet into the yard. As Blanchard had hoped, the garage had a back door. Running to this L-shaped corner, he crouched facing the door, his back pressed against the firewood. His luck held; the door appeared to be of thin wood with a hollow core and opened inward.

For a couple of seconds, Blanchard tried to catch his breath, the hot air choking more than helping. He shifted the Browning to his left hand, pressed its butt into this side, and used his right hand to mop his forehead. Still choking on the hot air, he pulled the vest as far from his body as it would go. The cooler air offered only teasing relief and Blanchard considered taking the damn thing off. But that would be stupid, and this was not the time to be stupid. He did need to hurry, though, before the heat and loss of fluids weakened him, maybe even clouded his judgment.

Inabinet had told him to come up with a plan. If Drum or whoever was monitoring the radio, he might not expect anything until the other unit arrived. At least, that's what Blanchard would tell Inabinet to justify what he was about to do. Inabinet, though, probably wouldn't believe him because he knew what had happened to Uncle Frank, knew that the doctor had told Aunt Melanie that by the time Frank reached the hospital there had been too much internal bleeding, too much additional damage to his organs, and if they had only gotten him there a little sooner he might have stood a chance. Only twenty minutes passed from the time Frank signed out until help arrived. Twenty minutes. This guy, Paxton, had already been in there a lot longer than twenty minutes. Blanchard should already be inside.

Assessing the situation, Blanchard asked himself what he would do if he were in the garage waiting to fend off an attack, and thought that he would either crouch in the back corner where he could watch both the front and back doors, or lay down in the doorway connecting the garage to the house. If someone waited in either of those places, Blanchard's only chance was a sudden charge that might allow him about an eye-blink of surprise. If he hesitated at all, he'd be as vulnerable as a cutout on a shooting range. Cautiously, Blanchard extended his arm full length and tried the door; it was locked. He would have to kick it open on the first try and let his momentum carry him far enough into the garage to get past the door—and hope to God that Drum had not put something in front of the door to trip him, because that's what Blanchard would do if he were waiting inside.

Carefully, Blanchard laid his sunglasses on top of the firewood and stood. He sucked in a deep breath of humid air, and said loudly in his mind, 'Okay . . . ready . . . now.'

Blanchard didn't move. He tried to swallow, but his mouth was too dry. A red glow of shame flushed his body even hotter. If he didn't break this paralysis, he knew he might walk with a permanent slouch all the way to the hereafter.

He thought again of how, for twenty critical minutes, Uncle Frank's life's blood emptied and darkened like the asphalt on which he lay. Without making a conscious decision, Dan Blanchard roared, "No." His right shoe crashed against the door beside the imitation-brass doorknob, splintering the wood around the knob, then he heaved his shoulder against the door, causing it to burst open and Blanchard to stumble forward into the dark garage. He regained enough balance after two steps to go into a crouch, the door into the house squarely at his back as he scanned the shadowy corners.

Luckily, the room was empty except for a few tools scattered around the walls, and it took Blanchard only a second to know it was safe.

Whirling to face the door, Blanchard lost his balance and ended up on his tail. The door was closed. Never taking his eyes from this door, he got to his feet and backed to the wide garage door. Groping until he found the lever, Blanchard lifted the door, flooding the empty room with sunlight. As this happened, the door to the house seemed to move and Blanchard jerked the Browning to his shoulder, squeezing the trigger to within a hair of discharging. He then realized the movement had been an illusion caused by the light. Lowering his gun, he looked out toward McGrady. The younger man squinted at him over the barrel of his own lowered shotgun that was still pointed straight at Blanchard. Scared and green and not told of the plan, McGrady had almost shot him.

Blanchard felt first a flash of anger, then a chill as he realized that if Will Paxton had stumbled through that door a moment ago, Blanchard would have blasted him into oblivion, no doubt about it, he was that close. Blanchard cursed himself. He had to be more cautious, yet the slightest hesitation could get him killed. Right now, the many hours of training to verify then fire felt like a game, while this was real. Maybe he should wait for Tucker, only another three, four, maybe five minutes. And if each second was tied to a weakening heartbeat? No. He would just have to be more alert, no more mistakes. And with the vehicle gone, Drum was most likely gone.

Blanchard signaled for McGrady to join him. When the young officer reached the garage, Blanchard said, "Stand in the far corner where you can watch the front of the house and the back door while I get us inside."

The door into the house was two steps above the garage floor. Crouched against the wall, he tried the knob; it was locked. Given the angle, Blanchard thought only a karate expert could kick it open, and checked the garage for a sledgehammer or heavy ax, but didn't even see a crowbar. He remembered the firewood. Positioning himself beside the back door, shotgun ready, he swung through, scanned, then quickly selected a thick, quarter-split log and hurried back into the garage. In the distance, he could hear a faint siren's wail. Standing to the right of the door, Blanchard slammed the log just above the lock, once, twice, and on the third time the door burst open, its locking mechanism hanging limply for a half second before clattering onto the top step. Flattening himself against the wall, Blanchard strained to listen for any noise inside, but it was difficult to hear over the siren. The loss of fluids was also taking its toil: his arms felt weak, his legs wobbly, and his pants were soaked as if he had urinated on himself and, to tell the truth, he was not sure that he hadn't done so.

He picked up the shotgun from against the wall, breathed as much humid air into his lungs as he could, then swung into a crouch low in the doorway and peered over the bluish-black barrel into a long, dark living room. The siren's harsh squall drowned all sound except Blanchard's heavy breathing. Weak light came through a door at the far end of the room and embers glowed faintly in the fireplace. In this near colorless dusk, Blanchard made out the forms of an easy chair, end table, and lamp, all positioned near the middle of the room. A door on the near side of the room opened into an area even darker than the living room. If trouble was here, he thought, it's through that door.

Blanchard was light-headed from the heat and exertion, and the siren's piercing blast triggered a dull throbbing at his temples. It took effort to think. Unable to be heard above the noise, Blanchard signaled for McGrady to move up, then surveyed the room one more time. With his eyes better adjusted, he noticed something on the other side of the chair that at first looked like a large, sleeping dog. Then he realized what he was seeing, and a rage more primitive than anything he had ever felt seized him. Fumbling, he pulled his radio from its holster just as Tucker's car screeched to a stop out front and, at last, the siren fell quiet. Pressing the radio's button, Blanchard yelled, "Officer down. Officer down. I have a visual inside the house and an officer in there is down. I'm going in."

II

SLED's communications room became very quiet. Stith paced and flicked impatient glances at the mute radio. Keenan leaned near the door, waiting for Blanchard's next report.

Pausing, Stith asked the dispatcher, "You got a smoke."

"No smoking in here," Sherer replied.

"I didn't ask you about the fucking rules, I asked for a smoke," Stith snapped.

With a resigned shrug, Sherer took a large cloth bag from a drawer, extracted a pack of Vantage 100s and a lighter, and handed them to Stith. He lit the cigarette and returned the pack to Sherer. "Thanks," Stith said as he resumed his clipped pacing, then muttered to no one in particular, "What could be taking so long?" After a hard drag on the cigarette, Stith stopped pacing, his blue eyes glistening and his scar hotly red. Staring at Keenan, he said, "That kid never would have been allowed to go there alone if he hadn't been put in charge. And I bet you had something to do with that, didn't you?"

Keenan met Stith's stare. "Yes, I did," he said, then lowered his head in full submission.

III

After reporting that an officer was down, Blanchard did not wait for a reply. Consumed by rage, gorged with adrenaline, he suddenly saw things with rare acuity. He also felt free of sanity's restraint and caution. Picking up the log that he had used as a battering ram, he hurled it through the door and charged after it, ready to blast anything that moved. Like a soldier out of the trenches, he never slowed as he swept through the dark door into a short hall and on into the darkest area yet, a small bedroom. He looked for, no, hoped for, the flash that would mean kill or be killed. Eyes and shotgun swept the room in unison as he moved deeper into it, almost tripping over the corner of a bed before reaching the far wall. He scanned, scanned again, and then noticed three feet farther along the wall, at head level, a pinhole glow of light. Sidling to it, he reached up, felt plastic, and pulled away a black trash bag that had been taped over a small window. Diffuse light filled the room and he saw . . . nothing. There was no one here. And as strongly as he had felt anything this volatile day, Dan Blanchard felt disappointed.

10

manhunt

I

"THE OFFICER is dead."

All activity in SLED's communications room stopped and no one spoke. Keenan leaned against the back wall, a silent no forming in his mind, hanging for a second as a fragile wish, then dissolving into hard reality. Stith stood hulking over the dispatcher. "Damn fool," he muttered, and grabbed the radio, but before he could transmit the drawl of Arnold Inabinet crackled, "You sure?"

"Yes sir," Tucker answered. "He has a wound to the stomach and a contact wound to the left temple. He had hemorrhaged from the mouth, but all bleeding has stopped and is starting to congeal. No vital signs, chalky color, peripheral digits feel slightly cool."

"All right. House secure?"

"Yes sir."

"All right. Let the paramedics check him. Don't disturb anything in the house. We'll have a warrant shortly."

"Sheriff, there were some remains of videotapes in the fireplace and I raked them out. One had fallen near the front and looks intact, but could have heat damage."

"Good. SLED HQ, I'd like your forensic unit over there. Also, notify Jones, Wincott, and Barnett."

"Already taken care of," Stith replied. "And we've put out an APB on Drum's vehicle. We'll update that we're looking for a cop killer."

"All right," Inabinet said, his voice barely audible.

Keenan stopped listening to the radio. He thought of the hole that had just come into the world of Marianne and Zack. Sadness swelled, nearly overwhelming him. The Communications Room suddenly felt hot and stuffy and he had trouble breathing.

Stith, still standing beside the dispatcher, shoved one of the rolling chairs noisily into the counter, then turned and charged toward Keenan. "This should never have happened," he said and thumped his index finger against Keenan's chest. His scar was bright red and spittle sprayed as he spoke. "Your boy should never have been put in charge. This is what that kind of bullshit gets you." Again, he drummed his finger hard against Keenan's chest.

Stith's accusation stung Keenan. Because of his own pride, Keenan had boosted Will into the storm's eye and he had floundered. His voice husky, Keenan managed to say, "I know." Then he looked away.

"Yeah, I guess you do," Stith said, staring at Keenan and obviously spoiling for a fight. When Stith realized that there was no fight in Keenan, not now anyway, he ordered, "I want you to go to the reception area and have whoever is at the desk canvas the building and get anyone that's here to the communications room. We're going to catch that bastard. Now get moving." Stith turned and, with his trunk tilted forward, stomped back to the dispatcher, saying, "I want the numbers for every jurisdiction in the state."

Keenan stared at Stith's back, and a sudden rush of anger blunted his other emotions and focused him. Anger is a much more pleasing feeling than sadness or pain or shame, so, in a sense, Stith had given Keenan the perfect salve. Keenan left the communications room and hurried down the polished halls to the reception area with his hands balled into fists.

II

Additional personnel arrived and soon SLED HQ bustled with a storm of activity. Using the chilly Communications Room as his command center, Stith stripped to his shirtsleeves as he coordinated the manhunt, his face red and hot-looking and wet circles forming beneath his arms. Stith worked with a berserker's zeal, shifting from telephone to radio to barking orders to studying incoming reports—bending the manhunt to his will. He wanted every jurisdiction personally contacted and asked that all bus stations and airports be covered, and that patrols on both primary and secondary roads be alerted, especially those near the state's borders. He also wanted each jurisdiction to send out extra units. "Make sure they know he's a serial killer and a cop killer; that'll get extra coverage," he told those assigned to make the calls.

Keenan contacted the FBI and orchestrated similar alerts in Georgia, North Carolina, and Tennessee.

At exactly 1:48, Keenan's unit began sending Drum's military records over the link. As the first couple of pages printed, Keenan and Stith leaned over them, shoulder to shoulder in what Keenan regarded as the smog of Stith's strong cologne. For weeks, both men had obsessed over any clue to this man's identity and now the printer was spitting out a portion of his life history. After glancing at the first page, Stith told Keenan, "Okay, this is your area. We need whatever you can pull from these, especially anything that tells us where he might run. Got it?"

"I know my job," Keenan replied, staring hard at Stith.

"Prove it," Stith said and turned back to his manhunt.

Keenan choked back his anger. He was used to working around law officers who were under pressure and had short fuses. But he intensely disliked Stith and was himself angry, so restraint took effort.

Carrying the military records to the corner he had claimed as his work area, Keenan began a quick review. Five years ago, just two months past his seventeenth birthday, Drum had enlisted in the army. His address at the time had been the Philip Weaver Home for Boys in Laurens, South Carolina. After basic training at South Carolina's Fort Jackson, Drum was accepted for Military Police training. Following more training, he was posted to Inch'on, Korea, with the rank of corporal. Six months later, he was reassigned to an off-base patrol unit in Seoul.

During this period, Drum had gotten pretty good performance appraisals on everything except his relations with peers; the longer he remained in service, the more his ratings in this area dropped. Then, in Seoul, came a major blemish. Six months after his transfer there, a prostitute charged Drum with assault. They assigned him on-base duty while they investigated the allegation, but even after it was dismissed, Drum never returned to active patrol. At that time, he had been approved to remain in Korea for the remainder of his enlistment, yet within three months they transferred him to a security detail at the military hospital in Wiesbaden—a drop in status from patrol. Drum remained in Wiesbaden until, three months from discharge, he returned stateside and finished his hitch on security detail at Fort Jackson's Moncrief Hospital. He received an honorable discharge this past November.

Keenan reviewed all the records, then carried his notes to where Stith was telling a computer analyst how to do his job. When Stith finished, Keenan told him, "Drum matches the profile. He's definitely the man we've been hunting."

"No shit," Stith sneered. "Do you have anything that's useful?"

"Do you want this information or do you just want to mouth off?"

Stith glared at Keenan. "All right. Do you have any idea where he might run to?"

Curbing his irritation, Keenan said, "When he enlisted he was living in a group home in Laurens, South Carolina. I can't see him running to Laurens, but alert the locals anyway. There's no family identified on his enlistment forms, so we need to get a court order to open his juvenile records."

Stith nodded. "That's doable."

"Two weeks after discharge, Drum went to work for a local security agency, the Midlands Guardians, and was stationed from 11:00 P.M. until 7:00 A.M. at a Hyundai dealership awaiting bankruptcy liquidation. The dealership is on Two Notch Road, probably not far from where Betty Reeves disappeared. You might want to have a couple of men check it."

"All right. What else?"

"Drum was an MP, so it's a good bet he knows standard pursuit tactics. You might ask yourself how you would run if you were in his spot."

"If it was me? I'd steal a car by any means necessary and stay on back roads until I was close to the state line, then hop on the interstate to cross. We have that covered. What else?"

"He had some martial arts training beyond standard MP courses. He's not a black belt or anything near that good, but he could give a single officer trouble. He also qualified as a marksman with the handgun."

"Marksman only means he went a little beyond basic firearms training. But I'll put it in the APB. What else?"

"I think that's all that might help us with the manhunt."

"Try to find out about his family," Stith said and, with a dismissive gesture, turned away.

Anger flaring anew, Keenan stared for a moment at the back of Stith's head while all around him the room crackled with hard-toned conversations; everyone seemed infected with anger. News of the shootings had been made public and jammed phone lines added to the tension. Yet, despite this torrent of activity, Isaac Drum had disappeared into the place where he had hidden all his life. He simply blended in with all the busy people going about their day.

11

a helping hand

I

POP PAULUS, a fifty-nine-year-old black man, drove his '54 Dodge pickup along an old logging road that was covered by pine needles. The truck was painted a deep green with black fenders. It didn't have air-conditioning so Pop had his arm resting in the open window, though today even the air blowing in felt hot.

Pop wore a ballcap with a bass stitched on it. He had a trimmed mustache that was flecked with gray. A lifetime working as a brick mason had given him thick upper arms and broad shoulders, though too many second helpings of his wife's cooking had nudged his shape into something akin to a potbellied stove.

Though Pop was eager to try his new Zebco reel, a Father's Day present, he'd almost stayed home today. He awoke this morning with a hitch in his back that kept hurting throughout church and Sunday dinner. But Pop believed that if you waited until you felt like it to do something, then not much would ever get done. As he drove, he distracted himself from his back pain by humming "Just a Closer Walk with Thee."

The road dead-ended in a loop that allowed plenty of space for parking. Here, the forest grew dense and the ground beneath the trees was clogged with vines and broad-leafed plants, except where well-worn paths led to Lake Marion. Only one other vehicle was parked on this loop. A fairly new maroon colored Chevy van. It was facing out from the woods with its rear doors open. As Pop drove past, a young white fellow with short dark hair stepped from behind the van and stood with his hands on his hips, watching Pop. The fellow wore jeans and a black T-shirt. He looked fit.

Pop brought the Dodge to a stop a couple of car lengths from the van. He'd scarcely had time to switch off the engine before the man walked over, coming around behind the truck until he stood looking at Pop through the open window. Up close, Pop thought the man, whose cheeks were scarred from acne, looked kind of pasty for a serious fisherman. Pop also thought the man stared at him a little too intensely for polite company; or maybe it just seemed that way because the man had the brightest blue eyes that Pop had ever seen.

"My battery's dead. Can you give me a boost," the man asked.

"Be happy to," Pop said and smiled. The man didn't smile back; he just kept looking at Pop like he didn't trust him. Pop, though, gave the fellow the benefit of the doubt and figured that he was probably acting so squirrelly because he was having car trouble. "I've got cables under my seat if you need them," Pop offered.

"I have some in the back of my van that we can use."

"Then I'll pull my truck over," Pop said and started the truck.

"Sounds like it runs good for such an old truck," said the man.

"It does," Pop answered. He backed out, eased to the front of the van, then switched off the engine, pulled the hood latch, and swung open the truck's door. He wanted to make sure that the cables were hooked up right so it didn't ground-out the Dodge's battery. Moving without hurry, Pop steadied himself by putting a hand in the open window and eased out. His back had stiffened on the drive here and he winced as pain grabbed him. Pop braced a hand on the Dodge's seat and waited for the pain to subside. "Been having back trouble," Pop explained to the man. "So I guess the Good Lord must be lookin' after you, 'cause it almost kept me home today."

"Is that right?" the man said and finally smiled, but it wasn't at all a warm smile. He kept watching Pop, his trunk tilted slightly forward and his hands held out a little from his sides, looking almost like he expected Pop to give him some kind of trouble.

Then Pop heard the van's engine popping from having recently been run and thought that that didn't set right with a dead battery. Something was wrong here. Maybe it was just that this man was a little strange. Or maybe he was up to something. Pop tried to never turn his back on a person in need, but his gut now told him that he should get out of there. "Now that I've stretched, I'm going to start my engine while you get your cables," he said, having decided that when the man went behind the van he'd drive away and go call the fellow a wrecker. Maybe he'd call the sheriff, too, and let a deputy check things out.

The man shook his head. "You're not getting back in your truck because I'm taking it," he said and reached to the small of his back and took out a dark gray gun with a matte grip. "So I'm going to tie you up in the back of my van." He then motioned with the gun toward the van's rear.

Pop looked at the gun and shook his head. He couldn't believe that he was being robbed of his truck.

"I said walk," the man ordered and, keeping a distance of about three steps, pointed the gun at Pop's face.

Pop stared at the gun, then nodded and began walking stiffly, lilting a bit to his left. He wasn't worried so much about himself as he was about that old truck. He pampered it like a grandchild, and now this young fellow was going to take it and probably hotdog it. "You take good care of that truck, you hear me," he said, as he rounded the van's rear panel. The seats had been removed from the cargo area. A canvas bag lay near the rear doors.

"Climb up in it, then turn and face me," the man ordered.

Pop stepped to the door and leaned in. It was like putting his head in an oven. With the doors and windows shut, the temperature in there might soon hit a hundred and ten or a hundred and twenty degrees. Pop looked at the man, who was careful to keep three steps between them. "Locked up in there, the heat could kill a man," Pop said. "Why don't we go back in the woods and you tie me to a tree."

"Old man, I don't' want to hurt you, I just want your truck. But if you don't do exactly what I tell you, I'm gonna hurt you bad. I don't want you found until I'm a long way from here. But I tell you what I'll do, I'll leave the windows down. So in you go."

Pop hesitated, then shook his head no.

The man steadied the gun with both hands and said, "Then fuck you."

"Okay. Okay," Pop said and leaned into the cargo area and leveraged himself up. His shirt already sopping, he crawled on his hands and knees until he had pivoted and faced the man, making sure he stayed close to the doors. Pop then eased back on his haunches, freeing his hands. He didn't trust this man to leave the windows down like he said he would. An open window would make it easier for someone to hear Pop banging on the truck's floor, or it might cause someone to come over and look in and this fellow knew that. He was desperate and didn't give a whit about anybody except himself. Pop now decided that if he got the chance he was going to grab the arm holding the gun. He was strong enough that if he got a hold of this fellow, the guy wouldn't be getting loose or pointing his gun anywhere except where Pop wanted it pointed.

"Now I want you to raise your hands," the man told him, "and press them against the roof while I get some rope from that bag near the door."

Pop thought his best chance would come while the man was fishing around in the bag. He placed his hands lightly against the roof and said, "See, I'm doing everything you want 'cause I don't want no trouble." He then took a deep breath and, realizing that he was about to tangle with a man holding a gun, he felt fear for the first time since this trouble began. His nostrils flared and the pain from his back was completely shut off. Silently, Pop prayed, "Lord, when the time comes please don't let me hesitate. Please, Lord." He then waited for the man to come closer.

The man, though, didn't come forward. He just stood there looking at Pop. Then he smiled and fired two gunshots, one into Pop's chest, the other ripping into his stomach.

Pop grabbed at his wounds and rolled onto his side, his shoulders and head leaning against the side-panel. This was wrong. He couldn't be shot. "No," Pop said; his voice sounded wet and weak. He was having trouble breathing. "No. Why?"

The man stepped closer and aimed the gun at the side of Pop's head. "You still think the Good Lord's looking out for me?" he asked, then fired again.

12

round o

1

ROUND O, South Carolina, is in the heart of pulp mill country. Its vistas are straight roads flanked by endless strands of evenly spaced southern pine that are interrupted here and there by murky stretches of black-water swamp. The people are a lot like the pine, rough barked and modest. Round O itself is little more than a wide spot on Highway 45 where an entrepreneur of sorts runs two businesses.

Located on one side of the road, Charlie's Diner is a long building with a wraparound porch whose wood has grayed from lack of protective stain. At the edge of the gravel parking area, a yellow porta-sign announces, "LIVE COUNTRY MUSIC ON SATURDAYS." Near the back of the property sits a forest green dumpster, and parked behind this dumpster on the Sunday afternoon Will Paxton died, was the idling patrol car of Colleton County deputy Duane Taylor.

Tall and lean, Duane stood at the dumpster's corner with a new citation in his book. On hot days like this most guys sat in their cars and ran radar out the window, but not Duane, he did it right, heat or no heat, which kept him among his department's top producers. From this spot, all Duane had to do was clock 'em, wave 'em over, and write 'em up—it was almost too easy.

Duane mopped sweat off his oval face. The ninety-eight-degree heat was wringing him out and he thought about cooling off in his squad car. Then, Duane's ready smile flashed as he considered walking across the road to Charlie's main business, which, except for three new-looking gas pumps, was a throwback to the fifties. Atop this boxy cinder block building was a bulky sign whose faded red letters announced to the world, "Charlie's Pit Stop." Below the name, smaller red letters read, "Gas. Groceries. Cold Beer. Bait." Hand-drawn signs plastered the store's front windows advertising specials such as "Watermelon $2.69," and one professionally done sign told anyone interested, "Hunting and Fishing Licenses Sold Here."

The more Duane thought about walking over to Charlie's to get a soda and cool off a little, the wider he grinned. Charlie wouldn't like it, not with all the men Duane had watched walking out carrying paper sacks. Everybody knew Charlie sold beer illegally on Sunday; he had been doing it for years. Smiling, Duane decided to go ahead and throw a ripple in that rebel-flag-toting redneck's enterprise. Since Charlie was breaking the law, he'd probably treat Duane real nice for a colored fellow, which was how Charlie referred to blacks, at least to their face. Duane would have a little harmless fun, take his time, chitchat with Charlie.

While thinking about this, Duane absentmindedly watched a Dodge pickup, maybe a '54 or '55 model, pull up at one of the pumps. He only noticed the truck because it was in good shape to be so old. Duane was about to step out from the dumpster when the truck's driver got out. He noticed the man's hand working at the small of his back and then he pulled his shirttail down—probably just shifting his wallet. But Duane thought it peculiar that this man wore an unbuttoned corduroy shirt over his T-shirt on such a hot day, and the man seemed to be looking around, checking out everything real carefully. Considering how Charlie's looked, who wouldn't be a little uneasy. Still, something about the man didn't seem right, so Duane eased back and watched as he unscrewed the cap and pumped in gas. When the man started inside to pay, Duane got a good look at him, and damned, if he didn't bear a strong resemblance to the picture on the APB that they'd passed out at the three o'clock briefing.

The bulletin had been a poor quality photocopy. Still, when Duane studied his copy, he thought the suspect, a man named Isaac Drum, looked ordinary, not at all like a mad dog killer, or even the run-of-the-mill pukes that regularly passed through the jail's revolving door. The report said that earlier today, without provocation or warning, Drum had gunned down a SLED agent named Will Paxton.

Someone at the briefing said they'd heard on the radio that Paxton had a wife and little boy. "What a shame," Duane thought. "What a damn shame." The APB also said Drum was a suspect in the serial murders that had been going on up around Columbia. What was it now, Duane tried to remember, five women that had been abducted and murdered. Duane shook his head; such perversion defied understanding.

Naturally, the report said Drum should be considered armed and extremely dangerous; he even had a little marital arts training from when had been an Army MP. And he was believed to be driving a maroon Chevy van, not an old Dodge pickup.

Before going inside to pay, the man carefully scanned the area again, and Duane ducked back. There was definitely something wrong about that guy. In his gut, he knew this was Drum.

Duane used his uniform's sleeve to wipe the sweat from his eyes, then peeked back around the dumpster. The man had gone inside. The only people visible were a father and two sons coming out of the L-shaped, cinder block alcove marking the men's bathroom, that was just a little up from where Duane watched. The sons hopped in a station wagon parked on the side of the pumps opposite the old truck, while the father went inside the store. Duane raced to his patrol car, grabbed the transmitter, and told the dispatcher he had spotted a man matching Drum's description who was acting real suspicious, and that he wanted backup. The dispatcher, a man named Mule Mellet, thought Duane must be having fanciful sightings and told him so. Mule said he wanted more details, told Duane that Drum drove a maroon Chevy van, and hemmed and hawed that the nearest unit was at least a dozen miles away.

"Look I gotta go if I'm going to maintain visual. Send someone. Out," Duane said, hoping Mule would have no choice but to send a unit. Mule had earned his nickname from being stubborn and more than a little lazy, so Duane couldn't be sure. Duane's hand shook a little as he took his Glock from the holster, popped the clip, checked the chamber, then slammed the clip back in place.

Duane switched off his car so it wouldn't give him away and, Glock in hand, returned to his vantagepoint at the dumpster's edge and peeked just as the suspect turned the store's corner, walking toward the bathrooms. Duane eased back to where he could only see a narrow sliver of space in front of the bathroom's L-shaped outer wall.

The APB said that without backup to maintain visual contact only. The family in the station wagon had gone and no one else was around. In a few minutes, the suspect would be back in his truck and Duane could not follow him on these straight roads without being spotted, which would give the suspect the upper hand. Once he had been seen, the suspect might slow down, let Duane get close, then slam on his brakes and swing out with an automatic weapon. Or maybe he had a scoped rifle and could stop farther ahead. Or he could take hostages. Or maybe he could push that old truck over terrain that would bottom out Duane's patrol car. If he did any of these things and got away, and killed again, Duane would live the rest of his life knowing that he had a chance to stop him and did nothing. And that didn't seem like such a good prospect for the next fifty or sixty years.

The man passed through Duane's narrow visual field. Duane counted off two seconds, and stepped clear of the dumpster, arms extended, hands tightly clasping his 9mm. Once across the sunbaked road, the parking area's gravel crunched loudly beneath his shoes, forcing Duane to stop, completely exposed. He used his sleeve to wipe the sweat from his eyes as best he could. A pickup truck with slat-board sides pulled up in front of Charlie's and Duane used the sound of the truck to ease forward with cautious steps that still sounded way too loud. At last, he reached the alcove and pressed his back against it while holding his gun at head level with both hands, ready, except there was a loud hiss in his breathing that he couldn't stop, and he felt a little light-headed, probably from the heat.

Muffled by the partition, Duane heard the toilet flush. A second later, the door opened and one, two, on the third step the man's shoulder came into view. With no time to wait, Duane stepped clear of the wall, aimed his Glock at the broadest part of the man's back, and yelled, "Police. Freeze."

The man stopped and stood motionless with his arms at his sides. His fingers fanned out and the bathroom key, which was connected by twisted wire to a thin wooden strip, fell on the gravel.

"Do anything sudden and I squeeze, understand?" Duane yelled, though not as loud as before. When the suspect did not answer, Duane repeated, this time louder, "Understand?"

"Yeah, man," the suspect answered, his voice husky, as if he had strained it yelling at a ball game. He was shorter than Duane, but stout and probably outweighed Duane by fifteen pounds. His short, dark hair was parted on one side and clumped with sweat. The suspect turned his head slightly and Duane noticed pockmarked cheeks. He also thought he caught a bit of bulge beneath the shirt near the small of the man's back.

"Hey man, I don't know who you think I am, but I can prove I'm not him. Just let me take out my wallet and I'll show you," the man said, and started moving his right hand toward his back.

"Freeze or you're dead," Duane shouted so loud his throat hurt. The man's hand stopped, but he left it poised about a foot from the small of his back. "I see the gun under your shirt," Duane said. "Move your hand away real slow, then raise them just as slow. Do it!"

The man didn't move. "Look, you're making a mistake," he said. "There's no gun. Just my wallet. Let me show you because you don't want to gun down the wrong man, do you? You don't want to make a mistake like that, do you? If you shoot me, you know what happens to cops in jail. You don't want . . ."

"Shut up and raise your hands."

"No."

"Do it or I cap a knee."

"All right, all right," the man said. But he still didn't move.

So Duane said, "Cop killer. Just give me an excuse." And Duane meant it. "I'm counting to three."

"No, man, no."

"One."

"We can work this out."

"Two."

"All right. All right," the man said and moved his hand back, but just a little. "There, you got what you want. If you won't let me, then you take out my wallet. Just ease it out and you'll see."

"Get your hands up. Now," Duane yelled.

The man still didn't move. Then things took a turn for the worse. From around the corner, a stove-bellied man, wearing bibbed overalls and a tight-stretched white T-shirt, staggered into view carrying a double-barreled shotgun. It was Charlie. Several days of white stubble covered the lower half of his beet-red face and rumpled tufts of gray hair stuck out from beneath a crooked and soiled cap that bore an emblem of the Confederate flag. Charlie walked with an unsteady gait that caused the shotgun to weave from side to side. If the gun went off, it could easily shred both Duane and the man he was covering.

"Boy, why you bothering this man," Charlie slurred.

"Go back inside," Duane ordered. "He's a cop killer. He's dangerous." Then he added, "He killed a white cop." In truth, Duane did not know if Paxton was white, but thought it might make a difference to Charlie."

"He's lying," the suspect yelled, and turned slightly so that Duane came into his peripheral vision. "This boy's trying to shake me down for money."

"For the last time, freeze," Duane bellowed to stop the man's slow turn. A few feet away, Charlie tottered, looking from one to the other, the two barrels moving with his watery eyes.

Then faint and distant, Duane heard the siren. So did the suspect. With his odds getting worse by the second, if the man was going to try something, it was now or never. He flicked Duane a hate-filled glance and, though his eyes were light blue, Duane thought they looked like a snake's eyes, empty and hard. The man turned his head a little more and now had Duane in view.

Sweat stung Duane's eyes, slightly blurring his vision. His breath hissed through his teeth, and he felt on the verge of hysteria. Charlie was saying something, but Duane couldn't split his attention.

"If you don't raise your hands by three," Duane yelled, "I'm going to shoot you. One."

The man turned a little more. His nostrils flared and he breathed as hard as Duane.

"Two."

The muscles in the man's jaw tightened, his eyes narrowed, he hesitated, and then . . . very slowly he began to raise his arms, and, as impossible as it seemed, the hate in his eyes deepened.

Duane ordered the suspect down, first on one knee, then both. A half-minute later, the man lay on the hot gravel. Simultaneously, Duane brought his knee into the small of the man's back and thrust the Glock between his shoulder blades with enough force that it had to bruise him. With his other hand, he removed a .32 Beretta Cougar that was snugged in the back of the suspect's jeans. Duane cuffed him and, just like that, it was over.

II

It was over. The menace ended. Yet, one more tragedy awaited discovery.

The Dodge pickup Drum had been driving was traced to John "Pop" Paulus of Elloree, South Carolina. When the patrol car pulled into the Paulus's yard, its grass worn short by the scuffing of six grandchildren, Mrs. Paulus met the officers at the door. They told her only that a criminal had been apprehended driving Pop's old Dodge. Mrs. Paulus just knew, with his truck stolen, that Pop was stranded at the lake, and she gave the officers directions to the old logging road that ended in a turnout about fifty feet from Lake Marion's edge.

They found the body of Pop Paulus inside Drum's van.

A different pair of officers returned to the Paulus homestead. Family had started to gather and Mrs. Paulus's thirty-five-year-old son, Solomon, came to the door with her, while others crowded behind them. When the officers delivered their news, Solomon held his mother tightly around her waist to support her. Mrs. Paulus asked the officers how it happened and they told her what they knew. Then she told them that Pop was too good of a man to die that way. He liked to laugh, eat, fish, play with his grandchildren. He never hurt nobody. And he was always helping the young ones who were starting out by giving them a little money if times got hard.

She had a lot more she wanted them to know. But the officers excused themselves. Mrs. Paulus thanked them for their kindness. And then, cradled in her son's arms, she began to cry.

13

a raindrop fallen to earth

I

THE MUFFLED rumble of thunder had grown more distant. Fierce thunderstorms, heat storms the locals called them, had rolled through the area all evening. In his hotel room, Keenan sat at the writing desk where he had laid out pictures of the interior of Isaac Drum's house. He glanced at the clock on the bedside table; it was a quarter past eleven, three minutes later than when he last looked. Sighing heavily, Keenan reached for the headphones, and his arm felt as if weighted by several layers of sopping wool.

Slipping on headphones, Keenan placed his thumb on the Sony's play button, then hesitated. The Sony held a copy of the tape taken from Will's pocket recorder. Keenan had probably listened to tapes whose horrors were much more graphic and prolonged. But he had never listened to the murder of someone he had known. In fact, he had only personally known two officers killed in the line of duty—Waylon Dupree died in a shoot-out with bank robbers in Miami, and someone had ambushed Mark Alverez on a logging road in Utah. He had not known either of these agents well, but had met them, and they were tribal family. For a while after each of these deaths, he seethed with impatience.

Keenan pushed the Sony's start button. A second later, the soft voice of Will Paxton filled his ears. "Sunday, June 14th, 11:23 A.M. Checking out at 51 Old Market Road to interview Isaac Drum, who was present in Andrew Scalaro's class on the night Mary Williams was abducted. This place sure affords a lot of privacy."

Moments passed, then a knock was heard. After several more seconds came the sound of a door opening. "Yeah?" a husky voice asked.

"My name is Will Paxton. I'm with the task force investigating the series of murders that includes Mary Williams. I'd like to talk with Isaac Drum."

"Uh, sure. That's me. Come in," Drum said. He sounded groggy or, perhaps, unsettled.

"I don't have much time and don't want to take up much of yours. I've just a couple of questions and I can ask them here."

"It's too damn hot to stand here and let the heat in," Drum replied—Keenan thought Drum probably interpreted Will's reticence as suspicion. "You're lucky I heard you. I work nights, and was sleeping fine until you woke me up. Now, I won't be able to get back to sleep until evening. So you can stay here in the heat, or come in and ask me whatever it is you want to know . . ." Drum's voice began to trail off and steps could be heard moving away, ". . . but I'm going to fix . . ." The sound of the door closing covered whatever was said here. ". . . just so all that heat's not coming in," Drum's voice again became audible.

Quickly, Keenan's eyes swept over a picture of the long living room. The only furnishings were a low-backed Naugahyde chair, matching ottoman, small end table, imitation brass pole lamp, its white shade still in the plastic protector, and a television and VCR on a low rolling stand in front of the chair. A few newspapers lay beside the chair. There was also a small fireplace, its bricks painted white, with built-in bookshelves on both sides. To the right, a door led into a small kitchen. On the left, another door opened into a narrow hall.

"Did you know Mary Williams?" Will asked.

"Naw. All I know is what I read in the papers. That crazy teacher really been doing all that stuff, killing all those women?"

"That's what we're trying to find out. You said you had no contact with Mary Williams?"

"I said I didn't know her." Drum's voice sounded distant and there was a barely perceptible sound of running water. "I'm curious about that teacher because I almost took his class. Newspaper said she was in it, thinks that's probably where he zeroed in on her." Steps could be heard approaching and Drum's voice grew louder. "Is that the way it was?"

In his mind, Keenan said, "Will, get out of there." Then he realized how irrational this was and how tightly he clenched his fists, so he opened and closed both hands to relax them.

"We believe the class is important," Will said. "I can't say much more because it's still under investigation."

"And that's why you want to talk to me," Drum said. "You want to know if I saw anything unusual, right?" He paused briefly. "Mostly, I remember that the teacher, this Scalaro, was strange and full of shit. There was something about him I didn't trust, so I decided not to take his class. Want some coffee?"

"No thanks. Did you see anything after class?" Will asked. Keenan thought Will sounded strained and telegraphed suspicion.

"Not really," Drum answered. "When the class ended, I had to be at work in an hour so I didn't stick around. You want my notes, right. I talked to one of the guys in the class, and he said you took his notes. They're in the bedroom. I'll get them. Just be a second."

"We've enough," Will said quickly, as the steps faded away. "We don't need . . ." Will's voice was cut off by a pop, as if someone had burst an inflated paper bag, followed by a loud "Uhh," and the sound of a table leg scrapping across a hardwood floor, and then a heavy thump.

For several seconds, the only sounds on the tape were labored breathing and moans of, "Oh God." Barely discernible beneath the struggling breath came the snap of a buckle being released and something hard sliding across leather as Drum first removed Will's gun, then his radio.

"How does that feel?" Drum whispered, close now. "You dumb bastard. Did you really think you could come in here and trick me? You're not that smart. I bet all you can think about right now is what a pathetic screwup you are. Huh? Isn't that right? Just a dumb screwup."

A loud gurgling came into Will's breathing. There was a rustle of clothing and a rasping groan, followed by metallic clicks as handcuffs were secured.

"You know, you're bleeding bad." The hushed voice sounded almost intimate. "I once saw a guy die from a stomach wound. Bad news. Takes a while. Stuff inside going where it's not supposed to, you get lots of choking."

For a couple of seconds, only labored breathing could be heard. Then, mockingly soothing, the voice sounded even closer. "I see a wedding band. What's she going to do all alone? Huh? Who all is going to keep her company at night? You know, maybe when things cool down I'll pay her a visit. I can get everything I need from your pockets. I can take your keys and let's see what's in your wallet . . . Well, look at this picture of a mother and child. She's cute. I'm definitely going to make her acquaintance."

Between gulping breaths, a gurgled "Please" and then "No" could be heard.

"She's mine now. So think about that as things start to get fuzzy. Think about how the only thing you've accomplished by coming here is introducing me to your family. And there is not a thing you can do about it."

"Please . . . I . . . anything."

"I wish I had time to enjoy this," the voice said. Then footsteps moved away.

The breathing became louder, more irregular. Brief episodes of rapid gasping began. Another two or three minutes, and the footsteps returned, followed by wood being dropped, paper being wadded, and the quick scratch of a match. Or maybe Keenan only imagined this last sound; it was very hard to hear anything except Will's struggle to breathe as his lungs filled with fluid. For two, three, four minutes, there was only the sound of Will's dying agony. So when the voice next spoke, its closeness startled Keenan—it was as if Drum stood close behind him, his whispers tickling the fine hairs on Keenan's ears. "Your time's almost up. Look at me. Damn it, I said look at me! That's right. This is the last image you'll ever see, because I hold . . ." Whatever was said here was lost in a spasm of wet choking. Then there was another pop, much louder than the first, followed by a slow exhalation as the gurgling weakened, weakened, stopped. Silence.

No, it just seemed like silence compared with the hellish suffering just ended. Fire crackled and muffled splashing could be heard as Drum urinated on Will.

A few more seconds and the footsteps receded, a door opened, shut, and only the faint popping of the fire could be heard.

. . .

Keenan took off the headphones. Sweat soaked his shirt and his own labored breathing replaced that on the tape. He moaned, "Ohhh." Moaned again, louder. Then strained to stop himself from moaning again, and his breath caught, and for a couple of seconds he could not breathe in.

Choking in a bit of air, Keenan tried to refocus himself by picking up the remaining packet of photographs and slipping off the rubber band. The first picture showed a chalk outline of a human form, the midsection broken by a large pool of drying blood. Its fetal shape reminded Keenan of a particular plaster cast he had seen over a decade ago, when he and his wife had gone to Pompeii. When Vesuvius's sudden violence buried that city beneath volcanic cinders, those who tried to run were beaten down by hot ash, while those who sought shelter choked on poison gases, though many held urns to their face and struggled for every precious breath. Run or seek shelter, struggle or lie down, their choice made no difference. Sometimes it was that way. Centuries later, archaeologists found strange cavities in the hardened gray ash. They filled the empty spaces with plaster, and human forms took shape. Keenan thought the chalk line in the picture like that, vacant space where life had ended.

The next picture was like one of those plaster casts. It showed Will's body, his hands cuffed behind his back, a large pool of blood at his middle, a dark ribbon running from a small hole in his left temple, his eyes open but vacant—a man reduced to no more than clay.

Then came a close-up of Will's head, and Keenan stared at the yellow droplets soiling Will's cheek. Drum had stood over Will's body and urinated. A pointless indignity. A desecration. Primitive rage swelled within Keenan. His breath came in heavy snorts. He wanted to piss on that son of a bitch Drum just like he had pissed on Will. Keenan wanted this as much as he had ever wanted anything, and promised himself that he would find a way to make Drum pay.

II

The hotel formed a shell around a spacious atrium with skylights and cascading plants. Centered on the ground floor, broad leaf plants and brass railings accented a handsomely appointed restaurant. Now past Sunday midnight, the hotel's public areas were nearly empty as Keenan walked briskly from the stairs into the lobby. He had taken the stairs from the fourth floor because the glassed elevator seemed too confined for his restless energy. After listening to the tape of Will's death, he became increasingly agitated and paced in his room, its air becoming unbearably stuffy. He needed the physical release of walking at a hard, tension-draining pace. For as long as Keenan could remember, he had vented his worst tension through such walks.

Keenan never slowed as he passed the young man and woman behind the front desk, and charged through first one set of glass doors then another, until at last he was outside. The night air remained steamy from the earlier storms, yet he immediately breathed more easily. He stood there for a moment filling his lungs with air, and noticed that fat moths looped and collided with soft thuds around the fixtures beside the doors.

Through the screen door Keenan saw moths bump around the porch lights. He was thirteen and stood behind his mother, who was tall and lean with angular features and wore a pale, peach-colored dress. Both stared through the screen at the beefy Virginia state trooper, his Smokey the Bear hat held before him like a fig leaf. This trooper had just told them that, while driving home in his pickup, Keenan's father failed to make a curve and veered across a double solid line, crashing head-on with a car driven by woman and her three-year-old daughter. All three were dead. "I might as well tell you now, since it's going to come out," the trooper said. "We're pretty sure your husband was drinking." In the awful silence, the moths fluttered and smacked against the porch lights.

The hotel was surrounded by highway sprawl. Looking either way, Keenan saw closed fast food places and the yellow beacon of a Waffle House. He set a hard pace in the direction he believed most likely to lead away from the congestion, and by the time he turned onto a road where he could see trees and mailboxes, his hair was soaked and his white shirt stuck to his body in dark patches. Keeping a hard pace, Keenan entered this neighborhood. The second house he passed had opened morning glories growing on the porch's ornate, ironwork columns. Keenan's damaged mental filters failed once again.

Keenan stood on a porch and could smell flowers. Through the screen, a gangly boy, almost as tall but not nearly so heavy, glared at him. The boy's lip was cut and the swelling and redness around his left eye had started to darken. The boy's mother stood behind him. Keenan's mother waited in the car, and he resented her for making him do this. She was wrong. She should stop butting in. This boy had called Keenan's father a sorry-assed drunk-driver killer. What angered Keenan most, and still did, was that he agreed with what the boy said. Stiffly, Keenan apologized for thrashing this boy and his words tasted bitter.

Later, Keenan sat at the kitchen table across from his mother. He refused to look at her. "You're going to become a large man, like your father," she said, and the comparison to his father flamed his anger. "So you could probably become a very good bully if that's what you want. But no one ever respects a bully," she told him. "Bullies think they're respected but it's contempt people feel. If you want respect, use your intelligence. Johnny, remember that a strong person always remains in control. Do this for me now. Later, you'll do it for yourself."

Keenan breathed hard as he pushed himself along the street past the mostly darkened houses. He rarely thought about the past, and never thought about his father, though he sometimes thought about his mother. She was the strongest person he had ever known. Despite all the pain his father must have caused her, he never once heard her complain or say one bad thing about him. Outwardly, Keenan followed his mother's example while inside his resentment grew. Thirteen years old and linked to his father by blood, he believed others searched him for the specter of his father's infamy, and that if he slipped even a little this would be seen as evidence of weak seed. He believed he could never let go and lose himself in a moment that might cause others to see him as anything like his father, so, throughout adolescence, he always held himself a little apart.

A sudden splash of light startled Keenan. Turning, he looked into a patrol car's blinding spotlight. The light stayed on him as a car door opened and a voice asked, "Okay, what are you doing in this neighborhood?"

Wet strands of hair splattered Keenan's forehead as he held his hands at chest level, palms out. "I'm FBI," Keenan said. "I can show you my shield. I'm uptight and need to unwind by walking."

At first, the officer didn't answer, then said, "Yeah, I know you. I've seen you on the news." The spotlight went off, as did the car's headlights, though the park lights stayed on. The patrolman walked to the front of the car and said, "You're consulting on the Saluda Woods case. You were a friend of Will Paxton."

Keenan's face flushed scarlet. It was irrational to think that this man somehow knew that he had let himself get distracted by personal feeling, had lost his objectivity, became careless, and, in so doing, had caused Will Paxton's death; yet, Keenan felt shame as if the officer knew all this. Shame because, in allowing his carelessness to cause another's death, Keenan had done the one thing that his whole life had been constructed to never do.

"I guess we're all uptight tonight," the officer said, and took out a cigarette. They stood almost directly beneath a streetlight and Keenan could see that the cop was a young man with soft baby-fat cheeks and short blond hair. "I've been driving around all night just feeling so damned angry myself," the cop said and lit his smoke. "A few minutes ago, I saw a couple of kids in a car smoking a joint, and I looked the other way. I didn't want to take them into custody feeling like I do now. You know, I don't want to chance anybody mouthing off to me. You know what I mean?"

Keenan nodded and huskily said, "Yeah."

The officer studied Keenan. To the patrolman, the FBI agent probably looked like a fighter who had taken the worst of it. "Yeah, I guess you do," the young man said. "Listen, I'll let the other units know you're out here. No one else will bother you. Walk as long as it takes."

After Keenan's mother finished her lecture, he left the house and walked down a dark road, pushing himself hard, trying to rid himself of his awful feelings. But no matter how fast he went, he could not outrun his shame.

14

first contact

I

ON TUESDAY evening, Keenan returned to the Jeffcoat Detention Center. He had spent most of the past two evenings in the dimly lit observation room, which was barely larger than a fair-sized walk-in closet and normally contained a small table and two wooden chairs. For Drum's interrogation, extra folding chairs had been dragged in to accommodate the wide jurisdictional interest.

The only person now in this room was Captain Oliver Treadle, who headed the interrogation team working Drum. Treadle had buzz-cut gray hair that clumped from liberally applied hair oil, and the droop of his jaws gave him a permanent sour expression. Treadle looked up as Keenan entered, then nodded toward the one-way viewing mirror and said, "You can have at the son of a bitch whenever you want."

On the other side to the viewing mirror was a glaringly bright interrogation room. Isaac Drum and his court-appointed attorney sat at a metal table. The attorney, a rail of a man with a humped nose, read from a sheath of stapled papers, while Drum, wearing a bright orange jumpsuit with JEFFCOAT DETENTION CENTER stenciled in large block letters on the back, slouched in an uncomfortable-looking straight-backed chair and smoked a cigarette. Below the table, shiny leg irons were hooked to a U-bolt.

Drum swept his hand through his short dark hair, which was becoming greasy and matted from restricted jailhouse showers. Keenan studied Drum. Drum was about five-ten, one hundred and eighty pounds and fit looking. He had been slightly sunburned on the day of his capture, but this had faded and his skin appeared pale; he was not someone who spent a lot of time outdoors during the day. On his cheeks, scarring from severe adolescent acne might be noticed. What those meeting Drum were most likely to remember, though, were his eyes. They were pale blue, yet there was something flat and reptilian about them.

Treadle pointed with his thumb toward the viewing mirror and asked, "What do you think you're going to get out of him?"

"Nothing tonight," Keenan answered, never taking his eyes off Drum. "Did you have a go at him today?"

"Hell no," Treadle said. He also stared through the mirror at Drum. "There's not a damn thing we need from him so I don't care if he never says another word until the night he fries."

For the past two nights, Drum had refused to speak to any of the officers attempting to question him. It made no difference if they acted solicitous, played good cop, bad cop, turned red with anger, or offered cigarettes, Drum would pick at his fingernails, smile at the mirror, do anything but look at the lawmen who questioned him. It wore on the officers that Drum, this zero, this nothing, this woman killer, felt so smug jerking them around. Drum was also a cop killer, adding volatility to the situation. Last night, a couple of officers ended up yelling at each other in the observation room, and Treadle pulled the interrogation team. Keenan agreed with this decision because they had more than enough evidence to put Drum on death row by the end of the year.

They had the tape recording of Will's murder and a wealth of damning evidence found in the death chamber set up in Drum's basement. Pushed against one wall was a cast-iron bed, the white paint rubbed bare on each post from handcuffs' chafing. Video cameras on tripods stood about six feet away on either side of the bed. In a padlocked closet, they found a cardboard box filled with women's clothing, and fibers linked these garments to every known serial murder victim. The same forensic ID held true for panties found in a drawer in Drum's bed-room. Also in the basement closet were four boxes of a strychnine-based rat poison, two oxygen tanks, ground charcoal, and handcuffs from which they had lifted skin particles matching three victims. Most damning was the videotape Dee Tucker had pulled from the fireplace. Unblemished, it showed Drum with Alicia Owens. Keenan had not yet viewed this tape, but the Jeffcoat County Solicitor, Robert Moore, told Keenan it was so awful that he would only use a few seconds in court. "But if the judge won't clear the courtroom and there's a chance that her family might see even one second," Moore had said, "I won't use it. I swear to God, I won't."

.   .   .

Drum stubbed out his cigarette, looked at the mirror, and exaggerated a yawn. Then he smiled. Keenan imagined that if snakes smiled, their smile would look like Drum's, with his lips pulled back without curl-ing upward.

Drum took a pack of Marlboros from his shirt pocket, extracted another cigarette, and tapped the butt-end on the table three times before lighting it. Keenan watched and waited as he smoked it. Before he finished the cigarette, Drum shifted in his seat and looked a little restless. Keenan continued to wait. When Drum crushed out the last embers, he strummed his fingers on the table, sighed, sat up in his chair, looked around the room, then slouched again and lit another smoke. Keenan waited until Drum finished this smoke, then unhur-riedly entered the interrogation room and sat directly across from Drum. Keenan did not say one word; he just stared at Drum, focusing intently on his hard eyes. As he had hoped, Drum stared back.

"I'm Brian Woolsy," the lawyer said. "And this seems irregular." Keenan ignored Woolsy and kept staring at Drum, like a boxer trying to stare down his opponent, or a rival beast circling and knowing that this was the real measure and whatever followed would just be for show.

Drum continued to smile, smug and confident.

"I said, this is irregular," Woolsy repeated. "First, who are you?" Keenan ignored him. "Mr. Drum, you don't have to do this." Drum also ignored him. "Ah, hell, what's the use," the attorney murmured and did not speak again.

Drum seemed to enjoy this game. Still smiling, he stood and braced his weight on the table so that as much as his leg irons and the table would allow, he hovered over Keenan. Keenan turned his head to track Drum, but otherwise remained motionless, his only expression the fierceness of his eyes.

Keenan had similarly remained expressionless this afternoon, when he had joined the long procession to the cemetery—a procession tailed by a line of police cars, their lights flashing and shimmering mirage-like in the ninety-eight-degree heat. He remained expressionless at the cemetery, where he stood well behind most others with dark sunglasses, his shoulders squared, and his hands clasped in front. Even when the bugler blew taps and many stared at the ground, Keenan remained unmoved. Nothing touched him—as long as he didn't look at Marianne and Zack.

After the service, he waited at a distance as well-wishers bathed Marianne with sympathy. Her thin, sandy-haired son had stood beside her, surprisingly still for one so young. Marianne looked small and fragile, yet she accepted what each person offered and gave comfort in return. "Thank you for coming," she said, again and again. "Yes, I'm doing fine." She defined grace. Keenan felt humbled.

Now, Keenan channeled all of his rage into staring at Drum. He wanted Drum to see this in him and know that he could never win. The magnified seconds ticked away. Drum's haughty smile began to look strained. He shifted where he stood, then shifted again. Keenan remained motionless, his gaze hard, intense, and steady. Finally, after six or so minutes, Drum raised his middle finger and said, "Why don't you go fuck yourself."

Slowly, Keenan stood. Being taller, he now looked down at Drum as he laid the card he had cupped in his hand on the table. "All right, we've played our games. My name is John Keenan and I'm with the FBI's psychological profiling division. When the time comes that you want talk to me, you better be ready because any bullshit and I walk. You'll only get one chance." Then, Keenan abruptly turned and left, knowing he had gotten what he wanted.

Drum would now remember him. After Drum's trials were over, Keenan would write him and request a profiling interview, and Drum would remember him. At first, Drum would probably turn down his requests. But Keenan would continue to write and twist Drum's perceptions to take advantage of his tendency to measure worth only by perceived strength. He felt confident that Drum would receive a death sentence and eventually face execution. For some men, like Ted Bundy and Elgin Cordell, only when they stood in the executioner's shadow did they become vulnerable enough to talk openly about their crimes. It was also a time when most men looked for someone strong to lean on a little. So when that time came, Drum would remember Keenan, remember his unshakable strength, and very likely agree to meet with Keenan in the days before his execution. And when that happened, Keenan would remember how Drum had stood over Will Paxton and pissed on him.

15

the sentence

I

ISAAC DRUM wore a bulky Kevlar vest and a waist chain that pinned his hands to his sides as frowning cops in protective armor ushered him into the courthouse. The trial was at the end of its second week, yet he still felt an emotional rush every time he made this walk. Cameras whirred, microphones on booms waved overhead, and photographers' flashes flickered like strobes. At the time of Drum's capture six months earlier, the headline, "KILLER MURDERS COP WHO SOLVED CASE" had snagged the attention of the national media, so big-time reporters were now among those shouting questions at him and calling him Isaac, like they were celebrity buddies. After a life spent blending in and barely being noticed, Drum thrived on being treated with such importance and passed through this mob each day with a half-smile on his face.

Today, the questions were the same as when he had left court yesterday: "What do you think of the verdict?" "Do you think so much publicity hurt your case?" "Do you expect to get the death sentence?"

Yesterday, the jury had returned a guilty verdict for the murder of Will Paxton—a separate trial would be held for the murder of Pop Paulus and yet another for the serial murders. Drum had stood when the verdict was announced, his eyes fixed above the judge's head, his chin jutting upward. When the foreman read, "Guilty of murder in the first degree," Drum had yawned.

He had expected to be found guilty. Little people with any kind of authority had screwed him his whole life. But to hell if he would let them think that anything they did mattered to him. Throughout the trial, Drum, wearing the same cheap blue suit every day, had slouched in his chair with his eyes half-closed. Rarely had he as much as glanced at any of the witnesses, and whenever that pompous asshole of a judge addressed him, Drum acted as if he didn't hear him. He wanted to show them all that nothing they did could touch him—though when the verdict was read, his stomach had tightened as if punched.

. . .

Minutes after entering the courthouse, Drum sat slumped at the defendant's table in Judge Raymond C. Wilcox's courtroom. His attorney, Brian Woolsy, stoop-shouldered with dark circles under his eyes, sat beside him as the prosecution opened the trial's sentencing phase by calling a psychiatrist.

The shrink was a smallish man with a clipped beard who droned on and on about Drum being a remorseless psychopath. He had tried to interview Drum, who had ignored him, just as he ignored everyone who tried to question him about himself or the murders, including his attorney. No matter who came at him with questions, tests, or the small-minded pigeonholes into which they wanted to categorize him, Drum dominated every one of them through his indifference.

In his cross-examination, Drum thought Woolsy spent too much time pestering the psychiatrist to get him to admit that Drum had not answered any of his questions. The shrink held firm, though, that he saw no signs of remorse in Drum's behaviors. Drum dozed during this exchange. He expected to be just as bored during the afternoon. They were going to sentence him to death no matter what Woolsy did. Big deal. So what? It meant nothing. With so much publicity, he would get a good attorney and get his sentence overturned. They would never actually execute him, he told himself once again. In fact, he had told himself again and again that a death sentence didn't really mean anything.

During the sentencing phase of a capital trial, members of a victim's family may tell the court how the crime has impacted them. That afternoon, the prosecution called Marianne Paxton. Drum raised his head and watched her walk to the witness box. On the first day of the trial he had gazed fixedly at her until she glanced in his direction and they had stared at each other. After that, he kept trying to make eye contact but she refused to look his way, looking anywhere except at him, a sure sign that he had succeeded in making her uneasy.

For a while, Drum had possessed a picture of her taken from the wallet of her dead husband. While waiting on the dirt road where he had killed that old black man, he had studied her picture, tracing her outline with his finger, and he had fantasized about taking her home and having her alone in his basement. Now, watching her settle into the witness stand, he felt as though they had a relationship of sorts—after all, he had profoundly shaped her future.

She sat with her hands folded in her lap. She wore a blue skirt and matching jacket that didn't show a lot. She had worn jackets every day so Drum couldn't tell what kind of tits she had, though it looked like she didn't have much.

The prosecutor, Robert Moore, a rangy man, moved in front of his table and asked in a voice that probably sounded gentle to everyone else, but grated on Drum's nerves, "What was your relationship to Will Paxton?"

"He was my husband," she answered, sitting very still.

"What kind of man was your husband?"

"Will was caring and warm, the kind of man who would never pass by someone who was broken down on the side of the road. And whenever he saw someone in pain, it bothered him and he genuinely wanted-ed to help. That's why he went into law enforcement, to help people."

"You have a five-year-old son?"

"Yes."

"How has your husband's death affected you and your son?"

"I'm very worried about my son, Zack," she said, and Drum thought she looked close to tears. It reminded him of how the women he had taken had looked when they cried and begged, and he hoped she would cry.

She regained her composure, though, and continued, "As far as Zack was concerned the sun rose and set on his father. Since Will's death, Zack has been having nightmares and he refuses to talk about his father. I try to get him to tell me what he's thinking and feeling. I tell him how important it is to talk about his feelings, but he won't talk about his father. He just won't."

Drum was bored with her moaning and about to shut his eyes and yawn, when she looked directly at him, her eyes wet and bright.

"All this happened because of that coward sitting over there," she said and pointed at Drum. "Because he's too inept and too scared to ever have a meaningful relationship with any woman, he wants to destroy anyone who can."

Drum pushed himself upright and leaned over the table, glaring at Marianne, his face flushed and his hands balled into fists. She stared back with equal intensity, her hands also tightened into fists, and said, "He's such a coward that I think he hated Will for being the man he could never be. And he's so pathetic . . ."

"Objection," Woolsy said.

". . . that the only way he can be noticed is by hurting others."

"Your honor, this is just purely inflammatory."

"Sustained. Mrs. Paxton, please restrict your remarks to how your husband's murder has affected your family," the judge instructed.

"But I took an oath to tell the truth," Marianne said, looking at the judge.

"Mrs. Paxton," the judge said, somewhat sterner, "please don't try this court's patience."

"All right," Marianne said.

The district attorney then intervened. "Mrs. Paxton, how do you think justice can best be served?"

Marianne again stared at Drum, her eyes fierce. "I beg this court to put that monster beyond where he can ever hurt anyone else. And I believe that justice demands sentencing him to death."

Marianne and Drum continued to stare at each other as the district attorney said he had nothing more to ask and Woolsy declined to question her. Marianne was dismissed. She held Drum's eyes a moment longer, then looked straight ahead and walked with defiant pride toward the gallery.

Drum watched the arrogant bitch come closer, hating her more than he had ever hated anyone. When she came abreast the defendant's table, Drum surged to his feet and the bitch flinched. A guard sitting behind Drum must have been ready for something like this because he was immediately between them, a stun gun in his hand. A second deputy also stepped in the way and the judge ordered Drum to sit down or be restrained for the duration of the trial.

Drum eased back into his chair but kept staring at the bitch as she moved into the galley and took her seat in the front row on the other side. She refused to look his way, but he could tell by the tightening of her jaw that she was aware of him. Drum stared at her until court was adjourned.

II

Three steps and turn. Three steps and turn. Drum paced his cell in Jeffcoat Detention Center's segregation area. Three steps and turn. He was the only prisoner now in this three-cell unit, put here under twenty-four-hour camera surveillance for the duration of his trial. Three steps and turn. Not even in the days after his arrest had a six by seven cell seemed so maddeningly small. Three steps and turn. He understood why a captive animal might attack the bars holding it with enough ferocity to break its teeth.

Drum paused and looked through the bars at the television pushed against the wall. Earlier, he'd yelled until someone came to turn it off after the local news showed him being escorted from the courthouse and claimed that Marianne Paxton had bested him in a courtroom showdown.

"I'm going to fix that bitch for humiliating me," he said to himself. He took a pack of Marlboros from his shirt pocket, tapped one out and lit it in one long draw, then resumed his pacing.

He had also paced last night, cursing both the jury and his attorney for the guilty verdict. But tonight the tension was worse. And tomorrow or the next day, they were going to sentence him to die. So what, it meant nothing, he told himself yet again.

Unable to stand the tension any longer, Drum sat on his bunk, its mattress so thin he felt the bed's springs. He stuck the cigarette in the corner of his mouth and rolled his left sleeve to his elbow. There were two scabbed-over welts on the inside of his forearm, both perfectly round, both from last night when he'd been pissed about the guilty verdict.

Breathing hard, Drum grasped the cigarette between his thumb and index finger and pressed its red ember into his forearm. The sharp stinging caused him to suck in his breath and his arm trembled. He smelled his flesh burning and pressed the cigarette harder.

Finally, Drum pulled back the cigarette and released his pent-up breath. Sweat ran down his forehead and his eyes watered. Burning himself had nothing to do with masochism; Drum would fuck over anybody who tried to humiliate or hurt or do anything to cause him discomfort. No, he burned himself because somehow, for reasons he didn't understand, the pain seemed to drain away his tension, it seemed to focus and calm him.

His hand still shook as he took a long drag off the smoke. He felt back in control now, stronger and ready to handle anything, and his anger now lay inside him as something cold and calculating.

Drum leaned back against the wall and looked at the new welt, which was red and runny. It's been over ten years since I did something like this, Drum thought. I was only eleven then, and was locked in a cell a lot like this one. Man, that was a long time ago.

Drum rested his head against the wall and shut his eyes and tried to recall exactly why he had hurt himself back then. If he understood why he did it then, it might make more sense doing it now. So he concentrated hard and tried to remember what his cell had looked like by recalling how it had been the same—the bars of that cell were painted white, just like this one—and then he recalled how things differed— back then, he'd had only a sheetless mattress on the floor and was stripped to his underwear. Drum kept concentrating . . . and lucid memories came.

I was a scrawny kid sitting in my underwear on a mattress so thin that the floor's cold leaked through it. I stared between the white bars at the heads of the staff sitting in their station. All day, they sat there and talked to each other and wrote in our charts about how we ate, how we slept, and how we took shits. They watched us, and we watched them.

A judge sent me here after I started a fire in the group home where I was being kept against my will—if I burned it down I thought they'd send me home. When I first got here, they put me in what they called a dorm, which was an open room with twenty-four bunks and grates on the windows. The first night they caught me climbing the back fence. A couple of weeks later, they caught me again, but this time I was ready for them. I had filled my knapsack with rocks and fought them off for a long time. After they overpowered me, they sent me here, to the Maximum Security Unit. I've been fighting them ever since. I especially want to get at the social worker from my regular unit. Just looking at her makes me angry. She told me my mother was coming to see me. She lied.

It was her, my social worker, that I was now staring at through the bars. She sat hunched over the counter in the staff's station, probably looking at my chart. She was a young woman with big tits and hips that were a little big, too, and she had long, reddish-blond hair that was real wavy.

She finished reading my chart and came and stood in front of my cell, keeping about three or four steps back where I couldn't reach her with anything. "Isaac, will you talk to me today?" she said, pretending to be concerned. "If you just stop fighting us, we can move you to a less restrictive place, and eventually put you back into a regular dorm where you can get out on the grounds."

I stared at her and imagined pushing her down and tearing off her clothes and forcing myself on her from behind while pulling her hair and hurting her and seeing pain in her face. Thinking these things excited me. I had been imagining doing this sort of stuff for a few weeks now. I didn't know why I started thinking about doing these things to women. All of a sudden, I just started thinking stuff like this. Of course, imagining myself getting even with everybody who ticked me off wasn't new. I'd been doing that ever since I was a little kid. Usually, I imagined doing dumb stuff like pushing them down or hitting them with a rock or killing their pet. I guess my imagination combined getting revenge and pleasuring myself because I was getting older and knew about sex. Why else would I think these things? And what did it matter, anyway?

"Isaac, please, let's talk, okay," my social worker said.

I answered her by tugging down my underwear and playing with myself while staring her. She sighed, shook her head, but didn't look away. "Isaac, think about it and maybe we can talk tomorrow, okay. Maybe if you can tell me about the things that have happened to you, we can find a way for you to get over it. Think about it, okay?" She smiled, then shook her head and walked back to the station to write in my chart.

Every time she came in here, I stayed mad for a long time afterwards. Especially when she said that crap about something having happened to me. All that happened was that my mother was tricked into sending me away. I'm not going to stop fighting them until they let me go home to her, because she's the only person who's ever really cared about me.

After my social worker left the unit, I sat with my back to the bars and scratched scabs off my forearms until they seeped blood. I'd been doing this every day since they put me in here. It usually helped me feel better. But it didn't help much today. I guess I was too mad.

At noon, a young black man with a goatee stopped in front of my cell with the lunch cart and took a tray from one of the slots. Today we got dried-out chicken with mushy green beans and carrots served on a plastic plate with a little plastic knife and fork—we couldn't be trusted with anything metal. As this guy popped the tab on a soda and poured it into a plastic cup, one of the unit's regular staff came out and leaned against the station's partition. He asked the guy serving our lunch, "I hear you're getting tight with Sheree?" The guy set the cup of soda on the tray and looked at the other fellow. "Man, I wish I knew for sure," he said. He checked to make sure that I was back in the cell before he knelt and unlocked the slot at the bottom. "She runs so hot and cold that I don't know what's going on," he said as he slid the tray into my cell.

Ol' lover boy there wasn't paying attention and screwed up. He held on to the soda can and put it back on his cart, but he left its tab on the tray. I saw this and hurried to grab my tray and sat with my back to him and, while pretending to pick at my food, wrapped my fist around the metal tab.

After the guy with the lunches moved on and I was sure that nobody was paying attention, I ran my finger along the tab's edge, which wasn't very sharp. But, I pushed the tab against the side of my stomach and started sawing until it broke the skin. I kept sawing, working it deeper and deeper until it was maybe a quarter inch deep, then I started working it across my stomach. I worked carefully and my stomach got real bloody. In a way, I felt the pain—it was both sharp and throbbing. But in another way, it felt distant, like it was outside of me. I also felt like time was sorta standing still and all the noise on our unit was blocked out. And I felt like I was in complete control.

When I'd cut a gash all the way across my stomach, I stood and backed up until I bumped against the bars. Blood had soaked the front of my underwear and some ran down my legs. I turned and stuck my bloody hands through the bars and when the staff saw me and started running towards my cell, I yelled, "Fuck you, you sons of bitches."

They patched me up with eleven stitches and sent me to a psychiatric hospital. I guess the shrinks there thought I was okay because a week later they sent me back to Juvenile Justice, where I was again stripped to my underwear and put in the same cell. My bitch social worker came by soon after I got back. She stood in front of the bars, out of my reach, and told me again how much she wished I'd talk to her so we could figure out what's wrong.

At first, I just looked at her and balled my hands into fists.

Then she said, "Please, Isaac, let me help you. Trust me and I won't let you down."

I kept my eyes on her face as I slid my hand across my stomach until I found one of the stitches and yanked it out. Then I jerked out another and another, and I kept tearing out my stitches until the staff came into my cell and restrained me.

Drum opened his eyes. The cigarette had burned into the filter and the ash had fallen onto the mattress. Leaning forward, he flicked the butt into the cell's steel commode, then sat back against the wall and lit another cigarette. "Fucking dumb kid," he said. "He didn't know anything. I can't believe I was ever that stupid."

He then remembered when they brought another kid into the Max Unit who was raging in much the same way, and Drum had seen how stupid and self-defeating it was to flail so aimlessly. After that, he turned quiet and watchful, and stopped fighting them, at least overtly. Eventually, they put him back in a regular dorm and the institutional routine gave his life a certain order that helped check the turmoil inside him. He still felt wary of his social worker and kept her at bay by answering her questions with "I dunnoh," or "I'm all right." Six months later, she left and the new social worker didn't pester him nearly as much.

Drum took a hit on his smoke and shook his head. He rarely thought about those years and when he did he had a feeling of being wrapped in a cocoon and looking at the world through a mask.

Whenever he thought of those times, he had a feeling of not really being alive.

"I was too fucking weak and powerless, then. Never again," he said. "Never fucking again."

He then stared at the bars of his cell, which were painted white, just like the bars confining him when he was eleven.

III

The next morning, Drum's attorney made his appeal for mercy by calling a psychologist who described Drum's history in juvenile justice and the army. The shrink claimed that, after a rocky period of adjustment, Drum had done well living in structured settings and should, therefore, adapt well to the controlled environment of prison.

Drum slouched in his chair as he had every day, except he kept glancing over at the Paxton bitch. She refused to look his way. But she knew he was watching her, of that he was certain.

When the shrink finished, Woolsy called Jeffcoat County's head jailer, who testified that Drum was cooperative and no problem, though he refused to talk much to anyone. His jailer also thought Drum would adapt well to prison.

Woolsy had no other witnesses to call so the judge gave the jury its final instructions. A verdict was reached by that afternoon. Drum stood and tried not to show any reaction when the jury foreman announced, "Death by electrocution." The judge then asked Drum if he had anything to say before sentence was pronounced. Drum turned his head and looked again at the Paxton bitch. This time, she looked back, her lips pressed in a hard smile. He stared for only a moment, then silently mouthed, "I'm going to get you for this."

Drum then turned and for the first time looked squarely at the judge, sitting so high and looking down on him. "Yeah, I got something to say," Drum said. "Fuck this court and fuck you."

PART TWO

Eight years later . . .

16

community problem

I

THE CONFERENCE room of the SLED Headquarters administrative area rested on a cushion of slate gray carpet and limited edition watercolor prints of Charleston mansions decorated the walls. The credenza and long table were dark walnut and the chairs a plush royal blue. A cart loaded with pastries and a coffee urn had been pushed into the corner below where the two walls of lightly tinted windows met. Keenan set his scuffed case on the table and shook his head. He wondered if Martin Stith was meeting in here to show off for Keenan's benefit, or if Stith habitually flashed the trappings of rank. Not that Stith's intentions mattered.

No one else had arrived. Keenan went to the cart, filled a cup with coffee, then looked out the windows onto a sparsely shaded lawn that was blanketed by tawny pine needles. In the distance, morning sunlight splashed on yellows and reds; autumn here had not quite reached its peak.

Keenan had last set foot inside SLED Headquarters eight years ago, on that harrowing Sunday when Will had died. It had been almost as long since he had been in South Carolina. A bit of gray now flecked his temples and nightly walks kept him somewhat trim. Keenan had prudently avoided returning to South Carolina by assigning requests from this state to agents who did not carry baggage here. He had taken this present case only because he was already scheduled to be here when the call for assistance came, and it would have been needlessly wasteful to send a second agent for such a straightforward request.

It surprised Keenan that he felt an edgy impatience, like returning to the scene of an accident. He had believed himself well past such feelings. For a while following Will's murder, his impatience had caused him problems. Back then, his eyes had never been sharper at spotting others' flaws. He became argumentative, clashing with those in his department, including Ben Lockhart. He also began finding nit-picking faults with Susan Chen, and their relationship ended.

A year after he and Susan stopped seeing each other, Keenan ran into her when she came to Quantico on a teaching rotation. It was an uncomfortable encounter, strained and overly polite. Susan did, however, suggest that Keenan call her sometime, trying to toss this off casually, though she avoided looking at Keenan for a couple of seconds after she said this. At the time, Keenan was in the middle of a very demanding case; he never called her. Two years ago he had heard that she'd since married and had a little girl. Good for her, he thought.

Turning away from the window and all the stirred-up ghosts, Keenan sat at the table, and took a file from his case. He began leafing though the reports, annoyed at himself for having difficulty keeping his mind on an active case. But his original purpose for coming to South Carolina had relentlessly tugged at his attention all morning. After leaving here, Keenan would go to Golgotha State Prison and begin four days of profiling interviews with Isaac Drum. Drum's case had gone pretty much as Keenan expected. Within a year of his arrest, Drum had received three death sentences—one for Will's murder, another for the serial murders of five women, and a third in Marion County for the murder of Pop Paulus. A few years later, the United States Supreme Court gave justice a hard shove when it singled out Drum's case as an example of drawn-out and abusive appeals tactics. Then last week, Federal Appeals Judge Franklin Shealey refused to issue a stay for Drum's latest death warrant. Two days after Shealey's denial, Keenan sent his eighth letter to Drum requesting that they meet; and this time Drum had agreed. As things now stood, Isaac Drum was scheduled to die in the electric chair in four days.

Voices sounded in the hall and Keenan heard a familiar gravelly voice speak his name, though he could not make out what was said. A moment later, Martin Stith strode into the room followed by three men and a woman. Stith tossed a folder onto the table and said to Keenan, "So you're not late, after all."

"Chief Stith," Keenan said, and rose to shake Stith's hand, catching a solid whiff of Stith's cologne as he did. Stith had thickened, especially in the neck, which bulged over his starched collar. Otherwise, he appeared unchanged. No gray showed in his dark-blond hair, which he still combed straight back and glistened with hair oil. His face was deeply tanned and his scar did not appear as red as Keenan remembered, but then Stith had been angry, his whole face red, during Keenan's last contact. In keeping with his advanced rank as chief of SLED's Criminal Investigation Division, Stith wore a dove-gray suit that looked sleek and tailor-cut.

"So this is how those up here on the second floor live," said one of the new arrivals, a young blond man as he looked around the posh room. Handsome by almost any standards, this trim man wore a blue suit with a red-striped shirt. "Wes Felton, he said, extending his hand to Keenan. "I'm SLED's liaison for this investigation."

Only one of the new arrivals wore a uniform and, pointing, Stith said, "Keenan, this is Jeffcoat Landing's sheriff, Howard Weiss." Keenan shook hands with Weiss, a tall lanky man with a hawk-beak nose and dark complexion that appeared lightly stained rather than tanned. The part in Weiss' hair was ruler-straight, with thin strands of dark hair combed across his balding scalp.

Keenan was then introduced to the two detectives from Weiss's department. After this everyone got coffee except Felton, who had brought a small bottle of orange juice, and Keenan and Weiss, who stood near the door chatting about who Weiss knew in the bureau.

"Okay, let's get started," Stith said and sat at the head of the table. Weiss laid his hat on the table and sat across from Keenan, each occupying the seats next to the table's head. The others sat farther down the table, a sign that they were here mostly to listen.

"The reason we're meeting again," Stith said, "is because Agent Keenan has come all the way from Quantico to give us his opinions about Gary Wilmet's murder. Keenan, since we're all professionals, I think you can dispense with any long explanations of how you come up with your particulars, okay? So, the floor's yours." Stith said and leaned back in his chair.

Keenan hid his annoyance at Stith's curt introduction by glancing down at the picture of Gary Wilmet attached to his case folder. He had been an eleven-year-old boy who, during the evening a week ago

Sunday, had gone riding his bike and never returned. A search was mounted and shortly before midnight a volunteer fireman discovered his body buried beneath some loose brush in a wooded area near a public softball field that was only five streets away from his home. The boy was dressed only in jeans and sneakers with the laces untied. He had been sodomized, strangled from behind but not fatally, had two teeth knocked loose, and was stabbed in the stomach six times with a large knife. Forensics found a usable semen sample and a couple of pubic hairs.

Keenan placed his forearms on the table and leaned toward Weiss. "Sheriff, I'd like to get your impression of the crime scene," he asked, "specifically, how careful do you think the killer was in hiding the body?"

Weiss also leaned forward and placed his forearms on the table, roughly mirroring Keenan's posture. "I didn't think he was careful at all," Weiss said, his accent decidedly rural. "It looked like he just dropped the boy's body in a little depression along with his underwear and then haphazardly threw brush and leaves over him. And judging by the pattern of blood on the boy's shirt, it seems the killer used that shirt to wipe blood and dirt off his hands, then to wipe down the knife. Then when he finished, he just tossed the shirt on top of where he'd left the body, like he didn't care about hiding it. That shirt's why we found Gary as soon as we did."

"And you never found Wilmet's bicycle?"

"No sir. We covered the area quite a few times and it's not there."

"That's what I thought. Sheriff, before I begin is there anything that you want to bring up?"

"Yes sir, there is. I know that a lot of the time when children are murdered that it's the parents did it; we've seen it in Jeffcoat Landing a couple times. But that boy was treated so badly . . ." Weiss gestured with his hands, palms out. "Well, I know his parents, and if you're going to tell me you think they did that to him, then you're going to have to make a strong case."

Most who go into law enforcement quickly learn that seemingly good neighbors sometimes do horrible things to their children. Yet, this is never an easy truth to accept. In this case, though, Keenan thought that the evidence pointed elsewhere.

"When parents murder a child," Keenan said, "they often try to stage things to look like an abduction or assault. Sheriff, there's nothing in this crime scene that looks staged."

Weiss nodded in agreement. "That's what I thought."

Keenan paused, then added, "I do think it's better for the parents if you go ahead and get a DNA sample from the father, just to put any talk to rest. For the same reason, you also need to rule out the volunteer fireman who found the body."

"We've already cleared the fireman," Stith said. He still leaned back but raised his chin from his knuckles and nonchalantly wagged his hand at Keenan. "And it seems a little insensitive for Weiss to further traumatize the parents, when he can already say with utter conviction that it's not either of them."

"That's right," Weiss said, and leaned back in his chair.

Not wanting to antagonize Weiss on such a non-critical point, Keenan shrugged and said, "It's your call, Sheriff. You know the community best." He wanted to keep Weiss open to his recommendations because he had some proactive ideas that he thought might produce a quick arrest.

"If there's nothing else, Sheriff, that you want to bring up, I'll tell you what I think."

"Let's hear it," Weiss said.

"I think the man you're looking for is a twenty-five- to thirty-five-year-old white male," Keenan began, now looking only at Weiss. "He came to the crime scene on foot and left on the victim's bicycle, which means he probably lives in the area. Given the closeness of the crime site to the ballparks, I think the perpetrator came there looking to commit sexual assault. He had thought about what he wanted and how to achieve it, but hadn't thought much about covering his tracks once he completed the rape. I think his decision to kill Wilmet came after the assault and was not part of his original fantasy, but done simply so Wilmet couldn't identify him.

"After the assault, I think the killer wanted to keep easy control over Wilmet so he told the kid to get dressed and then he'd let him go. Wilmet put his pants on and when he bent to tie his shoes, the killer tried to strangle him from behind. But he didn't know how hard it is to strangle someone and I think that's when he hit the kid. Then, while

Wilmet staggered or was getting up from being knocked down, the killer took out what was probably a large hunting knife, wrapped Wilmet's shirt around his hand to prevent getting blood on him, and began stabbing him."

"That makes sense," Weiss said, nodding and then rubbed his chin.

Keenan sipped his coffee to allow Weiss a little more time to absorb this. "Also, Sheriff, I think the killer showed a lot of sophistication in his use of violence. He stabbed Wilmet in the stomach below the chest cage and the wounds had an upward angle that indicates that he held the knife down like this"—Keenan formed a fist with his knuckles towards the ground—"and he used short, quick jabs. That's how a shiv is used in prison. I think this guy has done time, probably for arson or sexual assault."

Keenan paused again. He was somewhat surprised that Stith had not interrupted him. But no one said anything and Keenan continued. "Because the killer had not planned what he needed to do post-offense and he left the body at the site of the attack, I think we're dealing with a Disorganized Type offender. This means that if he has been in prison, he may have spent time in the prison's psychiatric unit or maybe served an alternative sentence at a mental hospital's forensic unit.

"That doesn't sound at all like the description of the man we've been hunting," Weiss said and leaned forward again. "We brought in a psychiatrist who is an expert on sexual abuse and pedophiles. He said the man who did this was older than what you said, probably between his mid-thirties to late fifties, and was known and well liked in the neighborhood. He also said the man was married, but had always felt more comfortable around children. And our shrink thinks some kind of upheaval, most likely infidelity on his wife's part, pushed this man to act more aggressive than he normally would in his sexual attentions towards a child. Afterwards, like you said, he knew he'd messed up because Wilmet could identify him, and he panicked. This psychiatrist also said the killer either had a job or volunteered at some activity that put him around children. And he said that covering the body was definitely a sign of guilt. Now, Keenan," Weiss said, and with his elbow on the table pointed at Keenan and looked over his finger as if sighting a gun, "that's the guy we've been looking for; so I'd like to know how you account for your differences?"

More and more, local police consulted psychiatrists and experts on sex offenders—an indirect nod to the growing clout of Keenan's department. Some consultants learned enough about forensics to do a credible job. Weiss's psychiatrist, though, had muddied the water enough to keep the investigation from having the kind of clear focus that might produce quick results. "Your psychiatrist did a good job describing the most common pedophile type," Keenan said tactfully. "My analysis differs because it's based strictly on the actual crime scene, and I've personally interviewed over a hundred and fifty predators to learn how to read the various clues." Keenan could have added that this information was part of his usual introduction to profiling that Stith had wanted left out.

"This was a brutal attack, but not a frenzied one," he continued, "which makes me think that when this man is stressed, he quickly turns to calculated violence to solve problems. That's one of the reasons I think we're dealing with what we call a Conditioned Pedophile; that's a sex offender whose formative sexual experiences came from being roughly sexually assaulted, and as a result learned to take out his anger by committing similar assaults on smaller kids. This man has developed a preference for rough, exploitive sex with smaller males— it's the dishing out of abuse that turns him on. When he strikes again, and he will rape again, I think he'll plan better, and he'll be more comfortable so we'll see more cruelty. I'm also afraid that now that he's killed, he may have a taste for it and murder will become part of his plan."

"Unless we catch him first," Weiss said. He again pointed at Keenan. "What about guilt from hiding the body? Do you disagree with that too?"

"Sheriff, anyone who says hiding a body is a sign of guilt, has obviously never considered the problem of having a body on his hands that a killer doesn't want to get linked with. It's a practical thing to do. The longer the body lies undiscovered, the more forensic evidence erodes and the killer delays the kind of heat that this case is now getting. If the killer had covered the kid's face, or put his shirt over his wounds, or laid him out in a peaceful posture, or finished dressing him, any of those things would indicate that this guy felt bad about what he had done. Nothing about this crime scene suggests guilt."

"So you think we should look for a jailbird who's crazy?"

Keenan shook his head. "It's more likely the guy you're looking for is so abrasive and argumentative that people generally regard his strangeness as done purely to annoy. He's been a problem in the community since he was a kid. He'll be a high school dropout who is either unemployed or works at menial jobs and has a history of frequently quitting or getting fired after doing things like arguing with his boss or stealing or doing something else along those lines. For that reason, he probably lives with a female who supports him such as his mother, grandmother, or aunt." Keenan had come to the crux of what he wanted Weiss to do. "Sheriff, I strongly recommend that you canvass the area door-to-door with that description and see who people point out. I think there's a very good chance that someone will name the killer."

"And what about the other description?" Weiss asked.

"Why don't you have one person from your team stay with the first description," Stith said from where he sat cocked back in his chair. "Then go ahead and saturate the area with Keenan's composite." It was a practical compromise that Weiss, who looked at Stith and nodded, would probably follow. Still, it annoyed Keenan for Stith to assume the role of judge.

"Just a couple more things, Sheriff," Keenan said. "When you do get a suspect, I think you might be able to break him. You might try putting a bulletin board in the interrogation room loaded with forensics, pictures, and maps. Really make a show of it and place it at forty-five degrees so he'll have to turn his head to see it. He'll want to study the board, but he'll try to conceal his interest, so that'll keep him tense and a little distracted. Let him know you've got more than enough forensics to get an easy conviction."

Weiss nodded. "All right."

"The killer is already blaming his victim for what he did," Keenan continued. "So once you get him good and tense, play along, say things like, 'I know you didn't want to hurt that kid but he must have done something to provoke you, something that didn't leave you much choice.' Or tell him you want to get his story on the record before the lawyers and politicians start making it look like you killed the child for pleasure. Tell him it's a matter of how bad he's going to look. He's not terribly bright, so if you get him tense and then offer him a chance to explain himself, he might start trying to sell you his warped version of how it happened."

"Weiss, you may want to reconsider this recommendation," Stith said and leaned forward, bringing the smell of cologne with him. Turning toward Weiss, Stith made small, wagging hand gestures as he said, "With the semen and pubic hairs, all you need is a DNA match. You don't need to suck up to this prick to get a confession. You have more than enough for a murder one conviction."

"You know how unpredictable juries are," Keenan said. "Nothing seals a case like a confession."

Without looking at Keenan, Stith said, "Weiss, ask yourself if you want his defense attorneys playing a tape showing how you tricked him so they can get that confession thrown out. And when they play it, that kid's parents are going to hear you kissing that scum's ass by putting down their kid and they're going to wonder what kind of man are you."

Stith's objections ran contrary to standard interrogation practices and Keenan wondered if Stith was saying these things just to goad him. "His parents will have a greater problem if the killer walks," Keenan said.

With a shrug, Stith leaned back. "It's up to you, Weiss. Personally, I wouldn't debase myself unless it made a real difference."

"I go along with Chief Stith on this one," Weiss said, and also leaned back in his chair.

.   .   .

The meeting ended and Felton stayed to talk with Weiss and his investigators about SLED's available resources, while Chief Stith walked Keenan out. As soon as they entered the stairwell, putting them beyond earshot of the conference room, Keenan asked, "What the hell is your problem? My recommendation is a common interrogation tactic that I know you've used dozens of times."

"We're talking about a child murder," Stith said, glancing back at Keenan without slowing as he led Keenan down the wide stairway. "Weiss lives in that community, and what you're telling him to do would disgust everyone he knows, and he'd be doing it for no gain."

"A confession is worth it, and you know it," Keenan said. At the bottom of the steps Stith turned and stood in front of the exit, and said with surprising feeling, "You Feds are too removed to understand what it's like to have a whole community brand a cop with shame. A man can spend his whole life earning a first-class reputation and then one thing can disgrace him, and that's all people remember."

It seemed out of character for Stith to be so concerned with appearances and Keenan wondered if becoming an administrator had turned him into a poor imitation of a politician.

"But . . ." Keenan began and Stith cut him off with a wave of the hand.

"Look, Keenan, you and I see things differently, okay. So let's quit while we're ahead. It's Weiss's call now."

Keenan and Stith stared at each other. But with nothing to gain by pressing the point, Keenan let it drop. "If there are any new developments, I'll be here most of the week," he said.

Stepping to the door and opening it with a flourish, Stith said, "If we ever want anything else from you, I'll be in touch."

Keenan walked past him and when he heard the door shut, muttered, "And to hell with you too." He would contact Weiss and let him know he remained available. It was probably best that way. Stith could still push his buttons, so the less he had to do with him the better. Keenan had felt a little edgy ever since he began reviewing Drum's records, and dealing with Drum this week might well scorch his detachment. Keenan felt confident, however, that he would adroitly handle Drum and, if necessary, Stith too.

17

the nature of things

I

EVERY STATE has a place like this. A place for the damned. A place for those who have done such evil that they have forfeited the right to a natural death. In South Carolina this place is the second tier of Cell Block 2 in Golgotha State Prison.

The first stones of this prison were laid in the decade before the War Between the States, and devout state leaders thought Golgotha an apt name for a prison. This biblical term refers to the place of crucifixion as a hill of skulls, and as a place of suffering, especially suffering of the spirit.

The next century ushered in an era of proudly large and regimented institutions, and Golgotha grew into a sprawling complex that housed eighteen hundred men. Later, as newer prisons mushroomed in South Carolina's fertile ground, Golgotha retained its reputation for housing the worst of the worst. And perhaps the deadliest concentration of these men lived out their remaining lives inside Cell Block 2.

Deep in this old prison's bowels, Cell Block 2 exists as a world unto itself, separated from the rest of the prison by a pair of metal doors, an elevator's width apart and designed never to open at the same time. Inside, six tiers, thirty-five cells per tier, rise seventy-two feet above a gray cement floor. Cell Block 2 is a place where the lights are never completely turned off, and a place of deep shadows. A place where the hard clash of metal and men reverberate in a tense static that is always too loud, and the sour stench of sweat, urine, and ammonia is ever present. It is a place where the only visible horizons are televisions anchored to a monotonous stone wall twenty-one feet from the tier's catwalks. Above all, Cell Block 2 is a hard place of stone and cement adorned by metal steps, nine-foot metal catwalks with four-foot metal railings, and behind all this, metal bars. And on that afternoon in October, hardest looking of all were the sullen men staring out from behind those bars as John Keenan walked past.

Most who entered this cavernous cathedral of the damned tiptoed, hoping not to disturb its slumbering menace. Most visitors, though, sneaked furtive glances at these men, as if they were sideshow freaks. Keenan did neither of these. He walked near the catwalk's railing, where spit or human waste might reach him but the distance discouraged the attempt. His eyes remained fixed straight ahead and he took long, self-assured steps. To many who watched him, his confident indifference was seen as a lack of respect. After all, many of these men believed that all they had left of value, at least in this world, was their stature as the ultimate junkyard dogs gone awry.

Matching Keenan stride for stride was Cell Block 2's charge officer, a black man with graying hair and a neatly trimmed mustache, whose blue nameplate read, "Lt. L. Jenkins." A handsome man, in spite of rough skin on his cheeks, Jenkins's forehead appeared creased by a habitual scowl. He wore a perfectly pressed white officer's shirt and carried himself with crisp precision right down to the way he had told Keenan exactly what he expected of him. Keenan pegged Jenkins as retired military in a second career, possibly a gruff master sergeant— he had the right temperament.

At the tier's end stood a Plexiglas-enclosed security booth. A few feet before reaching this booth, the two men stopped at a green metal door that Jenkins unlocked, then stood blocking the entrance and looked up at Keenan, who was about four inches taller than him. "You must remain seated as we bring the inmate in and again when we escort him out," Jenkins informed him. "And we prefer you stay seated while you meet with him. You may not have physical contact with the inmate and that includes passing anything to him or receiving anything from him. If you should want to exchange anything, then you signal the surveillance camera so we can check it first. The camera's mounted above the door. By law it can't transmit any sound, so you'll have privacy to talk. The inmate is allowed to smoke in there; if you don't like it, you'll have to take it up with him. When we bring him in, we'll remove his hand restraints but the leg irons stay on and will be bolted to the floor."

"I want all of his restraints removed," Keenan said.

Frowning, Jenkins said, "We do things according to strict procedures. You should know that; just like you should know that it's a thin line that keeps all hell from breaking loose in here."

Keenan felt a flash of impatience and stepped on this hard by taking a deep breath. He didn't want to antagonize this officer. Steadying himself, Keenan looked Jenkins in the eye and said with some force, "Have you ever seen a picture of a teenage girl's body left to rot in a drainage ditch? Or read a forensic report detailing how she was tortured? A lot of these guys make videotapes of what they do to their victims. Have you ever seen a tape like that? I don't recommend it— you're never the same afterwards."

Keenan softened his tone to one more confiding. "Right now, as you and I discuss this, we estimate that in the U.S. there may be as many as fifty guys out there trolling for their next victim. And they're not going to stop until we catch them. Lieutenant, I've spent a dozen hours planning how I can get this man to open up and maybe tell something that can help us stop one of these bastards before he kills someone else's son or daughter. If Drum is in restraints, he won't feel as confident and in control, so he'll be more guarded. For every concession that I ask you for, I have good reasons. Please, Lieutenant, work with me."

Jenkins's jaws flexed and a furrow appeared between his eyes as he studied Keenan's face for signs of sincerity, or insincerity. "All right," he finally said. "But you need to work with us too, you understand?"

Keenan nodded. "I understand. And thank you." The officer stepped aside and Keenan entered the room, satisfied that he had handled Jenkins well, simply by telling the truth. He also reassured himself that, when he needed to, he could nip the anger and impatient flashes that had come over him as his meetings with Drum drew near. Certainly, when he had started his vigorous pursuit of these interviews he had wanted some kind of revenge—back then, he had felt hot rage whenever he recalled the image of Drum's urine soiling Will's cheeks. In time, his hatred for Drum had turned cold and Keenan now felt confident that he would conduct these interviews with his usual detachment. Among his bedrock beliefs was that his head could always rule his heart.

Only those having official business with death row inmates could use the meeting room at the end of Tier 2. It had a twelve-foot ceiling and recessed lights to ensure that no condemned man, if somehow left alone, could cheat the state of its justice by committing suicide. An unblinking surveillance camera anchored to the chalky-gray wall also encouraged acceptable behavior. In the middle of the room, two chairs sat on opposite sides of a heavy table that was bolted to the dark tile floor. Soiled scratches mottled the table's fiberboard top and oily dirt packed under its metal rim. On the table sat a green aluminum ashtray, its center blackened from cigarettes pressed out hard.

Keenan pushed the ashtray to Drum's side, then took a small tape recorder from his jacket and placed it on the table as far from Drum's reach as feasible. This done, he hung his jacket on the back of the chair, sat, and began strumming his fingers in hard thuds on the chair's arm, near where tufts of cotton seeped from a crack in the tan padding.

While waiting, Keenan recalled things he had learned from Drum's Warden's Jacket, the term for an inmate's file. Drum had been on Zoloft for five years. He stayed awake nightly until three or four in the morning, then napped throughout the day. He kept his cell neat and washed his hands so often that in winter they remained red and raw. Both hand washing and masturbation, which he did several times a day, increased as rulings on major appeals drew near. When Drum read, it was mostly true crime magazines, the variety with bound, partially clad women on the cover. Occasionally, he read books and these were also mostly about crime. One note observed that Drum showed virtually no interest in the abundant pornography circulating throughout Golgotha, unless it contained pictures of bondage or forced sex, and these materials he hoarded and used during masturbation, along with the true crime magazines.

He regularly received sexually explicit letters from women, often accompanied by revealing photographs, though the number had dropped greatly from when Drum was first sentenced. This was a common phenomenon with notorious death row inmates, and especially common with sexual predators. Drum kept any photographs showing bondage. He wrote the sender's name and address on the back of all the other pictures and gave them away, to be passed from man to man throughout the prison and, perhaps, end up in the wallet of some inmate close to getting out. This act of generosity stood at odds with his usual lack of interest in other death row inmates. In fact, the other condemned men resented Drum because he came across as if he believed himself better than the rest of them.

The most unique thing about Drum, though, was his steadfast unwillingness to discuss his crimes, even to deny them. Most of the serial killers that Keenan interviewed showed one of four patterns. A small number of men, if treated as though they were important, responded with boyish eagerness to please and perhaps even came to see themselves as part of the investigation team. Of course, since truth meant nothing to these men, they told you what they thought you wanted to hear. Henry Lee Lucas's confessions pleased dozens of lawmen as they cleared the books of over two hundred unsolved murders. Many officers' careers were later damaged when Lucas's eager lies fell apart after he claimed responsibility for the Jim Jones massacre in Guyana. When asked how he got there, he said he drove.

More common were the extremely narcissistic killers who believed themselves so smart that if they just keep talking they think they will eventually convince others of their innocence—i.e., John Wayne Gacy. A subset of this type of narcissist were those who protested their innocence, yet badly wanted to brag about what they had done. These men often toyed with interviewers by making veiled admissions and using hints, such as, "Well, I imagine the killer might have felt very excited when he . . ." Ted Bundy loved this game.

Most common of all, however, were those men who described the gruesome details of their crimes with no more emotion than if they were telling you how to hook up a stereo. These men seemed completely unmoved, or perhaps unaware, of the horror of what they had done. They were also more likely to explode with anger if, for instance, they did not like the way a question was posed.

Keenan used different strategies with each type. But Drum did not fit any of the usual patterns. Whenever anyone mentioned his crimes, he became stubbornly silent, just as he had when first arrested. While exerting control through passive-aggressiveness is standard behavior among incarcerated men, Drum ranked at the high end of this already extremely skewed distribution.

·   ·   ·

Wearing prison-issue blue jeans and blue cotton shirt, Isaac Drum sat on his bed and leaned against the wall with one leg dangling over the side and the other foot propped on the bunk's edge. The hand holding his smoke was draped atop his crooked knee, and a jar-cap-sized aluminum ashtray, too flimsy to be honed into a weapon, rested beside him on the bed's green blanket. He had been sitting like this when John Keenan had strutted past without as much as a flicker of a glance his way. "Fuck you, you arrogant bastard," Drum had mumbled and crushed out his cigarette, half-smoked.

Placing both feet on the floor, Drum leaned forward and grabbed a fresh pack of Marlboros off a small desk that was attached to the far wall, and stuffed the smokes and a red plastic lighter into his shirt pocket. For eight years, he had lived in an area seven feet wide and maybe a couple of feet deeper. Furnishings consisted of a thin mattress on a narrow frame, a commode and sink, both of low-grade steel, a small desk with two shelves over it, and a footlocker. Through the bars he could watch a television attached to the distant wall beyond the catwalk and could hear it okay if there wasn't too much shouting or some asshole banging on the bars of his cell just to get on everyone's nerves. There was always noise here, locked in and echoing, and it played hell with Drum's already restless sleep. Even in the middle of the night, guys talked out loud to themselves, or sobbed, or some lowlife asshole would talk trash just to show that he had no respect for anyone. Things only quieted down on execution nights, and Drum for damned sure didn't sleep well then.

Yet, worse than the noise and the maddening frustration of being caged like an unwanted animal, was the numbing sameness of each day being a replay of the past thousand days and the thousand days before that. Normally, a person could tell himself that if he could get through a particular hardship for a certain amount of time, then things would be different or at least there would be something at the end to look forward to. But on death row the future promised only greater and greater monotony—except when last-minute appeals raced against approaching execution dates. Given such an existence, lethargy, dullness, and despair had crept in and beat him down until even his memories of the singular deeds that had put him here became dull and faded. Lately, he had even had trouble getting a decent hard-on. Well, all that would soon change, and not for the reasons those sanctimonious assholes trying to execute him believed. Soon, he'd be moving around the prison with yard privileges and such. And to some extent, he had John Keenan to thank.

Once he agreed to meet with Keenan, it energized Drum. He looked forward to matching wits and showing the bastard that he was not going to blink this time. He would prove that the tremendous pressure surrounding his arrest gave Keenan an unfair advantage during their only face-to-face contest. In fact, Drum had taken steps to ensure that he now had the inside edge. For instance, he knew, with his execution scheduled to take place in four days, that Keenan believed he had agreed to be interviewed because he was shitting his pants and looking for a buddy. Drum also knew that Keenan would try to play him along by pretending to be friendly and as eager as a horny school-boy to hear of his exploits. And, the arrogant son of a bitch believed that knowing Drum's case by heart would help him catch Drum in any lies. Drum knew all this because he had made his attorney obtain for him journal articles that Keenan had written on conducting profiling interviews, as well as Keenan's laughable profiles of him.

Knowing Keenan's mind, Drum intended to set him straight—that he had agreed to their meeting mostly out of curiosity, and that his consent had nothing to do with his pending execution, which wasn't going to happen, anyway. Besides, once he'd shown Keenan that he couldn't put anything over on him, Drum thought it might be interesting to rehash old times with someone as knowledgeable as an FBI profiler.

Things, however, had changed since he first consented to these meetings. The anticipation of Keenan's visit had shaken off his lethargy. Otherwise, he might not have recognized a golden opportunity. He planned to play along with Keenan for a while, then bring that arrogant son of a bitch to his knees and force him to do his bidding, which would be to get Drum's sentence commuted. This ultimate victory over Keenan would probably not happen this afternoon, but soon, very soon.

A couple of minutes had passed since Keenan walked by. Drum wondered why no one had come to get him. He took a round, palm-sized mirror from atop the desk and held it through the bars to look for the COs. Three correctional officers, one carrying restraints, sauntered this way, taking their sweet time. Galled at them for keeping him waiting, Drum watched until the COs came near, then moved back from the bars, put the mirror on the dresser, and waited until they stopped in front of his cell.

"Meeting time," the older, boss-man of the group said. "Let's have your hands."

Moving with deliberate slowness, Drum turned his back to them, unzipped, and urinated into the steel commode. He slowly shook himself a few extra times before carefully zipping up. Moving with great casualness, he turned to the sink and washed his hands with more care than a surgeon prepping, then splashed water on his face before methodically patting himself dry with a hand towel. After drying his hands with equal attention, Drum positioned the towel just so on the rack, and at last stepped to the front of the cell and stuck his hands and wrists through the slot. He did not say a word during all this; in fact, he rarely lowered himself to speak to guards. And whenever they chained him like a dog, as they did now, he always fixed his eyes above their heads to make sure that his chin tipped upward.

.   .   .

Keenan heard footsteps, barely audible above the prison's static roar, approaching on the catwalk. A dark figure, flanked by two brown-uniformed correctional officers, appeared in the door, hesitated, then shuffled inside with the baby-steps of a man in leg irons. Two correctional officers and Lieutenant Jenkins followed.

As the COs removed his restraints, Drum stared sullenly upward. In his prison-issue, blue-denim shirt and jeans, he looked strikingly different in almost every way than when captured eight years earlier. Back then, his dark hair had been scarcely longer than allowed by military standards. Now, he greased it straight back and had let it grow long enough to end in a ducktail just below the collar. Drum's stocky build looked somewhat fuller, though he did not appear overweight. His skin, scarred from teenage acne, had the odd paleness of those who rarely walk in sunlight. Drum's coming fate had etched an old man's creases across his forehead and at the corners of his eyes, while frequent and hard clenching had caused the muscles at the back of his jaw to jut like small gills. Keenan thought Drum, who had once been a chameleon able to blend into any community, had changed tones, blending now by looking jailhouse hard.

Casually, Drum walked to the table and slouched into the chair, not looking at Keenan until the door clanked shut and they were alone. He then slowly turned his head and began staring at Keenan, much like he had stared during their only face-to-face encounter eight years earlier. Drum's eyes were the aqua blue of glacial ice, and just as barren — windows to nothing, Keenan thought. He had seen too many eyes like these to chalk this observation up to his imagination. Others had also commented on it. One popular hypothesis proposed that the intensity of these men's inner rage burned out their core, leaving only cold venomous hatred — and expressionless eyes. Keenan, however, thought that what he saw was a void, existing where feelings that connected us to others should be. What these men lacked, he believed, doomed them to a permanent isolation that rendered human closeness alien and untouchable. As a result, they sought total dominance because it was the only human contact they understood, the only form of intimacy they could ever know.

Yet, as Keenan stared back at Drum his own eyes shone bright and fierce, the gray of his irises seeming flecked with light. He held Drum's gaze just long enough to tweak memories of his earlier victory, then casually turned away and clicked on the small tape recorder. "Thank you for meeting with me. As per our agreement, I'll be recording these sessions."

Drum continued to slouch and stare at him.

"I'm sure I'll ask some questions that seem picky or whose answer seems obvious. But if I don't ask such questions, I might misunderstand what you're telling me. Already, I need one of those picky answers. Even though you signed a consent form, I need a verbal okay to proceed with the taping," Keenan said, setting up the first of three critical points. Though Drum had agreed to cooperate and to discuss his crimes, his habit of refusal was deeply ingrained. Keenan intended to pop his stonewalling cherry by starting with a simple yes or no question about something that Drum had already agreed to do.

For a moment, Drum just kept staring. Finally, he spoke, barely louder than a whisper, "Yeah."

"I'm sorry, I didn't get that."

"Yeah, go ahead."

"Good," Keenan said. The second hurdle was to get Drum talking, so he now asked an open-ended question on what he believed would be an easy topic. He would word this question in such a way that it implied that the third and most difficult hurdle, getting Drum to admit his crimes, was a given. "Before we begin, there's something I'm curious about. To my knowledge, prior to tonight, you've never been willing to talk about your crimes, not even to deny them. Why stay silent for so long?"

Rather than answer, Drum kept staring at him, his eyes penetrating. Too early for a test of wills, Keenan said, "All right then . . ."

"You think that because Shealey denied my latest appeal," Drum said, his voice low and husky, "that I'm sitting here squirming so you can jerk me around."

"In the articles I coauthored, I called meeting with someone this close to execution 'talking in the hangman's shadow,'" Keenan said, holding Drum's stare. "It was also a recommendation in the post-arrest profile I did on you. I know your attorney gave you copies of my profiles and some of my monographs. So you know my thoughts on doing these interviews. And yes, your legal situation doesn't look good. And yes, near execution men often want to talk with me because they want to make sense of things. And yes, my profile on you was not flattering. But you knew these things when you agreed to meet with me." Keenan leaned forward. "I'm here because I want to talk to you, and I'll do anything reasonable to make it easier for us to talk. But whatever you tell me will be because you want to, not because I'm jerking you around," Keenan said and sat back in his chair, having undermined whatever advantage Drum thought he had gained from reading about Keenan's tactics.

Drum kept staring, probably trying to make Keenan uneasy. Finally, he spoke and Keenan could barely hear him. "I guess we'll see what 'anything reasonable' means."

Keenan resisted the temptation to lean farther forward in order to hear him. Influencing another's posture, tone of response, or timing of response are effective ways of controlling an interview and, thereby, subtly achieving dominance. Keenan would be the one to pace this interview.

Shifting his posture so that it more closely mirrored that of his subject—creating a subliminal impression of being attuned—Keenan repeated the question, "Why remain silent for so long?"

"Habit."

"It's an unusual habit."

"Well, it's like what you call the '*mask of normalcy*'—it's one of the smarter things you said. Because ever since they took me from my mother, I've been hiding what I really feel, what I really am. I've spent my whole life pretending to be like everybody else, because I'm different. And if you're different and don't hide it, they'll try to cripple you enough so that you have to depend on them."

"But after the trials, you were, ah, unmasked, so to speak, and everyone knew you were different. Why keep it up?"

Rather than answer, Drum unhurriedly took the red lighter and regular-length pack of Marlboros from his shirt pocket and tore off the cellophane. He hit the pack on his palm to dislodge a cigarette, then tapped its butt-end three times on the mottled table before lighting it with one long draw. "Most people who try to interview me bring cigarettes. Did you?"

"You didn't ask for any. So why keep up the silence?" Keenan pressed. He had cleared the second hurdle, tenuous though it might be, and now needed to establish a pattern of persisting until Drum answered what was asked.

Drum exhaled smoke through his nose, then asked, "You've been talking to the cops about that Wilmet kid, right?"

Keenan would not allow Drum to avoid questions by changing topics, yet he decided to go with this and see where it took him. "Are you interested in that case?"

"I thought that if you told me about it, I might be able to help you, you know, from an insider's perspective."

"What do you think is similar between Wilmet and your murders?" Keenan said, turning the question so that if Drum answered he would make his first ever admission of guilt, putting Keenan over the last and most difficult hurdle.

Drum shook his head. "No, you don't understand. I want you to give me details that aren't on the news. That way I can enlighten you with what I know."

"All the essentials about Wilmet were in the news. If you know something or have some ideas, I'd like to hear them."

Drum took another drag on the cigarette, then shook his head. "Later on," he said and pointed at Keenan with the fingers holding the cigarette, "I want you to remember that you had a chance to find out about Wilmet but played games with it. Remember that."

"All right, I will," Keenan said. "So, are you going to tell me about your silence? Or should we go to a different topic?"

Ignoring the ashtray, Drum flicked his ash onto the floor's dark tile, his eyes never leaving Keenan. Finally, he sneered, "You want to know why I kept quiet? It's simple. You listening?"

Keenan nodded.

Drum took a drag on the cigarette, his eyes never leaving Keenan's face, as he said, "Every son of a bitch with a clipboard wants to prove

I'm a freak. They've checked my blood, my enzymes, my piss, wanted to hook me up to machines to see if I'm brain damaged, and they've even tried to get me take those fucking psychological tests, all just to prove there's something wrong with me. If you want to know who's really fucked up, you should see those assholes from my perspective, see how they hide behind their clipboards." Drum shook his head. "How can some chickenshit like that understand me?"

"That's why you're talking to me. You want me to understand you," Keenan said, wording his statement so that it was also a suggestion, a technique he had picked up at a hypnosis workshop, where he had also learned about mirroring body posture and pacing techniques.

"Phhtt," Drum snorted. "I've read your crap and you've got too much wrong to understand anything. For instance, you cops didn't catch me. I caught myself by . . . by getting too carried away. And I don't hate women. Why would anyone take so much risk to possess something he didn't value? Huh? I just don't like how they act, you know, the way they use sex to control us. So I decided to set the terms. You see, your problem"—Drum took a final hit on his smoke and, again ignoring the ashtray, dropped the butt on the floor—"is that you don't have the guts to look at yourself." He crushed the butt with the toe of his sneaker, then leaned forward to the edge of the table. "Okay, tell me this. Don't we both hunt? Aren't we both relentless in getting what we go after? And don't tell me you don't feel a surge of power when you know your prey can't escape; I know you do because I saw it in you."

"That's right, I am that way."

"And that's the way I am. That's my nature." Drum touched his chest. "I don't repress my deepest desires because I don't have what you shrink types call an unconscious. I don't need one. You see, I'm not afraid of going after what I really want. And that means that the biggest difference between you and me is simply that I have the courage to take what I want. You'd see that if you had the guts to honestly look at yourself. Right?"

Keenan shrugged.

Drum leaned farther over the table and lowered his voice. "Look around you, Keenan, look at how your fellow men treat each other. Pick any place in the world and you'll find a history of savagery, and butchery, and cruelty. I am man's nature at its purest. And you can't accept that because of what it says about you and your own weaknesses," Drum said, and slouched back in his chair, looking pleased with himself.

. . .

Thus far, Keenan thought the interview was proceeding pretty much as he expected it would. Long, empty hours and the narcissistic nature of the men he studied usually resulted in such rehearsed posturing, similar to how one might think of conversation starters for an eagerly awaited first date. Every emotion shown so far was purely for effect. With genuine emotion, a person usually broke eye contact, if only for an instant. Yet, Drum's eyes never left Keenan as he watched for his reactions. More interesting, when Drum wanted Keenan to believe something, he leaned forward and increased his hand gestures. Later on, this enhanced emphasis could be useful for picking up lies.

Keenan had confirmed several guesses about Drum. His preferred phrasing included visual terms such as "see" and "look," instead of auditory expressions such as "sounds right" and "hear this," which meant that Drum's primary mode of processing information was visual. From here on, Keenan would judiciously frame his own statements and questions in visual terms, subtly increasing Drum's feeling of being understood.

Keenan also verified that their brief encounter eight years earlier had had the desired impact. His subject had drawn parallels between himself and Keenan, and had even used simple psychological theory to further imply similarity. Extremely narcissistic, he needed to believe that only someone of superior abilities, like a special agent of the FBI, could have caught him. And he expected Keenan to be tough and strong; that was what attracted him to Keenan. Of course, Drum would try to dominate him and jump on any weakness like a starving weasel on a baby rabbit. Unconsciously, though, Drum probably hoped Keenan could not be controlled, and as long as Drum did not get the upper hand he would probably remain engaged. The trick for Keenan was, when pushed, to shove back without forcing his subject into a corner by always allowing him a face-saving way out, preferably one that created a sense of "we're in this together."

The most revealing thing his subject said was an out-of-context statement about being separated from his mother. Having total dominance means others cannot reject or leave you, no matter what you do. Primitive abandonment fears were common in the men he studied and probably fueled this man's consuming rage. Now, with Drum standing on death's threshold, Keenan might be able to use Drum's fear of being deserted to exert leverage, perhaps a lot of leverage. He decided to test this edge by pushing a little.

Keenan placed his forearms on the table, leaned forward, and smiled the way a parent might smile at a child who is afraid of the dark. "Knowing what drives you is not as simple as that," he said, sounding like a slightly condescending professor. "No one can know for sure all that's hidden inside, that's the nature of defenses. It's been my experience that the more extreme the acts, the deeper and darker the pain. And what you did was so extreme . . . it makes me wonder if you can really afford to be honest with me? Most men aren't that strong."

"You think you're clever, don't you, Keenan."

"Talking to a stupid man wouldn't do you much good."

Drum opened his mouth to speak, stopped, then said, "And what good's talking to a clever man going to do me, huh? You better not forget that I'm the one who decides whether or not we talk, or you just might clever your way right out of an interview. In fact, I'm not so sure I don't need to think about it, let you know tomorrow if your rudeness is worth it."

"Rather than resort to being clever, I'd prefer we both talk straight," Keenan said. "I'm not here to bug you. I'm here because you expressed an interest in talking with me, and I have one in talking to you. We each have our own reasons, but for either of us to get what we want, you're right, we have to talk straight to each other. Either we both win or we both lose. So far, you've not really answered my question about your silence. If that's one of the things you don't want to discuss, fine, we can move on. But if you don't want to answer any of my questions or you want to quit before we even get started, then I might as well go out that door and never bug you again."

Instead of responding, Drum took another cigarette from the pack and lit it.

Keenan waited until Drum took a second hit, then turned his palms up and said, "Well, what's it going to be?"

Drum took another, shorter hit on the cigarette. He stared at Keenan, blew smoke through his nose, then slowly stood and leaned over the table so that he loomed above Keenan. "Okay, tell me, Keenan, since we need to be so straight with each other, in your opinion"—he emphasized the word *opinion*—"do you think I got a just sentence, do you think I deserve to die?"

"Yes," Keenan said without hesitation.

"And if during the interview, you hear something that might be grounds for a retrial or help my appeal, will you tell me?"

"No."

Drum took a deep drag, then blew a steady stream of smoke at Keenan. Smoke stung Keenan's eyes and the stench filled in his nostrils. Yet, he did not flinch, and when Drum saw this his lips pulled back in a humorless, snake-like smile.

"Now you tell me something straight," Keenan said. "It can be anything, just so it's straight."

A loud silence followed. Keenan waited. Drum took another drag off the cigarette, then stepped behind his chair and leaned on its back with both hands, the cigarette smoldering between his fingers. "All right," he said, "when I was first arrested everything was happening fast. I knew that anything I said would get twisted against me, so I played mute until I could figure out a strategy. That's when I saw how bad everybody wanted what I knew—the cops, the lawyer, TV people, jailers, other prisoners, you name it, everybody wanted to know what I knew. Well, any fool knows that as long as somebody wants something from you, you have the edge, at least until they get what they want. And the harder it is to get, the more they want it and the bigger the edge. So even though they put me in a cage and pushed me around, I was always the one in control. And I've stayed that way. Never once have I bowed my head by giving those pricks what they wanted, not once. That's straight."

"Why keep it up after the trial?"

"Nothing really changed." Drum waved the hand with the cigarette. "It's always a question of where you want to deal from. Tell me that you won't use some secret bit of information, identified weakness, or whatever gives you an edge to get what you want. Huh? You can't, can you? We both know you're either dealing from one-up or one-down, and anybody who tells you they want to deal as equals is either trying to sucker you or scared. Right?"

"That makes sense," Keenan said. The time had come to nudge Drum over the third hurdle, to get him to admit his crimes. "There's one more thing I've never quite understood. When you were ready to start killing, you started with a prostitute. She seemed so, ah, different from the others; she doesn't fit. Was she a friend of yours and you just got carried away? A lot of first kills happen that way."

Drum craned forward over the chair back and punched the air with the fingers holding the cigarette. "I didn't do anything I hadn't planned," he said. "And I don't hang out with whores. She was a practice run and nothing more. Easy to take, and if it didn't turn out like I wanted . . . well, no big loss. Any dumb son of a bitch can kill whores and get away with it. Big deal. Looking back I wish I hadn't bothered with her. It's embarrassing for people to think I've been with someone that trashy."

Keenan resisted the urge to smile. His tact to break Drum's posturing had worked seamlessly, erasing the nagging doubts that his hatred of Drum might have influenced this choice of such an aggressive approach. He would now zero in on the abduction phase of Drum's crimes—generally one of the easier areas to get at since it centered around cleverness, taking control, the fervor of hunting, and the final realization of consuming desires. Most often, the men he studied got off on describing how they had hunted. And learning how these men went about selecting and capturing victims had the greatest utility in aiding future investigations, so Keenan always started with the abductions.

"So, how did you prepare for the Reeves abduction," Keenan asked, switching from a confrontational stance to a more neutral approach that guided rather than challenged. Yet, a part of him, a feral watcher, continued tracking Drum's emotional jugular, just in case.

II

An hour later, cigarette butts littered the floor around Drum's feet and a smoky haze hung in the air. Keenan leaned back in his chair, his shirt-sleeves rolled halfway up his forearms, his chin propped on his knuckles, and his fierce gray eyes observing the minutiae of Drum's every move.

On the opposite side of the table, Drum sat more upright now, his chest rising and falling from arousal, his eyes glazed and dilated. For the past half-hour, his cigarettes lay untouched. Eager to push his mind's eye deeper into the past, Drum now readily answered whatever Keenan asked; yet Keenan's presence barely registered on Drum's awareness, the way a priest behind the screen might recede into the background during a particularly intense confession. Drum had described his first two abductions, remembering these terrible events with such clarity and punch that he had gone beyond the realm of memory to a state of mind where he completely reexperienced the nights when he had prowled.

"So after staking out three different places on Friday and coming up dry, I was almost frantic," Drum said, his voice husky as he recounted the build up to snatching Alicia Owens. "I couldn't shake the frustration; it was worse than I'd ever had it before."

"Can you try again to describe that feeling, the one you said you always felt before you went out trolling?" Keenan asked.

"It's like . . . okay, did you ever see a show where a football player is all keyed up before a game and starts smashing his forearm into a locker? It's like that. I was frustrated and angry and excited all at the same time. I couldn't stand feeling that way. I wanted to punch something or tear something apart or pick a fight with someone. And I was horny as hell. I've had feelings like that ever since I was a kid."

"Did these feelings only come on when it was close to your weekend off from work."

"Maybe. No. They were always there. I just kept them under wraps until I could do something about them. Then they took over and nothing calmed me except hunting. And as bad as those feelings were, there was a part of cruising that felt just as good; you know, excitement, anticipation, and all that. But if I didn't have any luck, the feeling got so bad I couldn't stand it."

"So, after coming up dry on Friday, what happened the next night?"

"I went out as soon as it was dark, around nine or nine-thirty. I planned to follow the same pattern, stay at each place for fifteen or twenty minutes, then move on. The first place I went to was this church parking lot that ran in back of a Quick Stop. That late on a Saturday night, there were few cars parked on the street in front of the church and no one was out walking around. I took that as a good sign," Drum said, his mind's eye gorging on the images of that night and his breathing again quickening from the dark sensations of his past.

He saw again the older streetlights with dim, half-dome fixtures hanging on arched arms. He saw all the shadows swelling around the brick buildings that squeezed close to the sidewalk, buildings with white-trimmed porches that were once homes but had been converted into law or realty offices or shops selling cutesy junk. He felt the May night air flowing across his bare arm as it rested in the van's open window. And he bristled with alertness as he drove slowly along this street, looking for a cleaning woman coming out of a building or someone walking a dog farther down the sidewalk, looking for anyone who might notice him, and maybe remember. And he felt truly alive.

A quarter moon's weak glow turned the church steeple pale blue. It was a good moon, not too much light. I eased past the church, checking one last time to make sure no one was around, then turned into the church's driveway between two enormous water oaks. The parking lot behind the church was covered with asphalt and would not catch tire tracks. I made sure that the lot was empty, then switched off the van's lights, excited and hopeful that I would not go home alone. On the side of the parking lot opposite the church I saw the boxy silhouettes of businesses that faced the next street, a street with good but not heavy traffic. One of these businesses was an older convenience store that I had scoped out earlier. Looping the van in a circle to avoid triggering its back-up lights, I stopped with the rear doors only a few feet from the convenience store's back corner and switched off the engine. The night came alive with the tense trilling of cicadas.

The Chevy van was a cargo model with no side windows that I had adapted for my work by taking out both rear seats. In case I needed to get away in a hurry, I left the keys dangling in the ignition. I also turned off the dome light so that no telltale glow showed as I slipped from the van. Nor did the light come on when I swung open both rear doors.

Though terribly excited, I worked carefully, aware that I could not afford even a small mistake. I unzipped a gym bag placed near the door and took out two sets of handcuffs, then climbed into the van and attached one end of each cuff to the forward tie downs, leaving the cuffs' other ends open. Crawling out of the van, I next took a towel from the bag, folded it once, and lay it across the latch where the doors met. This done, I pulled out a roll of duct tape and tore off a piece and lay it sticky side up on the van's metal floor. Last, I took a large hunting knife from the bag, slipped it into my belt, then put on a black jacket to hide its honed blade.

The prep done, I pressed belly-up against the store's back wall near the corner, breathing harder now. I already knew that this was a damn good spot with a narrow sidewalk that would make it easy for some lucky woman to come to me. And there were bushes blocking the view from the closed building next door.

Cautious, I peeked down the bare brick wall and saw some guy's shoulder at the far corner as he leaned against the building while his buddy talked on the pay phone that I knew was located a couple of feet from the corner. I jerked back and strained to listen, hearing enough to know that the guy was trying to get some girl to let them come over. "Aw, shit," the guy said and hung up. Those two guys made me want to spit, letting some girl jerk them around simply by withholding that little thing between her legs. They were such pathetic losers. I would never allow a woman to use sex to control me.

Moments later, I heard their car pull away and the waiting continued. After coming up dry the night before, I felt antsy and frequently shifted positions or paced in short bursts or tapped the fleshy bottom of my fist on the wall while listening at the corner.

After waiting there for twenty minutes, I was about to leave when headlights swung into the space in front of the walk. I ducked back and didn't look again until the headlights went off. Parked at the far end of the building was a red Camaro with steam spilling from the grill, not enough to be a broken hose, but a problem. The Camaro's door opened and a young woman with teased, shoulder-length blond hair got out. Alert and focused, I saw everything with slow clarity. Nicely dressed in a tan skirt and beige blouse, she didn't look much over twenty and when she crossed in front of the car, I saw that she had a slim figure and cute face, a sweet face, in fact.

My senses were so attuned that even though I was breathing hard I could hear everything, even the coin falling inside the phone. "Alvin, it's Alicia," she said. "The damn car's overheating. Will you come and get me? I'm at the Quick Stop on Martin Street . . . Okay . . . Thanks. See you in a few."

If I had my way, she would not see him in a few.

Quickly, I stepped to the van and slammed one of the doors, which clanked but also made a softer thump where it hit the towel and didn't latch. Yanking the door open again, I threw the towel out of the way, then grabbed the piece of duct tape, dropped to one knee, and began crying out in pain—my mating call.

Loudly, I moaned and begged someone to help me, and watched the corner until I saw her crane her neck around the edge, cautiously trying to see what had happened. The light coming from behind her caused the outline of her hair to shimmer as the little blonde stepped even with the corner, one hand touching the brick.

"Oh, God, my hand. I've broken my hand," I said, sounding like I was crying. I wanted to keep things moving too fast for her to think. "I stayed late to set up the church for tomorrow . . ." I paused, breathing hard, which I didn't have to fake. ". . . and then my van wouldn't start and I was looking for a flashlight and got so frustrated that I slammed the door on my hand. Oh, God it hurts . . . oh, it hurts."

She took her hand from the wall and stepped closer. It took all my willpower to remain hunched over and looking down rather than watching and taking in every inch of her. "Please, there's a flashlight near the van's door," I pleaded. "Please . . . get it, so I can see how bad it's hurt."

She hesitated.

"Please help, please? Oh, God, I can't move my fingers!"

Again she hesitated, then on impulse moved to the back of the van, which put her between me and the van's opened doors. The back of her leg brushed my shoulder and I could feel her body heat and even in the dim light see the seam of her stocking only inches from my face. It was such an exquisite and erotic moment that I could barely keep from grabbing her legs and pushing my hand towards her heat. But I knew I couldn't do that, not yet.

The little blonde leaned into the van and started patting the floor looking for a flashlight. I slipped the knife from my belt and stood, feeling a surge of primal strength; she looked so petite and weak. I clamped the tape over her mouth and showed her the knife, then pushed it against her throat. "If you don't do exactly what I say, I'll slice up your face," I hissed in her ear. "Go along and you won't get hurt." I knew that she would believe anything that offered hope, because the alternative carried *too much terror for her mind to even consider. Yet, she tensed, like she might try something. I shifted the blade and laid it against her cheek. "It's razor sharp," I whispered in her ear. I felt her tense even more, then she went limp and started whimpering, and I knew that she was mine. I lingered for just a moment, allowing myself to push up against her and smelling the floral scent of her hair. I wanted to run my hands over her soft places, but thought that might panic her before I had her secured. Rough enough to leave no doubt that I was in control, I pushed her on into the van and straddled her while snapping the handcuffs around her wrists. Working fast, I grabbed the duct tape from the bag and wrapped her ankles. When this was done, I took a third set of cuffs from the bag and hooked one ankle to a middle tie-down, forcing her into a fetal position that prevented her from kicking the sides.*

". . . so, seconds later, I eased out of the parking lot," Drum said, not so much to Keenan as to himself. His eyes remained glazed and wet, his breathing hard, and sweat beaded on his face, though the room was not warm. "And there was no traffic so no one saw a thing. It probably wasn't much over two minutes from the time she hung up the phone until I was out of there. Two minutes. Funny how quickly your life can change. I already had a feeling that things were finally starting to go right, and that she was going to be special."

Across the table, Keenan sat as he had throughout Drum's narrative, leaning back in his chair with his chin resting on his knuckles. Unhurriedly, he sat up and placed both forearms on the table, causing Drum to blink as Keenan's movement broke into his trance. "You had a gun with you, right, just like the other two abductions?" Keenan asked.

"Of course," Drum answered, sounding annoyed. "I had it in my lap as I drove away, just in case someone tried to stop me."

"So why use a knife during the abduction rather than the gun?"

"A knife's more personal, especially if held near the face." Drum shrugged. "And I think women are more afraid of having their face maimed than getting shot in the body somewhere."

"I see. Now, tell me this . . ."

Drum grimaced and waved his hands as if shaking Keenan off, yet his eyes became less clouded as he lost more of his hold on his dark memories.

". . . did you have any complications while driving with victims in the van?"

"Driving with them in the van was always the riskiest time. It was hard because I was so excited that I had trouble keeping my mind on observing speed limits and stuff like that. And driving with the little blonde was especially hard on me, having to concentrate . . . and wait." Drum stopped talking. Keenan asked something else, but Drum didn't hear him, as his eyes glazed again . . .

The only light inside the van came from the pale green dash lights and streetlights reflecting through the windows in front. I felt pumped like a fighter that's just beaten the shit out of an opponent; I wanted to roar and pound my chest. I knew that the little blonde was going to be special. Not like the first two; not a disappointment this time. I had such hopes.

I braked at a traffic light and twisted the rearview mirror until I could see her. I didn't say anything, just stared at her eyes. Enough light came though the front windows that I could see her watching me. Her eyes were so big and beautiful and tears ran down her cheeks. I loved the way she looked at me, watching my every move, wondering what I'm thinking, what I'm like, what I'm going to do to her. And I loved knowing that, from now on, I was the most important person in her life.

18

a lamb to the slaughter

I

JOE CAMERON thought the large room with its brightly colored plastic chairs and laminated tables resembled a school cafeteria, except that the windows were ten feet off the floor and covered with metal bars—but maybe that resembled some school cafeterias. Joe sat at the table closest to the open double doors separating this medium security visitation room from Golgotha's main lobby. From this vantage point, he watched a smattering of people coming and going through the bank of glassed front doors.

They had left Joe waiting here while some FBI agent met with Isaac Drum. Then, supposedly, Joe would meet with Drum.

Today, Joe was the only person in this large room, unlike yesterday when it had been crowded with Sunday afternoon visitation. Surrounded by all those feverish couples with their plastic chairs pushed together and their hands busy beneath the tables, Joe had blushed hotly and tried to look away from all the slurping kisses and blatant fondling. Yesterday, Joe had left after waiting for an hour, not because all the vulgar behavior around him made him uncomfortable—though it did—but because he knew he had been made a fool. Today, he expected to leave Golgotha just as he had yesterday, his head sagging and his feet scuffing the dark tiles, a far cry from his triumphant exit three days earlier.

Joe's strange odyssey began on Friday morning in the new gymnasium of Jeffcoat Landing's Baptist Church, where he served as associate pastor. Joe had been on his hands and knees scrubbing scuff marks from the lacquered floor when he noticed a stranger walking down the middle of the basketball court toward him.

"Joseph Cameron?" the man said. He was lean with a craggy face and wore a loose-fitting blue suit. His curly hair mixed equal parts of black and gray, and Joe thought he looked at least a couple weeks past due a haircut. His mustache also needed trimming.

"I'm Joseph Cameron," Joe answered and climbed stiffly to his feet. He tugged his gray sweatshirt down over his flabby stomach and wiped his sweaty palms on his gray slacks before shaking hands.

"I'm Mike Welch with the *Daily Record*," the man said. His voice had a deep resonance that reminded Joe of Texas cowboys, though Welch's accent was definitely southern.

"Really," Joe said, his hazel eyes appearing unusually large behind thick, wire-rimmed glasses. Joe swept his short brown hair back from his forehead. "Are you doing an article on our church?"

Welch shook his head. "If you follow the news, you know I've been able to get access to some previously sealed records on Isaac Drum, and from these records I found out that you were briefly matched with Drum as a Big Brother. What I'm trying to find out, Mr. Cameron, is not only what Drum was like as a child, but if there were points along the way where some sort of intervention could have made a difference so that he wouldn't have become what he did. I want your impressions and memories of Drum at that age."

"Oh, ah . . . I wasn't sure it was even the same Drum until just now."

"Okay," said Welch. He took a small pad from his jacket and poised his pen, ready to take notes. "So how did the match come about?"

"Ah . . . I guess his mother wanted him involved in Big Brothers because he didn't have a father."

"Now, the records indicate that his mother's acceptance was coerced after a teacher became concerned and asked the Department of Social Services to investigate. Reading between the lines, you might say that his enrollment in Big Brothers came about as a sort of plea bargain. I thought volunteers were briefed on such circumstances?"

"It . . . it was almost twenty years ago and I haven't thought about it for a long time," Joe said, hoping Welch would just accept this and go away.

But Welch kept standing there with his pen ready and said, "Well, what do you remember about Drum?"

"He, ah, he was quiet. He didn't talk much . . . but that's not unusual with new pairings. Our first outing coincided with a Big Brother-sponsored ball game, so we went. He didn't play or interact with the other kids. They told me to expect these kind of problems at first because a lot of kids emotionally can't afford to take a chance on being hurt so they withdraw. As a pastor I've worked with all sorts of youth and it's true. In fact, youth league is one of my duties."

"Why didn't things work with you and Drum?"

"Ah . . . it was my fault. After the first outing, I . . . ah, I was in my second year of seminary and school became very demanding. I couldn't keep up with everything so I . . . ah . . . withdrew my participation. I figured that since no real bonding had occurred, it was best to do it sooner than later. I guess that was wrong, but I've made up for it since then."

"Tell me about some of the things he did, or what you talked about. Be specific."

"I don't remember anything other than what I've already said," Joe said, and smiled at Welch to let him know he was friendly and would help him if he could.

"Okay, what was his mother like?"

"Ah . . . she was nice."

"How was she 'nice'?"

"Just nice. She, ah, didn't say or do too much. That's all I remember."

Welch lowered his pen and frowned. "Mr. Cameron, I wish you'd help me. Your experience is exactly the kind that might shed light on what could keep other kids from turning out like Drum?"

"Ah . . . there's nothing more to tell. He didn't want the pairing and I was having a tough year in seminary. That's all."

Welch shook his head. "Here's my card. Think about your time with Drum, okay? And if you can remember anything at all, please give me a call."

"Ah, sure," Joe said, and accepted Welch's card. As the reporter turned to leave, Joe said, "It was nice meeting you."

. . .

After Welch left, Joe got back down on his sore knees and crawled along the court from scuff mark to scuff mark. He could not stop thinking about the reporter's visit, especially his comment that Joe's experience might shed light on things that could have stopped Drum from becoming a killer. Welch made it sound like Joe was somehow responsible for the way Drum turned out. Sure, he'd been scared off as Drum's Big Brother, but that wasn't any of Welch's business, not really. And it was just plain crazy to think that he, Joseph Cameron, could have made any difference whatsoever to someone as seriously disturbed as that man Drum obviously was. Besides, Drum was only a child back then, an innocent child. Whatever set him off had to have happened years later, and there was nothing Joe could have done about it.

"I did the best I could," Joe muttered aloud, and realized that he was aimlessly rubbing the same spot. Climbing to his feet, Joe walked in a small circle to loosen his stiff legs. "That boy didn't want me as a Big Brother anyway. But that's the story of my life," Joe said, frustrated. He always introduced himself as Joseph, yet everyone called him Joe. At thirty-nine, he was ten years older than the other two associate pastors, but they treated him like low man on the totem pole. "I've given this church everything for fourteen years," he mumbled, "and my biggest responsibility is coordinating youth league, not that I'm complaining."

On and on, Joe paced and talked out loud to himself like someone in the loony bin. The more he paced, the more upset he became. In one breath, he blamed Welch for upsetting him; in the next he blamed himself for not doing more with Drum—and for not doing more with his life.

After almost an hour, tired from pacing and as frustrated as he'd ever been, Joe decided to take action, and hurried to his office before he changed his mind, the way he usually did. A friend from seminary, Bruce Tanner, was a chaplain at Golgotha. Prison information gave him Bruce's number and, on the second ring, Bruce picked up.

"Bruce, it's Joseph Cameron."

"Huh? Oh, Joe. This is a surprise. How have you been?"

"Good," Joe said. Already, he felt foolish for making this call. But now that he had Bruce on the line what could he do but go forward? Blushing, Joe leaned his elbows on the desk and said, "Ah . . . Bruce, I need a favor. I've just found out that I knew Isaac Drum when he was a child. I, ah, more or less briefly, ah . . . shepherded him. I can't believe it's the same person. But I need to see him."

"Hmmm," Tanner said slowly. "Honestly Joe, I don't know if I can help you. It's hard enough to get visitation with any death row inmate, but especially tough to see one who is under an active death warrant."

This was good news, Joe thought. He didn't listen as closely as he should while Tanner reminded him that Drum's crimes made national headlines because he killed the cop who caught him, and then again drew headlines when the Supreme Court singled out his case as an example of appeals abuse. Bruce then said something about getting bags full of petitions from people wanting a few minutes with Drum.

"You see, the media's following this execution more closely than I've seen them follow any death watch in a long time, and that includes the national media," Bruce explained. So our warden is keeping a tight rein to make sure Drum's execution, if it happens, doesn't get blown into a bigger circus than it already is."

"I understand," Joe said, trying to not sound too relieved.

"Hmmm." Tanner paused. "It's a long shot, Joe, but since no powers that be want to be accused of denying a condemned man his last shot at salvation, I might be able to get you in as his pastor. For what it's worth, I'll vouch for your character and sincerity. But I need to know what you mean by 'briefly shepherded.'"

"I, ah, was a Big Brother for him."

"Hmmm. That might do. But even if I get you official permission, I think pigs will fly before Drum agrees to see you. You see, he has the final say-so, and he's a strange bird, even for in here. He refuses to talk to just about everybody, including ministers. Either way, give me a number where I can reach you."

Joe gave Bruce his office number, thanked him, and hung up. He'd done all he could. If you can't get in, you can't get in. At least he tried.

With a little bounce in his gait, Joe returned to the gym and finished cleaning the court. Thirty minutes later, he went to lunch exuberantly humming "How Great Thou Art."

.   .   .

Joe still smiled and walked sprightly, as he returned from lunch. He'd had an inspiration for a new layout of the Sunday school bulletin board. The secretary handed Joe a message from Bruce Tanner asking Joe to call as soon as possible.

"I guess miracles never cease," Tanner said. "Drum has agreed to see you. I don't know why, but whatever his reasons, trust me, they're not good. Be careful, Joe, he can't be trusted."

Stunned, Joe could only say, "Okay."

"You're to see him at three o'clock, but you need to get here no later than two-forty. I'll leave word at the front gate, and have them bring you by my office first."

"I'll be there," Joe rasped, his mouth suddenly very dry. He forgot to thank Bruce for making the arrangements.

II

Well before he was due at Golgotha, Joe went home to change clothes. He first put on his best suit, a dark gray pinstripe with matching vest, but thought he looked overdressed for a prison. Then he tried tan slacks with a plaid jacket, but the jacket seemed too festive for death row. Finally, out of time, he left home wearing gray slacks with a navy jacket and a maroon striped tie. Fumbling, Joe dropped his keys while unlocking his Dodge Caravan.

Joe had driven past Golgotha State Prison all his life. Jeffcoat

Boulevard crossed the Saluda River and ran beside Golgotha's eastern perimeter. Approaching from the Jeffcoat side, the tall stone wall of Golgotha's back barrier came into view first. Covered with small vines, moss, and pale green lichen, it looked solid, dependable, reassuring— unlike the rest of the perimeter.

A hundred yards along the eastern side, the wall changed into thick-meshed fence laced with overlapping coils of razor wire. There were, in fact, two such fences, separated by a twenty-foot no man's land with tall gun turrets spaced along the way. These fences bothered Joe because you could see through them, not that he objected to the stone and brick buildings, each dotted with a myriad of small windows. What Joe did not like was the enormous recreation field a hundred yards or so in front of the main building. During the day, hordes of men played ball, jogged, or clustered in small groups doing who knows what. It reminded Joe of a huge mound of angry fire ants. And every time he drove past the prison, Joe remembered why it was best to avoid certain places after dark. He felt immensely grateful for prisons, he just wished they had put this one somewhere more out of sight.

Today, Joe drove more slowly than usual and kept glancing through Golgotha's fences, wondering how he had blundered so badly that he was not only going inside, but going into the building where the worst men were kept. And he had to do it all by himself. What if the men on death row were not locked in their cells but roaming around free? Joe's stomach convulsed and he almost threw up.

·　·　·

Golgotha's parking area was located on the opposite side of Jeffcoat Boulevard from the prison, with access via a covered walkway that spanned the highway's four lanes. Locking his car, Joe ambled to the walkway's entrance, where a large sign warned against contraband, cit-ing about a dozen categories. Dutifully, he walked back to his van and locked his small penknife in the glove compartment.

Crossing the walkway, Joe descended into a checkpoint manned by a black female correctional officer, who Joe thought very pretty. Under her close scrutiny, Joe blushed and stuck his hands in his pockets. The officer confirmed his name on a list, then picked up a telephone and called for an escort. While waiting, she asked Joe to hold out his arms and quickly ran a metal detection wand along his gingerbread-man outline. By the time she finished, a blondish-red-haired officer, his arms robustly pumping, bustled across the seventy or so feet of asphalt between the main building and the checkpoint. Short and pudgy, the man's face puckered as if he had just bitten into a crabapple. Joe hoped this guard was older than the twenty or so he appeared to be.

Addressing Joe, the officer said in a nasal voice, "Please follow me and do exactly as I say." Turning, he set a fast pace and Joe strained to keep up. "That enclosed parking area inside those fences is for top administrators and official vehicles," the young officer explained, and continued pointing out things as if taking Joe on a tour. At a sprightly pace, they walked to the main building, then up a short flight of broad steps to a bank of sturdy-framed glass doors. Above these doors, three-foot-tall, nickel-colored letters spelled out "GOLGOTHA STATE PRISON."

Inside, was a train-station-like lobby with a high ceiling. Thirty feet straight ahead, a double wall of iron bars blocked their way. "Through the nice doors to the left are the administrative offices," his escort said. "Most professional staff have offices in the long hall on the other side of that sally port." He pointed toward the double security bars. "The visitation area for medium security inmates is through the double doors to your left. And over here is a display of some of the things we've confiscated from inmates." His escort stopped walking and swept his hand like a game show hostess toward a large case enclosed by thick Plexiglas.

"Oh, lordy," Joe muttered. There were more than a dozen sharp, pick-like items with taped handles, butter knives with their ends filed to gleaming points, five or six real knives, a set of brass knuckles, a few metal tubes with holes drilled midway, several wooden clubs, several metal clubs, and, to Joe's horror, one snub-nose revolver.

"For every weapon we confiscate," his escort cheerfully informed him, "there are at least two dozen more hidden away. And this is only a sample of what we've found, so it's not surprising that we average over two violent incidents a month."

Joe's stomach tightened and he looked away from the case.

Noticing Joe's reaction, his escort added, "There's nothing to worry about. When you're walking through the general population, I'll be right beside you. Do what I say and everything will go all right."

This did not assure Joe. He wanted to tell this young man that it would not be necessary, that he had changed his mind. But that would take courage. Instead, Joe rasped, "Good. Thank you. I'm glad I'll be with a guard."

"I'm not a guard," his escort said testily. "I'm a correctional officer, CO for short. My job has a lot more responsibilities than just standing around watching inmates."

"I'm, ah, I'm sorry. I didn't know."

"Well you do now. This way," the CO said and, with renewed brisk-ness walked toward the metal bars. Proudly silent, his escort signaled for an officer in a control booth to release the first gate. Once this gate shut, a gate in the next wall of bars buzzed open. From there, they passed through a pale green hallway with offices all along both walls. Ahead, like the precipice of a waterfall, a long cement stairway led down to a broad landing, then more stairs.

When they came to a second landing, his escort halted in front of a door marked "CHAPLAIN" and pressed an intercom button. "Mr. Tanner, your visitor's here," he announced. Ten seconds later, Bruce Tanner opened the door and behind him Joe saw a small suite with at least three or four connecting offices.

"Thank you, Wayne." Bruce shook Joe's hand. "Good to see you, Joe. It's been a long time." A couple of inches shorter than Joe, Bruce was as lean as he had been in seminary, though his dark, wavy hair was a bit longer and sprinkled with gray. He also sported a mustache and tortoiseshell glasses. When Bruce looked at Joe, his eyes sparkled, seemingly with genuine interest.

"Thank you for helping me," Joe said, feeling a sudden and strong kinship with Bruce, and he wondered why such a fine minister was throwing his career away working in a prison.

"I'll walk with you the rest of the way," Bruce offered.

"That would be great," Joe agreed. Bruce locked the suite's outer door and the three men started down a final set of stairs.

"Why are we going down?" Joe asked.

"The lowest three levels of Golgotha were built below ground to provide a little relief from the summer heat," Bruce explained. "You see, there's no air-conditioning in the cell blocks."

Twenty feet beyond this last set of steps stood another security cage, and as he approached Joe saw prisoners walking around on the other side of those bars like it was nobody's business.

"I need to prepare you for the Tunnel," Wayne, his escort, said and turned to face Joe. "We're going into a passage that connects all the cell blocks to the chapel and cafeteria. Everyone calls it 'The Tunnel,' and anytime an inmate goes outside his cell block, he has to pass through there. At this time of day, all but maximum security inmates may move around in there, so we'll be walking through the general population, but most of the men are outside. I want you to walk between Mr. Tanner and me. All right, let's go."

Wayne signaled a CO inside another control booth and the first set of bars slid open. Once inside the sally port, Joe jumped as the gate clanked shut behind him.

"The Tunnel's the social center of the prison," Bruce explained. "It's a lot like main street." Bruce said some more things but Joe wasn't listening. He felt light-headed and things didn't seem quite real. The last barrier opened and they stepped into a wide, brightly lit hallway. Overhead, spaced about fifty feet apart, were three catwalks, each with a bored-looking CO on it.

"It's not as bad as it looks," Bruce said quietly. "Just do like Wayne says and stay close."

Joe did not need to be told to stay close. But he found it impossible not to sneak peeks at the smattering of tough-looking men who gathered in small groups, walked past, or lounged against the walls. Inadvertently, he made eye contact with a wiry man whose forearms were covered with tattoos of daggers and buxom women. "Who you looking at, lard-ass?" the man shouted. After that, Joe looked straight ahead, even as his escort pointed out various cell blocks.

"Those open wards are CB7 and 8; see how their beds are lined up military-style. They're for medium security prisoners. And ahead on your left is CB3, which along with CB2 and CB4 are maximum security. We've had more stabbings and assaults in CB3 than in any other cell block, and who knows how many rapes go on in there every day, because the inmates know better than to report them."

What a god-awful place, Joe thought, and wished that Wayne would shut up.

At last, they stopped in front of a green door with "CB2" stenciled in thick black paint. Pressing the intercom, Wayne announced,

"Pardue with a visitor for Drum." Then to Joe, "Death row is located in CB2. They'll explain what's expected. Mostly, it's commonsense stuff like having no physical contact."

"You mean I'm not going to be behind a glass?"

"No, Joe, that's not the way it's done here," Bruce answered. "You'll be sitting across a table from him. It's always tough the first time. If you prefer, they'll leave him in restraints. Usually, that's not a good idea when you're ministering to someone, but this man's used to it. And, Joe, whatever his reason for seeing you, it's probably not what you think it is. He can't be trusted."

The door opened and a hulking black man looked Joe over. "Let's go," he said in a bass voice

"Good luck, Joe," Bruce said. "And remember, you can't trust him."

"You got that right," Joe's new escort said. "You can't trust none of 'em."

. . .

Joe's new escort checked him again with a metal detection wand, then deftly padded him down, causing Joe to blush from being touched in such a personal way. This done, the CO led him up a flight of metal stairs and onto a gridded walkway with the officer positioned between Joe and the cells. Joe walked so close to the metal rail that he kept bumping it with his arm. He tried to listen as the CO went over the rules, most of which he didn't need to be told—of course he would remain seated and he had no intention of touching or exchanging anything with the inmate. As they walked, Joe couldn't help but peek at these children of Cain, and again accidentally made eye contact, this time with a longhaired man that he could smell all the way from the edge of the catwalk. "Don't you look at me, fat boy," the man yelled.

"Ignore him," his escort ordered.

But Joe could not ignore him. He'd had enough! Enough! Already enough!

III

At last, a haven. Dark, dirty, stinking of stale cigarettes, a haven with a scratched-up table and torn chairs. Alone in the meeting room on death row, Joe became giddy with relief. He wanted to stay right here, just like this. Oh Lord Jesus, yes, this was fine. A cell could be so safe.

His rapture lasted but a few moments before he heard footsteps on the catwalk and realized that he was about to be left alone with a vicious serial killer, and he had no idea what to do. "God, give me strength," Joe prayed with his hands clasped on the table. Joe then unclasped his hands, took them off the table, put them back on it, folded them again, unfolded them. The steps grew louder, and Joe's face rigidly locked in a broad smile like that of a Greek theatrical mask, or perhaps more like the indelible smile of a clown.

A man in chains came through the door followed by two COs. Joe stared with the same wide-eyed fascination as when he went though the reptile house at the zoo. As the COs removed his waist restraint, the man did not look at Joe, or look at anything for that matter. He just held his head up, like a big desert lizard. They left on the leg chains and the man shuffled to the seat across from Joe. Even after the COs left, the man still didn't look at Joe or say anything.

"I'm, ah, Joseph Cameron. I, ah, don't know if you remember me . . ."

"I remember you," the man cut him off. Slowly, he turned to stare at Joe with the bluest and meanest-looking eyes Joe had ever seen. The man slouched in his chair and just kept staring at Joe.

"Ah . . . ah, that's good. I'm, ah, I'm glad you could see me," Joe said. The man kept staring. Joe fidgeted in his seat until he couldn't stand being stared at anymore, and said, "I wanted to see you, but I wasn't sure you'd see me. I thought maybe . . . maybe . . ."

"That maybe you'd let me down. That maybe you'd gotten a little kid's hopes up and then you said screw him."

Joe cringed and Drum smiled.

"I . . . I thought maybe I had let you down," Joe admitted.

Drum leaned forward and in a hushed whisper, said, "You did."

Joe leaned forward so he could hear.

"And now you've come here, because you want to feel better about yourself by trying to make up for your failure. Right?"

"I, ah . . . that's not totally right." Worn down by everything that had happened, Joe felt confused and blurted, "I, ah, want to help you."

"You want to help me? Let me see. You're not a lawyer or a locksmith, so how the fuck are you going to help me?"

Joe winced at such language. With pressured speech he said, "I, ah, I want you to know Jesus. There's no joy like knowing God's grace. He can forgive all, if you just ask."

Drum leaned forward and laid his balled fists on the table. "So you want me to say 'Hallelujah, let's get down and pray.' Is that what you want me to do? You gonna try to slap your palm on my head and say 'heal' and purge my soul? I dare you to try slapping my head, you fat prick. I don't like you and I've got no reason to trust you, so why don't you turn tail and run like you did the last time?"

Looking down, Joe quietly said, "I'm not going to do that this time."

"Oh, yeah. So you're going to hang in there no matter what I do or say?"

"Yes."

"And if I yell at you, tell you to go to hell and hurt your feelings, you're not going to quit?"

"No."

"And you're going to keep coming back even if I refuse to see you?"

"Yes, I will."

"And you're going to do whatever it takes to get my trust?"

"Yes."

"Liar!"

"No. I'm going to do whatever it takes. You'll see. I'll prove it to you."

The man leaned back without taking his eyes off Joe. In a barely audible voice, he said, "We'll see. I can't take more disappointments. So if you're lying, get the hell out of here now."

"I'll not disappoint you," Joe said. He was breathing hard, and, as much as he had ever wanted anything, he wanted to prove himself, not only to this man, but also for his own sake.

Sighing, Drum slouched in his chair, then sat upright and leaned forward again. In a soft voice, he said, "Joe, I wish I could believe you. I really do. But I don't. You see, Joe, I'm in a bind. They're trying to kill me as quick as they can, and, just like your reasons for coming here, I want to square a few things. You can understand that, can't you?"

"Yes. Just ask Jesus for forgiveness and mean it. That's all you have to do," Joe said, smiling weakly and nodding his head.

"Is that right? Well, if that'd been enough for you, you wouldn't be here, would you? Huh? It's not enough for me. I've always been a man of action. And there's something I need to make right. You can understand that, can't you?"

Vigorously, Joe nodded yes.

"Joe, my problem is that there's no one I can trust to help me. You seem sincere enough, but frankly, Joe, I think you're a coward; you say you represent God's fucking power and yet you're a coward. So I know that when it comes down to helping me set things right, you'll chicken out. And it pisses me off for you to come here promising to help when I know you won't."

"You're wrong. Not this time. As God is my savior, I'm going to see this through."

The man stared down at the table, exposing the top of his head. It seemed a vulnerable position. Finally, he raised his head, fixed his eyes on Joe, and whispered, "All right."

Joe felt triumphant, complete, he was serving God's purpose by coming here, he truly was.

"What I want to do," Drum said, "is apologize to the families of the people I killed, especially the wife of the cop. Not ask forgiveness, just apologize."

"That's good."

"My problem, Joe, is that in here saying you're sorry is seen as a sign of weakness. Not only would they humiliate me, but in here being seen as weak is dangerous. Can you imagine what happens to the weak in here?"

Joe nodded yes.

"I've written a letter to that cop's wife, but I haven't known how to get it to her without putting myself at risk, because they screen everything I write before they mail it. Can you imagine these guards sitting in their little guard station laughing their asses off at me for wanting to square things. And they'd blab to the inmates, so it's too risky. Then, I heard you wanted to see me, and thought maybe I had one last chance. I have the letter with me, Joe." Still, leaning over the table, Drum seemed to scratch his belly just above his belt. Then he put both hands on the table, one atop the other. "The letter's under my hands. I want you to mail it for me."

"I don't think I can."

"That's what I thought. A coward and a liar. This might be a record for turning tail and running. So you don't want to get in trouble. Hell, if Jesus had disciples like you, we'd all be Muslims. Why did you come here?"

"I, ah, I meant I don't think they'll let me."

"They won't. Not without reading it, which they must not do. So, here's how we're going to handle it. We're going to bow our heads as if in prayer. Then, you're going to put your hands on top of mine and I'll pull mine away like I don't want you touching me, and when I do, I'll leave the letter under your hands. After the switch, leave your hands there for three or four seconds, then slide them back into your lap and keep them there until the COs come to take me back. While they're chaining me like a fucking dog, you can slip it into your pocket. That's what we're going to do. Right?"

"Er . . . ah . . ."

"Right!"

"Er . . . okay."

They carried out Drum's plan exactly as he had outlined it. Once they completed the transfer, Drum signaled to the surveillance camera for them to come and get him. As they led him out, he turned and asked, "Are you coming back tomorrow?"

"Yes," Joe said eagerly, seeing this as another positive sign.

Drum stepped through the door and Joe was alone. He had done it.

IV

On his way out, Joe asked Wayne to stop at Bruce Tanner's office. He told Bruce that Drum had neither accepted nor rejected his ministrations, but did ask him to come back.

"A lot of condemned men reach out when their time's short," Tanner said. "I hadn't pegged Drum for one of those."

"Just goes to show, you can't always tell," Joe chimed.

"Maybe. Just be careful, Joe. You're in rougher country than you're used to."

Joe knew Bruce meant well. But God had chosen him—not some-one else but him—to show this lost soul the light. Maybe he had been preparing for this mission his whole life. Maybe all his failures were to get him ready and bring him to this place.

Absentmindedly, Joe slipped his hand into his jacket pocket, touched the letter, and quickly jerked his hand away. He didn't want to think about that part of his mission. To be rid of this reminder, immediately after leaving Golgotha Joe drove to the Assembly Street post office. At the drop box, he hesitated and felt queasy. But Joe always felt queasy about this or that, so he ignored these feelings and mailed the letter. Then he put it out of his mind.

V

That evening, as Joe began dinner he kept peeking out the window over the sink. When his wife, Wendy, arrived home from her job at White's Department Store, he barely let her get through the door before he began telling her about his day—though he didn't mention the letter. He told her that going inside Golgotha had not been so bad, which seemed true now that he was far removed from that place. Mostly, Wendy, a petite woman who never seemed to have one strand of her chin-length blond hair out of place, listened. Joe figured she did not quite know what to make of her new man.

After Joe discharged some of his excitement, Wendy asked what Jeffcoat Landing Baptist Church's pastor, Mark Kemper, thought of Joe's mission.

"I haven't had a chance to tell him yet," Joe said.

"Joe, you need to tell him because there's something about that man, Drum, on the news almost every day, and you don't want Mark caught off guard."

Nodding, Joe agreed. For some reason, though, he felt queasy about telling Mark and decided to wait at least until after Sunday services. That would be plenty soon enough.

. . .

On Friday night, Joe stayed up late, sitting in his La-Z-Boy recliner and wrestling with tough questions, such as what he should actually try to do for such an evil man. It didn't make sense that someone could do the things Isaac Drum had done and then, perhaps with his dying breath, ask for forgiveness and receive it. Sure, Joe had always taught that this was possible; but he'd been thinking about people like the elderly folks he visited in nursing homes, people who might not be regular churchgoers but were basically decent folks. It didn't seem fair that a cruel man like Drum could sit in heaven beside someone who had devoted his or her life to living by God's word, maybe even sit beside someone he had tortured and killed. It just didn't seem right.

And even if it was right, how could he, Joseph Cameron, show such an evil man God's love? For every scripture lesson he thought of, there was a good reason not to use it. First, Joe thought of Mary Magdalene, the fallen woman, then, remembered this man's predatory inclinations toward women and rejected it. He considered the trials of Job, but worried that another's suffering might excite Drum. Jesus visiting the lepers? No, Drum might think Joe was calling him a moral leper, and Joe certainly didn't want to make him angry. Finally, he decided Wendy was right, and he should ask Mark Kemper's advice.

.   .   .

On Saturday afternoon, Bruce Tanner had the day off and, with no one there to look after him, Joe waited in the empty cafeteria-like room for over two hours before someone remembered him and told him that Drum had changed his mind about seeing Joe. Drum did ask that Joe come back tomorrow. On Sunday afternoon, Joe left after only an hour. By then, he knew that Drum was playing him for a fool, so there was absolutely no point in telling Mark Kemper. Others would probably find out about his folly soon enough—they always did—and Joe could hear them now, "You mean he actually went out to the prison and sat there everyday thinking that man wanted to see him." "That's right," would come the reply, followed by hearty laughter.

Well, it wouldn't be the first time Joe had been the brunt of a joke, but this one might feel like the biggest. And when it came, there would be nothing he could do about it except smile politely.

19

twice bitten

I

THE TINTED windshield and sunglasses deepened the late afternoon hues as Marianne Paxton slid the silver Mazda alongside her mailbox. She turned down National Public Radio, which was carrying an interview of a golfer struck eight times by lightning, then pulled the usual handful of bills, junk mail, and catalogs from her mailbox, unaware that she held venom in her hand.

Zack slouched in the passenger seat, his head bobbing to the music coming through his headphones. He was now thirteen and a recent growth spurt had bumped him taller than Marianne and turned his short hair a darker shade of brown. Baggy jeans and an oversized gray T-shirt accentuated how gangly he had become. Every day Marianne could see more of Will in his face.

As for herself, Marianne wore a rust-colored jacket and beige dress that was typical of how she dressed for work. She had become leaner over the years and long ago let the perm go out of her hair, which was now straight, shoulder length, and usually worn pulled back and clipped with a barrette. Already, she had started finding stands of gray, but not enough to begin coloring her hair as long as she didn't spend too much time in tell-tale sunlight. Marianne did believe her worry lines made her look older than thirty-three, though they still completely smoothed out on the scant occasions when she smiled.

Marianne stuffed the mail into the side pocket of a leather carrying case that contained lesson plans and folders bulging with third graders' work. The mail tucked away, she backed up and pulled into the driveway.

Without being asked, Zack carried the bag of groceries inside and placed it on the kitchen counter. Following close behind, Marianne slipped the straps of her case and purse from her shoulder and put them on the table in the breakfast nook. She signaled for Zack to remove his headphones, and as he did the tinny music was loud enough that she could make out the words if she tried.

"You know John Keenan's coming for dinner at six-thirty and I'd like for you to join us, okay," she said, then pressed on as if he had already refused. "He was a good friend of your father and he's helped me . . . helped us so much over the years."

"Okay," Zack said in the listless way that Marianne found so frustrating. As usual, she wanted to push him into a conversation, wanted to find out what was going on inside him, wanted to know what he thought was wrong between them. Zack slipped his headphones back on and shuffled from the kitchen, and she let it drop. The more she pushed, the more remote he became. They had briefly seen a counselor last year, when Zack had gotten in trouble for truancy, and she had told Marianne that most kids Zack's age withdraw somewhat from their parents and that such withdrawal was part of developing their own identity. Marianne had disagreed, informing the counselor that Zack's distance began with Will's death, when Zack had night terrors and first turned quiet. Over the years, nothing she did could get him to talk about Will. Desperately, Marianne wanted to fix whatever was wrong, but he kept her at such a distance that the best she could do was cushion him from further trauma. And when the counselor encouraged Marianne to stay in the *here and now*, Marianne believed the woman was ignoring the real problem. She canceled their subsequent sessions.

Marianne removed her jacket and laid it across the back of a chair, then emptied the bag of groceries. She left a liter bottle of merlot and Italian bread on the counter. The vegetables she washed and placed in a colander to be cut up later, after she put the pan of lasagna that she had prepared last night into the oven.

She very much wanted everything to go well this evening. Since Will's death, John Keenan had called her every week—though he had only visited once and that was to help with a problem seven years ago. Given all the national media interest in Will's murder, Marianne had quickly learned to watch what she said, even to friends and family. But whatever she told John stayed with him. He had become the sounding board that kept her sane through both the loneliness and seething rage. Mostly, he listened and encouraged her to trust her gut. She believed she owed him too much to ever repay him—hell, he wouldn't even cash the checks she sent to repay the loan he had given her to finish college.

With no prep to do for an hour, Marianne poured herself a glass of merlot and sat at the table to sort through the mail. Two credit card offers and a plea for money disguised as a survey from a political party immediately went into the stack for the trash. She next came to an envelope with a handwritten address and no return. Something about the block lettering caused her to feel uneasy. Then, she recognized the handwriting, which she had seen only once before.

Six months after she had challenged Drum in court, flushing out his true nature for the jury to see, she had received an unsigned letter that read, "I want you to come to see me so I can tell you personally how your husband begged for me to take you instead of him. If you don't come, I'll tell the press and they'll tell the world what a chickenshit coward he was. We're going to get to know each other real well. You have one week."

Keenan had flown down and assured her that Drum was lying, that everyone who had listened to the tape of Will's death could testify to Will's courage and loyalty to his family. She had already known that, but it was so good of him to come and offer his help.

She had also gotten help from Martin Stith. After Will's death, several SLED agents came by or called for a while, but gradually they all drifted out of touch, except for Martin. As soon as he found out about Drum's letter, Martin orchestrated a restraining order to have Drum's mail permanently screened.

Receiving that first letter galvanized Marianne's hatred of Drum into a crusade. She actively followed his appeals and made public statements whenever major rulings were pending. She even went out of her way to make friends with a Department of Corrections social worker, just to get an inside line about him. Marianne did not set the table, check the doors at night, or get the car serviced without thinking about Drum. And she frequently felt furious that he could do all the things—laugh, eat, watch television, lust, and even despair—that he had forever taken from Will.

In South Carolina, the family of a killer's victim can choose one witness to attend his execution. Drum's current death warrant was for Will's murder, and Marianne believed it her duty to be that witness. She prayed that justice would finally occur this Friday at one A.M., and that this would free her to get on with her life. She worried that some bleeding-heart judge would overturn Drum's death sentence and, in so doing, doom her to go on like this forever.

Over the years, despite Marianne's vigor in opposing Drum's appeals, she had never heard anything else from him, even indirectly—until today. "How dare that bastard do this," she said, and her hands trembled as she slipped a nail under the flap and raggedly tore open the letter.

20

threat

I

ONLY TWO other cars were in the roomy parking lot for Riverwalk
Park as Keenan eased the rented Regal into a space. On his way out of
Golgotha, he had asked the checkpoint CO if she knew of a good
place nearby to take a walk and she had directed him to this park,
located on the side of Golgotha opposite Jeffcoat Boulevard. Keenan
shed his jacket and tie, then started down a wide asphalt path bordered
by strips of mown lawn and evenly spaced crepe myrtle. To his left,
beyond this landscaped strip, stood a thick copse of bushes and
saplings, and fifty or so yards beyond this tangle of brush he could see
the top of Golgotha's fences, its razor wire and gun turrets tinted gold-
en by the late afternoon sunshine.

The path paralleled Golgotha's eastern perimeter until it neared the
prison's back wall, where the Saluda River came into view. Golgotha
stood in the apex of a sharp bend, so the river here was wide and shallow and strewn with boulders and small verdant islands, its character
more that of a mountain stream than a broad river. A smattering of
snowy egrets and great blue herons dotted the rocky ledges and clear
pools, and a refreshing coolness emanated up the banks.

Here, the path turned from Golgotha and followed the Saluda's
graceful curve for about two miles. Beneath a cloudless sky and
washed by soothing breezes, Keenan set a brisk pace. He wanted to
purge Drum's madness from his mind before turning his attention to
his third purpose for coming to South Carolina. Simply put, he did not
believe that watching Drum's execution would be good for Marianne.
Certainly, she was strong-willed and faced life's responsibilities without flinching; he deeply admired her for that. But her hatred of Drum,

especially her obsession in tracking his appeals, concerned Keenan. She believed that witnessing the execution would have a cathartic effect. His concern was that it could just as easily be traumatic and damaging. He had, at least in part, caused Will's death and could not stand idly by and allow her to be harmed by this final fallout from his poor judgment. He intended, therefore, to change her mind by offering himself as a substitute witness. After all, his rage had long ago turned cold and he certainly had proven an ability to handle horrific events.

. . .

Keenan walked at a hard pace for almost thirty minutes, then returned to his motel. While in the bathroom splashing cold water on his face, his cellular-phone rang. He dried his face with a hand towel as he went into the sleeping area and plucked his cell phone from the charger. "Keenan."

"John, it's Marianne. That bastard sent another letter. It's just like the one seven years ago, except now he's threatening my son. Damn him! Damn him to hell!"

"What does the letter say?" he said, flipping the towel onto his shoulder as he sat at the desk and picked up a felt tip pen.

He heard paper rumpling, then Marianne began to read, scorn encasing every word. "'I want to see you so I can tell you again how your husband pleaded for me to take you instead of him. He even told me your address and I still remember it. You think you don't want to see me, but you really do. You see, I have a friend on the outside that likes little boys, and he can be very, very cruel, in a slow sort of way. If you don't believe me, ask the Wilmet kid's parents. Unless you come, your son will soon have a new big friend. See you soon. Don't wear a bra.' That's all it says," Marianne said. "How dare that fucking bastard do this. God, I want him dead."

"Who else have you called?"

"I've just now opened it. John, I know you advise people all the time on how to handle this sort of threat. I'll do whatever you suggest, just so we keep Zack safe." Marianne paused. "Goddamn that bastard!"

It did not surprise Keenan that Drum had once again tried something like this. At his trial, Marianne had belittled Drum and pleaded for his execution, and, in so doing, became the focal point of the hatred that had earlier driven him to degrade, torture, and murder five women. With time running out, this letter was a last jab at revenge, as well as for sadistic pleasure. And he probably had other agendas; empty hours allowed a lot of time to connive and scheme. Drum would certainly try to use this threat for some kind of leverage, even though Keenan felt certain that Drum's threat was pure bluff. Careful to speak calmly, he said, "Marianne, I know this man. He's a loner with no friends inside or out. Everything in that note is a lie."

"How can you be sure? They're under a court order to screen that bastard's mail, yet this gets out. I can't take that risk."

"We're not going to take risks," Keenan assured her. "I'll call Martin Stith and ask him to arrange police protection for you until I find out what Drum's up to. And don't touch the envelope again; we may be able to pick up a latent print that can tell us who mailed it. After I find out what Drum wants, I'll come by. And try not to worry, everything will turn out all right."

"But I know from experience," Marianne said, "that things don't always turn out all right."

II

In rapid succession, Keenan called Stith, then Golgotha and arranged clearance for immediate access to Drum. Once this was done, he did not rush to the prison, but remained in his room weighing various strategies. When Keenan decided on a plan, he again called Golgotha and made additional arrangements. En route, he stopped at a drugstore and purchased a blank videotape. Before leaving the store he asked the young woman at the counter to write certain things on a label—so that it would not be in his handwriting—then he stuck the label onto the tape.

. . .

The stench of stale cigarettes saturated the meeting room and crushed butts still lay scattered around where Drum had sat earlier in the day. A stand holding a television and VCR set against the wall directly in Drum's line of vision. Keenan laid the videocassette on the table, a little off to the side with its label turned away from where Drum would sit. He then sat, pushed the on button of his tape recorder, and put it in his shirt pocket where Drum would not see it and possibly make an issue of being recorded.

While waiting, Keenan physically relaxed by slowing his breathing. It was crucial that he appear, if not nonchalant, at least not overly concerned. Earlier today, Drum had told him that the more others wanted something from him, the more leverage he tried to exert. The trick for Keenan would be to appear to want nothing from Drum, or at least not want much; otherwise, Drum would jerk him around. This strategy carried risk; if he slipped and Drum whiffed his eagerness, it would be near impossible for later strategies to succeed.

In full restraints, Drum appeared in the door, paused, and smiled at Keenan, gloating already. "Back so soon?" he asked, as he stepped inside. Still smiling, Drum held out his hands to have the chains removed. For this visit, Keenan had requested that Drum be left in full restraints and his leg chain fastened to the U-bolt in the floor, so Lieutenant Jenkins told him, "The restraints stay on." A heavy-gutted black man with a bushy beard put a hand on Drum's back and nudged him forward. Drum shrugged and shuffled to the chair and the CO secured his leg irons to the U-bolt.

Before the COs were out of the room, Drum smiled again, his blue eyes as bright as the eyes of a fighting cat. The stainless steel chain pinning his wrists to his sides chimed quietly every time he moved. "I guess you're ready to talk about Wilmet, huh? Well I'm not. You had your chance, remember, and you didn't take it." Drum shook his head. "What will people say about that?"

Slouched in his chair with his legs crossed, Keenan sighed as if he were bored. "I need to ask you what you want," he said, his voice flat as if he had little interest in Drum's answer.

"I want her to come and see me. And when she gets here, she's going to do tricks for me."

"She's not coming," Keenan said, as if he were merely going through the motions of a necessary chore. "Look, I know she pissed you off at your trial. So now you've said 'boo,' but nobody's jumping." Keenan sighed again, then sat up and leaned over the table with his arm on the table palm up. "I'm only asking you about all this because I don't want anyone else coming in here and screwing around so that you and I can't take care of our business. I'm not going to let that happen. If there was something to your threat it'd be different, but we both know there's not."

Drum stopped smiling and leaned forward. "Don't dick around with this. The threat's real. That bitch's son dies unless she does everything I want."

Keenan slumped back into this chair, his expression as bland as if he were sitting in a late-afternoon algebra class. "Even if your threat was real, you'll never get another message out, so there's no point to what you're doing."

"You think not! Well try this scenario," Drum said, his voice rising and his face red. "Unless my sentence is commuted to life, her son will also be under a death warrant."

Keenan smiled weakly and shook his head. "I'll be sure to get right on it," he said and snorted derisively.

"Fuck you," Drum said. "You better get the picture real quick and stop dicking around. You see, me and my friend have been planning this for a long time, including the timing of last Sunday's . . . incident. Hell, I even arranged for you to be here to handle the negotiations. So this is how it's going to work. My associate has all the information he needs. If my sentence gets commuted, he finds some other kid to be his friend. If not . . . let's just say that kid's appeals have run out and it's just a question of when."

"You know, that's really not a bad scam you've come up with," Keenan said and gave Drum a little nod of approval. He now knew what Drum wanted. He still needed to satisfy himself that Drum was indeed bluffing, so he said, "But even if I play along and pretend that you do have something to trade, there's a fatal flaw in your plan. Neither the governor, a judge, or anyone else in authority can give in to a threat, or else every man on death row would pull similar stunts."

"That's why I wanted you here. They'll listen to you. So, you better be real persuasive and change their minds, or else that kid dies. His life is totally in your hands."

Keenan rubbed his chin, then leaned forward and spoke as if sharing a confidence. "There might be a way we can pull this off," he said, then pointed at Drum, "but understand that I know your threat's crap and I'm only doing this so that nothing screws up our meeting; that's my condition. All right?"

"Yeah." Drum nodded, and leaned forward, eager now.

"Okay, here's the way things are. They can't give in to a threat, but might be able to reward a helpful citizen who identifies a killer, even if that citizen is on death row. You give me the killer's name and if it checks out, I'll get you a deal. But don't play with this. If you give me a false name, you're out of time and credibility. You only have one shot to make good."

Drum's eyes shined with anger. "I'm not stupid. You get a me a guaranteed deal, then I talk, but not before."

"If I take nothing to the governor, then all that will come of it is me looking like a fool, and I'm not going to make a fool of myself for you."

"When that kid dies, it'll be your fault, so what kind of fool will you look like then."

"All right, then, how about this?" Keenan said, ready to ask the question that counted. "I profiled Wilmet's killer. Prove you know something by describing his personality; that's information I already have so you won't be giving anything away. But you have to make it detailed enough to show that you have the goods."

"Why don't you make up something that fits?" Drum told him.

Keenan shook his head. "That would be aiding and abetting. There's no way I'll give you something like that to lord over me."

Chains clinked as Drum shifted positions, then shook his head no. "Well, I'm not giving you any peeks so you can steal my only chance. It's all or nothing."

"Then the hoax is up," Keenan said, and smiled sadly. "Sorry." If Drum had anything to trade, he would have proven it by teasing Keenan with some morsel of information. Even though Keenan was satisfied, he still wanted to bring an end to the hoax once and for all; it only took one gullible judge to award a stay; and there was Marianne's peace of mind to consider.

Casually, Keenan laid his hand on the videocassette and pushed it a few inches toward Drum. With his hand still on the tape, he said, "I don't blame you for trying to keep up the ruse because what's in it for you to drop it, right? So I'm sweetening the pot." Keenan turned the video around so that Drum could read the label, filled out by the sales clerk, which read, "Exhibit 43: Alicia Owens." "Since you can't give me a name that checks, admit the ruse and you can watch this video that you made."

Drum stared at the cassette, leaned forward, licked his lips.

"Come clean," Keenan coaxed, then pushed the tape forward a couple of inches and took his hand away, "and we could watch this later tonight. There's already a TV in here. All it takes is the truth, no tricks. And from what I heard this afternoon, I bet this was your favorite tape, you know, the little blond girl that was so special."

Drum breathed harder. "Show me the tape," he said, "and then I'll give you the guy's name."

"Prove you have something or come clean, then we'll watch it. But this is your only chance. I'll not bring it back after tonight."

Drum hesitated, then shook his head and looked at Keenan, his eyes bright with anger. "I'll teach you to try to fuck with me. You want the name? Then get my sentence commuted, give me that tape, and send the Paxton bitch in here, because she's the only one I'll tell." Still glaring at Keenan, Drum snapped his head toward the camera as a signal for the COs to come and get him.

"Think about it," Keenan said. "Nothing's going to happen unless you prove you have something to trade or drop the hoax."

"All or nothing," Drum said. Defiantly, he tried to stand but with his arms trussed and the table blocking him rose only a few inches before sinking back into his seat and wriggling against his chains in a momentary fit of impotent rage. Regaining some composure, Drum stared at Keenan, and hissed, "If you screw this up, that kid's blood will be on your hands."

III

Outside the meeting room, in CB2's cement and metallic vastness with its echo of raised voices and slamming metal, Drum stomped along the catwalk too fast for leg irons until he stumbled and the nearest CO, a big, bushy-bearded black man, steadied him by putting a hand on his denim-clad shoulder. Drum jerked his shoulder free and warned, "You touch me again and I'll take a dive and claim you pushed me."

"And if I let you fall, what are you going to claim?" the CO said. "Slow down or we put you in an arm lock."

Sullen, Drum shuffled at a safer pace. He found it inconceivable that Keenan should balk at his demands. Didn't he care about that Paxton kid's life? And he was sure that stuff about no one ever giving into a threat was bullshit. It couldn't be true. He just needed to put more pressure on that stubborn son of a bitch Keenan and force him to go along. Or go around him. Or both, Drum thought, suddenly seeing exactly how he could do it. According to state law, a condemned man was entitled to both morning and afternoon media interviews on each of the two days prior to the day of execution. If Drum made his demands public, Keenan could no longer dodge getting him a deal. And he would word things so that it sounded like he was offering help, not blackmail; at least Keenan had a good idea about that. Drum thought it might help if he also drew a very large, very public bull's-eye on that Paxton kid.

"Hey, Drum, what'd the Man want this time?" a scruffy-haired black man called out as Drum passed his cell. "He gonna keep you from fryin'?"

Drum glanced at Darnell Tramaine, without a doubt one of the strangest people on the row. Skinny and smallish, Tramaine talked to himself nonstop, calling himself Darnell Baby. Drum could smell Tamaine's body odor all the way from the end of the catwalk. He believed the sick son of a bitch belonged in a nuthouse rather than on death row. Tramaine had murdered a seventy-nine year-old woman for whom he had occasionally done yard work. He claimed that he had broken into her house to rob her, but she only had twenty-eight dollars in her purse and he went into a rage and crushed her skull with a commode lid, then raped her corpse. At his trial, Tramaine blamed his behavior on drugs, mistakenly thinking this might mitigate his responsibility in the eyes of the jury.

Tramaine asking him about being fried pissed Drum off even more. To hell if he was going to speak to that sick son of a bitch. Drum looked straight ahead and strutted the way Keenan had, at least he strutted as much as a man shuffling in leg irons could strut. When Tramaine saw Drum's snub, he spit at Drum, but his sputum fell short.

Drum reached the cell adjacent to his own and saw Allan Crenshaw lying on his bunk watching him pass. A pasty guy with short dark hair worn in bangs like one of the Three Stooges, Crenshaw had let himself go soft, so that his Roadrunner T-shirt stretched obscenely around his flabby chest and gut, causing his titties to look like a girl's. Crenshaw had gone on a spree, shooting a liquor store owner and his wife during a robbery, then two days later killing a pawn shop operator while the store surveillance camera caught the owner on his knees begging for his life as Crenshaw coolly put the gun against the man's head and pulled the trigger. What Drum found contemptible about Crenshaw, however, was that he had become a Bibleback, always spouting off about how he had been saved and how much he regretted what he'd done and that he was ready to pay for his crimes. Once, when Crenshaw, in his quiet way, was running off at the mouth about all that, Drum had asked him how long his conversion would last if he were set free, and Crenshaw quietly said, "I don't know, so it's best if I'm not released."

Drum now glared at Crenshaw because the son of a bitch was looking at him the way you look at someone who was starting to die. A lot of guys on the row had started to look at him like some bedridden cancer patient who was becoming more helpless by the hour. Drum knew that every man on the row now thought of him as a "Dead Man," and it pissed him off. He had watched other men make the sad walk out of here when it came time to be transferred to the death house. Every man on death row had looked at whatever bravado showed in these men's ashen faces and had witnessed his future. Drum had once overheard a CO say that, for many of these men, watching another's death walk was about as much empathy as they would ever feel. Empathy hell, Drum felt angry at these men for no longer being in line ahead of him. Now, the other inmates expected him to soon take that walk and looked at him as if he'd already been stripped of his manhood.

Well, he'd show the bastards. Not that they mattered, because every son of a bitch on death row ended up here from gross stupidity and poor impulse control, except him. He was different; he was not some stupid and impulsive loser aimlessly bumping around like a spinning top. He had clearly known what he wanted and then stood up and took it with cunning and nerve. Who else in here could say that? No one! And he was not about to desperately latch on to any wild scheme that offered a little false hope, the way most of the losers in here did. He was cunning—all the newspapers said so. He had a solid plan, a foolproof plan.

The COs released his leg chains and Drum shuffled into his cell. The bars slammed shut, closing him in. Drum pushed his hands through the slot and the COs finished removing his restraints and walked away. Drum leaned against the bars, lit a cigarette, and waited for Keenan to walk past so he could show the fucker how confident he felt. While waiting, Drum's frustration worsened as he thought about all the bloodthirsty bastards that were trying to murder him—they could call it what they want, executions were murder and those demanding his death were vile and less than human. And the most bloodthirsty and vile of them all was that Paxton bitch. Well, once they transferred him into the general population, he knew exactly how to fix her, once and for all.

Drum waited there for several minutes and Keenan did not walk past, so he figured they were keeping Keenan in here until mealtime traffic cleared the Tunnel. Drum sat on his bunk, lit another cigarette, and considered exactly what he should tell the reporter. But he had trouble concentrating because he felt as frustrated as he had on the nights when he had hunted and came up dry. Not an hour ago, he felt the best he had in years. His first session with Keenan had dislodged sharp memories and immediately after this session he had successfully masturbated twice thinking about the abductions. Now frustrated, those memories once again seemed vague.

Drum took a deep drag on his cigarette, and thought about the videotape that Keenan had brought, the one of the little blonde. The tape had not been used at his trial so his attorney could not get him a copy. He wondered which tape of her this was. On the first tape he made with her he had captured one of the most satisfying and peaceful moments of his life. Maybe, Drum thought, if I go slow and describe everything leading up to that moment the way I described things with Keenan, then maybe I can relax and escape this inhumane place by remembering that special time. Maybe I can even remember it with the same kind of clarity that I remembered the abductions.

Drum crushed out his smoke, then lay on the bed facing the wall and unbuckled his pants. Barely audible, he whispered, "My basement had a cement floor painted slate gray and there was always a weak odor of drain water. The cinderblock walls were unpainted but I hung a light blue sheet behind where I put the bed. It was a cast iron bed, painted white, and had diamond-shaped wrought work . . ." Drum stopped mumbling and breathed a little harder as he gained a clear image of the two photographer's lights set up a few feet from the bed. A VCR and television were placed to the left of the bed and Drum stood to the right of the bed's foot, adjusting the focus of a video camera.

She lay on the bed, her wrists and ankles handcuffed to the bedposts. Her nice outfit was all rumpled and her blond hair was so loaded with hairspray that it broke into clumps rather than becoming truly disheveled. She was breathing hard and I had never seen eyes open so wide. On the tape, it appeared that she was looking directly into the camera, but it was me, standing behind the camera, that she was actually watching. If her mouth were not taped, she would have begged me to say something, to let her go, to not hurt her. So far, she had not fought like the other two. She was being such a good girl.

I had not spoken a word since pushing her into the van; silence sharpens fear so much more than spouting off at the mouth. Now safe in my basement, I was in no hurry. Nor was I having weird thoughts or twisted desires or doubts about what I was doing. Of course, I was excited, but in a very deliberate sort of way. I could make her do anything I wanted. Anything! And there was nothing she could do to change her fate; she was completely in my hands. Only those who have held such God-like power can appreciate how erotic this feels; only they can understand why I take my time. And I had such great hopes for her, believed that she would be special, that she would not disappoint. As I watched her, I was nearly overcome by a sudden and deep affection for her.

I thought that her breathing had slowed a little, so I crossed the room and turned on the VCR and let her watch a few minutes of the video of my last guest. Her nostrils flared and there were tears all over her cheeks. When the tape began to get good, I stepped from behind the camera, holding out the knife, and slowly approached. At first, she didn't know whether to watch the tape or me. But when I reached the bed, she only looked at me. I put a knee on the mattress, then slid the blade under the bottom button of her blouse, lingered, and with a quick slash snapped it off. Her eyes grew wider and she started trembling—all on her own, without any poison, she trembled uncontrollably—and I felt such affection that I lay down and held her, keeping the knife a few inches in front of her face, and together we watched the tape. Never in my life had I felt such closeness and peace. But there was also a violence gathering inside, a brutality waiting until we were both ripe. We both knew this moment would not last; and neither would my loving treatment.

21

crosshairs

I

GOLGOTHA PRISON policy forbids anyone except correctional officers to be in the Tunnel while entire cell blocks saunter to and from the dining room. Thus, after confronting Drum, Keenan was required to wait in the meeting room on CB2 until eighteen hundred high-carbohydrate meals were served and each man leaving the dining hall turned in a knife, fork, and spoon under the scrutiny of a CO. During this wait, Keenan tried to call Marianne on his cell phone but, below ground and covered with layers of concrete and steel, he was in a dead spot.

Drumming his fingers on the table, Keenan felt certain of two things. First, if Drum knew anything at all he would have proven it by giving Keenan a taste—his threat was definitely an empty bluff. Secondly, he had brought Drum close to dropping his ruse only to have him entrench himself with new resolve, so he would be immune to the ploys tried tonight. To break Drum, Keenan needed more compelling leverage. Since he believed Drum's threat a hoax, breaking Drum would not matter were it not for the way it might effect Marianne.

Like many persons who've lost a loved one to murder, Marianne's radar locked on to every story of a convenience store clerk shot, every businessman abducted outside his motel room, every rape, every child molestation, every assault by a stalker. She never talked of fear for herself—her fear was that something would happen to Zack. Several times she had told Keenan that hardly a day went by that she did not see a news report about some horrible thing happening to a child. This

heightened sensitivity had prompted Marianne to begin regularly taking Will's service revolver to the range in an effort to restore some
sense of safety, as well as to regain a sense of control. His assurances
that Drum's threats posed no danger might not completely rid her of
doubt. He did not want her worrying every time Zack left the house
that brutal death might be lurking just down the street.

Almost as bad, Drum had put those who most wanted him dead in
the position of trying to save his life. If he died as scheduled, Marianne
and Zack would live with corrosive doubt. If his gambit worked, he
raped Marianne's spirit. Only catching Wilmet's killer or wringing the
truth out of Drum would spare her and Zack this anguish.

Determined to break Drum, Keenan turned his attention to the
"how." Years of experience with violent predators had taught Keenan
that the rage of these men had been stoked early in life. If he snooped
around in Drum's childhood, he might discover some fault line that, if
pressured, would break Drum. Drawing on his extensive knowledge of
Drum's records, Keenan compiled a short list of key persons who had
contact with Drum during his childhood and early adolescence. As
soon as he left Golgotha, he would contact Ben Lockhart and ask for
help in locating these people for phone calls or meetings. Of course,
this approach was a long shot and Keenan would keep working other
strategies, including taking another look at Gary Wilmet's murder.

II

At half past six, the last cell block left the dining room and, as the
evening count began, Keenan left CB2. He set a hard pace through
the Tunnel and up the three levels of stairs. Five minutes later he
reached the last security cage. Martin Stith leaned against the bars on
the other side, his arms folded over his chest and clutching a sheet of
paper in his fist. Keenan entered the cage and Stith turned and pressed
against the bars, demanding, "I need to know everything he told you,
but you're going to have to tell me as we walk." He waived the paper
and said, "We have a suspect."

In two steps, Keenan crossed the cage and asked, "Who?" At the
electronic buzz, he swung open the second gate and fell in beside
Stith, who had already started walking across the spacious lobby.

"For the past couple of months," Stith said, "Drum's only visitors were his attorneys, mostly Sammy Isgett, sometimes Jason Feldman. Then, out of the blue, a guy named Joseph Cameron shows up claiming to be Drum's minister. We ran his license and he lives in Jeffcoat Landing, about a mile or so from where Wilmet was killed. I'm on my way to question Cameron."

They passed out the front doors into a breezy and pleasantly cool evening. The western horizon had turned deep blue in the waning twilight. Floodlights lit the grounds and the distant athletic field looked as if it was ready for a high school football game, except that fences laced with dense coils of razor wire surrounded it.

"Are you checking to see if inmates or COs might have smuggled the letter?" Keenan asked.

Bent slightly forward from the pace, Stith said, "No inmates in adjacent cells have won a reprieve from the row and according to the staff most dislike Drum, anyway. I have a team pulling the records of every CO who has worked in CB2 over the past year, even those pulled to cover because the regular guy called in sick. We're going to start interviewing them tomorrow . . . if Cameron doesn't work out."

At the walkway checkpoint, Stith said, "Stith and Keenan leaving," and without slowing climbed the stairs two at a time. Shouting above the metallic echo of their steps, Stith asked, "So what did you learn from Drum?"

Keenan quickly told Stith of Drum's demands and the tactics he had tried. They exited the walkway and Stith, his face sweaty, stopped and continued to listen without interrupting, though he tugged at his collar a couple of times as if to stretch it from his bulging neck. When Keenan finished his summary, Stith said, "I figured that asshole was after something like that. So you think he's bluffing?"

"If he'd had anything at all, I'd have gotten a taste."

"Humph," Stith grunted.

Parked illegally in front of the walkway was a vintage Thunderbird, the floodlights igniting like dark star bursts on its black surface. Stith moved to the side of this car and unlocked the door. "We'll talk more about Drum later."

"I'm going with you," Keenan said and went to the passenger side.

Stith paused. "This is local jurisdiction."

"I'm not arguing jurisdictions but I can give you a good read on this guy."

"Suit yourself," Stith said with a shrug, "but stay out of the way." Then he reached across the car's interior and unlocked Keenan's door.

The car smelled of Armor All and was spotless with no paper wrappers tossed on the red leather seats, no coffee stain on the console, nor as much as a crumb on the floor. Even the two-way radio that hung below the dash looked polished. Keenan thought this car suited a peacock like Stith.

"So what do we know about Cameron?" Keenan asked.

Rather than answer, Stith said, "Watch it," and leaned past Keenan to unlock the glove box and take out two weapons. One of the guns Keenan recognized as a Sig Sauer P228—a good weapon, popular with law enforcement; Keenan had one locked in a box at home. Stith shoved the Sig Sauer into his shoulder holster. The other weapon was a holstered, palm-sized pistol. Leaning forward and brushing his jacket aside, Stith clipped this gun to his belt at the small of his back. "You packing?" he asked.

Keenan regularly violated agency policy by failing to remain armed. He did not feel comfortable locking firearms in cars outside of maximum security prisons, nor did he like leaving a gun in his hotel room. One of a lawman's greatest disgraces was to have a gun stolen and then later used in a crime. So, on trips strictly for prison profiling, Keenan usually left his weapon home, though he would never admit this to Stith.

"I can't carry when I go onto death row," he said and then changed the subject. "So what do we know about Cameron."

"Not much . . . yet," Stith answered as the T-bird's engine ignited with a low rumble that throbbed every time Stith touched the gas. The car slung in a backward arc, then spewed gravel and pushed Keenan back into the seat as it shot forward. At the parking area's exit, Stith barely slowed before lurching into traffic and accelerating. He weaved between two cars with only inches to spare, causing Keenan to clench his armrest, brace his feet against the floor, and he refrained from asking Stith anything that might even momentarily distract him.

The ride was mercifully short. They took Jeffcoat Boulevard across the Saluda River Bridge and blipped past the motel where Keenan was staying. Another quarter mile and Stith turned onto Tanager Street. He crept along, reading mailbox numbers until he came to Cameron's house, then stopped in the street and studied the modest, single-level brick home. It had a neatly edged yard and recently weeded flowerbeds. Light glowed warmly from the windows on the side of the house nearest the garage. Keenan thought it the kind of house you might drive by every day and never notice until something happened, like finding a boy's body buried in the backyard.

Stith eased into the driveway behind a Dodge Caravan and cream-colored Saturn. Outside the car, cicadas chirped loudly as Keenan followed Stith up a short, curved sidewalk to the front door. Rather than ring the bell, Stith pulled back the storm door and pounded the inner door with the side of his fist. A porch light came on, the door opened, and a pudgy man with round shoulders, light brown hair, and thick glasses squinted at the two large men on his doorstep.

"Joseph Cameron?" Stith asked.

"Yes," Cameron answered, looking from one to the other. Stith didn't say anything more. After a couple of seconds, Cameron nervously asked, "What . . . what do you want?" Still, Stith glared at him until Cameron wavered as if he were about to shut the door, then Stith held up his badge and said, "I'm SLED deputy chief Martin Stith and he's FBI special agent John Keenan. You know why we're here."

Cameron's mouth moved but no sound came out. Then, "Ah . . . no . . . Oh Lordy . . . oh no, I knew it. I'm sorry . . . I knew it was wrong . . . oh, Lordy."

"Step outside," Stith said. With his shoulders hunched, Cameron pushed open the screen and came out. "Turn around." When Cameron did so, Stith pushed Cameron's shoulder, throwing him off-balance so that he braced both hands against the bricks beside the door. As Stith deftly patted Cameron for a weapon, a petite woman, whose blond hair curled perfectly at the ends, came to the door and asked, "Joe, what's going on?"

"Police. Stay inside," Stith ordered. She put her hand on the door's handle but did as told, her face a mix of anger and confusion.

Stith grabbed Cameron by the shoulder and turned him so they stood face-to-face, but pressed his hand on Cameron's chest, forcing his back to remain against the bricks. "All right, tell me about it." Stith said.

Keenan put aside his distaste for Stith's heavy-handed approach and studied Cameron over Stith's shoulder, listening closely for any telltale hints of narcissism or distorted logic as he looked for the monster behind the soft facade.

Bugs began looping erratically around the porch light and sweat beaded on Cameron's upper lip. His eyes looked enormous behind his thick glasses. "Ah, I . . . I knew it was wrong but he made me do it. I couldn't help it."

"Are you saying Drum made you kill Gary Wilmet?"

"Huh?" Cameron said, his mouth open and his face wrinkled as if something reeked. "What? I don't understand?"

"Tell me what you did with Wilmet?" Stith said and his hand pressed harder.

"What? Oh, Lordy no," Cameron said, his expression pleading. He looked at Keenan, shook his head, then looked back at Stith. "All I did was mail a letter for Drum. He told me it was a letter of apology for what he'd done and that if anyone found out he was doing something nice, then the other prisoners would think he's weak and attack him. That's all I did. Honest," Cameron said, and his mouth quivered as if he were about to cry.

"Where were you last Sunday evening?"

"At church. It's the truth. As God is my savior, it's the truth."

"From when to when?" Stith said, each question coming fast, like a punch.

"Church starts at seven and I usually don't get away until at least eight-thirty."

"That leaves a window from six to seven unaccounted for, right?"

"He was here until six-thirty and then drove over," Cameron's wife said from the door. "I'm sure the other pastors will tell you he got there by quarter of seven at the latest."

"We'll see," Stith said and stared at Cameron for several seconds until Cameron looked away. Stith then thumped a finger against Cameron's chest. "Hey! I'm talking to you. Are you a pastor?"

"Yes. So you see, I'd never do anything to hurt someone," Cameron said and nodded as if trying to get someone to agree with him.

"Is that right? Well, we have a problem Joe. Is it okay if I call you Joe?"

"Uh, sure."

"The problem, Joe, is that letter links you to a planned abduction, and to Wilmet's murder." Stith moved closer, physically crowding Cameron. Though his voice coaxed, it also threatened. "So why don't you do yourself a favor, save yourself a lot of grief and come clean. We have hair and semen samples so why keep up the act? You don't want to put your wife through all this, even if she has done something to deserve it, you don't want that, do you, Joe? It's no good like this, you know that." With Cameron's back pressing against the side of the house, Stith inched closer and closer, and talked barely louder than a whisper as if they were exchanging late-night intimacies. He even put a hand on Cameron's shoulder. "If you come clean, you'll feel so much better. You must know how good confession is for the soul, all that pressure gone. I'll get you some help. I'll do that for you, Joe, if we end it now. So what do you say? Huh? Let's get it over with? Tell me what you did?"

Looking as though he were going to cry, Joe shook his head. "I didn't do anything except what I told you. Those samples . . . can they prove it's not me? Can they do that?"

"Are you saying you'll voluntarily give me a sample?"

"Yes, of course."

Pointing his finger inches from Cameron's face, Stith ordered, "Stay put." Then he went to his car, leaving Cameron breathing heavily.

His wife pushed open the storm door and came out, placing her arm around his waist. "Joe, are you all right?"

He put his arm around her shoulder and pulled her close. "It's just a mistake. It'll get cleared up."

Across the street, a porch light came on and Cameron's wife said, "Can we go inside?"

"Sure," Keenan answered and followed them through a small foyer into a formal living room with a floral print couch, matching easy chair, and walnut coffee and end tables that looked polished and dust-free. The Camerons sat on the edge of the couch, holding hands.

Keenan stood in front of the white gauze liner covering the picture window. Though, as far as Cameron was concerned, it was now a question of forensics, Keenan still wanted to probe a little. Casually, as if making small talk, Keenan asked, "Do you have any children?"

"Yes," Cameron answered, "a daughter who's a freshman at Clemson. She's always been a good student. We're very proud of her."

Keenan nodded. "And what exactly do you do at your church?"

After Stith's battering, Cameron smiled and looked grateful for Keenan's seeming friendliness. "Ah, I coordinate all youth activities," he said. "That includes organizing all team sports, trips, and arranging special programs and speakers. I'm also in charge of the bulletin boards. And troubled children come to me with their problems all the time. So you see, I like children."

"I see." Liking children did not lower Cameron's rating as a suspect. "Knowing children as you do, what do you think the Wilmet kid did to provoke that man into killing him?"

"What? I, ah . . . I don't understand your question?"

"What I'm saying is that that man probably didn't kill the Wilmet kid for no reason. I was just wondering, given your experience, what you think that kid might have done to provoke him?"

Cameron shook his head. "I don't know. Maybe he tried to run or something."

The storm door squeaked as Stith jerked it open. Fear showed on Cameron's face as Stith came into the living room. Scowling, Stith placed what looked like a small tackle box on the coffee table. Stith took out rubber gloves and snapped them on, then pulled a stoppered glass tube and packaged swab from the box. Tearing the paper from the swab, Stith bent over Cameron and ordered, "Open your mouth." He ran the cotton tipped end along the inside of Cameron's cheeks, then sealed the swab in the vial.

Stith then questioned Cameron about how he had gotten involved with Drum. Though Stith was now much more matter of fact in tone and pacing, he did make a pointed display of writing down the names of Bruce Tanner and Mike Welch, asking Cameron to spell them. Stith then questioned Cameron about whether Drum had mentioned anyone or hinted at anything that might be helpful, then repeated the same questions again in a different sequence.

Sitting on the edge of the couch with his eyes magnified by his thick lenses, Cameron didn't give them any useful information. Nor did Keenan, as he stood to the side listening for any slips, hear anything particularly damning.

Throughout the questioning, Cameron's wife sat beside him holding his hand in both of hers. A couple of times she looked at Keenan, a hard look, and Keenan wondered if her fierce loyalty was, in part, to bolster self-deceptions—he had seen such blinders many times before.

Stith finished his questioning and balled his fist around his pen and clicked it closed. He then pulled back his jacket, allowing Cameron a good look at his gun, as he slid the pen and small pad into his shirt pocket. "Don't even think about going anywhere because we're going to be watching you," Stith said, then let his jacket fall over his weapon. He stood and, looking down at the hapless minister, said, "And, Joe . . . if your sample matches, I'm coming back and I don't want any more bullshit, you got that?"

"Yes," Cameron said, looking down at his hands and nodding.

At the door, Keenan glanced back. Cameron sat with his head down and his wife's arm across his bowed shoulders.

22

siege

I

KEENAN SWUNG his rented Regal past the Columbia PD squad car parked at the edge of the Paxtons' property and pulled into their driveway. He pushed open his door and the patrolman flashed on his spotlight. Keenan held up his badge. "John Keenan, FBI. Now, get that light out of my eyes." Keenan's adrenaline had burned off, leaving him tired and a little irritable.

"It's okay," Marianne shouted as she walked from the front door toward Keenan. They hugged and her hair smelled of floral shampoo and her breath held a light bouquet of wine. She wore jeans and a dark blue blouse, and looked leaner than Keenan remembered. Moving back, her hand still touching Keenan's waist, she said, "John, it's so good to see you again. Come on, let's go inside."

She led him inside, talking as she went. "Martin called after he dropped you at your car and filled me in on everything." She shut the door behind them. "At least you were able to find out what he wants. Thank you, John."

In the brighter light, Keenan saw worry lines etched at the corners of eyes, which had once radiated interest and warmth and now shone with a hardness that seemed void of laughter.

"In case you're hungry, I've a plate warming for you," she said and led him down the two steps from the entry to the family room. The twilight-blue couch and matching easy chair were as Keenan remembered, though there were no longer plants in the room.

Zack sat on the couch, slouched so low that knee and shoulder were almost horizontal. His fingers rapidly worked a video game-pad held between his legs while on the television an animated tank blasted its way through a walled corridor. Zack did not look up as Keenan and Marianne entered the room.

"Hello, Zack," Keenan said.

"Oh, hi," Zack replied with only the barest glance away from the screen.

"You probably don't remember me. My name is John Keenan. I was a friend of your father."

"I know," Zack said, the frenetic manipulations of his fingers contrasting with his general listlessness.

"Zack, turn that game off," Marianne ordered. Zack ignored her.

"That's okay. Adults aren't terribly interesting. Good seeing you again, Zack," said Keenan, not wanting to make courtesy an issue when much greater concerns loomed over this family.

They started for the kitchen and Zack surprised Keenan by saying, "You can talk out here because I'd like to know if that man can really threaten us."

"You don't need to worry about any of this," Marianne answered. "We'll take care of it."

"Sure," Zack shrugged, and turned his slack-jawed attention back to the game.

Keenan had long suspected that Marianne was overprotective of Zack, and that Zack withdrew from her smothering concern in the same way that Marianne shunned those who showed her pity. Personally, Keenan thought it important that kids learn to handle life's hard knocks and had once suggested this to Marianne. She had rejected the idea, adamant that Zack had already had more than his share of "knocks." In other words, butt out of how I raise my son.

Keenan then thought that he was probably reading too much into what Marianne had just done. After all, what mother would not become extremely protective if a death row serial killer threatened her child?

Marianne closed the kitchen door. "I'm sorry, John. He's obsessed with those damn games," she said. Marianne continued talking as she went to the refrigerator, took out a salad, and removed the plastic wrap. "I worked out an agreement that as long as he keeps up his grades he can play for an hour each day, so he's very protective of his allotted time."

The kitchen looked much as he remembered, yet also different; there were no plants and the refrigerator's door remained bare of anything except a couple of coupons held by banana-shaped magnets. The nook's table was ready with a place setting, a bowl of bread wrapped in a cloth napkin, and hand-mixed salad dressing. Keenan sat and, surrounded by the smell of Italian food, his stomach gnawed with hunger.

"Would you care for some wine or a beer?" Marianne asked as she dished salad into a bowl.

"Water's fine," Keenan said, dodging, as he usually did explaining that he never drank alcohol. "How is Zack handling the threat?"

"I don't know." Marianne poured a glass of water and brought it and the salad to the table. "He doesn't seem to be acting any different. I hadn't intended to tell him that he'd been threatened, but he over-heard me on the telephone."

"Knowing will make him more cautious."

"I guess." Marianne returned to the counter and sipped from a half-empty glass of a dark red wine. "But he's been through too much already." She shook her head then set aside the wine and pulled a steaming pan of lasagna from the oven.

"You served lasagna the last time I was here," Keenan said.

"I'm sorry."

"No, it's very good. I'm glad to have it again."

"It was my specialty when Will was alive. I guess I haven't added any new specialties since then," she said, and heaped a generous portion of the pasta onto a plate and placed it before Keenan.

"How are you doing?" he asked, knowing well how Marianne put on a strong front.

"Better than I was earlier, thanks to you and Martin." Carrying her glass of wine and a two-thirds full liter bottle of merlot, she joined Keenan at the table. "I feel silly with all this protection around, but at the same time I'm glad they're here. There's another policeman out back. Martin says just their visible presence will scare off any would-be intruder."

Keenan nodded agreement, then tore off a hunk of bread and started on the salad with gusto. From living alone, he'd fallen into a habit of eating somewhat fast and heartily.

"Martin said you think Drum's bluffing and I guess that takes away a little of the fear, though Martin doesn't think we should back off until we're sure."

Chewing and swallowing rapidly, he said, "No one's backing off."

"Oh, I know. Martin is sure he'll get the truth from Drum tomorrow." Marianne sipped her wine. "I know I've told you that for a while after Will's death a lot of law enforcement checked on me, but only you and Martin have stayed in touch. So he knows how strongly I feel about Drum and wanted me to know that, in order to break him, we may have to make a deal."

On the ride from Cameron's house back to Golgotha, Stith had told Keenan that he intended to have a go at Drum tomorrow. When Keenan told Stith to leave Drum to him, Stith had replied, "You didn't get much." Keenan knew that arguing would do no good and, instead, he tried to direct Stith by suggesting common tactics that would prevent Drum from playing them against each other. Stith had brushed Keenan's suggestions aside, saying, "Drum's not going to play me at all." Nor did Stith share Keenan's conviction that Drum was bluffing, so he held on to the position that he might have to deal. Keenan expected nothing good to come of Stith's having a go at Drum.

He and Stith had agreed on one thing—to not inform the press of the threat. This would make it easier to keep pressure on Drum by feeding him only what information they wanted him to have. Keenan had a second reason for wanting to keep the threat from being made public. With the national media already gathering, he worried that some loser with a copycat mentality might think that carrying out

Drum's threat would bring instant fame and validate his sorry life. Granted, there was little likelihood of this occurring. But high-profile cases always carried some risk of copycats. And copycat violence was a phenomenon that had dramatically increased in recent years, as great numbers of the disconnected and overlooked sought ascendancy through terror and notoriety via the shallow glow of television.

"It makes me furious that that bastard murdered my husband," Marianne said, "and now puts me in a position that to save my son, I may have to ask the governor to commute his death sentence. God, I hate that fucking bastard."

Seeing a perfect opening, Keenan swallowed hastily and chased it with water. "I don't think we'll need to make any concessions. Maybe with everything that's going on . . . you should reconsider witnessing the execution."

"No, John. I'm going to his execution to show him and everyone else that I'm not going to roll over and be a victim," Marianne said, flashing anger. She took another gulp of wine, refreshed her glass, then shook her head. "I'm sorry. I shouldn't have snapped at you, and I know I should consider what you're saying. Martin said the same thing. He even offered to go in my place. I'm not thinking too clearly tonight, but when I'm calmer, I will consider it because I value both yours and Martin's opinion. All right? But even if I reconsider, I don't know if I want Martin taking on anything traumatic, at least not for a while. He took it hard when Arnold Inabinet . . . died three months ago."

"You told me about Inabinet," Keenan said. "I didn't know he and Stith were close."

"God yes. Arnold more of less saved Martin from himself. Martin's father abandoned the family when he was just a toddler, so Arnold was the closest thing Martin ever had to a father. That's why Martin worshiped him. So his . . . death was very hard on Martin."

Marianne stopped speaking and looked away, seeming close to tears. "I just pray that Martin can break Drum tomorrow because I don't want to feel scared every time Zack goes out the door."

Pushing aside his plate, Keenan reached across the table and took Marianne's hand. "Marianne, I'm going to learn everything I can about Drum, and when I do, I promise you that I'll get the truth out of him."

Moisture rimmed her eyes but no tears came, as if she would not allow them. "Thank you John. I'm so scared. And I'm grateful that you're here. You've no idea how much I count on you for stability, and for strength." Marianne put her other hand on Keenan's. "You may think I'm silly, but you always come when there's trouble and I guess I think of you as something of a guardian angel." She then drew back both hands, raised her wineglass, and said, her eyes now shining, "To you."

.   .   .

When Marianne walked Keenan to the door and told him good night, she kissed him lightly on the lips, lingering, he thought, for just a moment.

This kiss stayed in the forefront of Keenan's thoughts as he drove back to his motel. He felt foolish for having to remind himself that Marianne was merely expressing friendship and gratitude that were intensified by fear and several glasses of wine. Yet, this kiss left him buoyant, and this reaction caused him to feel foolish and to feel as if he were betraying Marianne's trust.

Several times during their frequent telephone conversations, Marianne had told him that she recoiled whenever she thought a man might be coming on to her. She thought this was crazy, but even after all these years the thought of being with another man made her feel she was being disloyal to Will—something she hoped might change after Drum's execution. On one particular Sunday night when Marianne had had several glasses of wine, she again confessed her loneliness but this time said that she was still a young woman and that she sometimes craved being touched and often hungered to satisfy her body. More than anything, she said she missed being held.

Concerned, Keenan had called her again two nights later and she had been as self-contained as ever. In fact, during this second call she only spoke about Drum's latest appeal having just gone to federal appeals judge Franklin Shealey, and how worried she was because Shealey had overturned a similar conviction last year.

Marianne never again mentioned her confession. And Keenan never confessed that as he had listened to her baring her soul, her voice slurred and husky with tones of the bedroom, that he had felt not just concern, but male desire. His arousal then had felt wrong, like a betrayal of her trust, and he chastised himself for feeling that way.

Now, as he drove back to his motel, Keenan's thoughts lingered on her good night kiss and he became aroused. Once again, his desire felt like a betrayal of her trust, and as disloyal to Will. The buoyant feeling persisted, however, gleefully mocking Keenan's noble intentions.

23

tuesday morning

I

AT EIGHT O'CLOCK the doorbell rang. Usually up by now, Joe Cameron still lay in bed, fitfully awake. He had been up and down all night, and every time he got up, wearing boxers and a T-shirt, he peeked through the living room curtains and saw that a police car kept watch in front of his house. Last evening, three neighbors had called to ask if everything was okay and Wendy explained to each that there had been a misunderstanding with a prison ministry Joe had undertaken, and that she couldn't really say more until it was resolved. Between these calls, Wendy had called their daughter, Faith, and told her what had happened and assured her that there was no need to come home because everything would soon be cleared up. Similarly, Wendy assured Joe that everything would turn out all right. Even the letter, she said, was a well-intended mistake and nothing would come of it. Still, Joe was scared to death.

So when the doorbell rang, Joe sat up in bed, afraid that that SLED agent had come back, and listened closely as Wendy answered the door. Joe sagged with relief when he heard Mike Welch, the reporter that he had talked to last Friday, introduce himself.

"He doesn't want to talk to anyone right now," Joe heard Wendy say. Wearily, Joe dragged himself out of bed. While he slipped on trousers and a sweatshirt, he heard Welch say something and Wendy repeat, "I said he doesn't want to talk to anyone. Can't you understand that?"

Welch then said, "There's strong accusations being made about your husband. I know him, and before I go public with these accusations I want to give him a chance to tell his side."

"I said no," Wendy said forcefully, as Joe came into the living room. The storm door was open and Welch had his knee pressed against the inner door. Petite and a head shorter than Welch, Wendy stood with one hand pushing on the door and looked angry.

"It's okay," Joe said and coming to stand beside Wendy put a hand on her shoulder. "I've nothing to hide. I'll talk to Mr. Welch." Looking past Welch, Joe saw that the patrol car remained parked in front.

Welch thanked Joe for talking to him as Joe led him into the kitchen while trying to smooth his sleep-ruffled hair. Joe poured them each a cup of coffee, then took the reporter out back to the patio that Joe had built himself. He was proud of the patio even though the bricks were unevenly spaced. It was a pleasingly cool morning. Sunlight dappled overheard on gold and red maple leaves and danced like fireflies on the patio. Joe wiped dew from the cushions of the metal-framed lawn chairs and they sat at the glass-topped table. The morning light showed Welch's creases to be deeper than Joe remembered and his curly hair grayer. The knot on his plain blue tie was loosened and a little crooked.

Welch sat back in his chair with his hand casually laid on the table near the coffee mug. "I'm going to get right to the point," he said in his resonant voice. "My sources tell me that you've been questioned in connection to Gary Wilmet's murder and I want to give you a chance to comment on it."

Shaking his head, Joe said, "Uh . . . it's all a misunderstanding."

"I'm sure it is," Welch replied. "What kind of misunderstanding?"

"It's all because I went to see Isaac Drum."

"You told me that you were not involved with Drum." Welch said, arching his eyebrows.

"I wasn't. But after talking to you I got to wondering if, ah, if maybe I could help him get closer to God, you know, since I knew him a little. So, I contacted someone I knew at the prison and saw Drum the afternoon after I talked to you."

"You better tell me all about it," Welch said, "in detail." And Joe did. He thought that telling his story would help get everything cleared up. He even told Welch about the letter and his reasons for mailing it, though when Welch asked what else he and Drum talked about, Joe said he couldn't say because it was a pastoral confidence. Welch asked how all this connected to Gary Wilmet, and Joe told him of Stith's visit and what Stith had said about the letter threatening an abduction and murder. Joe wasn't sure exactly how, but in some way this threat was linked to Gary Wilmet's murder.

Joe found it easy to talk to Welch, who was courteous and really listened to what Joe had to say without interrupting or rushing him.

"So, because you saw Drum, you became a suspect in the Wilmet case?" Welch asked.

"They have to rule me out, so . . . uh . . . they took a sample."

"Then, they must have some sample from the killer. What evidence did Stith mention?"

"Just a hair, I think." Joe didn't mention semen because he didn't want to be quoted in the newspaper talking about such things.

"Thank you, Mr. Cameron," Welch said in his courteous way. "You've given me useful information, so I'm going to look after you. Now, I have to report what's going on, but I'm from the old school, and I'm not going to twist your words to make you look bad the way some of these other reporters might. And they'll be here soon enough. If I were you, I'd be careful what I said to them; probably the less you say the better. But since I'm doing you a favor by giving you such a fair shake, it's only right that you return me the favor. As you know, I've been following Drum's case for a long time, and it would greatly help me to know what you and he talk about. Now, you can keep all the spiritual stuff to yourself, but Wilmet's murder and a planned murder are not pastoral, so I want to know what Drum says. You can be an unnamed source. If you follow the news, you know I'll go to jail before I reveal who you are. So how about it, do we have a deal?"

"I'm not going to see him again."

"You ought to reconsider. He's still facing death and I'm sure he needs spiritual counseling."

"Okay, I'll think about it," Joe said, though he knew that he was through with Drum, or, to be more honest, Drum was through with him.

"Good." Welch stood and put a hand on Joe's shoulder. "And watch yourself with those other reporters."

"Can I ask you something?" Joe said, squinting up at Welch in the flecked sunlight.

"Sure?"

"I've heard about DNA tests freeing men from death row," Joe said. "Are those tests accurate? I mean, could they make an innocent man look guilty?"

"I think they're accurate enough that an innocent man shouldn't have to worry," Welch answered and smiled reassuringly.

"I hope so. But who'd have thought that someone as law-abiding as me would ever be accused of such a horrible crime?"

"You'd be surprised," Welch said, "at what seemingly law-abiding folks sometimes do."

24

stith's deal

I

MARTIN STITH shaved carefully, as he did every morning, with a straight razor tracing the ragged edge of his scar. Like a mantra, he believed this ritual helped discipline the brashness of his nature. He had been a cop for twenty years and had never once crossed the line with any of the scum that he arrested or interrogated, though God knows there were plenty who deserved a good thrashing.

Stith rinsed foam from the razor's perfect steel and began the precise scraping across another inch of flesh, each stroke sounding like lightly rubbed sandpaper. His scar was what was known in the profession as "an identifying feature." He knew others used it to describe him—"Yeah, you've met Stith, the guy with the scar." As a signature, it was a manly scrawl, which was reason enough to keep it. Once an effeminate plastic surgeon approached Stith in a movie lobby and said he could reduce the scar to a hardly noticeable line, and Stith had told the man, "Why the hell would I want to do that?" In a stark and vital way, the scar confronted Stith with things in his nature that he had best not forget.

As a kid, Stith had been a scrapper looking to prove his toughness at every chance. From the time he could walk, he ran the streets of Jeffcoat near the trailer park where his mom did what she could to support them, which wasn't a lot with her scoliosis, emphysema, and three packs a day of Kool menthols. His old man ran out on them when Stith was an infant, so Stith made it a point of honor not to run from anything. He had been a resourceful kid who early on supplemented the family income, starting with a paper route that he walked every morning until he stole a bicycle.

By the time Stith turned sixteen, he stood close to six feet tall and had enough quickness and bad attitude to earn him a deserved reputation as a tough guy. Most of his money came from hustling pool in Ed's Pool Hall, and he had recently picked up a few bucks helping Ed collect on a bad debt.

All that changed on a rainy Thursday night, when Stith hustled a mouthy redneck at nine ball. The guy had stringy blond hair that needed shampooing and wore white socks with black lace-up shoes. Stith thought it was Ed's jukebox, loaded with country standards, that brought in this kind of riffraff. Of course, these yokels were easy money if you were smart about it; and being smart meant barely beating a mark so that it looked like you were just a little luckier in how the balls fell. But this guy kept mouthing off and getting in Stith's face even though the guy was down forty bucks. So Stith chalked his stick and ran the table with as much flash as he could muster. The guy must have taken offense at being suckered because, as Stith lined up the last shot, the guy came at him with a pool stick. Stith caught the stick and threw the guy to the floor without even breaking a sweat. He kicked the guy once in the ribs and was about to kick him in the groin for good measure, when the guy's buddy slashed Stith's face to the bone with a large hunting knife. Stith never saw it coming. The buddy—a hulk of a man with long dark hair and a jeans jacket that bore a Harley emblem on its back—had sat at a table all night just staring glumly into his beer.

Arnold Inabinet had been a patrolman then and was first on the scene. While waiting for the EMTs, he held Stith's face together with his hands and talked to him. Stith had been in shock, so later he couldn't remember what Inabinet had said, just that Inabinet stayed calm, looked him in the eyes, and talked to him like he mattered. A man had never treated Stith this way.

Inabinet came to see Stith in the hospital and told him that when he was well enough he had to do three months' community service by emptying the trash at the Jeffcoat police station. Whenever Stith later told this story, he always said that he'd been too dumb to know that only a judge could order community service. But he had known better, and he had gone anyway. It was the smartest thing he'd ever done.

Stith showed up at the Jeffcoat station every day to take out the trash and after the first week Inabinet managed to get him a little pay—or so he said, because Inabinet would just hand Stith a few bucks. Weeks became months and Inabinet stayed on Stith to finish high school and after Stith graduated helped him get hired as a Jeffcoat PD dispatcher. Later, when Stith made patrolman, he spent the first six weeks riding with Inabinet. Already, Inabinet was prodding Stith to take college courses. Stith would do anything to avoid disappointing Inabinet. And, when he was younger and more hotheaded, knowing that Inabinet would find out was the only thing that kept him from going over the line and doing something like slamming an elbow into the ribs of some mouthy perp.

Finished shaving, Stith splashed on aftershave, then went into the apartment's bedroom with its burnt orange carpet and matching drapes. This shit-hole was all that triple alimony left him able to afford—though he had salvaged the cherry bed and forest-green silk sheets, which were probably too domestic for a single man, but he didn't want Janet to have everything. He never could pick women and had decided that, in effect, he'd married the same woman three times. Not the same woman per se, but the same type: fun until they married, then bitchy—and they all blamed their bitchiness on him. Stith had vowed never to make that mistake again. From now on, he'd just rent to satisfy his needs.

Retrieving a small Chief's Special Airweight from under his pillow, Stith slid it into its holster, then clipped the holster to his belt in the small of his back. He next picked up the Sig Sauer from the nightstand and bounced its solid weight in his hand a couple of times. When the superiority of automatic weapons over the old reliable Smith and Wesson had become apparent, he talked Inabinet into making the change and the old man had bought a Sig Sauer P228, same model as Stith's. That had been a proud moment for Stith. Now, looking at this gun, he remembered what he most wanted to forget and his eyes became red and teary and he felt choked by sudden emotions.

"Goddamn you, Inabinet," he said, then shoved the gun into his shoulder holster. Grabbing his keys and wallet, Stith stomped out of the apartment, banging the door shut behind him, now on his way to have a go at Drum.

II

Stith wrinkled his nose at the ashtray-like smell of the meeting room. Otherwise, he liked the setup. He and Drum would be locked in here together with no barriers between them, just like your typical interrogation room.

Stith paced until he heard footsteps on the catwalk, then stood beside the table and watched Drum enter the room. He thought Drum looked like a jailhouse greaser with his hair combed back into a flip-up ducktail, and that he certainly looked more like a sleaze now than when first arrested. The COs unlocked Drum's wrist restraints and Stith noticed how the son of a bitch cocked his head up like he was royalty. He had seen other punks play that game and he half-smiled at the way Drum kept up the arrogant posturing with his nose stuck in the air as they put him in the chair and hooked his leg chains to the U-bolt.

Well, two could play at posturing. Stith remained standing until the CO's left, then unhurriedly pulled out his chair, sat, and studied Drum. He had watched Drum play mute when first arrested and thought he might try something like that today, so he got straight to the point, no bullshitting, no dancing around, no playing mind games like Keenan. "My name's Martin Stith. I'm a deputy chief at SLED. And I'm here to make a deal."

Drum cut his eyes to Stith. "Where's Keenan?"

"He doesn't want to deal. I do." Casually, Stith reached in his jacket pocket, took out a pack of Marlboros, a man's smoke, and tore off the cellophane. Stith thought that one of the great pearls of wisdom was a quip by Mark Twain that quitting smoking was easy, because he must have quit a hundred times. For almost a year now, the longest ever, Stith had gone smokeless. When Inabinet was first diagnosed with cancer, he had asked Stith to give up cigarettes. Now, telling himself that it would set the right tone, Stith lit a cigarette and inhaled deeply in a moment of pure visceral pleasure. He flipped the pack so that a couple of cigarettes stuck out the end and held it across the table. "Smoke?"

Drum hesitated, then shrugged and pulled one from the pack.

Stith leaned forward and lit it with a gold lighter. Thrusting the lighter and pack into a jacket pocket, Stith sat back and again filled his lungs with smoke. Having not smoked in a while, he could already feel the lift.

After exhaling slowly, he said, "Here's the situation. The governor cannot officially make a deal with you. You see, that would be giving into extortion and if he did that every pipsqueak on death row would try a stunt like this. Plus, it would be political suicide. I think Keenan explained all that and pointed out that the governor could generously reward someone who helped us catch a child killer. So the smart thing for you to do is be a good citizen and give me the name. Do that and I'll get your sentence commuted, no ifs, ands, or buts."

Drum took a hard drag and stared mutely at Stith. More seconds ticked off, but Stith knew how to undercut that kind of bullshit. "Take your time and think about it. You'll see I'm right." Stith took the pack of smokes from his pocket and tossed it on the table. "Like I said, take your time."

"Why should I trust a pompous ass like you?" Drum said, staring at Stith through the smoke from the cigarette pinched between his thumb and forefinger.

"Two reasons. First, if you think about it, you'll see I'm giving it to you straight. And the other reason is that you don't have any choice."

Drum snorted and tried to hook Stith in a staring contest but Stith took a pull off his cigarette and looked away. He had interrogated plenty of perps and knew enough to just relax and enjoy his first smoke in months while Drum sweated his options and became overly anxious. Patience is an interrogator's harshest weapon.

Minutes passed and Drum finished his smoke, then dropped it on the floor and rubbed out the embers with the toe of his sneaker. "Okay, I'll do it," he said. "You get me the deal and then I'll give you a name."

Stith shook his head and smiled. "You don't listen real well, do you? There's only one way we can pull this off and that's for you to be a good citizen and come forward with information first."

"No, I need a deal first."

"It can't happen that way. Use your head and you'll see that the only way for this to work is if you come across first." That's probably all Stith should have said. But he thought he might get better results if Drum wasn't so smug, and thought the quickest way to undercut that was to challenge his manhood. "It's time to cut the crap and deal like a real man," Stith said. "A lot of people think that roughing up women is about all you can handle? Here's your chance to prove them wrong by dealing like a man . . . if you can."

Drum stared at Stith, his eyes narrowed and his lips parted, showing stained teeth. Drum picked up Stith's pack of Marlboros, took out a cigarette, and lit it with his own lighter. Then, flashing an exaggerated smile, Drum shoved Stith's smokes into his pants' pocket.

For a few seconds Stith and Drum stared at each other. Finally, Stith unhurriedly stood and moved to Drum's side of the table, letting Drum's uncertainty and anticipation build.

"What're you going to do, slap me?" Drum taunted. "Why don't you do that, you sorry son of a bitch?"

Stith sat on the edge of the table, looked down at Drum, and shook his head. "I thought you were supposed to be a smart guy. Are you really this stupid? In two days they're going to fry your ass and you're in here playing kids' games."

Drum spit at Stith, missing his face but the sputum landed on Stith's lapel.

Stith remained motionless, his scar glowing red and his hands tightening on the table's edge.

Drum kept smiling. "You want to hit me? Go ahead. You know it would feel good."

What Stith knew was that if he so much as barely touched Drum, he would not only throw away his career, but at the very least delay Drum's execution while an investigation took place. Tasting bile from choking back his anger, Stith slowly rose and moved back to his side of the table. He took out a handkerchief and cleaned his lapel, then leaned on the back of his chair and stared into Drum's expressionless blue eyes. Without breaking eye contact, he said, "Let me refresh your memory. I'm the only chance you have to keep two thousand volts from burning your scalp black and cooking you inside until your liver splits open. So, use your head and give me a name."

Drum's only response was to blow a stream of smoke in Stith's direction.

"What's it going to be? Deal? Or die?"

"I already have a better option," Drum said and looked toward the camera and signaled for the COs to come and get him.

"You don't have jack-shit to trade; that's why you're doing this," Stith said.

Drum ignored Stith, not even looking at him until he was almost through the door. Then he turned and said, "By the way, thanks for the smokes . . . smart guy."

25

misspent youth

I

WHILE STITH failed to get anywhere with Drum, Keenan pursued a much different line of attack. He had awakened early that morning, as he did every day, with a burst of restless energy. Today, though, this energy had a ragged edge from fitful sleep. He had grabbed a quick breakfast and by eight o'clock sat at the writing desk in his motel room.

Three bulging files, each wrapped with a sturdy rubber band, lay atop this desk. The files contained copies of Drum's school, foster care, and Juvenile Justice records. Keenan had already called Quantico and talked to Wynton Carlisle. Carlisle had located most of the people on the list Keenan had given him last night, people who had had contact with Drum during his childhood. He had not yet found the most important person, however, Drum's mother. Carlisle had scheduled

Keenan for two meetings, one at ten this morning with the director of Psychological Services for the Department of Juvenile Justice, and another at three o'clock this afternoon with Drum's maternal aunt, Mary Bishop, in Greenville, South Carolina, which was about a two-hour drive from Columbia.

Keenan studied the telephone numbers that he had jotted down. Drum's maternal grandparents, Margie and Abraham Brazzell, refused to talk to him, though Carlisle had passed on their telephone number, anyway. Nowhere in the assembled records was there any indication that Drum had ever had much contact with the Brazzells. At this stage, however, Keenan wanted any glimpse inside this family, an apparently guarded clan, because he knew what most mental health workers knew—that family secrets, the kind that aren't talked about even within the family, are a fertile breeding ground for serious pathology. And, desperate for something to use against Drum, he was prepared to do whatever it took to steal these flawed secrets.

Keenan punched in the Brazzells' number and on the third ring a woman answered, "Hello."

"Mrs. Brazzell, my name is John Keenan. I'm with the FBI. My department contacted you last night. I want to talk to you about your grandson."

After a brief pause the woman whispered, "Mr. Brazzell said no."

"I'm aware of that, but I'm hoping I might change your mind. I'm not trying to exploit your grandson and you may tell us something that can help with another investigation. Lives are at stake, and I'm only asking for a few minutes. We can talk on the telephone. You'd be doing the right thing."

"Mr. Brazzell's washed his hands of anything to do with him," she whispered urgently. "He would be very upset if he knew you'd called. Please, don't call again."

"Have you washed your hands of him? Mrs. Brazzell, if you can just give me a few minutes. I'd be happy to take a message to your daughter, Rebekah."

In the background Keenan heard a gruff, "Who is it?"

"It's a wrong number, Abraham." Firmly, she said, "Please be more careful in the future and don't dial this number again." Then she hung up.

His lips pursed together, Keenan shook his head and thrust the telephone's receiver back into its cradle. His gaze fell on Drum's records and it struck him as ironic that such thick files held so few telling details about Drum's early childhood. He knew that Drum's father had been a chief petty officer stationed out of Charleston's naval base and that when Drum was six years old his parents divorced. A year later, his father died from head trauma when a cable snapped during resupply maneuvers in the Mediterranean, so, until Drum turned twenty-one, his mother, Rebekah Drum, received a pension for her son.

His school records proved only slightly more revealing. Beginning in the first grade, Drum attended three different schools in the Charleston area in as many years, and two other change of addresses were recorded that did not involve switching schools. Recurring comments in early school records included: "underachiever," "inattentive," "restless," "easily frustrated," "does not take correction well," "withdraws from social situations," "frequently falls asleep in class," and "inconsistent hygiene."

Two months before his eleventh birthday, Drum and his mother moved to South Carolina's midlands and he began the fourth grade at Jeffcoat Landing's elementary school. In late September, Drum attacked a boy at school and, soon afterward, a teacher named Eloise Whitten reported suspicions of neglect to the Child Welfare Division of the Department of Social Services. Three weeks later, Drum's mother abruptly yanked him out of school and sent him to live with her sister in Greenville, South Carolina. Nowhere in the records could Keenan find any reason for Drum being sent away. By then, DSS had completed its investigation and was not pressing for any further action. The abruptness and apparent mystery surrounding this change intrigued Keenan, especially because subsequent documents suggested that the separation from his mother had directly preceded the only documented time when Drum had spiraled completely out of control. Maybe it was only because of the sudden separation from his mother. Or maybe, something else traumatic and formative had happened. Keenan did not like pursuing such long shots, but right now it was the only blip he had so far identified in Drum's history.

Hoping for better results than from his last call, Keenan dialed the number of Eloise Whitten, the teacher who had filed a report with

Social Services. He was curious about what had prompted her to call Social Services and hoped that she might know the reason Drum's mother sent him away.

"Ms. Whitten, my name is John Keenan. I'm an FBI agent studying Isaac Drum."

"Yes, a polite young man named Carlisle called me last night and said that you might call today. I also read in the newspaper that you've been meeting with Drum," Ms. Whitten said. Her voice came over the line clear, unhurried, and friendly, with a light rasp of age.

"I'm interested in knowing everything that you remember about the incident that prompted you to call Social Services," Keenan said.

"I remember the incident very well. I had not yet retired when Drum was first arrested, so I went back into old records to see if it was the same person, though I knew in my heart that it was him."

"Was that because he was a persistent problem?"

"Oh, quite the contrary. Prior to the incident he struck me as a rather bland boy who could easily get overlooked. From what I remember, he never put much effort into assignments and I don't recall him showing much interest in other children, either. I realize that some of this may be hindsight from looking over my old notes, but I do distinctly remember him because of the attack."

"Please, tell me what happened?" Keenan asked, and fingered the pen lying atop his legal pad.

"Apparently, one of the larger boys picked on Drum during morning recess with a promise that he would get much worse treatment at lunchtime. I didn't see this, but other students later told me that Drum took the bullying without fighting back. At the end of the period, he lagged in the rear until all the students were in their seats, then came up behind the boy who had bullied him and grabbed that boy in a chokehold while pummeling his eyes with a handful of gravel. Mr. Keenan, I taught school for thirty years and never saw such ferocity in a child. As he pounded that boy with the gravel, he kept trying to bite his ear, and was screaming and . . . frothing may be a strong word for it, but you get the picture. And, Mr. Keenan, I'm a large woman, but I had trouble pulling him off. When I finally got them separated his face was red and contorted, and for a moment I thought that he was going to turn on me. Then his usual bland expression came over him as if nothing had happened, except that I could still see the anger in his eyes.

"I told him to come with me, and as I walked him to the principal's office I asked him why he had done that, and all he said was, 'I dunnoh.' Mr. Jarnitz, the principal, called Drum's mother and she accused me of making it all up. Well, Mr. Jarnitz didn't even dignify that with a response, and told her that because Isaac had not been in any other trouble, if she would come for a parent-teacher conference, then Isaac would not be suspended. Well, it's probably no surprise to you, Mr. Keenan, but she didn't keep the appointment. When I tried to call her about the missed appointment, the woman who answered the phone said that Mrs. Drum was not there and then hung up. I'm certain I was speaking to Isaac's mother; it's sad how often we see shenanigans like that. I tried again several times that day and no one answered, so I filed a report with Social Services. I didn't know what, if anything, they would do, but I thought someone should take a look at his home situation. Then . . . let's see . . . I guess it was about three or four weeks later that Mrs. Drum sent a note saying that she had sent Isaac to live with her sister in another part of the state. And I never heard anything more about him until his arrest."

"Do you know why she sent him away?" Keenan asked.

"Not a clue. The note was the first and last I heard about it. At the time, I do remember thinking that it might be in his best interest."

Though he was no closer to what he most wanted, Keenan thought the mother's response to problems informative. Preparing to hang up, he said, "Thank you, Mrs. Whitten, for taking the time to talk with me."

"Mr. Keenan, since I've tried to answer your questions will you tell me if DSS did anything with my report?"

"They did an assessment and then more or less required that Mrs. Drum enroll him in Big Brothers. Once she completed the Big Brothers' application, they deactivated the file," Keenan said. He had reviewed these records last night, hoping to find out more about Joe Cameron. What he learned was that Cameron had gone on one Big Brother sponsored outing with Drum, then quit. Considering Cameron's failure to follow through, Keenan added, "But I don't think much ever came of that referral."

II

Drum had been eleven years old when he came to live with his aunt, the former Mary Brazzell. At the time, she was married to Thomas Freeman and they had two sons, ages one and three. Three weeks after taking Drum, his aunt filed a petition asking the state to take custody, claiming that she was unable to influence Isaac's behavior and feared that he would harm her children if he remained in the home. She said Isaac had a terrible temper and asked that he receive professional counseling. She also said that she could not locate his mother.

Drum was placed in foster care with John and Laney Bowden, a couple experienced in dealing with children having behavioral problems. Ten days after taking Drum, the Bowdens demanded his immediate removal from their home. Mrs. Bowden told the social worker that after her husband left for work, Isaac had attempted to get in bed with her and she had sternly rebuked him. An hour later, her five-year-old son came to her crying because Isaac had done nasty things to him. She also said that she had disciplined Isaac three days earlier and, soon afterward, the family dog disappeared, and she was now convinced that Isaac was responsible. "Unless my husband is around, that boy is defiant of any suggestion I make," she said. "I don't know what's happened to him, but somebody else is going to have to straighten him out."

A second placement with Bud and Alice Larson failed after only three days. A fire broke out in the basement and the Larsons believed Isaac had set it. Mrs. Larson said, "I know he did it because, not an hour earlier, I'd given him a little spank with my hand. And he did it because he knew how scared I am of fires. You see, fire destroyed my parents' home when I was seven, so I spent a lot of time going over fire safety with him."

With foster care not working out, Drum was placed in a special needs group home. Records there described him as generally withdrawn, except for two incidents of picking on smaller boys. When he had been there twenty-six days, two days before Christmas, a fire broke out in his wing that was quickly extinguished. Two boys claimed to have seen Drum set it, and criminal charges were filed. Family court judge Richard C. Ardis, Jr., ordered Drum detained at the Department of Juvenile Justice's Chatham School for Boys until a social and psychological evaluation could be completed. After reviewing these evaluations, Ardis adjudicated Drum delinquent and returned him to the Chatham School for Boys with an indeterminate sentence.

At ten o'clock, Keenan was to meet with Neal Rasnick, Ph.D., the psychologist who had first evaluated Drum at Chatham nearly twenty years ago. Now director of Psychological Services for the South Carolina Department of Juvenile Justice, Dr. Rasnick's office was located, along with those of other DJJ administrators, on the twelfth floor of a high-rise in downtown Columbia.

Parking on Columbia's crowded streets proved more difficult than Keenan had anticipated, and after a brisk three-block walk he arrived ten minutes late for his appointment, breathing hard. The receptionist, a slender manicured woman with strawberry-blond hair, wearing a red jacket and matching skirt, immediately announced Keenan's arrival while he mopped his forehead with a handkerchief.

Walking with fluid grace, a fit-looking black man came out of one of the offices and extended his hand. "Mr. Keenan, I'm Neal Rasnick." Rasnick's hairline had receded a couple of inches, causing his forehead to appear especially prominent above his gold-rimmed glasses. He greeted Keenan in his shirtsleeves, wearing a forest green tie over a green plaid shirt and topped off by a friendly smile.

"Thank you for meeting with me, Dr. Rasnick," Keenan said as they shook hands.

"I'm very happy to help in any way I can," Rasnick replied, and ushered Keenan into his orderly office. On top of Rasnick's light oak desk, a stack of manila folders lay on one side of the green desk pad and on the other side was a flip-up binder containing about five inches of computer printouts. Also prominent was a picture of an attractive woman and two college-age girls. A baccalaureate from Emory University and doctoral degree from the University of South Carolina hung on the wall above the credenza. Behind his desk, a large tinted window overlooked the surrounding buildings and afforded a distant view of the Saluda River curving slowly between red- and gold-toned woods. Fortuitously, a neighboring building blocked any view of Golgotha.

Showing courtesy to his guest, Rasnick waited until Keenan sat down in a low-backed blue chair before settling behind his desk. "Mr. Keenan, I must admit that I've always been fascinated by your work," Rasnick said. "I remember seeing you on television a few years ago talking about an interview you'd done with Charles Manson. Your strategy was so interesting: you allowed him to sit on the edge of a table so he could be higher and you took a deferential attitude. How did you decide to adopt that tact?"

"Dr. Rasnick, I prefer we focus on your evaluation of Isaac Drum," Keenan replied. Normally, he would have readily answered Rasnick's question as part of the usual get-acquainted chat. Today, though, he felt too impatient for small talk, much like the impatience that had felt in the weeks following Will's death.

"Of course. I'm just professionally interested in your work," Rasnick replied, gracefully. "What specifically would you like to know?"

"As you reviewed your report on Drum, did anything about it seem unusual?" Keenan asked. He sat with both feet planted on the floor and his back straight.

Rasnick rubbed his chin, then said, "Well, maybe the 122 IQ on the Wechsler was a little higher than most of our students, since run-of-the-mill delinquents often aren't the brightest kids. But like most of this population, his lowest scores came in areas assessing social judgment. The majority of our kids have huge distortions in how they read social situations."

"I see. In your report, you said that abandonment issues had something to do with the problems that Drum was having. How did you come to this conclusion?"

"For one thing," Rasnick answered, "abandonment themes were prevalent in his CAT responses. Ah, the CAT is a test where I show him pictures and he makes up stories about them."

"I'm familiar with it," Keenan replied.

"Well, in my opinion, the separation from his mother shattered whatever tenuous self-control this kid Drum had been displaying. When I evaluated him, he was convinced that those who had taken him into their homes were part of a plot to keep him from his mother, and that if he forced them to kick him out, they'd have no choice but to send him back to her. At the same time, he was furious with his mother for sending him away but couldn't admit it, even to himself, because in his mind she was the only person who had ever genuinely cared about him. So, given his distrust for everyone else, if he didn't have a caring relationship with his mother, he was completely alone, and, by implication, unlovable. Therefore, he repressed his anger at his mother and directed it at other female caregivers."

Keenan nodded, then asked the question he most wanted answered. "Do you know why his mother sent him away?"

Rasnick shook his head. "No idea. When I reviewed the records this morning, I became curious about that myself and looked through the social worker's notes. Soon after he was sent to Chatham, his social worker managed to track down the mother, who had recently moved back to Charleston. She arranged for the mother to come for a Sunday visit and planned to formally interview her at that time, but the mother never showed. According to this social worker's records, it appears that Drum had been fairly withdrawn up until his mother's no-show, then that night they caught him trying to climb the back fence. He threw rocks and then tried to club staff with rocks and was placed in the Maximum Security Unit, where he went completely out of control. While in the Max Unit, he spit at staff, threw handfuls of urine on them, and he tried to grab or scratch staff. He also screamed curses until he was hoarse and made a dozen or so accusations of physical abuse, all of which proved unfounded, of course. He also scratched his arms with his fingernails until they oozed blood, something that I had noted when I first evaluated him—we see quite a bit of that—and then he began to mutilate himself.

"Our physician patched him up and we sent him to the children's state psychiatric unit for assessment. A week later, they sent him back saying his self-mutilation was not a manifestation of psychiatric disorder but aggressive and manipulative in nature and, therefore, a part of his conduct disorder, so we were best suited to treat him. They do that with every kid we send them. I'm not kidding, Mr. Keenan. Even when we send them a kid who is hallucinating, they send them back saying his primary problem is conduct disorder.

"My apologies, I didn't mean to digress," Rasnick said with a wave of his hand. "It's a persistent sore point."

"What do you think makes a kid like that self-mutilate?"

Rasnick paused and rubbed his chin. "I don't think anyone understands it completely. The kids themselves often say they do it as a way of getting rid of tension. But over the years, I've noticed that a lot of kids self-mutilate when they're at war with the staff. I think kids who self mutilate are very angry kids who don't feel a lot of control. Put a kid like that under tight controls, such as in a Maximum Security Unit, and they're very much at risk to harm themselves in some way. I think, at least in part, kids like Drum do it to show us that we couldn't control them. But, that's just my opinion." Rasnick shrugged and smiled.

"Then, after banging himself and staff around for a few weeks," Keenan said, "he suddenly stopped all of his aggressive behavior. Why?"

"Who knows?" Rasnick answered and shrugged again. "Drum was bright, so he might have figured out that beating his head into the same wall wasn't getting him anywhere. Whatever the reason, I think that the same control that he'd had before the separation from his mother, suddenly latched back into place and from that point on we had relatively few problems with him."

"And after that, he spent six years in your system without further incident?" Keenan said, his mouth set in a hard frown.

"Yes. By age fourteen he was doing well enough to transfer to a group home. At sixteen we put him in a halfway house where he could learn basic life skills such as using a checking account, driving a car, ordering a meal in a restaurant. While there, he passed the GED and earned an Associate Degree in Criminal Justice. Two weeks after he turned eighteen, he was accepted into the army and we closed the file."

"In our request, we asked you to contact others who might remember Drum, especially his first social worker."

"It's been twenty years, Mr. Keenan. I have no idea where she is. I did contact two other social workers who managed Drum's unit at different times, and of course they both knew from the newspapers that Drum had been at Chatham, but neither had any specific memory of him."

For a moment, Keenan looked past Rasnick, staring out the window at lazy clouds. When Keenan again looked at his host, his irises seemed flecked with light and he leaned forward, near the edge of Rasnick's desk. "So you're telling me, Dr. Rasnick, that with a history of setting fires, explosive aggression, and, as you yourself documented, a deep anger at women, that Drum wasn't in some type of individual counseling and that none of your staff can recall such a volatile history?"

Rasnick's face tightened, though his voice remained calm. "Unfortunately, Mr. Keenan, counseling is but one of a myriad of things we expect from our social workers. Let me see," Rasnick said and, turning to the flip-up binder on the side of his desk, began shifting through its sheaths. "Here it is, this week's census for Chatham. In C Unit, we currently have twenty-eight young men sent there for offenses that include sexual assault, armed robbery, attempted murder, assault and battery, and I have four with some history of fire setting, though only one is charged with that particular offense." Rasnick looked up from the file. "There are five other units on that campus with boys there for similar crimes. In each of those buildings, we have one social worker, *one*, Mr. Keenan, who's responsible for each of those kids' therapy, as well as discharge planning, administration of the building's activities, and supervision of the staff who work in their building. For the most part, the staff that each social worker supervises are large men who can physically handle the bad-asses housed there. Now, most of these men are dedicated and do a damn good job. But even the best ones, after they've been spit on, punched in the face, and kicked in the balls a few times, lose some of their compassion. So faced with an assembly line of broken people and a conveyor belt that never slows, the staff deal with the biggest problems and do what they can with the rest."

"So you're telling me," Keenan said, his face red, "that a predator passed through there untouched because you have burned-out social workers? If I did my job like that, I'd quit."

Meeting his stare, Rasnick retorted, "Drum killed four people after you started hunting him? Does that mean you should quit? Or that you have a damn tough job?"

Biting back another pointless reply, Keenan rose. "I won't trouble you further, Dr. Rasnick. Thank you for your valuable time."

"A bit of advice, Mr. Keenan," Rasnick said and also rose, but did not offer his hand. "When people try to help you, you may want to extend them the same courtesy that you showed Charlie Manson."

26

exposé

I

DRUM HARDLY noticed his escorts' firm grasp on each arm as they led him to the chair in the dank meeting room. And to hell with remaining aloof, he could not take his eyes off the woman seated at the table. She was slender, like a cat, with dark, satin hair parted on one side and falling in slow, loose waves to the nape of her neck. Her black skirt had seemed molded around her firm, pumping hips as she swished past his cell. She now sat with perfect posture that made her little breasts jut beneath a black jacket that perfectly matched her skirt. Her hands rested one atop the other on the table, disappointingly motionless, though Drum thought there might be some satisfying whitening of the top hand's knuckles. All the while, as the CO hooked his leg chains to the U-bolt, Drum fixed his eyes where the top two buttons of her silky, cream-colored blouse spread open and a single pearl on a gold chain nestled between the barest hint of fleshy mounds, just begging to be stared at. The way she exuded her sex, he had every right to look where he pleased.

The COs left the room and Drum reminded himself that too much was on the line to allow her womanliness to distract him this way, and lifted his eyes to her face. Her petite nose turned up ever so slightly at the tip and dark red lipstick made her lips appear slick. Leaning forward, chains clinking softly, Drum stared at her eyes, their blue deepened by lightly applied eye shadow, and his arousal turned completely hard.

For a moment, Amanda Slade stared back. She had already done a couple of prison reports and had prepared herself for this type of ogling, especially since death row inmates were rarely in the presence of women, and this man was a sexual predator. Also, Amanda Slade, born Amanda Sladkus, harbored no illusions as to why Drum consented to be interviewed by her—it wasn't her reportorial skills or the fairness and intelligence that she tried to bring to her stories. Regardless of his reasons, she was very excited. For although Amanda Slade considered herself savvy and tough, she still needed a big break if she was to move permanently from World Network News to one of the major networks while still in her twenties.

She had worked hard for such a break last month, when she had endured a week of insects and diarrhea in the Colombian jungle before being blindfolded and badly bruised during a jolting jeep ride, only to spend the next hour looking down the barrel of an AK-47 as she explained to the guerrilla leader why he should talk to her rather than shoot her. After all this trouble and risk, her producer did not think this insurrection enough of a hot-button issue to warrant being featured on either of WNN's news magazines, so all Amanda got was a minute and a half airtime on the Eight O'clock World News Summary. Her earlier prison reports, however, had earned her this plum as on-site reporter covering Isaac Drum's execution for WNN's parent network. And now she had scored an exclusive interview with Drum, a man who had never before talked to any journalist. Amanda Slade knew that she could turn this interview into a break, perhaps even get a segment on one of the parent company's prime-time magazines, or maybe even parlay it into a broader feature on sexual predators.

Her ambitions had been hampered somewhat when Drum vetoed having a cameraman present, probably so that it would just be the two of them, alone. Too bad, she thought, because he had strong presence with his paleness and scarred cheeks and the way he greased his hair back in a style that was remarkably common among prisoners—he certainly gave off a sufficient impression of danger to grab and hold the viewer's attention. And those eyes—Amanda Slade was surprised that the rumors of them being penetrating and unsettling were true.

After meeting Drum's stare just long enough to show that she wasn't afraid, Amanda Slade averted her gaze to turn on a tape recorder and said, "I'll be tape-recording our conversation, though I wish you would reconsider having a camera present."

Drum kept staring without speaking and Amanda Slade, concerned that he might have just met with her to ogle, met this head-on by say-ing, "I hope this isn't all you intend to do."

In a low husky voice, Drum said, "It's okay for you to stare at me. It's natural for you to want to. Hell, unchain me and put me in a room with anyone, even the goddamned President, and I'm the one that any-one else in that room will be watching, especially if it's a woman, like yourself. So go ahead and look; I don't care."

Amanda Slade knew that to get an unguarded answer you have to set up the questions you most want answered, preferably by getting your subject a little off balance, then spring the crucial question. She had one particular question that she very much wanted to ask, but not until the time was right. So she started trying to tip Drum off balance by probing his own juicy declaration. "Why is it important to you that people, and especially women, want to watch you?"

"I don't give a shit one way or another," Drum said. "It's just the way things are."

"But it's the first thing you've told me, so it must have some impor-tance for you," she pressed.

Drum's eyes narrowed at her impertinence and felt tempted to show her that he was not some pipsqueak on whom she could use her sex like a ring through the nose. He considered dangling just a bit of the scoop that he was about to hand her, and then make her earn the rest by taking off her jacket and showing him a little more tit for his tat. Pointedly, he stared again at where the pearl lay between the barest shadow of cleavage and thought that she didn't have enough breast to be so smug. Drum shook his head, trying to shake off her allure, and again reminded himself that too much lay on the line to allow her to sidetrack him. As distasteful as it was, he had to stay focused and ignore her attempts to belittle and control him. Still, his erection did not sub-side completely.

"We only have a half hour," he said, forcing his eyes back to her face, "so there's no time for this petty shit if I'm going to tell you what's going on. It'll be the biggest scoop of your career."

"By all means, please, go on," she said nodding.

Drum thought this sounded condescending and glared at her. She looked interested enough though, the way she leaned forward and watched him with bright, attentive eyes. He decided he should go ahead before she squirreled his whole plan. "Okay, here's the situation," he said. "All I care about right now is getting a fair shake on my appeals. It's what every citizen should be entitled to, right? But ever since my trial, Marianne Paxton has been squawking to the media about how she wants to stop any fair-minded consideration of my case; if you don't believe me just look at all the things she's said over the years. And now that my appeals are finally getting a lot of last-minute attention and there's a very good chance that someone will recognize the serious problems with my conviction, what does she do? She enlists a SLED agent named Martin Stith to make up lies about me. You see, Marianne Paxton has put this guy, Stith, up to claiming that I had something to do with the murder of a twelve-year-old named Gary Wilmet. And if that's not enough, Paxton also has Stith making accusations that I'm threatening to have her son, what's his name, Zack, killed. They think that Wilmet's killer, or maybe some other guy with a lot of nerve, is out to get the Paxton kid because it will make whoever kills him the most famous criminal in America."

Leaning back in her chair and frowning, Amanda Slade asked, "Why would such a murder make anyone particularly famous?"

"Because I'm scheduled for execution as the result of a wrongful conviction for the murder of Paxton's father. With all you reporters here, if some bold guy kills that kid close to my execution, it would get huge media coverage. But that's not my fault, though Paxton and Stith are claiming that it is, and have even manufactured a letter trying to link me to all this, just to sabotage my appeals. If only I hadn't . . ." Drum stopped talking and shook his head.

"If only you had not . . . what?"

"I've already said too much," Drum said, shaking his head and dropping his eyes from her face. Then he looked back at her and shrugged. "What the hell. It's going to come out, anyway. I let it slip that I knew who killed the Wilmet kid."

"Do you?" she asked and leaned forward.

"Yeah, I know exactly who killed Wilmet. And I'm afraid this guy's not going to stop. And he may be after the Paxton kid."

"Who is he?"

Drum shook his head. "I've already said too much. You see, I can't tell you without also telling the bastards who are trying to execute me.

And why should I tell them a damned thing when all they care about is murdering me as fast as they can? Personally, child killers disgust me. But I'm not going to help a bunch of bloodthirsty bastards who refuse to show one bit of mercy. You tell me, what sane person is going to help his murderers look good just so they can get ahead in their bureaucratic careers?"

Amanda Slade cocked her head to one side. "So what you're actually saying is that if your sentence is overturned, then you'll tell who killed Wilmet? Is that what you're offering?"

Drum shrugged and pursed his lips. "I guess if . . . let's say my sentence was commuted to life, that I'd be very grateful and do everything I could to stop more kids from being brutally raped and murdered. But that Paxton woman and Stith are gonna make sure that's not going to happen, so there's no point in even talking about it. That is . . . unless you help me get the word out to counter their lies."

Drum sighed and watched the woman as closely as he dared. He knew she believed that he had granted her this interview merely because she oozed sexuality, and he had played to that conceit by doing what came natural in her presence. But when he had watched her on the news last night, having never seen her before, he thought that she came across as a little pissant hungry for a big story—the bigger the better—so their interests overlapped enough that he could use her. He had also mistakenly thought he might enjoy himself at the same time; instead he was having to tolerate her impertinence.

Amanda Slade leaned back in her chair, studying Drum. "I'll certainly report everything you've said and play portions of the tape," she said and gestured toward the machine. "But I'll also have to get rebuttals from people who are going to argue that your claims are nothing but a desperate scam to try and avoid the electric chair. So unless you give me a name, how do you prove it's not a scam?"

Enraged at her questioning him this way, Drum regretted not using a man for this errand. He had lost sight of how a woman, the instant she realizes that you want something from her, starts jerking you around with this kind of bullshit. He leaned forward, coming over the table, and stared hard and pointedly—something the tape recorder would not pickup—yet managed to keep his voice quiet and husky. "I guess I better give you the killer's name, then," he said. "But I'm paranoid that

Stith has bugged the room; he was in here alone for several minutes. So you'll have to come over here and let me whisper it in your ear." Drum smiled his hard, humorless smile.

Amanda Slade shook her head. "I'll not get that close to someone who hates women."

"Then be sure to report that I offered to give you the name and you refused. And I don't hate women."

Amanda Slade also leaned forward, putting her forearms on the table and coming to within a couple of feet of Drum, her eyes glittering as she asked the question that she had come here wanting to ask. "You torture, degrade, and murder women. Of course, you hate them. And what people most want to know is why do you hate women?"

Added brightness came into Drum's eyes. "Just because I won't let some cheap wannabe trash like you walk all over me," he said, "doesn't mean I hate women."

Their eyes locked; Amanda Slade leaned even closer. "It sounds as though you're afraid of women. Are you only afraid of strong women? Or do you generally feel you don't measure up? Is that what's caused you to hate so much?"

Drum's hands clenched into fists and he strained against the chains holding his wrists to his side. He could barely curb the impulse to head-butt this bitch or do something else that might undermine what he needed to achieve here. No, doing that would give her what she wanted, and allow her to humiliate and destroy him. Drum restrained himself and put her in her place by using something that she would never broadcast on the air. "Have you ever thought about what the men in here do while you're on television?" he said. "Think about it the next time you go on air, because it's the only reason they show you. If you don't believe me, on your way out look into all the cells and see what they're doing. We'll see how much death row exposé you really want."

To make sure that she did not provoke him into doing something stupid, Drum signaled for the COs to come and get him and he refused to speak to her again, even though she pressed him with more pathetic questions.

A couple of minutes later, sandwiched between COs and shuffling slowly along the catwalk, Drum told every inmate he passed that the news-bitch had just called them all losers and that she would be walking by in a couple of minutes. Once back in his cell, he pressed close to the bars with the mirror held out, waiting to see what bodily fluids the bitch picked up along the way from the likes of Tramaine.

The COs had also heard Drum's tip and knew exactly what he was attempting to orchestrate and, as Amanda Slade left death row, a tight, three-man formation shielded her from the inmates' fluids. Surrounded by these large men, Amanda Slade walked with jouncy steps. She had asked Drum about his hatred of women and gotten better material than she had even hoped she might.

27

hardscrabble weed

I

SHAPED LIKE a narrow shoebox, the Cedar Lane Cafe offered subdued lighting, dark linoleum floors, and red vinyl booths. Potted ivy and wandering Jew hung in the plate glass windows framing the door. Keenan, sitting in a booth near the back, checked his watch, then looked back at the door.

There was a good chance that this trip to Greenville would be a waste of time. When he had called his department this morning, Carlisle had told him that it took hard persuasion to get Drum's aunt, Mary Bishop, to meet with Keenan. She had said that neither her husband of three years, Hank Bishop, nor anyone at the mortgage loan company where she worked as assistant manager knew that she had a nephew on South Carolina's death row, and she wanted to keep things that way. She had agreed only after Carlisle promised that after this meeting no one else from his agency would contact her. Still, she might not show.

The door opened and a slender woman with wavy, shoulder-length brown hair stepped inside the café. Her hand still on the doorknob, she scanned the few patrons. Keenan stood beside the booth and waved. The woman hesitated, then approached with tight, assertive steps that did not conceal her nervousness.

"Mrs. Bishop, I'm John Keenan." he said, extending his hand. She wore a navy blue jacket and skirt, and white blouse with a cameo brooch at the collar. A noticeable odor of cigarettes hung on her. Keenan thought her attractive, though her face bore deeper worry lines than one would expect of a forty-one-year-old.

"Please sit down," he said and gestured toward the booth, gently taking control. A pot of coffee with two cups set on the dark Formica tabletop, along with the usual condiments and metal napkin holder pushed against the wall.

"I don't know why I'm doing this," she said, as she slid into the seat opposite Keenan. "Mind if I smoke?"

"No, go ahead. Coffee?" Keenan asked and poured.

While Mary rummaged through her purse for a pack of Vantage 100s and Bic lighter, the waitress, an older, buxom woman with curly red hair, sauntered to the table as if her feet hurt from the noon rush. Mary told her that she didn't care for anything and the waitress moved away and resumed topping off the salt and pepper shakers.

Mary lit a cigarette, then held it in her fingers, twitching it up and down. "I don't know why I feel like I'm doing something wrong," she said. "I don't like it. I don't want you bothering me after today, all right. And I don't want you bothering my mother again."

"I understand your desire for privacy. But it's public knowledge that the Brazzells are his grandparents, so I don't understand why your mother refuses to talk to me."

"I'm not here to talk about my mother, all right?"

"I understand," Keenan conceded. He very much wanted to talk about Mary Bishop's family, but it was too soon to push. Keenan leaned forward and clasped his hands at mid-table. "I've reviewed the records and it's obvious that when you took in Isaac he was beyond what anyone could control," he said. He wanted this woman to know that he understood, that he had not come here to blame her. He wanted to put her at ease. Again and again during the two-hour drive here, he had reminded himself that he needed to check his impatience so that he would not have another angry and shameful lapse like he had had with Rasnick.

"I'd like to know how Isaac acted when he first came to live with you?" Keenan asked, starting easy to get her talking.

Mary took a quick puff of her cigarette and blew the smoke to the side away from Keenan. Then her eyes flickered over his face, wary. "All right," she said. "He was quiet, withdrawn, seemed to be pouting. I figured he was hurt and needed time, so I didn't ask much of him. I knew what kind of childhood he'd had. Pretty quickly, though, it was obvious he wasn't going to do one thing I told him." Mary took another drag on the cigarette.

"Can you give me some examples," Keenan nudged her to talk.

Mary sighed. "Let's see . . . things like, if I asked him to straighten his room, he'd mess it up more. And he'd hardly let me touch him. He got some bad scratches on his forearm and wouldn't let me check it. I asked him how he hurt himself he said, 'I dunnoh.' Then he got a worse cut in the same area and acted the same way. I know this is such little stuff that it must sound silly," she said, watching Keenan.

"I assure you, I will not find anything you tell me silly. I know how difficult it is to deal with a kid like Isaac. How was he with your husband?"

"He'd mind Thomas. In fact, he always seemed to be watching Thomas. I thought it was because his father had died and he wasn't used to living with a man in the house."

Keenan sat back against the booth, seemingly relaxed. "What other things did you notice during those first few days?"

"Honestly? He was sneaky. He'd disappear for an hour or two then claim he'd been there the whole time. Or I'd hear him at night moving around in the house, and if I got up to check on him, he'd hide. This worried me because my children were young and I couldn't be sure what he was up to. You see, I hadn't been around Isaac for four years. And he seemed so . . . wild. A couple of times I know I heard him outside our bedroom when Thomas and I made love, not that we did it that often. We weren't getting along so great then, and having Isaac in the house wasn't helping; I know it wasn't right to think that, but I did—but that's not why I sent him away," Mary added quickly.

"Mrs. Bishop, I've talked with other families who have taken in boys similar to Isaac. They all spoke of difficulties. And there are cases where these boys did hurt children, a few seriously. So I know it was difficult, and that you did everything you could."

Mary looked at her hands, which had finally become motionless. Then she looked up, her eyes moist, and said, "Thank you."

Having earned a bit of trust, Keenan pushed the interview deeper. "Now, we have to get over a hurdle," he said. "I know there was some incident that scared you. And my guess is that you've never told anyone what happened."

Keenan paused, and waited until Mary slowly nodded yes.

"I need to know what happened."

Looking down, Mary shook her head no. Keenan waited. She snubbed out what was left of her cigarette, then took another from the pack. "I'm usually not a chain smoker," she explained. "I just feel so damn nervous."

Keenan smiled. "I know this is difficult. I wouldn't ask if it wasn't important. It's time to get it all out. Please, tell me what happened?" he said.

Mary took a slow drag off the cigarette. She looked down, then said in a quiet voice, "He . . . he didn't assault my children, but I was afraid he would. He . . . he tried to assault me. I know that sounds crazy. I didn't think anybody would believe me if I said an eleven-year-old had tried . . . So I didn't tell anybody." Looking up, Mary's eyes pleaded for understanding.

"You were right to be afraid," Keenan assured her. "And it's a sexual assault we're talking about, isn't it?"

She again looked down, sat very still, then nodded yes. Pulling a tissue from her purse, Mary dabbed at her eyes, slightly smearing her eye shadow. A minute passed before she gathered herself, and, sniffling, said, "He didn't succeed. Not by a long shot. But by God, that's what he was after. I didn't think anybody would believe me. Maybe if I'd told them . . ."

"It wouldn't have made any difference," Keenan cut her off. "It's hard for anyone to accept that kind of rage in one so young. Will you tell me what happened?"

Using a fresh tissue, Mary blew her nose. "It was the first night my husband had worked the midnight shift since Isaac came to live with us. I had put the kids to bed and was in the living room having a couple glasses of wine and watching Johnny Carson, except Joan Rivers was the guest host so it wasn't too good. Isaac came into the living room and seemed to be acting different, like maybe he wanted to talk or something. I asked him if anything was wrong and he said no. Then he came over and sort of snuggled up to me on the couch and put his head on my shoulder, right here." Mary patted her right shoulder just above her breast. "I figured he was missing his mother, so I put my arm around him. It was the first time he'd ever let me show him any affection. Then he took his hand and . . . at first I thought it was an accident . . . but he started fondling me. I told him he shouldn't do that and moved his hand, but he moved it right back. When I tried to push it away again, he resisted, and then tried to grab me with the other hand and climb in my lap. I pushed him away and stood up. He came at me again and I pushed him away again, and that's when he picked up an ashtray and threw it at me. God, it gave me a terrible bruise, right here," she said, touching her left hip. "Then he started hitting and scratching, and it was all I could do to hold him off, so I finally pinned him to the floor. For the longest time, he squirmed like some kind of rabid animal, trying to bite and kick until he tired himself out. And the whole time I kept thinking, what if he turned that anger on one of my kids.

"When he finally quit, I let him up and asked him why he'd done that. He wouldn't say anything. I told him to go to bed, but he just stood there with his little fists clenched, staring at me. So I told him that if he didn't go to bed and stay there, that I'd call Thomas and tell him what he'd done and Thomas would be furious. I could see the hate come into his eyes. You can't imagine what that looks like on a little boy—like the way that girl in *The Exorcist* looked. Finally, he did what I told him and I gathered my kids into my bedroom and stayed awake all night. The next morning, as soon as he was on the school bus, I dropped my kids off with a friend and went to Social Services. I guess you know the rest."

Mary Bishop stopped speaking. She sat motionless, detached. Reaching across the table, Keenan touched her arm. "Mary, I know talking about what happened was not easy. And tomorrow, you may regret it, that's a common reaction. But by telling me these things, in time, you may be able to let it go," Keenan said and withdrew his hand, anchoring the suggestion.

Keenan wished he could stop here and not push for the family secrets that are not talked about, even within the family. Such secrets, he believed, were a necessary incubator for Drum's kind of pathology.

But he now wanted Mary to betray the silence that her family valued more than love. "There are a few more things I need to know," he said. "You said you knew what kind of childhood Isaac had. I need to know what his childhood was like."

"Is this really necessary?" Mary asked, her expression hardening a little.

"If it wasn't important, I wouldn't ask. I know your sister was a lousy mother, so you won't be telling me something I don't already know. But I need the details. I need for you to fill in the gaps."

"Why don't you ask her?"

"We haven't been able to locate her. There's an old address in the prison file, but the phone was disconnected over a year ago."

"I have her address." Mary dug in her purse and took out an address book. Opening it to the D's, she slid it toward Keenan. "There. I haven't talked to her for at least two years. But I sent her a Christmas card and it wasn't returned, so maybe the address is still good."

"That's the same as in the file," Keenan said. "I'll check it tomorrow, but I still need for you to tell me about Isaac's childhood. Even if I locate your sister, I don't think she can accurately tell me what kind of mother she was. As much as I wish it were otherwise, you're the only one who can."

Mary roughly stuffed the address book back into her purse, then stared hard at Keenan. "What does all this have to do with a child's murder. That's all the man last night would tell me. Isaac's in prison. So what's this about?"

"Drum claims to know the identity of a man who has been raping and murdering young boys. If I can understand Drum better, maybe I can get him to tell me the killer's name. If not, he claims that another child will die this week."

Mary sighed, then laid her head back against the red vinyl with her eyes closed. She shook her head, opened her eyes, and said, "All right. What do you want to know?"

"What type of contact did you have with your sister after Isaac was born?"

"My parents lived in Jeffcoat and Isaac and Reba—that's what I call my sister—were in Charleston so I'd only get down to visit four or five times during the school year and then maybe a week or two during the summer. Reba never came home. And Momma would just drop me off, she wouldn't go in."

"Why didn't she and your parents get along?"

"Look, this doesn't have anything to do with Isaac, all right?" Mary said and glared at Keenan.

"All right," Keenan replied, and raised his hands slightly as a sign of concession. Then he slowly sipped his cold coffee to let the tension linger and sharpen her inclination to make up for this refusal by telling him other things. Putting down his cup, he asked, "When you visited your sister, what concerned you about the way she cared for Isaac?"

"Everything."

"Everything?"

"Yeah. Everything." Mary took out another cigarette and lit it. She turned aside and exhaled a long stream of smoke, then looked at Keenan, her expression angry. "She didn't know how to be a good mother, all right. She was only sixteen when she had Isaac. She was a kid, a wild kid who had been running away from home three or four times a year since she was twelve, and when Mickey said he would marry her . . . I think she had Isaac just so she could finally get away from my father."

Mary held up her hand to keep Keenan from asking her another question and looked away. Keenan waited. After a moment, Mary sighed, then continued. "Reba was the kind of mother who only cared for Isaac when she felt like it. Sometimes he'd be soiled and she wouldn't change him until the soap she was watching ended or she finished polishing her nails and letting them dry. That's the way she was. And it was probably worse when I wasn't around, because I thought she tried a little harder with me there just for show, though she was still no good at it. Once when Isaac was maybe three or four, Momma dropped me off and when I went in the house, Reba was gone. She had just left Isaac alone and didn't come home until the next morning. She said she'd had a date and knew I was coming, so she knew I'd be there to take care of him. I was so ashamed of her. And so sorry for Isaac."

"She had a date?" Keenan asked. "Was this after she separated from Mickey Drum?"

"I don't remember. She's always been boy crazy. Even while dating Mickey, if he couldn't get a weekend pass, she'd go screwing around with someone else. And that didn't change after she got married."

"How did she and Mickey get along?"

"I only visited a couple of times when Mickey was home. They fought a lot. But Mickey was almost never around. When he wasn't at sea, he'd go off most weekends with his buddies, fishing or driving up to Atlantic City to gamble. But he expected Reba to take care of Isaac and got pissed when she didn't. Not that Mickey was father of the year or anything."

"How did he treat Isaac?"

"You ever know anybody that kept a dog in their backyard and they pat its head for a couple of seconds whenever they come home and that's the last time they notice the dog until the next time they come home. That's how Mickey treated Isaac."

"Did either of them use much physical punishment?"

"No. Not much. Some. Mickey yelled sometimes and Reba was real inconsistent. It depended more on how she felt, than on what he did. I remember this one time when she was getting ready for a date and Isaac started sprinkling the cat with whatever was in his little juice cup. Reba laughed like it was the funniest thing in the world, so he kept doing it until the cat jumped up on a dresser where he couldn't reach her. Her date never showed, and two hours later Isaac did it again and this time she slapped him and said, "You little bastard, don't you ever do that again." But she didn't do things like that too often. Mostly, she just didn't pay much attention to him. Then sometimes she'd laugh at something he did and talk to him or play with him or sometimes even read to him, though she screwed that up too—she wouldn't read him kids' books, but those trashy novels she liked. But she only did any of those things when she was in a real good mood."

"What else concerned you?"

Mary shrugged, then said, "She drank a lot."

"Were you ever aware of any sexual abuse?"

"No."

Keenan leaned back in the booth, and asked, more for her than for his wanting to know, "What kind of relationship did you have with Isaac?"

"I tried to play with him, talk to him, pay attention to the things he did. But he was hard to get close to. Even when he was a baby, I'd try to pick him up and he'd squirm and stiffen up; he just wouldn't cuddle. As he got older, he didn't talk much or ask about things. I don't think I ever heard him cry after he was four or five. He seemed so . . . independent.

He had his little routines that he followed the same way every day. Later, when I found out he'd gone into the army it didn't surprise me because back then I used to think of him as being like a little military man.

"When I turned sixteen and Isaac was five, I lived with Reba for a couple of months. By then, she'd separated from Mickey. When I'd been there about a month, Isaac started bringing me things he wanted me to see or he'd take me in the yard to show me something. I didn't have much money, but I bought him a few puzzles and children's books. Then I finished high school and moved back to Jeffcoat so I could take classes at Jeffcoat College during the day and waitress at night. I didn't have much time to visit Reba, but when I did, Isaac never again would have anything to do with me.

"Then, at about the time I got my AA degree, Thomas and I decided to get married. I called Reba and asked her to my wedding. She said she'd be there, and then asked me if I'd take Isaac. I talked it over with Thomas, and he didn't want us to start out with a kid, so I said I couldn't, not now. She said okay, she'd see me at my wedding, but she didn't come. After that we fell out of touch. I guess it was four years later when she called and asked if I'd take Isaac for a little while. She sounded desperate. By then I had two of my own, so I said yes. You know the rest."

Finally, Keenan asked what he most wanted to know. "What was her reason for wanting Isaac to come live with you?"

"She said Isaac was causing problems with her boyfriend. Big problems, she said."

28

ductwork

I

UNIFORMED OFFICERS kept onlookers at least a hundred yards from where a narrow road passed over a small creek. Late afternoon sunlight tinted everything golden, especially the weed husks that grew beyond the mowed strips adjacent to the road. Stith left the pavement and followed a path trampled through the knee-high weeds that grew along the rim of the steep bank. Sunlight no longer reached the creek bed below, which consisted mostly of dried mud, rocks, and tangled patches of silt-coated sticks—it was more drainage ditch than creek, thought Stith. Stagnant water pooled at the mouth of a round cement conduit that passed beneath the road. Twisting out of this culvert with a shoulder and face submerged in the shallow pool and the arms stretched above the head, lay the upper torso of a body dressed in a black T-shirt and nude from the waist down.

The victim was a sixteen-year-old named Jimmy Gilpin, by all accounts, a tough kid. He had been reported missing this past Saturday. Earlier today, someone called a television station and told them where to find Gilpin's body, and the caller identified himself as Gary Wilmet.

Even before Columbia PD investigator Bob Marshall inspected the crime scene, he had told Stith that there was absolutely no relationship between the murders of Gary Wilmet and Jimmy Gilpin. Marshall insisted the caller used Wilmet's name just to get media attention, because criminals love to hear about their crimes on the news, and possibly to misdirect any investigators who weren't bright enough to know better. Marshall called Gilpin a hoodlum whose lifestyle had finally caught up with him. He said Gilpin's first arrest came at age eleven and his rap sheet listed arrests for petty theft, shoplifting, vandalism, marijuana possession, bringing a knife to school, and one B&E. "And that's only the stuff we caught him doing," Marshall said.

Marshall also told Stith that he had only called him because the perp used Wilmet's name, so he needed to cover his ass, the one thing at which Stith thought Marshall—a man who sullied nepotism's reputation—showed any talent.

Standing at the top of the steep bank, Stith squeezed small drops of menthol vapor rub onto the inside of a painter's mask, then returned the tube of vapor rub to a plastic bag that he stuffed into his jacket pocket and slipped on the shell-like mask. Bending his knees and leaning forward like a skier crisscrossing a slope, Stith followed the recently trampled path down the tricky bank. Despite the mask and vapor rub, as soon as he dropped below the diluting breezes he caught enough stink of human remains to cause his eyes to water. A hump of shale ran beside the finger-deep pool that was tinted blackish-green by silt and algae. Stith stirred up a halo of flies as he stepped onto the shale, squatted, and studied Gilpin's swollen remains.

Gases from decay formed large blisters on the body's forearms, cheek, and bloated legs. A slight movement drew Stith's attention to a large brown spider, camouflaged at the T-shirt's edge, that had come to prey on flesh-eating insects. Gilpin had been dead at least two days, more likely three.

A ridge of cracked mud clumped in front of Gilpin's hip. With his arms stretched above his head like that, it looked as though someone had recently pulled the body halfway out of the culvert. Most likely, the killer got tired of waiting for Gilpin's body to be found, so he came back and moved it, then called in the location. Also, he had used Gary Wilmet's name knowing this would get lot of media attention. And he had called a television station rather than police. Marshall was right about this guy wanting to hear his crimes reported on the news.

Stith used a handkerchief to protect the knee of his suit, then lowered his head until his cheek almost touched the rock and looked along the body's chest and stomach. At the abdomen, he saw small tears in the shirt surrounded by crusted blood, and a little surge of adrenaline kicked in. Those tears could be . . . no, they were knife wounds in the same place and same pattern as Gary Wilmet's stab wounds. The boy's hip tilted downward so Stith couldn't be sure, but it looked like there might also be genital mutilation.

Standing, Stith brushed the dust from his hands, then wiped them with the handkerchief, all the while kicking himself for accepting Marshall's glib assessment of the crime and not calling out SLED's tech-team. There was nothing wrong with Columbia PD's techs, except that Marshall received their reports first. The identical pattern of knife wounds in Gilpin and Wilmet pointed to the same killer, and that made this a multi-jurisdictional case — Wilmet in Jeffcoat Landing and Gilpin here at the edge of Columbia's city limits. Instead of merely offering support services, SLED could take the lead. Weiss wouldn't buck it; in fact, he already did pretty much as Stith told him. And Marshall? Piss on him.

Tromping up the bank, Stith tried to reconcile the two cases. After Wilmet's murder, they had thought they were hunting the neighborhood pervert. This killer, however, ranged and could take down a streetwise tough. Keenan's suggestion that the guy could be a low functioning jailbird might fit. It galled Stith that Keenan's profile might be right and that he should probably get Keenan's read on this latest murder. What a lousy day, Stith thought. In fact, the only remotely good thing so far had been satisfying himself that Drum was bluffing, or else he would have gone for Stith's deal, so the Paxtons were not in danger. But that son of a bitch Drum had been so smug! Well, if Stith played his cards right, he would be at Drum's execution and would see how smug the bastard was when they strapped him in the chair.

Stith reached the top of the bank and spotted Marshall sitting on a galvanized guardrail upwind of the culvert. In the distance, news crews mingled with onlookers outside the yellow ribbon, their cameras recording everything. On the other side of the road was parked a tech van with three men leaning against the front panel, waiting.

"You done?" Marshall asked, as Stith came near. In his early thirties, Marshall had light brown hair that lay in kinked waves and a thin mustache of the same color. The bulk of his head sagged into his jaws and double chin, his head forming a mirror image of his pear-shaped body. He wore a short-sleeved white shirt and loud tie, and vigorously chewed gum, even when he talked.

Stith removed his painter's mask. "Yeah," he said, as he wadded the greasy mask into a ball and stuffed it inside the plastic bag where he kept the vapor rub and put it all back into his pocket.

"All right," Marshall said, pushing himself to his feet and waving to the men at the tech truck. "Time for you to go down. And, hey, do me a sketch and measure while I consult with this officer, okay? And hurry, I want to get him bagged and get out of here." Stith now stood beside Marshall, who said quietly so only Stith could hear, "No need for me to climb back down there."

Though Stith now privately regarded this as his case, he could not officially take over until forensics confirmed the connection. Yet there were things that needed to be done quickly, things Stith thought more likely to occur if he got Marshall's fat ass bumped off the case. For now, though, he would have to direct Marshall, or rather push him to take appropriate action.

"What do you know about the Rosewood Video Arcade," Stith

asked. That was where Gilpin had last been seen. He had gone there on Saturday night at around nine P.M. with a pal named Nathan Kinder. Kinder said they each did their own thing, and he lost track of Gilpin. Sometime around ten o'clock, Kinder said he started looking for him and realized that both Gilpin and his car were gone. Kinder said he caught a ride with a friend and didn't think anything of it until Gilpin's mother called the next day because he had not come home.

"That arcade is nothing but a magnet for little hoodlums," Marshall answered, chomping on his gum. "We have a lot of trouble there. Mostly fights and drugs."

"Would someone who is not a kid stand out?"

"Only if he was straight. The building's partitioned; the arcade's on one side and the other side is a bar that attracts bikers and riffraff with tattoos. A lot of those guys go into the arcade, supposedly to play the games, but we know there's a lot of drug dealing goes on. My guess is that Gilpin tried to hustle a biker on a drug deal or something like that."

"You think Kinder knows more than he's telling? "

"Bingo," Marshall said, and sat back down on the guardrail. "He was Gilpin's Tonto, so you bet he knows who did it. And I can't wait to squeeze that little bastard."

"Any sign of Gilpin's car?"

"Nah. Probably in some biker chop-shop," Marshall said.

"All right, Marshall, you squeeze Kinder as much as you want, but there's some other things you need to do," Stith said, careful to keep his demeanor and voice matter of fact in spite of his contempt for this man. "You need to get Crime Stoppers to offer a reward to anyone who might have seen something, either here or at the arcade. I'm going to put out an ABP on Gilpin's car, and you need to keep that car's description in the forefront of your patrols' minds."

"You're not my boss," Marshall said.

Ignoring this, Stith said, "You also need to canvass this area and see if anyone saw anything on either of the killer's two trips here."

"You hard of hearing or just hardheaded? You're not my boss," Marshall repeated. "And what the hell are you talking about, two trips here?"

Marshall tried to rise, but Stith stepped closer so that Marshall could not stand without knocking into him. "The killer came back and moved the body before he called it in. Now, the other thing you need to do is get some ears in both the bar and arcade, and your investigators should play up the fact that we're looking for a child killer because some of those guys don't have much tolerance for that."

Finished with the things requiring Marshall's full attention, Stith stepped back and Marshall pushed himself to his feet. "You're not going to tell me how to run my goddamned investigation. And Gilpin's hardly a child."

"The same guy killed Wilmet, and that makes this case multi-jurisdictional."

"Bullshit," Marshall said, chomping hard on his gum.

"When the forensic report comes back, this is my case. Until then, I'll let you know what you need to do so that you don't embarrass yourself."

"Fuck you," Marshall said, and Stith nearly came unhinged. Stith did not tolerate fools well under the best of circumstances, and, today, the fiasco with Drum had left him seething. Plus, it offended him whenever a cop embarrassed himself or herself; his belief in the brotherhood of cops ran deep, to his very core. Not that he regarded Marshall as a real cop, but merely the city manager's son playing with something his daddy had given him. Yet, Marshall's ineptitude could give a black eye to cops in general. And a cop could be devoted, skilled, and a model of integrity, and then one thing could destroy his reputation. Look at what people most remembered about Inabinet!

His face red, Stith crowded close, forcing Marshall back until he almost fell over the guardrail. Inches from Marshall's face and struggling for restraint, Stith said, "If you handle this case half-assed and some other kid gets killed, I'm going to make sure it lands square on you. And your old man will cut and run, because that's what political types do from high-profile dung."

"I doubt that," Marshall said.

Stith could not stand looking at Marshall as he chewed gum with his mouth open, or listen to his sassy voice for another moment. He remembered how sweet physically manhandling someone had felt when he was a kid. Just a little push on the chest and Marshall would topple backwards over the rail. And who would care what Stith did,

anyway? Probably not one goddamned person now that Inabinet was-
n't around anymore. At the thought of Inabinet, Stith felt ashamed.

"Just do your job," he said and quickly walked away.

29

long slow burn

I

ONCE AGAIN, Keenan marched down the catwalk's metal alley, his
expression stern and his eyes fixed straight ahead. Beside him,
Lieutenant Jenkins kept pace. Keenan slowed as he neared the cell,
and when their eyes met Drum stopped pacing and Keenan nodded in
a friendly sort of way, then moved on. When out of earshot, he asked
Jenkins, "Has he been pacing much?"

"Most of the afternoon," Jenkins answered.

"What about taking his meds?"

"This close to execution, he could have some pretty strong sedatives
but so far he's declining. He's still taking his antidepressants, though."

They reached the meeting room and Jenkins unlocked the green
door. The odor of an overloaded ashtray wafted from the room, smothering death row's pungent aroma of sweat and ammonia. Once again,
Jenkins lingered in front of the door and scrutinized Keenan's face.
"You sure you're in a mood to properly conduct yourself with this man."

"Absolutely," Keenan answered, though it concerned him that
Jenkins had so easily pegged his foul mood. When he had gotten back
from Greenville, Keenan had called SLED. Stith was in the field so
Wes Felton took his call. As expected, Stith's session with Drum had
been a complete failure. Felton then told him about Jimmy Gilpin's
murder and Stith's belief that the same man killed Gilpin and Wilmet.
The publicity seeking shown by Gilpin's killer worried Keenan. Every
high-profile case carried a small risk that some loser might think he
could hop onto a slingshot to fame by doing something messy, splashy,

and similar to a crime that had already gotten so much attention. Gilpin's killer showed such a penchant. Granted this was a meager risk, but a risk nonetheless.

Keenan had learned of an even worse development, however, when he caught the evening news before leaving for Golgotha. Appalled, he listened to segments of an interview with Drum that cagily focused a potentially deadly spotlight on Zack Paxton. Drum had attempted not just to snag the attention of Wilmet's killer, but of any loser who thought headline-making violence might validate his sorry life; and by doing this, Drum may have actually put Zack in danger.

Now seething, Keenan had to conceal every hint of his anger if he was to successfully work Drum tonight. Despite the meeting room's stink, he sought to calm himself by breathing in deeply. Keenan also tried to empty his mind of everything except working Drum.

. . .

Tonight, Drum held out his hands to expedite the CO's removal of his restraints and even glanced at Keenan a couple of times as this was done, eager and hopeful. He wore no belt and his sneakers splayed open from having the laces removed—because he was scheduled to be transferred to the death house in less than twenty-four hours, standard suicide precautions were in effect.

As Drum's restraints were removed, Lieutenant Jenkins placed a plastic water bottle with an accordion straw on the table. Drum didn't wait for Jenkins and his men to leave the room before sitting, and the moment the door shut asked, "Do you have a deal for me."

Keenan sat slouched with his legs crossed. "I delivered your message and recommended they reward any help you give—which is really the only thing they can do. After that, no one's asked or told me anything," he said, and waved his hand nonchalantly.

Drum's face went slack. "Fuck," he said. Pushing himself to his feet, he began pacing, then stopped and looked Keenan. "I guess it'll take a little while for tonight's news to cause enough public outcry," he said. "Don't you think?"

"Maybe," Keenan said.

Turning, Drum looked at the surveillance camera and pantomimed drinking something held between his thumb and forefinger, then he resumed pacing.

Keenan waited, silently watching Drum pace. A couple of minutes later, the door rattled and a black CO, bushy-bearded with arms ready to burst his uniform's sleeves, came in carrying a small tray bearing a shot-sized paper cup filled with what looked like watery orange juice. Drum met the CO and drained the cup, then the CO left.

"What are they giving you?" Keenan asked.

"I can have a hundred mil of Seconal every four hours. But I held off in case we had to deal."

"I would have held off too," Keenan said, painting a little parallel between himself and Drum. "You still taking Zoloft?"

"They switched me to Elavil because the Zoloft jacks me up a little. But neither one does shit for me."

Again, Keenan nodded, as Drum resumed his restless back and forth circuit. The Seconal was a bit of good news. A strong barbiturate with effects much like alcohol, it made one hazy, impulsive, and more open to suggestion. Keenan thought he could coax Drum into a trance. True, all hypnosis was self-hypnosis. A subject had to put himself or herself into a trance. But Drum had put himself into a trance yesterday when he relived the abductions, and that would make it easier for Keenan to nudge him into a similar state, especially if under the influence of a strong downer.

Waiting and watching Drum pace, Keenan considered going for broke, pushing for a deep trance and demanding the truth. But he knew the limitations of hypnosis too well to try something so brash. A person could not be made to do anything that he or she was strongly opposed to doing. Stage hypnotists succeed in getting people to make fools of themselves because their volunteers expect to act foolish and, therefore, implicitly accept the demands of the situation. If Keenan tried to coerce the truth out of Drum, Drum would most likely pop out of the trance and become more entrenched and guarded than ever.

Hypnosis, though, could make emotionally laden memories more accessible. At one workshop, Keenan saw a car accident victim, who was unable to remember the crash, go into trance and recall every detail from the way the hood crumpled against the bridge's cement buttress to the sounds, the pain, and the fear at seeing his own blood. This person, however, could only remember those things while in trance. Afterward, the memories were once again blocked as protection against being overwhelmed by images and feelings that were too traumatic to handle–a pure example of unconscious defense mechanisms at work.

A common trait among the men Keenan studied, especially the preening narcissists like Drum, were defenses more formidable than steel and razor wire blocking recall of the traumas that had made them feel especially weak and vulnerable. These men could describe in grisly detail the torture and mutilation born of their hands, yet balk and deny and completely repress any recall of things such as being eight years old and having their face pushed against a rough blanket while being raped. Keenan intended to tear at the seams holding back any potentially overwhelming memories.

Drum's gait became sluggish and he finally plopped heavily into his chair. Moving more slowly than usual, he pulled a fresh pack of Marlboros from his shirt pocket. After tearing off the cellophane and taking out a cigarette, he tossed the pack on the table and tapped the butt end on the mottled top three times before he lit it. His eyes looked sleepy.

"Do you ever wonder where the desire that landed you here came from?" Keenan asked. If he guessed correctly, he was pushing Drum directly toward repressed material; and pushing someone toward things repressed produces considerable anxiety and avoidance. Keenan planned to trip both of these, then offer Drum a means to escape what he most wanted to avoid by going back to an earlier time in his life, a time before the trauma.

"I've already told you," Drum said, his words a bit slurred, "that I took what I wanted because I'm not afraid of my natural desires."

"Yes, you did," Keenan agreed. "But I'm not talking about the decision to take. I want to know where your unique desires came from, the ones you could only satisfy by feeding women strychnine. I want to help you make sense of your life. Finding out where such desires came from is the reason most men want to talk to me."

"Look, I only wanted what everyone wants but is too chickenshit to go after," Drum said, his voice sharper. "That's all there is to it. End of story. You got that?" Without taking his eyes off Keenan, Drum took one hard drag on the cigarette, then another.

"I was just wondering," Keenan said, stretching each word and speaking in a soft rhythm with no inflection, "back when you could play outside and feel sunshine on your cheeks . . . remember how good sunshine felt on your cheeks . . . and arms . . . and soothing and warm on your hands . . . and legs. Back when things were easier and you were seven . . . or six . . . or five . . . or four . . . or three . . . back when you were very young. I was just wondering what it was like when you and your mother lived in Charleston. I want you to remember . . . like you remembered things last night . . . when you were young and lived with your mother . . . back when you were seven . . . or six . . . or five . . . or four." Drum's eyes were half-closed and dreamy looking. "I want you to remember . . . now!" Keenan said with some force.

Speaking in his normal voice, Keenan asked, "What was it like for you back then."

"Like everywhere else. Everybody had it in for us."

"Let's say, you're five or six and someone ticks you off? What would you do?"

Drum looked at the cigarette in his hand, turned it as if studying the other side, then leaned forward and rubbed it out in the ashtray. "As long as I can remember," he said and settled back in his chair, his voice softer and higher pitched, "when someone ticked me off, I'd spend hours imagining all the things I could do to get even."

"Such as?"

Drum picked up the water bottle and took a slow drink. "Mostly stupid things like pushing somebody down or hitting them with a brick or stabbing glass in their eye. I'd think about stupid stuff like that."

"What's some of the first things you actually did?"

Drum thought for a moment. "Okay. There was this kid that lived a couple houses down and he got a new bicycle for his birthday or something, and it ticked me off that he had a bike and I didn't. So this one night, I saw it lying in his backyard and my mom was out. Then when it got real late I sneaked in there and took it. I knew I couldn't keep it 'cause he lived too close, so I got a hammer and smashed it up and then put it back in his yard."

"I see," Keenan said, nodding and smiling. "Did you ever get caught doing things like that?"

Drum shook his head no. "If anyone started asking us about stuff, Mom would get real mad and yell at them. We didn't take shit off anybody."

Keenan smiled and nodded. "It was like that for me growing up, too," he lied, creating another false parallel between them.

Warily, Drum cocked his head and looked at Keenan, then nodded back.

"I bet you did things to you mother, too, didn't you?" Keenan asked.

"No. I was special to her. She told me I was the only one she could count on. And that she was the only one I could count on. We took care of each other. Like her getting mad if someone accused me of something."

"That's good. But I bet you worried about her?"

"Sometimes."

"I worried about my mother when she went out," Keenan said.

"Yeah, me too. And . . . maybe sometimes I did get a little mad. The men she hung out with were no good; they just wanted to use her. She was always saying that there'd never been one man born who was any good. Then she'd tell me that women were worse. And she'd tell me, 'Nobody will ever treat you as good as I do.' I guess she was right."

"What about your father?"

Some of the edge came back into Drum's voice. "What about him?"

"Was he like those other men?"

"Worse. The only good thing about that prick was that he wasn't around much. When he was, he'd come strutting through the door and start ordering me around, saying shit like 'Snap to it, boy,' as if his uniform made him some stud or something. And he'd use Mom like all the other assholes. He was nothing to me, less than nothing. No wonder Mom kept telling me she didn't want me turning out anything like him."

Keenan sat relaxed in his chair, placing himself in Drum's awareness only enough to guide him. "Later, we'll talk more about the men who used your mom. For now, I want you to remember when the ways you thought of getting back at people changed. Let's say you're at the age when you first hurt something that was alive. Tell me about when you began to hurt living things."

Drum sipped his water, then shifted and crooked his right leg over the chair's arm. "We were still in Charleston, living in a house that had a broken-down grape arbor in back. I'd crawl under it, and when the leaves were on it was like being in a teepee—I could see out, but no

one could see me. I'd put stuff in there that I found in the neighborhood, stuff like a bird feeder, grass clippers, kids' toys, I even had a pink
flamingo. Sometimes, when my mom had a man staying over, I'd take
my blanket and sleep out there. It was a good place."

"What happened there to change things?"

"I was coming to that."

Keenan nodded. "Go on."

"There was this fat yellow cat that liked to go under the grapevine
and catch lizards that were usually green but sometimes turned brown.
Anyway, that cat was real unfriendly, wouldn't let me touch her. But
sometimes we'd watch each other. This one morning while I was waiting for my mom to come home, I watched that old cat as she crouched
under some leaves, perfectly still until one of the lizards came to within a few inches and then she jumped. You'll never guess what she did
next. She let it go, let it think it was getting away, then she caught it
again. She'd crippled it enough that it couldn't get away. So she kept
doing it—let it go, catch it, let it go, catch it, until the lizard got too
weak to get away anymore. Then she took it in her mouth and carried
it off. The whole time she played with it, she was so fierce. I knew
exactly how she felt, because that's how I felt. I got really excited, and
I remember that I even got hard.

"So the next time my mom stayed out all night, as soon as it got light
I took a paring knife and a can of tuna and kneeled under the
grapevines with the tuna a few inches in front of my knees and waited
just like that old bitch cat. Even when my knees started aching real
bad, I didn't move, but on the inside I was real excited. And when that
cat came close enough for me to stick her, I didn't know that anything
could feel so good. I didn't get to play with her too long, because I
jabbed the knife in too deep. For a little joke, I left her on our front
steps where my mom would find her when she came home. And do
you know what she said? She said, 'Damn it, Isaac. I don't want to have
to listen to those pricks behind us bitch about this.' So she put the cat
in a plastic bag and that night dropped it in one of the neighbor's trash
cans and made me promise not to tell anybody because she said if I
did, they'd raise hell and try to get money or something out of us. She
said she knew it was an accident, but other people wouldn't believe
me. So I never told anybody, until now."

"Did she do anything else to correct your behavior?"

"She told me not to do it again. But after that, when somebody ticked me off, I'd hunt—cats, dogs, baby birds, frogs, I even found a chicken one time. It always made me feel better. I didn't share any more of my kills with my mom and I was careful not to do it too often because I didn't want people to start watching and make a fuss—that'd make Mom mad. But whenever I'd see an animal in the neighborhood, I knew it had been put there for me and I'd think about what I could do to it that I hadn't done before. I kinda thought I'd outgrow it."

"Did you ever have sex with these animals before or after you killed them?"

"No! That would be nasty. I'd just think about it later and doodle with myself."

"How did you know about doodling with yourself?"

"One of my mom's boyfriends taught me."

"I see. How?"

Drum frowned and firmly shook his head no while staring at his hands.

"That's okay. Were you having fantasies like the ones you had as an adult, the ones you tried to bring to life by abducting those women?"

"No. I didn't start having those until later."

"When did those fantasies start?"

"I don't know; puberty I guess. Can't say," Drum said in a much firmer voice.

"Okay, we'll talk about that later," Keenan superficially conceded, while implanting a suggestion. "You said you didn't share any more kills with your mom. Did you find other ways to share with her? Maybe play jokes on her with your kills?"

Drum cocked his head to one side. "How'd you know?"

"I've talked to guys who have done similar things. What'd you do?" Keenan asked and grinned.

"Well . . . sometimes I'd save a little blood in a mayonnaise jar and then put it down in the toes of her shoes, just a little, not enough to be messy, so she'd be walking around in blood and not know it."

"Any particular shoes that you liked to put blood in?"

"Yeah, her best shoes; the ones she'd wear on dates."

. . .

Keenan uncrossed his legs and leaned forward, resting his elbows on the table. "You said that you and your mother looked after one another, and you told me how she looked after you when someone accused you of something. How did you look after her when men were around?"

Even though he was regressed, thus far Drum had remembered the things Keenan asked as one might remember any past event; these episodes lacked sufficient allure to achieve the vividness of last night's flashbacks. Still, for Drum it felt surprisingly good to tell about these things and have someone smile and nod. Before tonight, everyone seemed too caught up in trying to act better than him or in telling him what he could or could not do. Keenan, though, just sat back and listened without judging; he was not at all like every other tight-assed adult. But now he was asking about the men who had taken advantage of his mother, and for some reason this made Drum mad. "I kept my eye on them, that's about all I could do," Drum said, a hardness coming into his voice.

"Tell me about one particular man and what you did to look after your mom."

Drum shrugged and looked down at his hands lying on his lap. "I don't even remember what any of them looked like."

"If I snap my fingers, you'll have a clear memory," Keenan said and snapped his fingers.

Drum kept watching his hands. Then, his mouth twisted into an angry pout as he remembered using a kitchen chair to climb up onto the counter to check the cabinets.

All I found was a quarter box of cornflakes so I took that down and went back to the refrigerator. Other than catsup, mayonnaise, and mustard, there was a half pack of baloney that had turned a little green around the edge and a jar of pickles. I carried the baloney and cereal into the living room, which was small with a worn and uneven hardwood floor and sparse furnishings. In fact, there was only a TV, a rickety coffee table, and a matching chair and couch that were greenish-white with prints of fancy green leaves that Mom called a French design. The couch had several big stains and a few brown burns from cigarettes; some of them I made while playing around. I sat on the couch and started eat-

ing a piece of baloney and watched the door to Mom's room. The sun had been up for hours, and the house was getting hot and stuffy 'cause the only air conditioner was in Mom's bedroom window. I hoped she would wake up soon, and that the man with her did not hang around. I didn't know which I hated most: Mom staying out all night or bringing a man home.

I had just pulled out a second piece of baloney when the door from Mom's room opened and a blond man in a wrinkled sailor's uniform came out tucking his shirttail inside his pants. As he walked past he said, "See ya, sport," and picked up the box of cornflakes and dipped his hand, eating them dry as he went out the door and took the box with him. I gave him a mean look and wished I was bigger so I could fix that no-good bastard, which was what Mom would probably call him when she got up; after they had gone, Mom always called them no-good bastards.

But that was not what she called them at night. A lot of nights, she'd leave the bedroom door open and I'd stand in the dark living room and listen to them laughing and grunting; and sometimes I'd watch them if they left the lamp beside the bed on.

With the man gone, I got off the couch and went to the bedroom door and wrinkled my nose at the stale stink of booze. The sheets were thrown off and Mom sprawled naked on the bed with one arm over the side and her legs spread. I went and stood beside the bed, but because she would probably wake up soon, I didn't touch her the way I sometimes did if she'd just gone to sleep after drinking a lot. When she did wake up I knew she'd be in a bad mood and would probably stay in her room all day. On the nightstand, in front of a frilly lamp with a baseball-sized bubble midway in its clear glass base, was a bottle about a third full of brown booze and a twenty dollar bill laying beside it.

Mom stirred but didn't open her eyes and said, "Oh, Jesus, fuck." I picked up the booze to take and pour it down the sink. I also grabbed the twenty; that way she was less likely to allow last night's man to come back.

A voice intruded, "What are you thinking about?"

"Huh?" Drum said, and shook off the memory.

"You've been remembering something," Keenan said from across the table. "Probably what I asked you about your mother's men friends. Tell me about it."

Drum's lips pressed together. "They weren't her friends," his voice was deeper, more adult-like. "And I can't remember a one of them because they were nothing to her, or to me. Understand?"

The memory disturbed Drum, and he suddenly felt annoyed by Keenan's questions. "Talking about this childhood stuff is a waste of time."

Keenan decided not to push for more background on Drum's childhood; he knew enough. And this last memory had shaken the trance, leaving Drum agitated and wary. Before Drum completely shook off the trance, Keenan thought he would take a stab at the separation from his mother, not expecting to succeed, but perhaps setting up things for a later assault. "You're right," Keenan said agreeably, "we have spent enough time on those things. So let's get away from Charleston and jump ahead to when you were almost eleven, and you and your mother moved to Columbia. Tell me how things were different after this move."

Drum glared at Keenan. "It was the worst shit hole we ever lived in. We hated it."

"Yes, that was a difficult time, a most difficult time. All that frustration and shame. But you can have all those bad feelings disappear if you tell me why your mother sent you away."

"She didn't send me away," Drum snapped, his eyes glittering with if-looks-could-kill intensity.

"Then why did you go live with your aunt?"

"Because my aunt tricked us by saying she wanted me to come visit for a while and then wouldn't send me back. And why the fuck are you asking about this crap? It doesn't matter, it means nothing." Drum reached for his cigarettes and lit one; a sign that he had escaped back to the present. Without taking his eyes off Keenan, Drum took a long pull on his smoke, then said, "I'm sick of this childhood shit."

"Okay, we can talk about it later, when you're ready for these memories to come back . . . and when they do . . . you will describe them," Keenan said, once again seeming to concede while implanting a suggestion.

"The fuck I will," Drum said and blew a stream of smoke directly at Keenan, now completely out of trance and away from leaking memory portals. "I don't know what kind of mind games you're playing, but I've said all I'm going to say until you get me a deal."

Drum signaled the camera for the COs to escort him to his cell. He felt anxious to get out of here and away from Keenan, though he was not sure why.

30

molting

I

DRUM LAY on his bunk and stared at the ceiling until he heard the footsteps of Keenan and Jenkins pass and grow faint. He was sick of Keenan and his sneaky questions. Pushing himself to his feet, Drum lit a cigarette and began to pace—three steps forward, three steps back; the bars and walls seeming to close in as his enemies pushed him into a smaller and smaller corner. He felt strangled and teetering on madness, much like he had felt when first shunted into death row. And before that he had felt this way when they forced him into the Max Unit at Chatham and hammered him down until getting out of that cage mattered more than proving that they could not beat him.

Through the bars Drum saw a CO stop in front of his cell and, for a moment, thought he was about to get more Seconal, thought he might escape into numbness. Then he noticed the officer's clipboard—standard suicide precautions required that they check him every few minutes at irregular intervals.

"Bring me more Seconal," Drum ordered.

"Next dose isn't scheduled for an hour," the officer replied, made a note, then moved off.

He should have known the stingy, trailer-trash bastards would make him wait, just to mess with him. Little men trying to feel big.

Drum sat on the edge of the bunk and crushed out his smoke, then grabbed the plastic water bottle from off his desk and sipped from the flex-straw. If the bastards had their way, he might never touch a glass container again. Drum slammed the bottle back onto the desk, frustrated with himself for such defeatist thinking. Jerkily, he lit another cigarette and silently cursed Keenan for bringing on this raunchy mood. If Keenan really wanted to know where things started, he should have asked about Korea. Drum could have gotten off on telling him what happened there—well, telling him most of it. Everything had finally come together and, for a while, Korea was probably the happiest time of his life.

Yeah, Korea was definitely good for a while, Drum thought and leaned against the wall. He took a hit off the Marlboro and blew a bluish-gray smoke ring, then shot a smaller ring though the first, something he had not done since his hitch in the army. Smiling, he remembered how he had not at all been scared going off to a foreign land, just like he hadn't been scared going off to basic. It was a new beginning, like shedding a cocoon—an institutional cocoon of layer upon layer of restraint weaved around him that had begun in lockup and not ended until he left the group home. In retrospect, it seemed that he had survived adolescence by burying himself deep inside a husk and existing only as someone who watched life go by and mindlessly did as he was told. Once basic training was behind him, however, there was no one looking over his shoulder every second; it was his first taste of real freedom and all things seemed possible. Brainwashed from growing up in an institution, he believed he would eventually acquire all the things he had seen in movies and on TV—a respected career, an impressive house in the suburbs, a loving and virtuous wife, and obedient kids. He had a chance to become anything he wanted; it was merely a matter of deciding what—a decision he had made while in Korea.

First stationed with the 19th Theater Command at Taegu, Drum started his tour as an MP standing at the main gate and checking IDs and passes. For the first few weeks, he was paired with a corporal a couple of years older who liked to talk and so all Drum had to do was pretend to listen and they got along okay. Quickly, Drum discovered how much he liked being able to tell someone to show his ID or to stand and wait while he took his time looking over a pass, and he especially enjoyed doing this with the Korean women who worked on the base. His partner, though, was a slacker and would say things like "Aw, she comes through here every day, let her go." Drum greatly resented this guy undermining his authority, but things were going so good, enjoying real status for the first time in his life, that he decided to overlook these little affronts, at least at the start.

During this honeymoon period, Drum used his free time to study procedural manuals so that he would know the proper response to any situation. His required paperwork was always complete and detailed. He also frequently volunteered to freeze his ass off at the main gate at two A.M. because some hungover jerk-off claimed he was sick. Six months after arriving in Korea, Drum's exacting work habits earned him a transfer to the 8th Army in Seoul and a step up to off-base MP patrol.

In no time at all, Drum came to see his new patrol duties as nothing more than herding rude and offensive drunks. He ended most patrols bristling because he couldn't do a thing to any of these obnoxious men without being reported. That is, unless he were alone with some mouthy asshole who had passed out, then he might stomp the guy's toes or spear his ribs with an elbow, because drunks were always injuring themselves without knowing why. But he couldn't even do those things very often without raising suspicions—and he had learned while incarcerated in Juvenile Justice the critical importance of not being caught. He had also learned how easy it was to convince yourself that you're too smart to get caught, and then let this thinking lead you to do something sloppy and stupid.

During this time, an even worse rub came when Drum had to stand around while Korean detectives or warrant officers investigated some petty criminal complaint such as theft or some GI slapping a whore. Drum fumed at the way these big shots walked in and began ordering everyone around, including MPs. He began studying forensic and criminal procedural manuals, but not because he intended to stay in service long enough to earn an investigator's rank—he now had too many resentments to extend his current hitch by even one day. Drum studied these manuals because as soon as he was a civilian, he planned to become a cop. The thought of patrolling alone with all that authority seemed perfect. Once he decided upon this career direction, Drum bought himself a pair of mirrored sunglasses to wear when off duty.

Within a couple of months of his transfer to Seoul, things started to slip in even more profound ways. Almost every day, patrol took Drum into the bars and brothels catering to GIs. He regarded Seoul as a modern Sodom and Gomorrah, and came to see all Koreans as lewd and corrupt, especially the women; they had no shame.

Ever since Drum was first locked in Juvenile Justice's Maximum Security Unit, he had had violent sexual fantasies. He didn't know how these fantasies had first formed or where the idea for the particular type of sex that most excited him came from. He didn't think it mattered. Back then, if a social worker or nurse challenged him in any way, he would later masturbate and imagine overpowering the offending woman, forcing total submission and then punishing her with humiliation. Most often, the imagined humiliation involved callous anal assaults because he believed that this was the ultimate way of putting a woman in her place.

These fantasies continued when they transferred him to the group home. There, mingling with delinquent girls in the group home's self-contained school and on its large campus, Drum saw how these girls brazenly flaunted their sex with no bras, bare midriffs, and raunchy talk. Drum's disgust with their whorish behavior turned to hatred when a couple of these girls taunted him about the red and oily eruptions scarring his face. Girls who treated him nice, however, left him confused and anxious, and he deeply distrusted them. One girl, a heavy girl who was homely with coarse hair and early-developed breasts that stretched her worn sweaters, was particularly friendly. She often smiled at Drum and spoke whenever they passed and once handed him a note asking him to meet her after dinner. Of course he didn't meet her, but he began to think of her whenever he masturbated, fantasizing about callous anal assaults that paired sex and violence, violence and sex, again and again and again and again . . . until nothing else excited him.

Over the years, the frequency of masturbating to these violent fantasies rose during stressful periods and eased up when things were going well. Drum thought he would always think about these fantasies but could never actually do what he imagined; like the way men jacked off looking at women in *Playboy* that they knew they could never have. For a while after entering the army, when things had seemed to be going unusually well, the fantasies had stopped, only to return when he was confronted daily with bar sluts.

Well, maybe they had come back a little earlier. After growing up in institutional settings, Drum was curious about women—not delinquents and sluts—but normal, virtuous women. He believed these women would be different in every way from delinquent girls, and thought that virtuous women would excite more normal desires in him. His curiosity had been stroked by watching the Korean women coming on base and smiling demurely whenever he checked their passes. So even before the transfer to Seoul and the provocative bawdiness he saw on patrol, Drum began going to parks and shopping districts to watch women. Sometimes, he'd follow them just to see what they did, how they acted, where they were going, where they lived. After doing this for a few weeks, he began returning at night to the residences of the women living on ground floors or in basement apartments that he found most attractive, and he would then peek through cracks in their blinds and masturbate while watching them. He told himself that he was simply curious and trying to learn, but it was also terribly exciting, though not completely satisfying. He was careful and did not prowl too often—but that changed after his transfer to Seoul.

Before Seoul, Drum rarely went to bars and never to a brothel. Most GI bars were both. And every time he went into one of these pits, he left feeling turned on and angry, choking on contempt for the young GIs he saw making fools of themselves. As a release for these feelings, Drum began prowling whenever he could, even rearranging his schedule and claiming he was sick in order to spend more time following women and looking in their windows. Because he was chronically sleep deprived, his work standards slipped and he often awoke the next day wondering if he was losing his mind by taking such risks. And what most scared him were the growing urges to do far more dangerous things, because the more he peeped, the less satisfied he was.

Finally, Drum returned one night to an apartment that he had surreptitiously visited on several occasions. It was a basement apartment hidden by thick bushes and shared by two Korean girls who worked on the base. One of the girls always left her bedroom blinds up a couple of inches. On this night, Drum waited for an hour after the lights had been turned off, then jimmied the lock with his ID and entered their living room, his heart racing and breathing so hard he thought they might hear him. Standing in the dark, with the only light slipping past the edge of the room's small, high blinds, Drum felt overwhelming excitement and arousal, and began masturbating. Before he could climax, one of the girls coughed and this panicked him and he got the hell out of there. When safely away, he couldn't believe that he had done something so risky, something that could ruin his life and send him to the stockade or some hellhole Korean prison. He vowed to never do anything like that again. For two weeks afterward, he stopped his voyeurism, and even stopped going to parks and shopping districts to watch women. Repeatedly, he told himself that he'd learned his lesson and from now on would keep himself on the straight and narrow with a career and a future.

Yet, he couldn't stop thinking about the drenching excitement he had felt while inside those girls' apartment. Nor could he stop thinking about those young women sleeping in their beds, and his urges rose like a fever. He began to wonder if maybe his real problem was that he had not been bold enough in how he sought to satisfy himself. Then he would think of the consequences of this leap forward, and compensate for his lagging willpower by volunteering for late-night patrol. During his nights off he stayed on base, even if it meant going to the same movie two nights in a row. But whenever he masturbated, which he now did four or five times a day, he always imposed his callous fantasy on the one or both of the two girls in the basement apartment. During these times of strong arousal, Drum berated himself for being cowardly, telling himself that unless he showed a little guts, he'd never have anything.

While vacillating with his inner struggle, Drum's so-called superior ragged him during a quarterly performance review because he did not socialize with other members of his unit and, his so-called-superior claimed, this hurt cohesion. Bristling because the asshole had no right telling him how to spend his free time, Drum went straight from being ragged to the PX and bought duct tape and a Randall hunting knife. While making these purchases he felt relaxed and chatted easily with the clerk, as if someone else had taken over. On the way back to his barracks, he calmed some and realized what he was preparing to do, and again felt scared and thought he should find some foolproof way to occupy himself that evening, something that would prevent him from yielding to his distended urges.

. . .

Still leaning against his cell's wall, Drum opened his eyes, shook his head, and muttered, "Dumb kid." If it wasn't so pathetic, it would be laughable the way that kid had tried to beat back his true nature, he thought, seeing his earlier self, confused and lacking courage, as some-one else entirely. The Drum who existed now would have found a way to fix the stiff-assed lieutenant who gave him such an unfair perform-ance review, and done far more to those girls than that kid intended.

A CO sauntered in front of his cell to record on a clipboard—just to cover their ass, Drum thought and Drum flipped the guy a bird. Unfazed, the CO made his recording and moved off.

Picking up his smokes, Drum knocked one out, then noticed that his flimsy little ashtray was overflowing. Stretching forward, he dumped the butts in the toilet and slammed the handle to flush them. He leaned back against the cement wall but didn't light up. Remembering things that he'd not thought about for years did help pass the time, but he wanted to skip ahead, away from frustrations like that unfair perform-ance review and then being mocked by a woman that very night. He wanted to go forward, to a night when only good things happened, to the night when that same woman dared not mock him at all. He want-ed to remember the night when he had elevated himself into a new being and had first known the intoxication of God-like power.

Yet, when Drum closed his eyes, like a released pause button, he slipped back into the memories that he had just stopped, and saw him-self trapped in the back of a taxi between two members of the hot-shit clique. For some reason, this image caused a little swell of panic, but Drum found himself just as unable to extract himself from the taxi now as he had been on that night, so many years ago.

In the taxi's backseat I was wedged between a guy named Mike and another guy called Davy. Mike reeked of cologne and cocky confidence, sitting with one arm laid across the back of the seat like he owned it. Lights from passing cars played slowly across his face, highlighting prominent cheekbones and a square jaw; he had the all-American good looks of a jock. I despised the casual way that Mike carried himself; talk about conceited; and I despised the way the other jerks in the barracks played up to him. Crowding me on the other side was Davy, a boot-camp thin boy with a bony face, freckles, and a swath of short brown hair above nearly shaved sides. Davy was getting on my nerves by leaning in front of me so that he could see Mike while he chattered nonstop with-out ever really saying anything worth hearing.

"We're going to get you initiated," Davy told me, grinning. "I bet
you're a cherry, ain't you? Huh? Come on, admit it. It's okay to tell us."

"Lay off," Mike told him.

"Sure. Sorry. I was just trying to get to know him."

Mike turned and looked at me, passing car lights catching his half-
smile. "So where you from, Drum, and what do your folks do?" he asked.

I told him what I told everyone. "I'm originally from Texas. My
father's an oil well rigger and my mother teaches school."

Mike nodded and smiled. "Then your old man must be one tough son
of a bitch," he said. "He ever take you out to the oil fields?"

I shrugged. "Sometimes." I thought they were making a fuss over me
like I was a stray dog they'd picked up on the side of the road—and I
resented it.

Mike and Davy composed half of a tight clique of assholes that were
a couple of years older and, like me, lived in the barracks designated for
MP's. Everyone in the clique had little minds and spent their free time in
the shit-hole bars they patrolled—getting drunk and getting laid was all
they cared about, and their whoring disgusted me. Because I felt so much
contempt for them, I kept to myself—just as I had kept to myself while living in the group home, surrounded by lowlife delinquents. When those in
my barracks saw that I wasn't going to let whores make a fool of me, it
made them jealous and they razzed me by calling me the Seoul Virgin.
That's why it surprised me when I returned from the PX carrying a bag
containing duct tape and my new knife, and Mike called out, "Hey
Drum, I see you not on the roster tonight. Want to go out with us?" I was
feeling real scared then because of what I was planning to do to those girls
in the basement apartment, so at the time it seemed as if fate was offering me a chance to save myself. "Sure," I said, "that'd be great."

We were taking the taxi to Sunny's, a bar and brothel run by a little
yellow pimp named Sun something. Everybody called him Sunny.
Sunny's was among the more popular places catering to GIs and had a
reputation for keeping clean women who had regular medical checkups.
Just as cops have places where they congregate, the younger MPs favored
Sunny's because Sunny was shrewd and occasionally offered MPs sexual freebies that he called "specials." That way, on or off duty, the MPs
stopped trouble in his place before it ever got started. From time to time,
patrol had taken me into Sunny's, but I always turned down his offers to

come back for a "special." Though Sunny just shrugged, I knew that he respected me for not allowing myself to be manipulated.

We stepped from the open-doored alcove into Sunny's, and Mike put his arm around my shoulders, guiding us to one of the few available tables near the back, and I wondered who the fuck he thought he was touching me like that. I went along, though, trying to fit in and prove that my so-called superior was wrong. But this shit-hole bar felt all wrong; it made me tense. The air was thick with smoke and the smell of spilt beer, and the room was a roiling sea of glassy-eyed nineteen-year-olds, gesturing, laughing, wobbling pathetically to and from the bathroom. A jukebox could scarcely be heard above their boisterous voices.

We settled in a corner at a table with a black laminated top and red padded metal chairs. Glowing on every wall were American beer signs— Bud, Coors, Miller, Busch, and even Pabst Blue Ribbon. In fact, everything about the bar seemed American, except the people working there.

A squat and wrinkled Korean woman with toothless gums came to our table and asked, "What want?" This old hag was typical of the waitresses, but there were also a dozen or so attractive bargirls, most with eye shadow thicker than their see-through blouses, moving through the room and hustling the roaring GIs to buy them watered-down champagne at four-star prices. Their presence also kept all the guys acutely aware of what could be had in the cribs in back of the bar.

Along both sides of the alley behind Sunny's stood two-story buildings, each containing about twenty small cubicles that the Koreans called apartments. You could reach them by going out Sunny's back door or directly from the alley. I often passed these apartments on patrol; in fact, I went there a lot, walking along and looking though the opened curtains that signaled the occupant's availability. But I never found this particularly enjoyable because the women inside brazenly looked back.

Rather than order beer, Mike told the waitress we wanted set-ups for tequila shooters and paid for a whole bottle. "We're going to celebrate tonight," he said, smiling and slapping me on the shoulder.

"Let's go get some women first," Davy suggested, raising his voice to be heard over the general melee. "Then we can come back and drink all night."

"Go on, if you want," Mike said, as if he didn't care. "Drum and I are going to get primed first. Right Drum?"

"Yeah, sure," I agreed, not intending to do either. The oozing sexuality of the bargirls had me thinking of those two young women in the basement apartment, decent and clean girls. Maybe after having a drink or two, I would leave and go my own way.

"Well, I'll get primed too," Davy conceded.

It intrigued me the way Mike controlled Davy by not seeming to care what he did, and how this made Davy hungry for Mike's approval, which Mike only gave in dribs and drabs. As for myself, I had already figured out that Davy was nothing but a bootlick who didn't matter and decided not to waste any more energy listening to his irritating chatter. Mike, though, I had reason to watch.

One night on foot patrol, while passing a muddy alley, I saw Mike facing a couple of drunken soldiers that he had backed against a wall. Mike stood with his feet planted wide and tapped his baton soundly against his palm, and even though I could barely see his profile I could tell he was smiling. As soon as the trapped men saw me, they pointed to me and when Mike glanced my way his expression changed to one of disappointment. Stepping around a mud puddle, Mike ordered the two men to come stand directly in front of him, which put them ankle deep in muck. He checked their IDs, then told them to beat it. "Just getting their attention," he said as he walked past, scarcely glancing at me. I sensed something in Mike that was kindred, but never gave it much thought, until now, sitting here beside him in Sunny's. I leaned back in my chair and affected just as much casualness as Mike, determined not to let him control me.

The stubby waitress deposited a bottle, three tall shot glasses, lime slices, and a red and white box of Korean table salt. Mike filled the glasses, then told me to watch. He poured salt onto the back of his hand between the knuckles of his index finger and thumb, then raised the shot glass. "Salute," he said, and tossed the salt in his mouth, then threw back his head, emptying the glass before banging it down and sucking on a slice of lime. This done, Mike opened his mouth and made a loud, "Ahh." He looked at me, his eyes watery. "Now you try it."

I did just as Mike had demonstrated, right down to slapping my empty glass on the table. The tequila burned and I had a retching feeling from my first taste of alcohol other than an occasional beer.

Mike promptly refilled our glasses, even before Davy took his turn. We downed the second round and Mike poured a third, and with each round I came closer to retching.

"Let's give it a few minutes to catch up," Mike told me, smiling and looking amused, "then we'll do a couple more."

"How'd you like it?" Davy asked. "I bet you never done tequila before, huh?"

It bugged me the way Davy grinned; I thought the skinny prick might be laughing at me and decided to completely ignore him.

"Hey," Davy said, tapping my upper arm with the back of his fingers, "I'm talking to you."

Real cool and casual, the way Mike might do it, I stared at Davy and said, "So what." It felt good putting that little pissant in his place. In fact, I felt pretty good in general, warm with a sense of well-being and confidence.

Davy screwed up his face, which had turned red and sweaty. "All right, smart-ass," he said. "If you're so tough, why don't you tell me why we never see you in bars? Huh? Where do you go at night?"

"Give it a rest," Mike told Davy. "We need to allow Drum, here, time to get to know us before we . . . start asking personal questions."

I felt grateful for the way Mike seemed to be looking after me. Yet, feeling as confident as I was, I didn't need anybody looking after me; I felt as though I could handle anything and wasn't about to take shit off anyone, especially a little brown-nose like Davy. I thought it strange that I had avoided alcohol all my life and, for some unknown reason, had once gotten royally pissed when I accidentally came upon a group of sluts passing around a bottle behind the group home's gym. Maybe I'd been mistaken in avoiding booze all these years because this wasn't so bad. And it wasn't so bad hanging out with Mike. I decided he was being so smug because Davy was such a kiss-ass. I felt special the way Mike obviously preferred me over Davy.

I enjoyed these feelings while Mike and Davy gossiped about guys in our unit, something I didn't care a thing about. I looked around and noticed one of the bargirls weaving between tables, smiling at the young soldiers, and moving in our direction. I could see the shadow of her pubic hairs though her sheer white dress and it got me hard. I guess I kept staring at that dark patch because she kept coming our way until she stopped right in front of me and when I looked up, she was smiling at me. Then, this slut, this whore, laid her filthy hand on my shoulder and said, "Join you for drink?" I guess she saw from my expression that she couldn't treat me like a fool because she stopped smiling and jerked her hand away, then moved off.

"Buddy, you'll do better if you smile at them," Mike said, having watched us. "I think it's about time for a trip out back." He refilled the shot glasses and said, "Salute." We clinked glasses and simultaneously downed the tequila. Mike's face was flushed, his eyes wet and shiny. "One more," he said, "then we go get some pussy."

I shook my head. "I don't think I want to do that."

"Salute," Mike said, again touching glasses with me, but winking at Davy.

The glasses smacked on the table and Mike leaned closer, something in his expression putting me on edge. "So how come you don't want any snatch?"

"I only want clean women, decent women, not these tramps," I explained and swept my hand to indicate all the bargirls.

Still leaning close, Mike said, "If it's because you've never been with a woman, just admit it and we'll take care of that problem tonight."

I felt sudden anger at being pressed, and said, "I told you I only want clean women. Not sluts."

Davy, smirking now, said loud enough for the surrounding tables to hear, "Could be you're queer, like everybody thinks you are. Is that it, Drum? You a queer?" He almost shouted this last question.

Hissing through clenched teeth, I said, "I told you I only want clean women."

I expected Mike to tell Davy to lay off. Instead, Mike shook his head and clamped a strong hand on my shoulder. "That's exactly the kind of thing a queer would say," Mike said, his eyes glistening. "You see, we've had a problem with you for a while because you're a strange bird, Drum, and the whole unit's been trying to figure out what's strange about you. Maybe it's from growing up in some stinking group home—I've seen your file; Texas oil rigger, my ass! But maybe you're strange in a different way. And that makes all the guys uncomfortable going to sleep with you still up and moving about." Mike's face was red and he put a finger in my face. "So, buddy, you have to prove yourself tonight—one way or the other."

I felt like getting a gun and blowing their fucking heads off. And if I were armed, I would have killed them both right then. I did have extra martial arts training, so even though Mike had me by a couple inches and outweighed me I thought that I could take the son of a bitch, make him apologize and promise to never again doubt my manhood. But I didn't do any of those things; I didn't even tell him to fuck off. At the time it seemed like the only thing that mattered was putting an end to their insulting accusations, and that later I could find a way to get even. My teeth still clenched, I said, "All right. Let's do it."

We stood and Mike put his arm around my shoulder, rough and controlling and pushed me unsteadily toward where Sunny sat at the bar. On the way, Mike said in my ear, "Time to become a man. You might even like it. But I'm still going to have doubts because you're such a chickenshit coward."

I could feel my jaws grinding. I wanted to fix that son of a bitch so bad, if only I could think more clearly.

Weaving slightly, we stopped beside where Sunny sat, wearing his usual tan pants and jacket with an open-collar floral shirt. "Drum here wants a 'special,' or I'll pay if you want." Mike said.

Lean and small, with dark strands of hair swept across his balding head, Sunny's expression never changed as he studied me for a moment. "I've fresh girl just in from the county who treat you nice," he said, finally.

I couldn't stand the thought of some innocent young girl. "I want someone older."

"Okay, go room five. She treat you right," Sunny said and wrote something in Korean on a piece of paper and slid it toward me. "Give to her."

Mike's arm stayed tightly around my shoulder as we walked unsteadily out the rear exit and to room number five, a ground-floor unit. Mike knocked, then he and Davy retreated to the edge of the building, weaving and watching; Davy laughing and smirking; Mike with his cruel smile. I hated them, wanted them dead or worse, and thought of the knife stored in my footlocker and that they now had a real reason to worry about falling asleep.

The door opened and a young Korean woman looked out. "Hi, Joe. Come in," she said and pushed the door further open. Her hair was parted on one side and fell well below her shoulders and she was younger than I had asked for and a lot smaller than I thought she'd be. I didn't feel any attraction and would have left except for the snickering assholes watching at the corner. She again gestured for me to come in and smiled, but even when she smiled her mouth looked sour and unhappy, and her eyes remained dull and lifeless, a sharp contrast with the festive blue design of her silken robe.

I thrust the note at her and heard snickers from the two assholes, so I brushed past her into the room, careful not to touch her. That's when I saw that she had a kid. A crib was pushed inside a small cubby and a kid with dark hair shooting straight out from his head stood holding the crib-rail and staring at me with large dark eyes. This kid looked like he was between a year and a year and a half old; I wasn't sure, though, because I don't know jack-shit about kids. The young woman finished reading the note, then crossed the small room and cooed something in Korean to the kid before closing a curtain over the cubby. But that kid could hear everything. What kind of worthless slut would treat a kid that way? She disgusted me.

Wobbly and a little sick from the booze, I felt confused and over-whelmed when she came at me and placed her hand on my chest. "What you like?" she asked. I didn't answer, so she stuck the tips of her fingers into the top of my pants and tried to pull me toward the small bed with its rumpled sheets that looked filthy. I stiffened and resisted her tugs. This was not at all how I wanted it to be. I wanted to be the aggressor. I wanted her to be softer and do everything I told her, but only the things I told her. But I figured this was how whores did it. So I stood motionless with my fists clenched as she stopped trying to pull me into the bed and, instead, unbuckled my belt and slid down my zipper. She kneeled and slipped my pants and underwear off my hips then ran her hand softly across my stomach. She worked her hand lower, touching me, and I drew in a hissing breath. She looked up, smiled her unhappy smile, and said, "Relax, Joe. It okay. I help." Then she took me into her filthy mouth and all I could think about was that kid, listening.

And she didn't do anything right, couldn't even get me up, so after less than a minute I grabbed her shoulders and pushed her back. Still kneel-ing, she smiled up at me. "That okay, Joe. You okay guy. No hurry." I knew that she was making fun of me, mocking me. She stood, undid her robe, let it fall behind her. Small and tight-nippled with not much pubic hair, she was more a little girl than woman, like the delinquent sluts that had made fun of me. Pointing to the bed, she said, "Lay down, be more relax." Then she came at me again, this time trying to grab my wrist, and I hit her with my fist, spinning her and knocking her onto the bed face-down. I moved up behind her and grabbed the hair on the back of her head and pushed her face into the blanket and yelled, "You filthy whore." Her ass was rubbing against me, my pants still down, and I cold feel her legs pumping against the sheets beneath mine, and I became hard and took her in the way that I most wanted to take a woman.

At first, she resisted and the tightness of her muscles increased my excitement. After a few moments, though, she just lay beneath me sobbing until I finished, which didn't take long because I was so excited.

Once I climaxed, I felt confused, as if the booze had just hit me, and not knowing what to do stood looking down at her as she cried, sobbing like a child and begging me not to hurt her anymore. I told her to shut up and not say another word. The side of her face was red—she was going to bruise—and I had investigated enough dumb jerks knocking around whores to know that Sunny would report me. In a panic, I pulled up my pants. "If you say anything about this, I'll come back and get you," I warned; it was all I could think of saying. Then I ran from the room, the alley, the bar, the district. I felt very drunk and wobbly, and walked around for over an hour to sober up. As my head cleared, I realized that I'd fucked up, that Sunny was extremely protective of his merchandise. If those pricks hadn't fed me so much booze, I would have been thinking clearly and gone straight to Sunny and squared things by paying for the damage. Too late, now.

And just as I feared, ranking MPs were waiting on me at the main gate.

. . .

Drum opened his eyes and breathed in sharply. His throat felt dry and his shirt damp with sweat despite the coolness of CB2's great cavern. His hand trembled as he reached for his cigarettes. These things he had just remembered . . . that's not the way they happened. He had confidently walked into that whore's room and told her what he wanted, and she had sassed him and told him to go to hell—that's why he hit her, to put her in her place. That's how it happened, really.

Yet, tonight's memory seemed more vivid than he'd ever recalled this incident before.

Rising from his bunk, Drum began to pace. Hell, why think about that first time? It was so . . . incomplete. Instead, he should make himself feel better by remembering how he had outsmarted everyone by claiming that after sex he had caught the little sleaze stealing his wallet and they had struggled and that he only hit her after she pulled a knife. And the anal sex? He claimed he'd paid her for it, arguing that you can't rape a whore who has already made a deal for sex. It came down to his word against hers, with his unit conducting the investigation; the charges were deemed unsubstantiated.

So what, if his future with the army was over. And so what, that they even put him back on gate duty—big fucking deal. None of that mattered, for every time he thought of the little Korean slut pinned and struggling beneath him, he felt a chest-pounding surge of power that was primal and addictive. He now knew that he could have that kind of satisfaction over and over, as long as he was careful enough to never again get caught. Nothing else now mattered. And with nothing else mattering, Drum found all the courage he needed.

After that night, there was but one more step to be taken. Over the years, whenever he remembered going back to that little whore's room, he remembered doing it simply because things with her were incomplete. Now, unable to shake the last few minutes of remembering, unable to truly convince himself that these were false memories, Drum recalled the little Korean slut trying to humiliate him by lying and claiming that he became angry when he couldn't function sexually. Somehow, this had gotten out and Davy embarrassed him by braying in front of others in the barracks that Drum couldn't handle his booze or his women.

Drum stopped pacing, took a hard drag on his smoke, then flipped it into the cell's commode. He put both hands on the back wall to brace himself and stared at the wall's blankness. What the hell did it matter why he returned to her apartment. That decision had changed him, and whatever weaknesses he had before were shed because from the moment he decided that he could kill anyone at any time, he set himself above all the rest of humanity, an entirely new breed. From that moment on, he made his own rules and enjoyed a freedom and power that removed him from all the petty concerns and games of the small-minded. No one's opinion could touch him. So what if his former self had been a little shaky? He had been reborn.

A voice behind Drum called, "Drum, your meds." Turning, he saw a CO pushing a tray with a little cup on it through the slot in the bars. Lurching forward, Drum seized the cup, yet he hesitated before drinking its contents. Zonked on meds, he could completely lose himself in a memory worth recalling, and could probably go as deep as he had yesterday. Maybe he would relive the Monday night he had stalked the alley outside that little prostitute's cubicle, and then at zero-four-hundred hours jimmied her lock and entered wearing gloves and carrying duct tape, a rubber, and his new knife. Maybe he could feel again the incredible excitement as he strangled that tiny woman while anally raping her; it was everything he had hoped it would be—she struggled ferociously—except that it was over too quickly.

And after recalling all this, maybe he could unwind by tapping the smugness he had felt as he once again outsmarted all the investigators. Sure, he was suspect number one right from the get-go. But they had no prints, no semen, he had shaved his pubic hair before the assault, and he was never charged. Two weeks after the prostitute's murder, they transferred him to Germany with nothing except the unsubstantiated first complaint on his record. Knowing that someone had probably snitched to his next duty commander, Drum outsmarted them again by refraining from any further assaults until after he left the army—all the while studying forensic manuals.

Yeah, maybe with the meds he could relive all those highs, right up to the night, while working hospital security in Wiesbaden, that he had helped the medics carry in a stupid GI who'd gotten a Dear John letter and tried to kill himself by taking rat poison. As the guy bent double with spasms, Drum had imagined what a woman would look like doing that, and thought that fate had blessed him.

Drum touched the paper cup to his lips, anticipating all the powerful and worthwhile things that he might relive. But his hand froze and trembled; he could not make himself take the meds. Suddenly, he threw the paper cup toward the commode, missing and splattering the orange liquid on the floor. Infuriated, he lay on his bunk facing the wall. He could not risk zoning out because of the way these unnerving flashbacks kept happening; it was as if his mind was leaking . . . and he sensed something terrifying yet lurking inside.

31

porter

I

ON WEDNESDAY morning, Joe carried his newspaper to his patio, his stomach churning at what the paper might say about him. A banner headline read: "DRUM CLAIMS APPEALS BEING SABOTAGED." Beneath it, the subheading said: "Condemned Killer Accuses Wife of Victim and SLED Agent of Lying." Reading slowly and carefully, his mouth silently forming each word, Joe read Drum's outlandish claims and official rebuttals, all saying that Drum was a desperate liar.

Near the end of the article, Joe found the part about himself, and it wasn't too bad. It said that Joe's name had briefly surfaced during the investigation because, other than law enforcement and attorneys, Joe was Drum's only visitor. It then said that Joe had voluntarily submitted for DNA testing and had been conclusively ruled out. Welch did not mention that Joe had smuggled the threat-making letter. (The threat was described in a separate feature with its own heading.) Overall, Welch portrayed Joe in a good light by explaining that Joe had contacted Drum because he had once been Drum's Big Brother. "Now, Reverend Cameron has once again entered Drum's life as his personal pastor," Welch concluded the article, "with the hope of bringing some comfort in the final days to a man who has treated others so cruelly."

Joe liked this ending. He thought Welch had caught the essence of his Christian faith. Maybe after reading this Kemper would recognize Joe as a man of deep faith and welcome him back. Maybe he would even give Joe expanded duties. Joe felt guarded optimism that everything would, at last, work out fine.

Yesterday afternoon, the patrol car parked in front of his house had pulled away and he called the Jeffcoat Landing Sheriff's Department and found that the first DNA panels produced a negative match. Even with this good news, though, Joe knew that he needed to tell his pastor, Mark Kemper, about everything that had happened before he heard about it on the news. Filled with dread, Joe had put on slacks and a jacket but no tie, and drove to the church.

Once he arrived there, Joe ambled down the long hall to Kemper's office, passing the high arched windows with his head down and his eyes fixed on the royal blue carpet. The door to Kemper's office stood open and Mark sat at his large cherry desk, rubbing his chin and studying what looked like a draft of Sunday's sermon. As usual, no stacks of files or loose papers lay on Kemper's orderly desk. In fact, Joe could never remember seeing as much as a phone message stuck in the green blotter's edge. Kemper kept himself much the same way. His light-brown hair always had a severe part and his white button-down oxfords looked impervious to wrinkles. Though Kemper was not a small man, his leanness made him seem so compared to most other Baptist ministers that Joe knew. Most ministers, Joe thought, also showed a little more jovial gusto at church socials than Kemper seemed to allow himself. Maybe it had something to with Kemper eating Tums like candy when he thought that no one was watching.

Joe reached in and tapped lightly on the door. Kemper glanced up. "One second, Joe." Using red ink, Kemper neatly crossed out a half-line on the draft and wrote two words above it. Finished, he aligned the sheets perfectly and lay the copy to the side of the blotter and asked, "What's up?" Then noticing Joe's flushed face, added, "You don't look well. Maybe you should go back home."

Joe sat in one of the high-backed, red-leather chairs and looked down at his clasped hands. Barely audible, he said, "Uhm . . . I've taken on a personal ministry that may be a problem for our church."

"You're not . . ." Kemper hesitated, choosing his words carefully, " . . . getting us into a situation like the one last February, are you?"

Kemper referred to the Sunday when seven men, presumably Mexican migrants brought in for spring planting, came unannounced for church services. Jeffcoat Landing Baptist Church was a meat and potatoes congregation, for the most part staunchly aligned with the moral majority's vision for America, and affluent enough that their Sunday best came from the area's finer shops. To many of those present, the visitors, dressed in clean but worn plaid shirts and dungarees, looked as unsavory as a police lineup, and tense whispers had pulsed though the chapel even as Kemper delivered his sermon.

The following week, Kemper had been inundated with parishioners' phone calls and visits, all expressing concern, advice, or demands to know how he planned to deal with "those outsiders." Most were tactful or oblique, such as asking if those men might be better served by a Catholic church. Some were not so polished, like Adeline Cornish. She was a matron of the church generally known to be among the first to visit those in the hospital or show up with a pot of soup when death visited a family. She had cornered Joe after Wednesday night's services and warned, "The only reason those men came to our church was to steal from the offering. So, if they come back, don't you dare pass the plate down the row where they're sitting."

Fortunately, "those men" did not return. For several weeks afterward, Joe thought Kemper's sermons skirted topics of brotherly love, perhaps out of concern for being mistakenly regarded as snide.

"It's nothing like that situation," Joe explained to Kemper. "I'm only ministering to one person. But ah . . . but ah . . . he's in prison,"

Tilting his head to one side and leaning forward, Kemper asked, "How do you know someone in prison?"

Joe looked down at his white knuckles. "When I was a student, I was briefly his Big Brother."

"I see," Kemper said and, placing the tips of his fingers together, rested his chin atop them. "He's not planning to settle in this community when he gets out, is he?"

"Ah, no . . . he, ah . . . won't be getting out."

"I see," Kemper said slowly. "And what, may I ask, is he in for?"

"Murder."

"All right, Joe, tell me everything I need to know."

His throat dry, his voice barely louder than a whisper, Joe said, "He's Isaac Drum."

"You know Isaac Drum?"

Joe nodded. "And he's claimed that he knows something about the

Wilmet boy's murder, so everyone who has seen Drum is being questioned," Joe said, suddenly feeling hot and sweaty.

Kemper blew a silent whistle, then leaned forward. "Are you telling me that you're a suspect in Gary Wilmet's murder?"

"Ah, no. I've been ruled out. They just wanted to know if Drum mentioned anyone."

Kemper again put his fingertips together and rested his mouth against them. It seemed to Joe that Kemper sat this way for a long time, looking at Joe the way his father used to look at him. Like the time Joe was in the library and someone dented the fender of his father's new Mercury. When Joe told his father, his father gave him that look and accused Joe of being too damn stupid to even tell a good lie. His father was always pointing out the stupid or inept things Joe did. When Kemper finally spoke, Joe thought he sounded a little like his father used to.

"Obviously, Joe, you cannot be at the church, especially around the children, until this is completely cleared up."

"But I have been cleared," Joe said. "And you've never had a complaint about me."

"Joe, until this is completely resolved you could bring a lot of negative attention to this church. Also Joe, consider . . . some of that man's victims lived in our community. We may even have distant family of victims among our parishioners. So some in our congregation may take exception to your being involved with him. I have to consider that, Joe, because as you know, the congregation is the final word in our church. Therefore, I am formally asking you to end your involvement with that man, Drum. Don't you agree that's best?"

"Uh, I don't plan to see him again."

"Good. That may make a difference. I'll call you when it's . . . appropriate for you to return. And, Joe, when you got involved in all this, what were you thinking?"

. . .

Joe lay the newspaper atop his patio table and looked toward his house. Surely, Kemper would have read the paper by now. Joe pushed himself from his lounge chair and went inside to call Kemper and find out if he had had any change of heart.

The answering machine's message light blinked. Joe thought it was probably more reporters, but then it could be Kemper, calling after he read the newspaper. Joe hit the play button and listened through five reporters' messages and one from Adeline Cornish. Mrs. Cornish sounded upset and Joe worried that something may have happened to her husband, Bud, who had a bad heart. Promptly, he dialed her number. "Mrs. Cornish, this is Joseph Cameron. You called a little earlier?"

"I certainly did. I want to know why you've turned your back on our church by getting involved with . . . with such an evil man?"

Caught off guard, Joe stammered, "I, ah, just wanted to give him a chance to, ah, know God's love and, ah, at redemption."

"Do you mean to tell me that you think that monster can be saved?"

"I, ah, don't know. Maybe."

"Well, I've never heard such an absurd thing in my life. You're saying that even though I've spent my whole life living in accordance with God's will, that in heaven I might have to sit before God beside that . . . that sex fiend. Do you actually want him to be among the chosen few who get into heaven, because you know as well as I do that only so many will be selected? So who's place would you have him take? Mine? My mother's? My children's? Maybe you should give him your place, that's what I think. And, Mr. Cameron, you can rest assured that your lurid interests will be seriously considered at our next review of pastor performance. And I don't think I'll be the only one with concerns. In fact, I've already talked with Reverend Kemper and he took what I had to say quite seriously. Goodbye. I have more calls to make," she said and hung up.

Stunned, Joe sat with the receiver in his hand. He had always looked after his parishioners. He cared for them, and thought they cared for him. He needed for them to care for him. Tears formed in Joe's eyes.

Mrs. Cornish's threat was not a trifling one. Southern Baptist ministers serve at the pleasure of their congregation, and all congregations hold periodic reviews of pastor performance. His church did so on a twice-yearly basis. If a congregation became displeased, they could release a pastor for reassignment by the Baptist Foundation, the church's central administrative organization. Once released, a pastor's future employment depended upon another church accepting him — but if others shared Mrs. Cornish's attitudes, Joe would be a pariah.

Joe put the receiver back into its cradle. He felt as if he were a distant observer of his life. He had felt this way once before when he was a teenager. On a warm Friday night in early spring, he had gone out with three friends. Young, they were inebriated only with the night's possibilities. Joe drove his father's big Mercury—thanks to unusually strong intervention by his mother. The powerful engine pushed Joe's buoyant mood higher, until hedges, picket fences, and mailboxes blurred past as the car seemed to float along a rolling country road. For a little while, the car's power was his and all things seemed possible. Then, and he never knew how it happened, a swerve, a fishtail, and the car plunged through a grassy field, completely beyond his control. Strange, but as the car approached a utility pole with unnatural slowness, Joe felt no fear, no panic, no emotions; he became a spectator of his own life. He heard no sounds as the car split the pole. This silence lasted for a moment after the accident, then time again claimed Joe with noise, confusion, and anxiety. By God's grace, no one was hurt.

Joe had pushed too far and not been able to hold it on the road. It was the story of his life, his motto, his fate. Joe's father knew he couldn't handle the big Merc, and Joe had proven him right for the umpteenth time. His father had yelled like a sideshow barker about how Joe was too stupid to even drive a car, and how he was such an embarrassment, and how he would never be able to make a man out of Joe. Afterward, Joe was certain that his father would not let him use his new car, so Joe never asked.

It was the same thing now. Joe had attempted to stand among men and failed at every turn. The only option left was to crawl on his hands and knees to Kemper and other church leaders and beg to be allowed to once again take his place as the porter for men who make a difference. "Yes, sir." "No, sir." "Right away, sir."

Maybe in time, the resentment in his eyes would fade.

32

rode hard and put away wet

I

ONE OF the nation's oldest cities, Charleston's public face is aristocratic grandeur. Beneath the fine silk surface, however, are all the rough-hewn hustlers, toughs, and dealers in human wants that enliven port cities with a rich decadent heart. When the naval base left Charleston, a part of that fabric died. Those with smarts or grit loaded up their vans, Mercedeses, or battered Oldsmobiles to follow the money. Left behind, like so much human detritus, were many already on the fringes who lacked the resources or perhaps some rudimentary pioneer initiative to take risks and seek a better place.

Near the abandoned ports of North Charleston, Keenan, in his rented Regal, crept through a neighborhood of abject poverty. He was having difficulty finding Hebron Street because many street signs were torn down or badly bent.

On his second pass, Keenan determined that a sign bent at a ninety-degree angle read Hebron Street. He turned into a dead-end street where decay marked every house. The mesh of most screen doors was stretched or torn. In many of the small houses cardboard replaced at least one windowpane. Rusting cars that looked one jump-start away from a salvage heap dotted the curb. And two children not old enough to go to school played unsupervised in the middle of a street that otherwise looked as though it had not yet awakened.

With so many house numbers missing, Keenan counted and stopped in front of the fifth house on the left. It was a small clapboard house with no screen door, badly peeling white paint, and a closet-sized door stoop.

Before getting out of his car, Keenan breathed in slowly and deeply.

He was seething anger at the thought of how gleefully the media was wringing every ounce of sensation from Drum's outlandish claims, and hawking the bull's-eye that Drum had drawn on Zack.

Perhaps the bulk of Keenan's frustration, however, arose from the sheer desperation of the plan that he was about to attempt. If he could, indeed, locate Rebekah Drum this morning, Keenan intended to take her back to Columbia and deposit her in the Warden's office or some other suitable place while he met with Drum. In exchange for admitting that he had lied about the threat, Drum could see his mother. Of course, that would probably not be a sufficient enticement for Drum to abandon his only chance at avoiding execution. So Keenan would also inform Drum that unless he got the absolute truth from him, his mother would be told that Drum refused to see her and then taken back to Charleston. This threat could rattle Drum if he thought his mother might become angry enough to openly reject him, which would kick straight into the teeth of Drum's rigid self-deceptions about his mother being the only person who had every truly cared for him. How much was holding on to such a core illusion worth? Keenan was betting life itself. Admittedly, this was a long shot, but so far it was the best plan he had devised. At least it would likely cause Drum some pain, make him pay a little. At least, Keenan could do that.

In three steps, Keenan crossed the cracked sidewalk to the house. He rapped solidly on the door, pleading under his breath, "Please, Rebekah Drum still be here."

No one answered and he knocked a second time. A few moments later, the door opened six inches and a woman peered out. Long strands of brown hair fell across a face that appeared too wrinkled to be a forty-five-year-old woman. Her face was somewhat rounded, her skin rough, and mascara had smeared around her blue eyes. "Yeah?" she demanded. Her breath smelled of stale booze.

"My name is John Keenan. I'd like to talk with Rebekah Drum."

"It's too early. Come back later, okay, sugar?"

She started to close the door and Keenan pushed one hand against it while taking out his shield with the other. "I'm with the FBI. Are you Rebekah Drum?" He studied the worn face and now thought he saw a resemblance to the file photograph of Drum's mother.

"I ain't done anything," she said.

"No you haven't. I need your help to solve a case."

"Well, come back later, all right?"

"I've driven two hours to get here. I'm hoping you can help me with your son."

She pushed strands of hair from her face, then opened the door wider and looked over Keenan while clutching together the top of a worn pink housecoat. "What's this really about?" she asked.

"Your son claims to know the identity of a child killer. He doesn't trust police, but maybe with your help I can get him to tell me the killer's name."

"We've fallen out of contact," she said. "I can't help you."

"When was the last time you heard from him?" Keenan asked, buying time to find some way to entice cooperation.

Rebekah Drum shrugged. "He wrote me once and told me he'd been in the army, but that was years ago. But I remember that it was around Mother's Day because he sent me a necklace with some kind of fish on it that had a real diamond for its eye. It got here late, but it showed that he turned out good. But that's the last I heard from him, so I can't help you," Rebekah Drum said, and once again moved to close the door.

Keenan kept his hand on the door. The pendant she described matched the one that Alicia Owens had worn on the night of her abduction. Many killers gave victim's jewelry to the women in their lives; it was a subtle form of deception and degradation. "That pendant sounds beautiful," he said and smiled. "May I see it?"

"Honey, I lost that thing years ago. Someone must have taken it. Look, I can't help you, okay."

Close to losing her, Keenan tried a tactic he would rather not use. Rebekah Drum's sister had described her as man-crazy. Keenan put his hand high on the doorframe, leaned forward a little and said, "I bet that pendant looked great on you. At least let me come in and tell you how you can help me." Keenan smiled.

Still she wavered. "I don't know."

"I'll pay you twenty dollars to talk to me for ten minutes," Keenan said.

A half-smile, not that different from her son's smile, formed on Rebekah Drum's lips. "All right," she said. "But you pay first."

Keenan opened his wallet and took his time, allowing Rebekah Drum to see the hundreds and twenties that he always carried when traveling. She stuffed the twenty into the pocket of her housecoat, then smiled and pushed the door open. "Do come in. And how about if I fix us something to drink?"

"I hope you will help me, Mrs. Drum. If it wasn't important, I wouldn't bother you," he said as he went inside and she pushed the door shut.

"Call me Becky." She slipped her hand under Keenan's arm and guided him toward a boxy couch with a floral-print throw cover that was faded and marred by several brown stains. Pieces of nacho chips littered the hardwood floor around a flimsy coffee table on which sat an overfilled ashtray and a couple of glasses. "I probably shouldn't tell you this," she said, suddenly adopting an exaggerated southern belle accent, "but I have a special thing for big men. Should I be telling you that?"

"If it's all the same, I'm going to sit in the chair," Keenan said, forcing a smile as he gently disentangled himself. "I prefer to face people while . . . we talk."

"Any way you want it, sugar."

Keenan sat and she put her hands on the chair's flat arm and leaned toward him. Her housecoat fell open, exposing full breasts that had dark, taut nipples and, despite stretch lines, looked decades younger than her face. Beneath the heavy aroma of last night's alcohol, Keenan smelled her musky body odor.

"Not many decent men dressed in such nice suits come to see me. So you let me know if there's anything you'd like," she said and brought her face to within inches of Keenan's, which caused him to look up from her breasts. Smiling wryly, Rebekah Drum casually closed her housecoat as if she had caught him sneaking a naughty peek.

"I'd like some coffee, if you have any," Keenan said, tactfully trying to get her away from him.

Instead of moving, she whispered, "Cream? Sugar?"

"Black, please," he answered and frowned.

Still, she did not move and, reflexively, Keenan slid down a little in his seat. This brought a gloating smile to her face. She then stood and made a display of tightening her housecoat. "Be back in a sec," she said and languidly left the room.

Keenan wondered if he had gotten himself inside by opening a Pandora's box, both from the kind of attention she was showing and his reaction to it. He had been celibate for a long time, but now had the stirring of an erection. Shamed by his arousal, Keenan shook his head, though mental images of her breasts lingered, and so did his arousal. He forced himself to think strategically. He needed to backpedal to a workable distance without overtly rejecting her—he did not believe Rebekah Drum would take rejection well. In case things did turn sour, Keenan wanted to protect himself against possible retribution from messy false allegations, so he placed his Sony recorder on the coffee table.

Fifteen minutes later, Keenan seethed with impatience before Rebekah Drum finally sauntered back into the living room. She now wore cut-off jeans and an oversized white shirt with the top four buttons unfastened. She had combed her hair and applied a thick layer of eye shadow and scarlet lipstick. Rings adorned every finger, two on some. In one hand she carried a steaming mug, in the other a half-empty bottle of George Dickel and a jelly glass, already a quarter filled with bourbon. "I feel much more presentable now," she said.

Walking to the other side of the table, Rebekah Drum bent and set the coffee in front of Keenan, again lingering and exposing her breasts until Keenan forced himself to look away. Only then did he notice that she had ruined his coffee by putting cream in it. She settled on the couch and Keenan noticed several bruises on her legs as she curled them beneath her. Again, she leaned farther forward than necessary and topped her glass to half. " I hope you don't mind if I have a little drink. You see, sugar, I don't meet many decent men so I'm a little nervous." She smiled coyly. "And the drink will loosen me up."

Ignoring this, Keenan bent and turned on his tape recorder. "Do you mind if I record our conversation?"

"That might be interesting," she said, and took a hearty drink of bourbon. She then stretched out her leg and began running her toe back and forth on the table's edge.

Keenan thought it best to get right to his pitch. "I need for you to go to Columbia with me, so together we can ask your son to help us catch the child killer I told you about."

"Oh, I can't do that, sugar. I have a friend . . . well, not really a friend, but a man coming over this evening." She looked at Keenan over the top of her glass. "Maybe we could do it next week."

"We can't wait because your son is scheduled to be executed on Thursday."

"Executed? They shouldn't do that to him," she said, and took another sizable drink. "You know they lied about him. He was a good boy. He'd never embarrass me by doing all those things they say he did. But let's not talk about him. Why don't you tell me about yourself."

"Please," Keenan pleaded, "it's vital we see him today. And I promise I'll get you back by late afternoon, so you won't miss your friend."

"I don't want us to spend an afternoon cooped up in a car," she said, drank more bourbon, and slowly licked her lips. Her eyes had become watery and she wobbled a bit as she leaned forward and brought the glass back to half. Settling back, glass in hand, she asked, "Were you looking at my breasts again."

"Listen, children are dying," Keenan persisted. "I need your help. Please?"

"Well, I don't know those kids," she said and took another swallow. "And their parents should take better care of them, that's what I think. I always knew where my son was—not like some people I know." She tried to lean forward, but her forearm slipped off her knee, sloshing liquor.

Irritated, Keenan said, "Don't you think you should go easy on the booze?"

Rebekah Drum's smile disappeared and her expression became one that a grizzled seaman might show in a tough bar. "My check came yesterday, so I don't have to watch the mail . . . and I don't see anything else worth doing," she said, her southern belle accent shifting to one decidedly more rural and her words starting to slur. Sitting upright, she made a display of pulling her shirt closed. "Just because I'm not educated, you don't think I'm good enough for you. Well, I'm good enough for you to keep staring at my goddamn tits. And I've never had a problem finding better men than you. So, Mr. High and Mighty, fuck you."

"No thanks," Keenan replied, regretting this impulse as soon as he said it.

Pointing a ringed finger at Keenan, Rebekah Drum yelled, "Get the fuck out." Then she flung the remaining bourbon, over a third of a glass, into Keenan's face.

Startled, and barely containing his anger, Keenan rose and hurried for the door as she yelled, "Not one of you limp-dicked assholes has ever given me one bit of pleasure."

With strained dignity, Keenan walked from the house, his face red, his hands clenched and trembling slightly. Never had he allowed an interview to go so badly. Then, just when Keenan thought he could not become any angrier, he remembered that he had left his three-hundred-dollar tape recorder on Rebekah Drum's coffee table.

33

trapdoor

I

EVERY MORNING at eight, Stith held a briefing with the four department heads who reported directly to him. Attendance and punctuality were mandatory. So was brevity, and the meeting often ended before anyone's coffee cooled enough to sip.

On Wednesday, Stith once again wore too much cologne and the same dove gray suit that he had worn on Monday—alimony and four maxed-out charge cards having thinned the quality in his closet. He waited until all four had gathered in the conference room before he joined them. Careful to appear relaxed, Stith sat at the table's head and looked slowly around the room, his face red and moist as if with unabsorbed lotion. "I'm sure that each of you has heard Drum's allegations either from the news or gossip," he said and paused to look each man in the eye. "I met with Chief Jones this morning and he assured me, as I am now assuring you, that everything is going to run as usual. As for my personal feelings, if Drum wants to keep pissing in the wind, let him. We have work to do, so let's get down to business."

Stith wanted his men to see that Drum had taken his best shot and nothing came of it. He subscribed to the school of thought that a leader should never show doubt or appear worried. He also believed in a strict chain of command and that a leader should not have to explain himself, so he had said all he was going to say about the allegations. He had said even less to the reporters waiting in front of SLED HQ this morning, calling Drum's allegations "the desperate lies of a psychopath."

Sure it would feel good to unload and rant about what a worthless piece of shit Drum was, or to chew out someone. But Inabinet had repeatedly warned him that such reactions diminished rather than increased one's power. Yet, it seemed to Stith that all he did anymore was make assignments and put his signature on forms, and that this was slowly strangling his street brawler's heart. And Inabinet sure turned out to be a fine one to talk about restraint.

Stith's scar reddened as he listened to his top officers' reports. Each man had worked with Stith long enough to note the redness of his scar and the splotches where his neck bulged over his collar. Today, their status reports were more succinct than usual.

Five minutes after entering the conference room, Stith dismissed everyone and called in Wes Felton to update him on the Wilmet case. He sat back in his chair with his chin resting on his knuckles as Felton opened the accordion folder that he had brought with him. "They bitched and moaned, but Parole and Community Corrections finally sent the mug shots and rap sheets for every felon released from midlands prisons over the past four months. They promised the rest of the state by Friday. There are so many because, in addition to the dozens who walk every month, over six hundred inmates were cut loose a couple months ago to mitigate an overcrowding lawsuit."

Stith nodded. As much as he detested most of Keenan's psychobabble, Wilmet's killer had used a knife the way an ex-con might, so he gave Felton this assignment, just in case.

"I plan to review them this morning and start a sub-file for those with any kind of sex offenses in their records," Felton said. "Then I'll start calling the parole officers to ask about incidents that might not have brought charges."

"All right," Stith said, getting to his feet. "Bill said the preliminary on Gilpin should be ready by noon. Stay on it and . . . ."

The wall phone buzzed. It was the duty officer, who said that Frances Kinder and her son, Nathan, were in the lobby and wanted to talk with Stith about Jimmy Gilpin's disappearance. Stith told Felton to stay and had the Kinders escorted to the conference room.

Nathan Kinder shuffled into the conference room with his head down. He was a lean kid dressed in dark gray jeans and a glossy black jacket over a gray T-shirt. His mother followed a step behind, a hand on her son's shoulder as if she were pushing him along. Pale with bony hands and frizzy, unmanageable dark hair, Frances Kinder's shoulders curved forward beneath a thin white sweater over a shapeless peach-colored dress. When they reached the table, she uneasily looked around the posh conference room.

Stith asked if either cared for something to drink and both declined. Then he sat back and listened as Kinder's mother explained that Nathan thought his friend, Jimmy Gilpin, had willingly gone off to score some money and Nathan had covered for him by not telling the truth.

"When Nathan found out what had happened to Jimmy, he felt terrible and wanted to set things right," she said, her hands on the table, clasped in a knot. "But there's this Columbia investigator that has it in for him, so he thought it would be safer coming here. Nathan didn't do nothing wrong except not tell everything. But the way that investigator goes on, I ought to get a lawyer. But it's tight enough raising a son when you don't make much over minimum. You probably can't understand that," she said to Stith, then, as if shamed by her impertinence, looked down. "I'm sorry."

Stith thought this woman looked worn out, in general by life, and more specifically by a son headed in the wrong direction. He did understand her dilemma, very well. "I'm not after your son unless he had something to do with Gilpin's murder," he told her.

"No. Not at all . . . he wouldn't . . ."

Stith held up his hand and she stopped pleading. "As long as that's the case, you've nothing to worry about. So I'm going to have my man take you to the break room and get you whatever you want while your son and I talk."

She opened her mouth to protest and Stith again held up his hand. "He may have things to tell me that he'd be uncomfortable saying in front of you. So just go on; it'll be all right."

Alone with Nathan Kinder, Stith studied him, making his scrutiny obvious. Kinder had shaggy dark hair whose waves crimped in sharp ridges. Fuzz spread below his sideburns because he was putting off starting to shave, and wisps of hair grew over his lip in what Kinder might mistake for a mustache. He also had a few red scabs on his face from picked-at zits.

Looking at kids like Kinder always disturbed Stith, left him edgy, mirroring as they did how he must have looked to Inabinet when they first met. Stith had shifted from local law enforcement to SLED so that he wouldn't have much direct contact with adolescent perps. Stith didn't know a damn thing about kids, and usually couldn't see much good in these shabbily dressed delinquents—he had decided long ago to leave looking for the good in these punks to people like Inabinet. But Inabinet wasn't around anymore.

Stith got up, walked slowly to the credenza, taking his time to let tension build. Without saying a word, he opened a can of soda and put it and a cup of ice in front of Kinder. When he was seated again he said, "You're here because you want us to catch the son of a bitch that killed your friend. And that's what I want. So as long as you tell me everything that happened that night, you and I won't have any problems. And I promise you that I'm not going to charge you with any petty shit. Do you understand?"

Staring down at his hands, Kinder nodded and said, "Yeah."

Rising partially from his chair, Stith leaned over the table and did what Inabinet had done the first time he visited Stith in the hospital, he put his fingers under Kinder's chin and lifted his head. "I want you to look at me while we're talking."

"Okay," Kinder said.

Stith eased back into his seat. The boy's head started to sag and Stith motioned with his finger for Kinder to look up. "That's better. The best way to do this is to just go ahead and say whatever it is you have to say. If you don't hold back anything, you walk out of here with your head up because you've done all you can do for your pal. All right? So what happened that night?"

Kinder licked his lips, opened his mouth once and didn't speak. Then he said, "I didn't say anything before because we . . . because Gilpin was doing a little dealing."

"Dealing what?

Kinder's head sagged and Stith said, "Raise your head and look at me."

Kinder did as he was told. The rims of his eyes looked wet. "He had a half dozen Jim Jones for sale, and about as many for his own use."

Jim Jones was marijuana dipped in PCP and laced with cocaine. "That's righteous stuff," said Stith. "One hit and you're flying, right?"

Kinder nodded and started to lower his head, then jerked it up and looked at Stith.

"All right. You've got the toughest thing to admit out of the way. Now tell me the rest of it."

"Jimmy was pretty high when he met this big guy and they struck up a deal and went out to the parking lot. When he didn't come back, I thought he'd taken off with the guy because Jimmy thought he was really cool. You know, the guy had hair halfway down his back and claimed that he'd been a top dog in prison and could put Jimmy in touch with some good connections. But he said he'd only do business with Jimmy alone; that way, if Jimmy ever tried to roll over on him it would be his word against Jimmy's."

"Did you get this guy's name?"

Nathan shook his head. "No, and I'd never seen him before . . . but I'd recognize him if I ever saw him again, that's for sure."

Stith then had Kinder run through everything a second time, starting at the end and working his way backward, pressing for more details, and checking his story against itself. When satisfied that Kinder was giving it to him straight, Stith pushed the folder that Felton had put together containing the mug shots across the table and told Kinder he wanted him to look through those photographs very carefully.

All in all, Stith thought Kinder had done well, answering every question without becoming a bit mouthy. On an impulse, Stith did something that seemed flaky as soon as he did it. "Look, Nathan or Nate or whatever the hell you go by," he said. "You need to get involved in some group or do community service. Something that'll give you a change of scene before you end up like your pal. You need to do that for yourself," Stith said, though he had no idea what sort of thing Kinder might do. Felton knew a social worker, though, so maybe he could come up with something. "If you want to do that, I'll put you in touch with the right people. So what do you say?"

Kinder looked down and this time Stith let him. "I don't think so," Kinder said, shaking his head no.

"All right, no big deal," Stith said. "Take your time with the pictures. I'll be waiting in the second office down the hall." Face flushed, Stith left the room, wondering why had he coddled the little shit ass? And who the hell did he think he was to suggest community service to this kid?

. . .

Stith did not have to wait long. In less than five minutes, Kinder had a hit. The perp was a jailbird released from Kirkland Prison six weeks ago. His name was Wayne Allen Rawson.

Studying the stat sheet, Stith turned and started from the conference room, when Kinder said, "If you got any leads on a job, I'd be interested in that."

Preoccupied, Stith dismissively flicked the back of his hand without turning. Stith then heard the elevator door open and Felton and Frances Kinder came around the corner. Her eyes caught his, pleading that everything was okay and that her son was not in any kind of trouble. Stith suddenly felt angry that this woman had to shoulder so much. "This is nuts," he muttered, then turned back into the conference room and gruffly told Nathan Kinder, "No promises. But I'll ask around and see if I can get a line on some kind of job. And if I do, you damn well better make the most of it, you understand?"

II

Felton drove the unmarked blue Caprice while Stith studied the additional records faxed by Parole and Community Corrections. An unmarked van filled with a SWAT team followed. They were en route to Gatti's Appliances on Rosewood Drive where Wayne Allen Rawson worked. Gatti's was less than a mile from the arcade where Jimmy Gilpin had met Rawson. Forensics had not yet established that Gilpin's and Wilmet's killer was the same man, thus making this case multi-jurisdictional, so Stith had to notify Bob Marshall, who said he would take charge of the second SWAT team being dispatched to the halfway house on Huger Street where Rawson had lived since his release from prison.

At first, Wayne Allen Rawson's sheet looked like the history of so many other career criminals who were small time, stupid, and sometimes deadly. He was twenty-six years old, six foot one, and weighed one hundred and ninety pounds. He had a dragon tattoo on his left forearm, a claw on his right shoulder, and his initials, WAR, inscribed in block letters on his left shoulder. His mug shot showed him with shoulder-length dirty-blond hair and several days' beard stubble. Kinder said he still looked that way except that his hair was longer.

Rawson's first charges came at age twelve for truancy. Within a year, he racked up additional arrests for petty theft, vandalism, and shoplifting. A complaint of forced sex with a much younger boy landed him in a secure facility of the Department of Juvenile Justice. Eight months later, he was released to his grandparents, who were raising him because Rawson's father was in prison and no one knew his mother's whereabouts. Then came a charge that caused Rawson to stand out from the run-of-the-mill punk. Three months after release from DJJ, Rawson shotgunned both grandparents. His defense claimed the old man had been sexually molesting him for years, though Rawson admitted his only reason for shooting his grandmother was to keep her from snitching. Only fourteen years old and claiming to be a victim of sexual abuse, Rawson was sentenced as a juvenile. He remained in a DJJ facility until age seventeen and then a prison for young offenders until released on his twenty-first birthday.

Within two months of being released, Rawson was arrested for armed robbery of a convenience store. While out on bail awaiting trial, he was arrested again for trying to rob a liquor store and badly pistol-whipping the sixty-eight-year-old owner. He drew nine, served five. The prerelease report rated him a high risk to repeat.

Also noteworthy, Rawson served his entire sentence at Kirkland without ever going near Golgotha. It seemed very unlikely that he and Drum were buddies. Stith felt vindicated. So what if Drum shot off at the mouth after Stith pressured him. It was only hot air with no one listening.

III

Rawson had not been at work for the past two days. Stith left Felton to garner what he could from Gatti and his employees, while Stith swerved through traffic to the halfway house on Huger Street. Before he reached the halfway house, he learned that Rawson was not there, either.

A crowd had gathered around the boxy, two-story building with huge sun-dappled oaks in front and most of the packed yard dusty and worn clear of grass. A half dozen squad cars and a white van were parked inside the twisted yellow ribbon. Black-vested SWAT officers talked in small groups or moved about in no particular hurry with their vests uncinched.

Stith hung his badge from his jacket's breast pocket and pushed his way inside. The house's interior brandished worn grandeur. It had high ceilings, but dust coated the frosted light fixtures. The windows were tall and broad with many gaps in the dried putty and a couple of cracked panes. The hardwood floors were worn and the gold-and-green-plaid living room suite looked dusty and threadbare.

Bob Marshall sat on the back of the couch talking to a young man with a thatch of black hair and dressed in a loose-fitting madras shirt, its sleeves rolled up, revealing muscular forearms. Noticing Stith, Marshall said to him, while still working over a piece of gum, "He left at around nine this morning and nobody knows where he went."

"I'm the house manager, Ray Chavis," the young man introduced himself to Stith. Chavis had blue eyes and a rough handsome face. "I thought he had gone to work. But I'm not really surprised he's in trouble."

"Tell me about him," Stith said.

"It's like I told the other officer, he'd become hard to deal with. For the past two weeks he's gotten more and more touchy and arrogant. I figured he was working himself up to reoffend. That's usually the way it goes, their attitude takes the dive first. For instance, he violated curfew on Saturday and . . ."

"You sure it was Saturday?" Stith interrupted.

"Documented on Saturday's log." Chavis smiled and Stith thought him a little too cocky. "Anyway, when I confronted him," Chavis continued, "he started talking about how I was the problem, that I had it in for him, and if I'd just treat him fairly there wouldn't be any problem. Then he said he had too much pride to let me jerk him around. I took that as a serious threat. Rawson's a big guy, over six feet, and I could tell he hit the weights in prison."

"How else did he cause problems?"

"Earlier in the week there'd been friction between him and a couple of the guys. The big thing, though—what I was about to boot him for—was that he stopped paying his rent. We're a service organization and most of our funding comes from the community. That allows us to only charge these guys fifty a week for room and board, and we don't even do that until they get a job. Rawson must have been clearing at least one fifty a week, but he kept telling me he was short because he was helping his grandparents. Yesterday, I checked with his parole officer and Rawson's grandparents are long dead."

"No shit," Stith said. "Go on."

"So, yesterday evening, I pressed Rawson for the rent and he told me that I was a liar, that he'd already paid me and I'd stolen the money. I told him I'd give him until he got paid on Thursday to square things and if he didn't I was going to ask his parole officer to remove him. Frankly, I'd feel better with him out of here."

"Well, he didn't go to work, so any guesses where he might have gone?" Stith asked.

The young man shook his head. "A couple of the guys said that as went out the door this morning he told them that they'd soon be bragging to people because they knew him."

. . .

At the top of the stairs, a uniformed officer stood outside Rawson's room. Stith took rubber gloves from his pocket, snapped them on, then walked into the middle of the room and slowly looked around. Furnishings consisted of a narrow three-drawer dresser, worn writing desk, chair, and single bed with a badly sagging mattress. The closet door stood open and Stith saw a few shirts and jeans on hangers but that was it; no extra shoes, boxes, or even a duffel bag. On the desk lay an open phone book, a pencil, and a small writing pad with newspaper clippings beneath it. A newspaper also lay on the floor beside the chair.

Stith squatted over the newspaper and saw that it was opened to Drum's interview. He felt a queasy stirring in his stomach. He checked the clippings beneath the pad; they were all about either Wilmet's or Gilpin's murder. That made sense; perps love reading about their crimes. Stith studied the phone book and noticed that the ragged remains of a torn-out page stuck from the crease. The left page ended with Pavlik and the right began with Peele. Stith's breathing picked up and he shook his head. He did not like where this was going.

Squatting again, he looked across the pad and saw an indentation. "To hell with waiting for the techs," he muttered, and gently rubbed the side of a pencil's lead across the pad.

Stith stared at the pad, his face hot and sweaty. "Damn it!"

Ever since he was a child, whenever Stith felt a trapdoor open beneath him, it focused and spurred him to decisive action. It had been that way after Will Paxton's death and again when he discovered his second wife's infidelity. His clear-headed decisiveness had earned him a reputation as a good man in a crisis, the kind of guy you want backing you up when you crash a door with guns drawn.

Three months ago, the trapdoor had opened and Stith fell through; but that time he had been confused and unsure. It happened on a Saturday morning when Arnold Inabinet asked him to come over, said it was important, said he'd be in his workshop out at the barn. It had been tough watching Inabinet shrink to a pasty, husk of a man, staring off more and more, and frequently complaining as cancer ate the hard knuckle of his character along with his flesh.

At the barn, Stith had just gotten out of his car when he heard the shot. He knew immediately. He didn't run into the shop or pull his gun, but walked with slow wooden steps while the only tears he ever shed as an adult streamed down his face.

Inabinet, his arms sprawled at his sides as if making a snow angel, lay in front of the workbench. His Sig Sauer—the same model as Stith's—was a few inches from his hand, a last wisp of smoke twisting from the barrel. Blood and brains splattered across Inabinet's tool board, workbench, and the envelope with Stith's name on it. Below this was another letter to Inabinet's wife; Stith's letter had shielded it from the gore, just as Inabinet had called Stith to shield her from finding him and her having to see any of this.

For Inabinet to call on Stith to deal with his suicide had been a nod to Stith's toughness, and an indication of how much Inabinet trusted him to handle things. How many times had Inabinet told him he could handle something? But whenever Inabinet had said that, he usually gave Stith a few suggestions. But ever since that Saturday morning, Stith felt himself dangling with his legs churning on nothing but empty air.

Now, looking at what was revealed in the white furrows on Wayne

Rawson's pad, Stith felt the trapdoor give way again, and he slammed his fist into the wall, pushing in a ragged circle of plaster.

Written on Rawson's pad was the name and address of Zack Paxton.

34

aces and eights

I

THE GREEN interstate marker read: "Columbia 50 Miles." Keenan bent to sniff his jacket's lapel; it still reeked of bourbon, just as his mood had remained foul since leaving Rebekah Drum's house. In an effort to stop chewing on his frustration, Keenan took his cellular phone from his jacket pocket and punched in SLED's number. He did not really expect any new developments but hoped that focusing on the case might distract and settle him. The switchboard patched him through to Wes Felton, who was in the field.

Sounding excited and breathless, Felton told him, "We know that Gilpin was killed by a recent parolee named Wayne Rawson and that at some point Rawson wrote down the name and address of Zack Paxton."

Almost on top of an exit, Keenan barked, "Hold on," and swerved onto the exit ramp for Route 176. All around were large fields whose grass and weeds, except the thistles, were chewed short by grazing cows. The only building in sight was an abandoned gas station, its windows covered with graffiti-marked plywood. Keenan shot across Route 176 and lurched to a stop beside the raised cement and rusted nubs of what had once been a gas island. He slung open the car door and got out, his cell phone pressed to his ear. Whirling breezes, further whipped up by noisy trucks on the interstate, ruffled his hair and lapels as he began to pace beneath the stark afternoon sun.

More slowly this time, Felton told Keenan how they identified Jimmy Gilpin's killer as Wayne Allen Rawson and about the empty-handed raids. Felton then explained how Stith found evidence in Rawson's room that he had written down Zack's name and address.

Felton finished his update and Keenan told him he would get back to him. Roughly, Keenan tossed the cell phone onto the seat through the Buick's open door and said, "Goddamn it!," as he kicked at loose gravel atop the crumbled asphalt. New anger piled onto Keenan's frustration and he began to breathe in short snorts, like a bull impaled with pikes. He wanted to tear, kick, slash; and he did kick again at the gravel.

"Think! Think!" he told himself. Maybe the danger to Zack wasn't so great, after all. Trying to abduct a specific target, especially an alert target, was much harder than taking a victim of opportunity. Maybe Rawson lacked the boldness and determination to pull off a targeted attack. Maybe his interest would never go beyond fantasy. Keenan needed to find out how bold Rawson had been in the past and how badly Rawson wanted to become famous, because that was the lure that caused him to target Zack. He also needed to know how much, or how little, Rawson believed he had to lose.

Rawson's Warden's Jacket and parole reports might answer some of these questions. Keenan stopped pacing and leaned into his car to retrieve the cell phone, intending to arrange access to all materials on Rawson. Felton had said that Rawson was never in Golgotha, so they could forget about Drum.

Drum! Keenan froze, his hand inches from the phone, then stood, wind whipping his hair, a sour frown creasing his mouth. Drum had caused this threat by enticing this guy, Rawson, into considering Zack an appealing target. And now that Rawson was the focus of attention, Drum would be left alone to gloat and possibly come up with some other malicious ploy to hurt the Paxtons. He had already threatened to slander Will, and the press would trumpet any lie, no matter how outrageous. And everyone would assume his death sentence was sufficient, so Drum would never be punished for causing this latest round of suffering. Hell, thought Keenan, everyone around Drum will be intent on minimizing his suffering and pamper him until he enters the death chamber, numb and probably sedated. Where was the justice in that?

As much as Keenan had ever wanted anything, he wanted to make Drum pay. It was a palpable desire that twisted his insides and gorged him with angry frustration because there was nothing he could do. His plan to break Drum was in shambles and he had no leverage, whatsoever.

Keenan slammed the fleshy bottom of his fist against the car's roof, then hit the roof again, denting it each time. Abruptly, he stopped and straightened. *Drum was within his reach*. The disastrous trip to Charleston had been unnecessary; Keenan had been conscientiously crossing t's and dotting i's, when a bold stroke was best. He saw now how he could make Drum pay, at least a little for causing so much trouble, and it would not take very long; and afterward, he would have plenty of time to develop a profile on Rawson.

Yet, Keenan hesitated. Going after Drum served no purpose except to emotionally wound and maim him, and that would be a violation of Keenan's sworn code of conduct. He had always abided by rules. At the moment, though, his morals felt like a straightjacket and he resented how they held him back.

Caught between his desires and his code of conduct, a memory pushed into Keenan's mind's eye. Vividly, he recalled the close-up photograph of Will Paxton with Drum's urine soiling his cheek, and remembered his vow to avenge Will's death by pissing on Drum. And finally, Keenan faced a simple truth—for these past eight years he had been stalking Drum with revenge always in the back of his mind.

Keenan's hate swelled again, and gathered force as other photographs flashed in his mind. He again saw the bruises and vulgar pose of Alicia Owens's body at the dumping site, and then her pale autopsy photos, and finally the portrait of her smiling so sweetly.

Then images from other cases, images Keenan thought he had cataloged apart from his feelings, began to assault him, and he braced both hands against the roof of his sedan. He saw the junior high cheerleader, an honor student, lying on golden leaves with her skirt pulled up to cover her face while exposing her mutilated lower body. He saw the toddler wrapped in a burlap sack and tossed into a dumpster, and then recalled the autopsy photo of his mangled anus. There was the grandmother abducted while working in a convenience store, the runaway hitchhiker with orange socks, the nurse found on a golf course, prostitutes, druggies, and freckle-faced kids—how many had there been? Each one burned indelibly into his mind. Unforgettable. Tragic. Too painful to think about. Too volatile to bottle up forever.

At last, the rush of memories stopped and Keenan raised his head, his eyes glittering with white-hot rage. For too many years, he had concentrated only on his small goals and never really considered the bigger picture. There were moral issues far greater than petty rules and the rights of monsters. The rights of monsters! What an absurd concept!

Keenan leaned into the car, his movements so deliberate they seemed casual, and rummaged in his case until he located his black address book. He sat on the seat with his legs outside, found the number for Golgotha, and punched it in. As the phone rang, Keenan wondered why it had taken him so long to see the world with such clarity.

II

SLAMMING METAL doors and a legion of jangled voices echoed in the cavern of CB2, all but swallowing the tapping of Keenan's shoes as he trotted up metal steps behind Lieutenant Jenkins. On the second tier's catwalk, Keenan maneuvered to walk on the side closest to the cells and set a slightly faster pace than usual. He had asked that Drum not be told that he was coming, so there was a chance that Drum, on some whim, would refuse to see him. To counter this, he intended to whet Drum's eagerness to meet.

They neared the twelfth cell, Drum's cell, and Keenan slowed enough that Jenkins went a step ahead of him. Abruptly turning, Keenan moved close to the bars and looked into the puny space that had confined Drum these past eight years. Drum lay atop his bunk facing the wall where he had propped a copy of *True Detective* magazine. A picture on the magazine's cover showed a bound and gagged woman, her eyes wide with terror. Drum's trousers were loosened and his right hand actively tucked inside.

"Excuse the interruption," Keenan said loud enough to startle Drum, who left his hand inside his pants and twisted to look at Keenan. "I have some news for you," Keenan said, and nodded as if it would be good news, then walked on.

Through clenched teeth, Jenkins hissed a warning about following procedures. Keenan didn't care about warnings by Jenkins or anyone else. The rule makers lacked the will required for true justice. He, at least for now, did not lack such will and felt completely warranted in doing whatever justice required. By enticing Drum as he had, he

ensured not only that Drum would see him, but that he would probably come with his guard down hoping for good news about some sort
of reprieve.

On the videotape that Drum had made of Alicia Owens, Drum had
told that poor girl that unless she pleased him, he would one day kidnap Alicia's daughter, Jennifer, and do the same things to her. Tortured
by poison and by Drum, she had bravely tried to meet his demands,
only to be told that she wasn't good enough and had failed her daughter. He gave her false hope, then crushed it.

Keenan wanted Drum to taste his own brand of cruelty.

.   .   .

The ashtray had been emptied and the floor swept, yet the worn meeting room still looked dirty and smelled of stale ashes and smoke, like a
kind of incense from hell.

At the door, Drum paused and smiled cockily at Keenan, already
preening from his presumed victory. His smugness momentarily
lapsed as the COs pushed him toward the chair without removing his
restraints and then hooked his leg irons to the U-bolt. Rather than take
the hint that he was not about to be handed a victory, Drum did not
wait for the COs to clear the room before he looked at Keenan, smiled,
and arched his eyebrows. "So, what do you have for me?"

Keenan took his time, honing Drum's anticipation. He even smiled
and nodded a little, then calmly said, "The game's over. We know who
killed Gary Wilmet." He paused to let the full meaning of this land
upon Drum.

"You're just trying to trick me. Well, it's not going to work, so forget
it," Drum said, though his smug smile disappeared and his eyes
searched Keenan's face.

"We'll probably have him in custody by this evening or tomorrow
morning. That leaves you a very small chance of getting something out
of this." Keenan unfolded a piece of paper with WAR written on it and
slid it toward Drum "These are his initials. It's now or never to prove
you know something. What's his name?"

Drum leaned forward, his chains clinking softly, and stared at the
paper. The muscles in his jaws flexed, then he leaned back in his chair.
"Looks like you got him," he said.

"His name," Keenan demanded.

"You're not going to jerk me around. You see, I know where he's . . . waiting. So if you want to find him before it's too late, you'll get my sentence commuted."

"We both know you don't have anything to trade, so here's the only deal you're going to get." Nothing in Keenan's voice or face hinted at any emotion or his pleasure in toying with Drum. He remained as still as a viper enticing its prey closer. "I have your mother in the lobby. She wants to see you. If you admit this was all a ruse, I'll bring her to you."

Drum looked away, considered, then said, "Why should I care? I haven't seen her in years."

"If you don't fully cooperate, I'll tell her that you refused to see her. And since you don't care, maybe I'll claim you called her some juicy names."

Drum stared and the gill-like muscles at the back of his jaws flexed.

Keenan leaned forward and placed his forearms on the table. "The game's over. There's no point in the charade. It's time to come clean."

Drum shook his head.

"If that's the way you want it," Keenan said and rose, "have a good execution."

"All right," Drum said. He looked down and rocked back and forth, and a hissing sound came in his breathing. Finally, he looked at Keenan, his mouth quivering, and said, "I was just jerking the Paxton bitch around, all right." Drum kept rocking and said, more to himself than Keenan, "She and that guy Stith violated my rights. That's enough to get me a reprieve."

There was one more thing Keenan officially wanted to know. His department did have a legitimate interest in learning about Drum's ploy, because such a well-publicized case would inevitably spawn copycats. "How did you come up with the idea?" Keenan asked.

Drum stopped rocking and looked at Keenan. "I'd heard about the Wilmet kid's murder on the news, so when this minister said he wanted to see me, I saw a chance to get back at Paxton for all the things she said at my sentencing hearing. Then, bang, it hit me that this was a way to get my sentence commuted. And if she had any decency, she'd have been begging the governor to commute it. Shows what a tramp she is." Drum started rocking again, breathing noisily with his chains rattling softly.

As he had set out to do two days ago, Keenan had broken Drum and, so far, everything he had done remained consistent with his mission. He could stop here and never have crossed the line, never have violated his golden code of these past sixteen years. A feeling that he was about to do wrong caused Keenan to hesitate from taking the next step.

Drum rocked for several seconds, then stopped and looked at Keenan. "As soon as my sentence is commuted," he said, "I'll get that bitch. When I'm put back in the general population I'm going to find a pervert close to release and get him to finish it with her and her brat. That's been my plan all along. She'll never know when it's coming, but please let her know that it is, because, goddamn her, I'm going to teach her that she can't walk on me like I'm dirt."

Of course Drum would do something like that if he ever won an appeal. Keenan had not anticipated this threat, but it now seemed obvious. Something deep in Keenan's core dropped a few degrees and he felt what a snake might feel at the moment it strikes.

He leaned forward, resting his forearms on the table, and said in a voice that was quiet and calm, "I lied to you about your mother being here. She refused to come." He waited for this to register.

"What the fuck are you trying to pull?" Drum asked

"I did talk to her and pleaded with her to come here and see you one last time, but she refused because some man she despised was coming over for a good time."

"Bullshit!"

"You know it's true. You know you've been in her way your whole life. When you were ten, she sent you away to get rid of you . . ."

"Shut the fuck up."

". . . because you were in the way."

The anger contorting Drum's face was not his usual sneering anger but a vulnerable wet-eyed fury. "I said, shut the fuck up," he shouted.

Keenan shrugged. "Hell, she even told me that you're an embarrassment and that she never wants anyone to know she's your mother. But . . ."

"Liar!"

". . . that's all she said about you, because the rest of the time she was too busy coming on to me."

"Liar! I ought to kill you." Though he wore restraints, Drum rose a few inches from his seat.

Keenan leaned back in his chair and smiled the way Drum had smiled at him on the first night. Then Keenan flung Drum's own words back at him. "But don't worry. I don't associate with whores."

Drum tried to lunge across the table, but the leg irons hooked to the U-bolt cut him short and he fell hard on the table's top, wriggling like a fish slapped onto a cutting board.

In a surprisingly fluid motion for so large a man, Keenan rose and, with his back to the surveillance camera, clamped his hand onto Drum's head to prevent Drum from head-butting him as he leaned close and hissed in his ear, "After Will Paxton's murder you weren't try-ing to escape. You were working your way to Charleston so you could murder your mother, probably to rape her, too—I'm going to assume you were because that's what you really wanted when you murdered all those women."

Drum almost twisted free and Keenan slammed his head hard against the table. "If you do anything else to harass the Paxton family, or say anything hurtful"—Keenan's fingers closed around Drum's hair and he lifted his head a few inches and then bashed it against the table—"or if you file any formal complaints, I'll tell the whole world that in your last hours of freedom you were trying to rape and murder your mother."

A key clicked in the lock and the door swung open, banging hard into the wall. One after the other, two beefy COs rushed into the room followed by Jenkins, who demanded, "What's going on?"

Keenan stepped back from the table and the COs put themselves between him and Drum. "He tried to attack me and I acted to protect us both from injury," Keenan said calmly. "Your surveillance tape will confirm it. We're finished. Get him out of here."

Jenkins bent to unhook Drum's leg irons while the two COs posi-tioned themselves on either side of Drum, each gripping his upper arms with both hands. As they did this, Keenan said, "I forgot to mention that I did tell your mother what you were really after while on the run."

Now unhooked from the floor, Drum tried to squirm free but the COs' experienced grip held. Glaring at Keenan, Drum promised, "I'll get you for this."

They started pushing Drum toward the door and Keenan said, "One more thing."

Jenkins looked warily at Keenan but held up his hand for his men to pause.

In case rejection and worry were not enough to keep Drum in purgatory for the next thirty hours, Keenan wanted one more inner conflict to twist Drum. "If you go to your execution without trying anything else, I'll visit your mother again and tell her something different from what she now thinks. I guess you'll have to trust me. And by the way, I won't be seeing you again, ever."

Once again Drum struggled and the COs' grips held. As they shoved Drum out the door, he looked over his shoulder and stared at Keenan with naked hate. Keenan, his head tilted regally upward, stood beside the table staring back, a humorless, snake-like smile on his lips.

35

untouchable

1

EVEN WITH a four-dollar city map, Joe Cameron thought he would never find Hebron Street. Normally, he would stop and ask someone for directions, but Joe was not about to unlock his door or roll down the window. This neighborhood looked like a war zone, with weed-covered lots, boarded-up buildings, and battered grates on every storefront. It was late afternoon and there seemed to be a lot of people just hanging out doing God knows what. The women reminded Joe of women he'd seen when delivering donations to the Salvation Army Thrift Store. And the men . . . well, they reminded him of the men he had seen inside Golgotha—except there were no guards here and not a policeman in sight. This was certainly not the kind of neighborhood where Joe expected mothers to live.

Joe slowed to check a bent street sign above the heads of three black teenagers who wore red bandannas and clothes that were preposterously too large. All three pointedly looked at Joe and one shouted,

"Hey, mothafucker, who you . . ." Joe didn't hear the rest as he sped away and once again hit the lever to lock all the doors on his Caravan, just in case one had jiggled loose or something.

Why did he let Bruce Tanner talk him into coming here? It made no sense. So what, if Drum was angry and throwing things around in his cell because he believed that the FBI agent, Keenan, had told his mother lies about him? So what, if he wanted to see her so he could straighten things out? It was crazy for Joe to do this when it might even cost him his job—he had promised Mark Kemper that he was through with Drum.

When Bruce had called him, Joe had suggested that someone just phone her and tell her that her son wanted to see her to straighten out a few things. Bruce explained that she didn't have a telephone. Then Bruce had said that the Warden—not some assistant, but the Warden—had told Bruce to call Joe and ask for his help. Apparently, Warden Edwards did not believe sending someone to see Drum's mother was the prison's responsibility, but rather the kind of thing Drum's personal minister should do.

Joe found it difficult to disappoint the Warden, and told himself that technically he wouldn't actually have contact with Drum. And he would be doing a good thing for an unfortunate woman whose son was on death row. At the time Joe agreed to this trip, he had genuinely felt sorry for Drum's mother. Now, driving through the kind of neighborhood that he always avoided, Joe's promise seemed typically naive and overly optimistic. He had met Rebekah Drum once—and on the drive here he had had plenty of time to remember that brief encounter.

.   .   .

On the third pass, Joe figured out that the bent sign read "Hebron Street" and turned. On one corner was a pawnshop, its mesh window covers looking as though someone had attacked them with a baseball bat. A dilapidated Laundromat stood on the other corner. A smattering of people, who looked as though they had nothing better to do than lie around all day, sat on the front steps of houses or leaned against rusting cars.

Joe thought that a week ago he would never have gone into a neighborhood like this, and felt a twinge of pride. Mostly, though, he felt nervous.

Street numbers were missing on many houses, so as near as Joe could tell the fifth house on the left was the one he wanted. A rusting blue Oldsmobile, with a twisted wire where the antenna should be, was pulled onto the sidewalk in front of the house. Easing his Caravan in behind this boat of a car, Joe hesitated, got out, and carefully locked his door. As he turned toward the house, a tall, scruffy-haired black man sauntered from the adjacent yard and walked directly toward him. Joe tried to act like he didn't notice him, but the black man said, "Hold on, man." Slowly, Joe turned to face him. The man wore an unbuttoned black shirt with black pants, white socks, and black sneakers. Three fake gold chains dangled on his bare chest and real gold gleamed from one tooth.

"How you doin?" the man said.

"All right."

"Glad to hear that. Yes sir, glad you're all right. You know, I was just admirin' your car. Nice car like that shouldn't be left unprotected in a neighborhood like this. You know, bad elements and all."

Joe thought this man looked like one of those bad elements.

"Yeah, sure be a shame if somethin' happen to it," the man said, shaking his head. "You know, I seen thieves strip a nice car like that clean in less time than it takes to piss."

"I, ah, I've got to go into that house, so I guess I'll have to take my chances," Joe mumbled and took a step.

"Hold on," the man said and stretched his arm in front of Joe. "That's the good news I come to tell you. You don't need to be takin no chances 'cause I'm here and I'll watch it for you for twenty dollar."

"Uh, I don't know, twenty dollars is a lot of money," Joe said, which was part true because he and Wendy lived on a budget and never spent money foolishly. Mostly, though, Joe didn't trust this man and wondered what kind of fool he thought Joe was.

"Man, your insurance deductible be a lot more'n twenty dollar. But I understand your hesitatin,' 'cause you don't know me and I don't know you, right?"

Joe nodded agreement.

"So here's how we work it. You tear a twenty in half and give me half and you keep the other one. When you finish your business in there, if your car's okay then you give me your half. It's up to you, man. But like I say, it'd be a shame if somethin happen to your nice fancy car. Deal?"

Suspecting that a certain bad element would surely do something to his car if he did not make the "deal," Joe nodded 'yes' and reached for his wallet. As he slipped out the twenty, he tried to hide the rest of the contents without appearing to do so. Tearing the bill down the middle, he gave the man half. With a smile the black man said, "Now you go have your fun and don't worry about a thing." As this man walked back to join two other men waiting on his porch, he did a little dance step and Joe overheard him loudly tell his friends, "I'm making more money off these fools than that raggedy old whore over there." All three men laughed, and Joe realized what this man thought he was here for and he blushed enough to glow in the dark.

.   .   .

At the door, Joe raised his hand to knock, and hesitated. He had met Rebekah Drum when, as a Big Brother, he'd gone to pick up Isaac. She was young then and very good looking in a reckless sort of way. And she had flirted with him right in front of her son. In fact, it had seemed to Joe that she was competing with Isaac for his attention. But she was very good looking, and it was hard not to like being flirted with, though he could tell it made Isaac mad. Maybe that was why he and Isaac had such a bad afternoon.

The worst, though, came when he took Isaac home. He did what the Big Brother agency recommended and went inside to touch base with the mother. A man, whom he assumed was Rebekah Drum's boyfriend, sat shirtless at the kitchen table drinking a beer. A big man, he had a deep copper tan and lots of freckles. Tattoos covered both arms and his hair came down almost to his waist. As Joe came through the door, this man looked at him and wanted to know what the hell Joe was doing there. Joe tried to explain, but the boyfriend cut him off, telling Joe that Isaac didn't need a Big Brother because he was there. Then he said that Becky didn't want Joe coming around and that if he ever saw him there again, he'd kick his ass all the way to Sunday. The boyfriend suddenly stood and Joe ran from the kitchen and never went back. Joe never told anyone, not even Wendy, about his cowardice, he was too ashamed. Maybe, if he'd had more courage things would have turned out differently for Drum? Maybe Drum would not have killed all those people? Joe would never know.

With surprising firmness, Joe knocked on the door. When no one answered, he knocked harder. A minute later, the door opened about six inches and a woman with strands of hair across her face and clutching a pink housecoat peered out. Her eye shadow and lipstick were badly smudged.

"Mrs. Drum?" Joe asked. If this was the same woman, Joe thought, then life had ridden her hard.

"Whatever ya want, I'm busy," she slurred, alcohol heavy on her breath.

"My name is Joseph Cameron," he said hurriedly. "Your son asked me to . . . come here."

Releasing her robe and showing sweaty cleavage, she brushed her hair from her eyes, and squinted at Joe. "You a reporter?"

"I'm a minister"

She squinted harder, then smiled. "Yeah, you look like a preacher. Well, I'm real busy. Why don't you come back some other time."

Afraid she would shut the door, Joe said as fast as he could, "I've driven from Columbia, and won't take but a minute. I'm your son's minister and he wants to see you."

"What?" she slurred.

"Your son wants to see you. He thinks an FBI agent told you lies about him and he wants to talk to you and straighten things out."

"Huh? FBI?" Then she looked angry. "I threw that fucker out," she said louder than Joe thought necessary. "I caught him looking at my tits," she added, gesturing toward her very visible cleavage.

"What the hell's going on," a gruff voice demanded from somewhere in the house.

Turning, Rebekah Drum yelled, "Keep it in your pants, I'll be back in a minute." As she turned, two things happened. The door opened wider and Joe saw a fat, naked man with stringy gray hair and a scraggly beard, and Rebekah Drum's robe fell open, revealing most of one breast. Joe knew he should look away, but did so too late to avoid being caught.

"And you a preacher." Rebekah Drum smiled and gathered her robe back together. "I gotta go, sugar. You come back some other time."

"He'll want to know when you're going to go see him?"

"I don't know. Come back next week."

"But they're going to execute him tomorrow night."

"I can't help that."

Others were depending on Joe, and he was sure that he must not have explained it right, that she really didn't understand that there was no time to go later. "But you don't understand," he tried to explain, "he's your son . . . and if you care about him you have to come back with me today."

Rebekah Drum's expression hardened and she opened the door wider and stepped toward Joe, causing him to take a step back. "Who the fuck do you think you are?" she slurred. "You think that because of your fancy suit that you can come to my house and put me down and treat me like trash. Get the hell out of here."

"No . . ." Joe started to tell her she was wrong about him, but she cut him off, screaming, "Don't you tell me no. Get out. Get the fuck out." She lurched at Joe and he raised his arms to ward her off and began running down the sidewalk with her pummeling his back, like a blue jay swooping down on the cat who raided her nest. "You fucking pervert, get out of here. You goddamned pervert," she screamed.

Fumbling, Joe dropped his keys as she stood behind him yelling, "I'm calling the cops and tell them you tried to get me to go off with you. That'll teach you."

Finally, Joe scrambled into the sanctuary of his van and slammed down the lock. Shaking, he had trouble getting the key into the ignition. To Joe's great relief, Rebekah Drum walked back toward her house, her hands wildly slashing the air. Shifting into reverse, Joe looked behind him and saw that his troubles were not over. The tall black man had his face and both hands pushed against the rear glass. Joe could not back up without running over him and the Oldsmobile blocked his way in front. Once the man's eyes caught Joe's, he wagged a long finger at him, then casually walked to the driver's door and gestured for Joe to roll down the window. Hesitantly, Joe opened it about two inches and began digging in his pocket, trying to pull out the other half of the twenty, anything to get out of here. His face burned with shame—he had never before been attacked by anyone.

Bending over, the man peered through the opening, his expression sour. With a flourish, he swept his hand to the window and flipped his wadded-up half of the twenty through the opening. As the bill fell onto Joe's lap, the man said loud enough for his friends to easily hear, "There, man, I don't even want to touch your money."

36

skink

I

AMONG THE firehouse red brick buildings of Kirkland Correctional Institute, a maximum-medium security prison, is a general purpose facility with rooms used for GED and college credit classes, as well as AA meetings and services by religious persuasions as diverse as the Holiness Church and Black Muslims. This building also contains a canteen and a nursery that is decorated by inmate art and becomes lively and crowded during Sunday visitation.

In a room with two bulky tables pushed together and blackboards lining one wall, Keenan sat leaning back with his legs crossed and his chin resting on his knuckles. It had been almost four hours since he had torched Drum, yet, his state of mind remained like that of a redneck strutting back into a bar after a fight, ready to prove himself again should anyone care to try. His mood had worsened when he reviewed Rawson's Warden's Jacket. The more he learned, the more he thought Rawson might actually go after Zack.

Given Keenan's combative state, the man sitting across from him was a disappointment. He much too readily allowed Keenan to have his way. Paunchy, with a pasty complexion, dark thinning hair, and black-rimmed glasses, Wayne Rawson's former cellmate looked and moved like a lazy accountant getting paid by the hour. Forty-two-year-old Trent Coover wore the prison-issue jeans and blue shirt that he had worn for almost half his life. A mechanic by trade, Coover had twice served seven-year stints for burglary. Now, tripped by a state three-time-loser law, he had currently marked five of the minimum twenty years laid on him for his third B&E conviction.

Keenan sat with his back to the mesh-covered windows, forcing Coover to squint into the sunset's red-tinted rays whenever he tried to look at him. On the table lay a medium-sized paper bag and an aluminum ashtray that, as with all the prison ashtrays, lacked enough stiffness for anyone to hone it into a weapon. "I'd like to help you, John," Coover said, "but I'm not a snitch. You see, snitching goes against the prisoner's code, and mightily increases your chance of having a 'prison accident.'"

With seeming nonchalance, Keenan pulled three cartons of Marlboros from inside the paper bag, opened one, and tossed a pack across the table.

Greedily, Coover slipped the pack into his shirt pocket, then looked at the cartons, licked his lips, and said, "My brand. Well, what the hell. Everybody snitches when there's something in it for them. And Rawson was nothing but a stupid blowhard, anyway. You know, the kind of guy that if you disagree with him, he wants to fight. Nobody liked him."

Keenan thought Coover a contemptibly weak man for rolling over so easily. Fresh from his victory over Drum, he knew how good it would feel to rub Coover's nose in his own weakness. Keenan squelched this impulse because it would not help him find out about Rawson.

"My impression is that Rawson wants to make a name for himself," Keenan said.

"You got that right," Coover said, and twisted to his side and slipped his hand into his jeans' pocket to take out a rumpled near-empty pack of cigarettes and red plastic lighter. Slouching in his chair, he lit a cigarette and held it between his index and forefinger, gesturing and leaving little trails of smoke, as he explained, "Rawson's one of those guys that believes he deserves special respect but can't get it, so he hates anybody that's earned a little status or reputation. For instance, Rawson was always bitching that the guys on death row, especially those who got a lot of press coverage like Drum or Pee Wee Gaskins, hadn't done anything all that special. And, man, I hated it when somebody got him started about Manson."

"You mean Charles Manson?"

"Yeah, Charlie Manson. If someone mentioned Manson he'd start pacing and bitching about how Manson was a fraud, that he'd never lifted a finger and that he didn't deserve any fame. And you know what?" Coover said, pointing the fingers holding the cigarette at Keenan. "*Helter Skelter* was the only book I ever saw Rawson pick up. And I'm pretty sure he sent Manson at least one hate letter."

"Did he ever say he wanted to do something like Manson?"

"Not that I recall. But I wouldn't put anything past him. He was a real son of a bitch with anybody that was smaller than him."

"Such as?"

Slouched in his chair with his shoulders hunched forward, Coover shook his head. "I ain't saying nothing that might get me subpoenaed."

Keenan casually lay his hand on the cigarettes. "Speak hypothetically."

Coover took another hit and eyed the cartons. "All right. Let's just say that he was the kind who might rape the weaker new jacks—that's young first-time inmates. And let's say that taking wasn't enough, that he liked to rough them up, that even if they went along, he'd do something to hurt them a little. Get the picture?"

"Was that why he was stabbed?" From reviewing Rawson's Wardens Jacket, Keenan learned that two years into his sentence, someone stabbed Rawson in the thigh. A year later, he took a shiv in the back that cost him a kidney and almost ended his life.

"Nah. He got stabbed because he was mouthy and asking for it," Coover said. "It would have happened sooner except that at first nobody would touch him because they were afraid of his old man."

"So bad blood developed between Rawson and his old man?" Wayne Rawson's father, Keith Rawson, was also at Kirkland doing life with no chance of parole.

"I ain't saying anything about Keith Rawson," Coover said and shook his head.

Keenan smiled, hard and humorless. "It seems to me, Trent, that you already have said something about Keith Rawson. I know the old man's tough." A dark furrow formed between Keenan's eyebrows and he leaned forward and stretched one arm across the table. "If you don't help me, I'll call Keith Rawson in here and ask him if it's true what they say about bad blood between he and his son. Do you think he'll know that I just finished talking to you?"

Perspiration beaded on Coover's upper lip as he took a quick puff. "Ain't no need to do that," he said.

"What's it going to be?" Keenan demanded and leaned back in his seat.

Coover took a slower drag, studying Keenan. "This stays between us, right?"

"Absolutely."

Coover shrugged. "What the hell. Here's what I heard. Like I told you, Rawson was mouthy and wasn't showing much respect to some very bad Aryan biker types—that's who Rawson's old man runs with. The first time they just stuck him in the leg to warn him that he better start shaping up. Word had it the old man protected him on that one. The second time his old man must have been fed up because it was a serious attempt, right through the kidney, and after Rawson recovered the old man started forcing him to be a nobody."

"How?"

Coover took another quick hit, and again gestured with the hand holding the cigarette. "In here, you can only have a nickname if you earn status. Little Rawson had been going around calling himself Snake. Everybody knew he was doing it because one of the old man's nicknames was Cottonmouth—that's because when Keith Rawson gets pissed, he talks to you real soft before he strikes. So after Little Rawson recovered from the stabbing, the old man told him that his name wasn't going to be Snake, but Skink, after a friggin blue-tailed lizard. And Skink stuck; that's what the tougher inmates started calling him. And man was Rawson ever pissed at his old man, but he had sense enough to let it ride, what with one kidney and all. But that's when he started talking about doing something big and got all fixated on Manson. I figured that sooner or later Rawson would try something flashy and stupid. I guess he finally did it by killing the Wilmet kid. But you know, that just shows how stupid Rawson is, because that made him a Chester—that's what we call child molesters—and Chesters are the lowest of the low. So unless Rawson does something else really big, he's stuck with that. And he knows it. If he has a lick of brains, there's no way he'll let himself be taken alive. No, sir. Not with what he knows is going to happen to him if he ever comes back in here," Coover said and took a final hit on the cigarette, singeing it down to the filter prison-style, then he stubbed it out.

Keenan's questions had been answered. If Rawson could find a way, he would try to get at Zack. And with his judgment probably impaired by the cocaine-and PCP-laced joints he taken from Jimmy Gilpin, he might ignore bad odds and do something mutually destructive. Keenan felt an urge to smash something.

"And that's about all I can tell," Coover said.

Keenan looked at Coover. The man was a career criminal and small-time gossip who wore his weakness like a bull's-eye. He had probably become too institutionalized for prison to be much of a punishment. Keenan could easily add a little discomfort to Coover's life, have him looking over his shoulder scared to death that the bogeyman, Keith Rawson, was planning to thrust a stiletto into his kidney. On the other hand, burning Coover would serve no purpose — Rawson was the threat and Keenan needed to put his energy there. He was also nagged by the code of ethics, though at the moment he regarded these ethics as handcuffs.

Keenan struggled with these conflicting feelings. He then shoved the three cartons of cigarettes across the table and told Coover, "Take these and get out of here. Now!"

37

venom

I

THE TWILIGHT was rapidly fading and Joe did not think the ample floodlights surrounding Golgotha's vast parking area made going inside after dark any less scary. He was surprised at how lively the parking area seemed tonight, especially in the vicinity of a white transport truck with a satellite dish on top. This truck and several other news vans were corralled behind a forty-foot barricade with police cars parked at both ends and a couple of bored-looking Columbia cops leaning against the nearer car. Behind the barricade, twenty or so reporters sat in lounge chairs or in the opened side doors of vans. Joe nodded approvingly as he drove past the media's curtailed hunting ground. Their confinement, however, did not keep the reporters from shouting a volley of questions as Joe left his van. Acting like he didn't hear them, Joe hurried into the walkway.

It had taken Joe two hours to drive back from Charleston and he still felt shaky after being chased off by Rebekah Drum. All he wanted to do now was go home, shut the door, and not have to deal with anything else. Instead, he came as promised to report to Golgotha's warden.

An escort left Joe in the Administrative Suite, which was surprisingly well furnished with two comfortable couches and a smattering of healthy-looking plants. Joe sat and slumped forward with his hands clasped between his knees as he waited to tell the Warden that he had failed.

After a wait of perhaps five minutes, a man with brown curly hair and a bushy mustache, both seasoned with gray, hurried into the suite followed by a stern-looking CO. Joe thought the CO, a stout black man, walked and stood like a drill sergeant. "Reverend Cameron, I'm Warden Clayton Edwards and this is Lieutenant Jenkins," Edwards said as he shook Joe's hand. Edward's suit looked as though he had slept in it, his tie was loosened, and deep creases etched his face.

Edwards led Joe into his office and gestured for Joe to sit in a high-backed chair facing the desk. Lieutenant Jenkins stood beside these chairs, his feet wide and hands clasped in front, as if at parade rest.

"I've just met with Drum to go over a few details like disposition of his belongings, last meal, and explained the procedures that we'll be following tomorrow night," Edwards said as he settled in behind his desk. "Do you know he's named you as his witness at his execution?"

"But I don't want to do that."

"Then you need to tell him. But I hope you'll reconsider. Reverend, we may have a problem. Right now the inmate's agitated and telling officers, including me, that he's going to fight to the bitter end tomorrow night. No one wants that to happen. So we need your help because this man does not like his attorneys, and has no other visitors. Other than you, Mr. Cameron, the frame's empty. I do hope you will seriously consider being his witness. It seems to me that it would put you in a position to possibly help this man, which is what I thought you came here wanting to do."

Joe had never been able to say no to people in authority because he so wanted to please them. And rarely did anyone ask him to do anything important. Also, the only saving grace for him in this whole fiasco was that he had not quit. "Okay. I'll do it," he said.

"Good. As his minister you will have unlimited access to him tomorrow. And excuse me for saying the obvious, but your job will be to comfort the condemned man and to help prepare him to meet death with dignity. Please believe me when I tell you that it's better for him if he does. Now, have you arranged his mother's visit?"

"She won't come."

Edwards frowned and leaned back in his chair. "Do you know why?"

"She, ah . . . doesn't want to make the trip."

"Are you sure you can't change her mind?"

Joe shook his head. "She won't come."

Absently, Edwards picked up a pencil and tapped its eraser a couple of times on the desk blotter. "All right, then," he said. "Maybe we can arrange to get a cell phone to her. I'll see what I can do." He then leaned forward and nodded toward the CO. "Lieutenant Jenkins will be in charge of the Capital Punishment Facility tomorrow night and can answer any questions that might come up later. Of course, it's imperative that you do exactly what he tells you. As you know, Mr. Cameron, we're charged with seeing that everything runs smoothly. For that to happen, everyone must carry out their responsibilities, including you. In other words, you need to handle yourself like a professional, because this is no place for amateurs."

Blinking, Joe's eyes appeared large behind his thick glasses. All he could think of saying was, "I see."

"Reverend Cameron, I'm certain you're up to the task. We're all counting on you," Edwards said and rose and again shook Joe's hand. "It would be good if you spoke to the condemned man tonight; I think the news about his mother would be received better coming from you; maybe you could ease it by telling him some other things about her. Lieutenant Jenkins will take you to him. Good night, sir."

. . .

Jenkins said very little until they passed through the security gate and started down the stairs toward the Valley-of-Evil-like Tunnel and the stalled purgatory of death row. "I know you never been through nothing like an execution," said Jenkins. "Even if you had, it still ain't easy. Publicly, they say the officers working an execution are volunteers; truth is, we ask our most reliable men to volunteer. So whether he fights or goes easy, we'll handle him. Most men, though, want to go out with a little dignity. It's better for them."

Joe nodded.

"Now, tomorrow, except when he's meeting with someone or wants privacy, you can stay with him all night. He'll probably have some things he wants to say; most men do. We'll start our prep work at eleven-forty-five. You can be with him then, but you gotta do exactly what we say and get out of the way if things turn rough. You can walk with him into the execution chamber, but since you're not an employee, after his final words we'll put you in the witness room. Any questions?"

"No."

"It'd probably be a good idea in the morning to take things easy and do whatever helps you get ready. And it you need anything at all tomorrow, let my men know, all right?"

"All right."

They reached the bottom of the stairs. Jenkins's stopped and looked at Joe. "Mr. Cameron, remember that you're not alone. For what it's worth, if there comes a time tomorrow when you need to talk, I can listen, or get you some privacy and a telephone. You just let me know."

"All right," Joe said. He felt reassured by Jenkins solid calm. "I . . . ah . . . I won't let you down."

"The secret," Jenkins said, "is to not let yourself down. Manage that and everything else falls in place."

Joe wished Jenkins had recommended a different secret, one that did not depend on him.

II

Left alone in the grim meeting room, Joe chewed his fingernails and watched the door. As the COs led Drum in, one tried to direct him by grabbing his upper arm and Drum roughly jerked it free.

"You do that again and we take you back to your cell," the CO warned. "What's it going to be?"

"Go ahead," Drum croaked hoarsely.

It seemed to Joe that the COs were extra careful as they removed the cuffs and waist chain, and then bolted Drum's leg irons to the floor. Before the CO's cleared the door, Drum muttered, "Bastards." He then took out a pack of cigarettes and lighter, and only after he blew out a hard stream of smoke did he finally look at Joe—and boy did he look angry.

"Did you take care of it?" Drum asked.

"Ah, not exactly."

"What's that mean?"

Tense, numb, and unable to think enough to be tactful, Joe blurted, "She won't come."

"Because she believed that lying bastard Keenan?"

"No. She said she threw him out because he . . . insulted her."

"And you still couldn't get her to come? You must not have asked her right."

For what seemed like a long time, Drum stared at Joe, his only movement a slight flexing of the muscles at the back of his jaws. Finally, he leaned back and his hands trembled slightly as he tapped off the cigarette ash. He took another drag. "Everybody thinks they can jerk me around. Well, I'm going to show them they can't. And you, you fucking idiot, you can't do one simple thing without fucking it up."

Joe knew better than to say anything. But Drum kept looking at him like he could kill him, and when Joe couldn't stand it anymore, he said, "Ah, I guess you don't want me to be your witness tomorrow night."

"I'm stuck with you."

"Ah, what about your lawyer? Don't they usually do things like that?"

"I'm sick of hearing Isgett cry about how wrong the death penalty is. Hell, if he weren't so incompetent he wouldn't have to sweat it. And I'd be ashamed if people thought I couldn't get anyone better than Isgett, or any other lawyer."

"Well, what about . . ."

"Shut the fuck up, you incompetent prick. She'd have come if you weren't so inept," Drum said, his head lowered like a dog about to bite.

Joe felt like crying. First Drum's mother. Now this. He couldn't stand much more.

Drum took a drag and blew the smoke directly at Joe, who rather than wave it away, cringed. And Drum just kept staring at him for the longest time. "I don't want any more fuckups, you got that?"

"I'll try," Joe promised.

"All right then. Since we're going to have to spend so much time together, I'm going to have to put this behind me, be a bigger man than I should have to be." Drum dropped the half-smoked cigarette and snubbed it out with his toe, then slowly extended his right hand across the table. "No hard feelings?"

With relief bordering on ecstasy, Joe forgot that physical contact violated prison rules as he eagerly returned the handshake, saying, "No hard feelings."

Drum smiled, then with the suddenness of a snakebite he squeezed rock-hard on Joe's hand and pain, simultaneously dull and sharp, flared between Joe's knuckles. Joe tried to free his hand but Drum's grip was too strong. Smiling, his stale breath in Joe's face, Drum said, "Stop fidgeting and act normal or I'll really hurt you."

"Please," Joe whined and crumpled forward until he almost lay on the table.

Drum's smile broadened. He squeezed harder, then eased back a bit and ordered, "I told you to straighten up and act normal."

"Okay," Joe said, doing his best to comply.

"How does my mercy feel?" Drum whispered, then squeezed so hard that Joe knew his hand must be damaged. "Does it feel like God's mercy?"

"Please," Joe whined.

"Tell me, Joe, at this moment, is there anything more important to you than me?"

"No. Nothing."

"Not even God?"

"No."

"That's right. And do you still feel so damn smug and righteous? You fat egotistical prick! Do you really think you can just walk in here, screw up my life, and then feed me all your mealymouthed crap?"

The pressure on Joe's hand seemed to increase with each angry word until he crumbled again, leaving a sweat spot where his forehead hit the table. "Please stop. Please."

"I'm telling you one more time to act normal. Now put your other hand on top of mine and bow your head."

Joe did as Drum said.

"Say hallelujah."

"Hallelujah," Joe whimpered.

"So you've come to save me. All right, then save me, Joe," Drum mocked, his face close, his breath stained with cigarettes. "Come on, Joe, save me. Save me, you fat-assed fuck. Or are you too wrapped up with saving yourself?" Drum hissed, squeezing still harder.

"Please, please," Joe sobbed through clenched teeth. Tears filled his eyes and he studied Drum like he had never studied anyone, trying to figure out what this cruel man wanted. This was insane. It was madness. It made no sense. "Please. Please, I'll do anything," Joe begged. "Tell me what?"

The door clattered open and Drum released his hold. At that moment, Joe felt overwhelming gratitude, even affection, because Drum had stopped the pain.

"Amen," Drum said, as a CO hurried into the room.

"Is everything all right in here," the officer asked.

"It's been a long time since anyone's prayed for me like that, pastor," Drum said loudly. "And it's been a long time since anyone has shed tears like that for me. Thank you, pastor. Our confidences are sacred, aren't they?" Drum smiled.

"Mr. Cameron, is everything all right?" the CO repeated, and looked disapprovingly at Joe.

"Everything's fine," Joe croaked. Joe felt as though he was going crazy. He could not look at Drum. Nor could he look at the CO, because that man would surely see through him and know what happened. Joe didn't know why, but he felt ashamed and never wanted anyone to know what happened. He wanted to hide where no one could see him. But there was no place to hide, except to shrink inside himself, to become so tiny and so small that surely no one could see him, no one could even know he was there.

A strained grin cinched Joe's face as he repeated, "Everything is fine."

. . .

After they led Drum out, Joe heard him shouting and the sounds of a scuffle on the catwalk. The racket continued, getting farther away and then moving out of the cellblock. When Joe left, protected by his fig-leaf smile, he saw that Drum's cell was completely empty, no maga-zines, no clothing, no toiletries, not even any bedding.

Joe's trip out of Golgotha seemed longer than Moses' journey through the dessert. His legs felt rubbery as he descended the steps to the parking area. Again, reporters shouted and waived their arms like trotline hooks. Without thinking, Joe flipped out both hands as if push-ing them away and hurried to the safety of his van. He turned the AC up full blast and only then became aware of how badly his hand throbbed. He could not fully flex or extend his fingers. Maybe he should see a doctor. But what could he tell him? Shut it in a door? Not likely. He couldn't tell the doctor what really happened. Joe knew it didn't make sense to feel so ashamed. He hadn't done anything wrong, he was attacked. But no one, not even Wendy, must ever know about the attack. No one. Not ever.

Pushing his face closer to the AC vent, Joe told himself, "If I just hang in there, God will take care of me and everything will turn out fine."

III

Wendy heard Joe in the driveway and had his dinner out of the oven before he came into the kitchen. "How did it go?" she asked.

"Fine," Joe answered, still smiling, though his jaw muscles ached with fatigue.

"Are you finally through with that man?" she asked.

"He wants me to witness his execution," Joe said flatly.

"Oh, Joe, no. You've got to tell him you can't," Wendy pleaded and put her hand on Joe's shoulder.

"I have to do it," Joe replied, and moved back because Wendy being this close to him felt intrusive. "I'm tired, okay. I just need to eat, take a nap, and then everything will be fine."

. . .

Joe carried a wooden tray bearing his warmed-over food to the living room. The food tasted bland, overcooked. Setting the tray aside, he pushed back his La-z-Boy and shut his eyes. But his belt felt too tight, his shirt pinched him under the arms, a toe stuck through a hole in one of his socks, and his hand still hurt.

Frustrated, Joe pushed upright and grabbed the newspaper from the coffee table. Ignoring the articles about Drum and Golgotha, he scanned the other headings. In Miami, a woman from Denmark, a mother of two, had been shot in what was described as a random act of violence. In Tennessee, another black church had been burned. In Chicago, a stray bullet from a gang member's automatic weapon killed an eleven-year-old girl as she slept in her bed.

Bad news, Joe thought, nothing but bad news. Roughly he turned the page and scanned the World Capsule Summary. In Athens, a terrorist bomb killed twenty-three. New ethnic cleansing shattered the fragile Eastern Europe peace. Thousands died from starvation and cholera as a result of a resurgence of civil war in Rwanda. Throwing the front-page aside, Joe picked up the state and local section, only to find more of the same. A Columbia cab driver was robbed at gunpoint and then hammered in the face with the pistol butt. Two con men bilked an eighty-one-year-old woman out of her life savings. And in Charleston, two men were arrested for throwing a puppy from their truck as they drove across the Cooper River Bridge.

Joe, who prided himself on never getting angry, threw the newspaper on the floor. When he shut his eyes, he saw Drum's face, with his stale breath, looming inches from his own. What Drum had done to Joe was nothing compared to the tragedies in the newspaper and . . . it was much too painful to think about what Drum's victims must have endured.

None of those victims deserved to be stripped of their humanity. How could a merciful God allow such atrocities? How could an all-powerful God sit on his hands? What could possibly be tested or taught through such inhumane abuse? Surely not lessons in faith. Surely not lessons in love. If this was part of a plan, it was as deranged as anything that Isaac Drum could conceive, because only the truly mad—or truly evil—could so abuse those who love them.

38

good intentions

I

FLOODLIGHTS GLOWED at both corners of the Paxtons' house and two squad cars flanked the driveway. Keenan had scarcely switched off the Buick's engine when a patrolman tapped on the window to verify his ID, while a second officer positioned himself at the opposite rear fender. Tonight, thankful for this protection, Keenan treated their thoroughness with strained courtesy.

The night's pleasantly cool air resonated with the sound of cicadas and moths pinging around the outdoor lights. Keenan's tie was loosened and his eyes red and dry. He rang the doorbell, then surveyed the shadows on neighbors' lawns and found way too many blind spots. Sooner or later, a determined stalker might find gaps in anyone's protection. How many scores of agents paved the way and then guarded the president, yet in Keenan's lifetime two presidents had been shot and others came close. To hell if he was going to sit back and wait for Rawson to try something.

Keenan was about to ring the bell again when Zack opened the door. "Oh, it's you. Come on in," Zack said and led Keenan from the landing into the living room. He wore gray sweatpants and a baggy navy blue T-shirt. "Mom's in the kitchen on the phone with Martin Stith. She said to tell whoever was at the door that she'd be out in a couple of minutes. Have a seat."

Keenan settled on the edge of the recliner and leaned forward with his forearms on his knees. Zack plopped on the couch and picked up the video joystick. Rather than activate the game, Zack looked at Keenan and complained, "She's talking in the kitchen so I can't hear. Mom never tells me much. She thinks that because I lost my dad that

I can't handle anything. She needs to stop treating me like a kid. I am thirteen."

To Keenan's raw mood, Zack's complaint sounded like whining. Annoyed, he asked, "So what should you know that everybody's not telling you?"

Still holding the joystick, Zack shrugged, then said, "I'd like to know if that man is really going to try to hurt us." He then looked down at the controls in his hands and shrugged again. "I was just wondering about that."

Keenan stared at Zack for a moment, then averted his eyes and berated himself for bringing his belligerent mood into this house, this family. Of course, Zack had good reason to want to know what was going on. Through no fault of his own, this kid had been marked by a psychopath to be bound, raped, and mutilated. And while everyone else came together, their efforts to shield Zack left him alone with his imagination. Though tired and angry, Keenan thought he should have realized all this before walking into the house. He also needed to remember that whatever of Zack's flaws resulted from the absence of a father to guide and model for him were, at least in part, Keenan's responsibility. He had as much obligation to help this boy as he did to help Marianne, probably even more.

"That's a fair question," Keenan said. "But if you want me to answer it, you'll put down the game controls and look at me." At first, Zack acted as if he hadn't heard Keenan. Then he languidly set the remote on the coffee table. "Now look at me," Keenan said. "That's what adults do when they talk, they look at each other. Thank you. To answer your question, yes, I think this guy, Rawson, is trying to find a way to hurt you."

"Why? That's crazy."

Keenan nodded. "It is crazy, but he's a nothing man who wants to be big and thinks that hurting you will make him famous."

Zack thought for a moment, then said, "Like these three guys who got caught vandalizing the school and everybody knew about it so they started acting like they were rock stars or something, when before nobody hardly noticed them."

"Exactly," Keenan said, pleased. Zack's understanding reminded him of the way Will had quickly grasped dynamics. "So until Rawson is caught, you need to be careful. This is not a game."

"Okay," Zack said, nodding. He shifted and leaned forward, roughly mirroring Keenan's posture, except that he looked down for a moment, then raised his head and said, "Can I ask you something else?"

"Anything," Keenan said, which brought a look of surprise to Zack.

Before Zack could ask his question, the kitchen door opened and Marianne came out and, spotting Keenan, said, "John, I'm glad you're here."

In a hushed voice, Zack said, "What I want to know is private. Maybe later."

"It's up to you," Keenan said, then rose to greet Marianne.

She wore a maroon blouse and jeans, and Keenan noticed more than he usually did the snug fit of her jeans and the graceful lines of her breasts. Marianne hugged him, quick and formal, and still standing near the kitchen door, said, "Martin just filled me in on how he identified Rawson. He keeps telling me they'll have him in a day or two. I wish I could be as confident." Marianne shook her head. "We also talked about tomorrow night and I'm going to follow your advice and let Martin take my place at the execution."

Keenan had wanted Marianne to change her mind about witnessing the execution, yet he resented Stith advancing himself as a substitute before Keenan had the opportunity to offer himself. In spite of his resentment, Keenan nodded and said, "I'm glad you're not going to be the witness."

"Martin also said that Drum finally admitted that he had been lying all along. I guess that was your doing because he said you and Drum had some sort of altercation. Are you all right?"

Given how Marianne felt about Drum, she would probably applaud anything that might increase his suffering. Yet, Keenan did not want Marianne to know what he had done; he wanted to keep his vengeful actions hidden. He didn't exactly feel ashamed. It was more a feeling that Marianne and others might not fully understand. So, he simply said, "I'm fine. After Drum confessed to lying he realized that he was out of options and became frustrated and tried to lunge across the table. I held him down until the COs arrived, that's all. No big deal. Anyway, I've just finished talking to Rawson's old cellmate and . . ."

"Wait, let's go in the kitchen," Marianne said.

"I need to hear too," Zack said from where sat on the couch, watching and listening.

"I don't think so," Marianne replied emphatically.

"Mom, our counselor said that if you quit treating me like a little kid, we might have more to talk about."

"It may be worse on him not knowing and imagining the worst," Keenan said. "And if he doesn't know what's going on he might inadvertently stumble into something dangerous."

Marianne bit on her upper lip as she considered, then sighed and said, "All right, John. If you think it's best." Keenan found it both gratifying and wrong that Marianne trusted him so completely.

She went to the couch, sat beside Zack, and put her hand on his. Zack pulled his hand away, saying, "I'm not a kid." Marianne then folded her hands on her knee and asked, "Okay, should we be worried about this man?"

Keenan again sat on the edge of the recliner and twisted to face them. "Yes," he said. He then told them what he had learned from Rawson's cellmate and what he thought it meant.

". . . so on top of being reckless and stupid," Keenan concluded, "he's probably staying high on the cocaine and PCP he took from Gilpin. Add the pressure from the manhunt, and I think he's so agitated that he's coming unraveled, and that increases the likelihood that he'll try something bold to reassure himself that he's still in control. Plus, what he most wants is notoriety, and the perfect opportunity to thrust himself into the spotlight comes tomorrow night while the national media are gathered here for Drum's execution. I'm certain Rawson will try something then. And if he believes that Zack is too well protected, he'll probably go after someone else."

"Shit," Marianne said and balled her fists. "There's no way we can win. If we're protected, then someone else gets hurt. Shit!" She shook her head and looked intently at Keenan. "John, do you have any ideas on what we should do?"

"We can make sure that neither happens," Keenan said. "I want the two of you under heavy guard tomorrow night. But we can also misdirect Rawson, make him think you're going to be somewhere you're not and that you've given up your protection. That might lure him into a trap."

It had not been made public that Rawson had written down Zack's name and, therefore, may have targeted him. With that in mind, Keenan suggested that Marianne tell the press that because Drum had admitted the threat was a hoax, she no longer believed her son in danger and wanted privacy tomorrow night, with no reporters and no police intruding. Marianne liked the plan, and especially liked using Drum's own admission to undercut the evil he had sicced on them. After some discussion, they decided that Marianne's mother's house offered a believable place that was rural enough to allow a tactical team to saturate the surrounding area. Obviously, Marianne's mother would be elsewhere and an assault team would housesit.

Keenan next asked Marianne where she planned to spend tomorrow evening and she said she wanted to go to Bradley Miller's gathering. Over the years, several family members of Drum's victims had formed a tight-knit group. Bradley Miller, Alicia Owens's father, had become a vocal advocate for the rights of victim's families and on the night of the execution wanted other families of Drum's victims to gather at his large country home.

Based on Marianne's descriptions, Keenan thought Miller abrasive and rigid. Yet, Marianne had grown close to several in this group, especially Alvin Owens, who in the weeks following Will's death had reached out to her the way Will had tried to reach out to him. Given the volatility of her hatred for Drum and strain from the current threat, Keenan thought it wise for Marianne to be among those who could offer a uniquely deep support. He knew she also wanted to cushion Alvin from any abuse heaped on by his father-in-law, Bradley Miller, who blamed Alvin for not accompanying Alicia on the night of her abduction. Alvin already felt guilty about this without any help from his father-in-law.

They ironed out a few other details, then Keenan said he should go back to his room and call Stith to work out tactical plans while Marianne returned calls from reporters and set up the misdirection. They all stood and Keenan looked at Zack, who had listened without interrupting, and asked, "Do you have anything that you want to say or ask?"

Zack shook his head. "I think it's a great plan; I really do. And thanks for what you're doing. I'll see you tomorrow, okay?" he said and shuffled toward his room.

Marianne then walked Keenan to the door. "John, we're going to the cemetery tomorrow to remember Will. I'd love for you to go with us."

"Of course," he told her.

"Would you also go with us tomorrow night to Bradley Miller's gathering. If you need to be elsewhere, that's fine, but I've . . . always admired your strength and felt safe around you. I hope it doesn't show, but with everything coming to a head . . . I need someone to lean on just a little."

They reached the door and stood facing each other. Keenan thought her eyes as bright as on the night he first met her. His voice husky, he said, "I'll do anything for you."

They hugged and Keenan felt her breasts pushed against his chest and for the second time that day became physically aroused. When they parted, yearning tugged at Keenan, yet he hesitated. A kiss tonight would be telling; he felt too much desire for it not to be. But Keenan just stood there feeling awkward until Marianne broke the uneasiness by touching his cheek and saying, "When all this is over, there's a lot of things I need to sort out."

"It will be over soon," Keenan promised, seemingly reassuring her but actually emotionally distancing himself.

"Well, I guess I need to go call some reporters," Marianne said, then stepped back and folded her arms as if hugging herself. "And let's pray that man doesn't get a chance to hurt anyone else."

. . .

Keenan walked to his car feeling both loss and relief. He always sought control of situations, yet had felt awkward and waited for Marianne to choose what happened between them. For years he had been a friend and sounding board for Marianne, but he tried to keep the giving one-sided. To find pleasure in any way that resulted from Will's absence seemed taboo, and his desire for Marianne felt like betrayal. He was probably misreading friendship and trust made urgent by fear, anyway.

Frustrated with his lapse in clear-eyed detachment, Keenan willed himself to push everything out of his mind except for Rawson and the threat, and to keep his goddamned emotions under wraps. Yet, in the car as he turned on the ignition, he thought again of Marianne's breasts pushing on his chest and his erection would not go away.

39

hydra

I

KEENAN BOLTED upright in bed and only the sudden onrush of darkness kept him from running, flailing like a madman against the horrid images still fresh in his mind. Vice-like tightness squeezed off his breath, worsening his panic. Drenched in sweat, Keenan strained until he finally gulped in a hiccup of air and then another and another until he began to breathe in rapid snorts. Keenan then forced each breath a little deeper than the last until the squeezed feeling around his chest eased and the nightmare's terror receded. Yet the room still seemed sweltering, the air barely breathable. He dressed quickly, glanced at the clock as he did—it was almost two A.M.—and hurried from his room into the damp night air, and immediately breathed more easily.

Walking at a good clip, Keenan left the motel's parking lot and crossed the empty lanes of Jeffcoat Boulevard, then proceeded onto the Saluda River Bridge, its turn-of-the-century streetlights fuzzy in the dewy night. Above Columbia's skyline, a three-quarters moon peeked between a smattering of cumulus clouds. Below the bridge, low-lying fog blanketed the river and muted the sound of water rushing past rocks and small islands. And across the way, the dark stones of Golgotha's back wall rose above the fog's ghostly plain, like the walls of hell forever keeping in the damned.

Refreshed by the cool air emanating from the river below, Keenan stopped midway on the bridge and filled his lungs. Calmer now, he leaned with his forearms on the cement railing and tried to make sense of the nightmare. The dream was based on an actual videotape confiscated from two serial killers, Charles Nunez and Fletcher Van

Owen. Nunez and Van Owen had used ads for inexpensive electronic equipment to lure the unsuspecting to their wilderness cabin, where they raped and tortured their victims over several days. They video-taped everything and later sold the tapes on the shadowy snuff-film market. Van Owen died resisting arrest, but the elusive Nunez escaped. Keenan had studied several of their tapes while preparing a profile on Nunez. It was one of his first assignments after going to work for Ben Lockhart and, not yet inured to such horrors, had haunted him for weeks.

On the particular tape from which tonight's dream was drawn, Nunez slowly raped, mutilated, and then cut the throat of a pretty brunette with shoulder-length hair. Throughout the assault, she wept and begged her tormentor to stop, while her bound-and-gagged husband was forced to watch everything.

In his dream, it was Keenan helplessly bound in a chair and forced to watch. But tonight, rather than Nunez and Van Owen, Drum's face leered above the camera, cold and sadistic, while Wayne Rawson wielded the knife. And the woman was Marianne, her eyes remaining on Keenan, silently pleading for help he could not give. Her anguish and torture were not enough to awaken Keenan from his nightmare before she died. Only when the bloodied Rawson turned toward him, smiled, and started slowly approaching with the knife held before him did panic finally catapult Keenan out of this nightmare, his heart pounding and his chest squeezed by a choking band.

In the weeks following Will's death, a variation of this nightmare had awakened Keenan exactly seven times. On each awakening, he continued to feel suffocated until he escaped into the open night. To make matters worse, Keenan's difficulty breathing indoors spread into other areas of his life. Even moderately crowded rooms seemed so unbearably stuffy that when heading to a meeting Keenan always checked for the quickest exit and felt more comfortable sitting where he could see the door. When he traveled, he began staying only in motels where but a single door stood between him and breathable air—atriums, elevators, and long hallways had felt like a pillow pushed over his face. It was also during this time that seething irritability marred his relations with peers.

To cope, Keenan began pushing himself nightly on hard walks. He also made his first call to Marianne, determined to help her in any way that he could—but from a distance. These calls, more than anything else, seemed to let off some of the pressure in him. Within three weeks or so, the dreams and other problems subsided. The walks and calls, however, became fixtures in his life, as did staying in motels where he could step through only one door and be outside.

It made sense, Keenan told himself, for this nightmare to return given his concerns for Marianne and Zack's well-being and all the things that had been stirred up from confronting Drum. He simply needed to keep tight control over himself through tomorrow night, when everything should get resolved, and Drum would be dead.

Keenan raised his head, stared at Golgotha's jagged silhouette, and wondered what Drum, a nocturnal creature, was now doing. Pacing? Plotting? Perhaps suffering? As Keenan thought of Drum, he felt a longing to be at Drum's execution. He wanted the last thing Drum saw to be the contempt and gloating in Keenan's face. He had wanted this ever since he began pursuing deathwatch interviews with Drum eight years ago. Now, Stith had stolen his place.

He thought it would be easy to unseat Stith. He could simply tell Marianne that he wanted to be the witness and she would most likely go along. But he would rather keep the full extent of his bloodlust hidden from her. Another way might be to pull Marianne aside and express concern that Inabinet's recent death might make Stith too vulnerable, and then offer himself as an alternative. And bloodying Stith's arrogant pride promised echoes of the chest-pounding power he had felt after breaking Drum. But what good would come from giving into these desires?

A car drove across the bridge, slowing as it passed Keenan. At this lonely hour the driver possibly thought him a jumper. The car moved on and Keenan straightened from where he had leaned on the rail. The night air passed easily through his dress shirt, pleasantly chilling him. He felt tempted to set off in the direction of Golgotha, pushing himself and all his pent-up tension hard and sweating into the night. Instead, he started back to his room to get what sleep he could before tomorrow's long day.

As he started walking, he glanced back at Golgotha. The moonlit fog and shadowed stones came together like a juncture of heaven and hell, good and evil, right and wrong.

40

thursday morning

I

DRUM LAY on his side atop a mattress that had no sheet on it and a thin pillow with no pillowcase. Though he lay with his eyes shut, he knew that COs were watching him from the control booth that was directly across the polished hall from his cell, and that they logged everything he did. Worse than being continuously watched, however, was the oppressive quiet here in the death house. It raked his nerves more than the relentless noise in CB2 ever had.

He had dozed some but now lay awake and wondered if the sun had come up yet, but felt too listless to open his eyes and look at the clock mounted above the control booth. What the hell did the time matter, anyway? His attorney, Sammy Isgett, couldn't get him out of here until the courts opened. So Drum intended to lie there with his eyes shut until they brought him breakfast.

As he lay there, it occurred to Drum that getting a last-minute reprieve might make this the best day of his life. This started him wondering what had been his best day, so far. Certainly, those days when he had taken women were the most important days of his life; he had felt powerful then and completely alive. But he had also seethed with anger, and he did not believe he ever felt true happiness while having his way. Had there ever been a time when he felt genuine happiness? Drum thought about this until he became drowsy and began drifting from consciousness. Then, in sleep's twilight, a clear memory emerged from among the fragments and images floating in his mind, a memory of what might well have been the happiest day of his life. Drum became fully awake as he remembered.

I was nine years old and we were living in Charleston and it was the

*afternoon of my school's Christmas show. I didn't want to be in this stu-
pid show but the teacher didn't give me any choice. I was a shepherd and
had one line, "A star led us here."*

*We were all behind the stage getting ready and there were a lot of kids
talking loud and showing off. I had only been in this school since
September and pretty much kept to myself, which suited me just fine
because most of the kids here were stupid.*

*I had on a stripped cloth that was supposed to be a robe and this girl
from my homeroom came over and said that it wasn't pinned right. She
didn't ask me, she just started straightening the robe and putting the pins
in different places. I expected her to stick me with a pin but she didn't. I
had never liked this girl. She was the teacher's pet, always showing off by
answering questions and getting good grades. "There," she said. "You
look good. And don't be nervous, it'll be fun." Then she smiled and went
on to help someone else. After that, I kept watching her as she went from
person to person, helping them or saying something or laughing. I kept
watching her and imagined what it would be like if she and I were
friends, maybe even best friends. And the more I thought about it, the
more it seemed like we were already friends.*

*It came time for the play to start and I went with the other two shepherds
to the steps at the front of the stage. The auditorium was crowded. A lot of
parents had come, mostly mothers but there were several men there, too. I
knew that my mother wouldn't come to something so stupid. And I was glad
because I didn't want her wasting her time by coming to this dumb play.*

*A couple of late arrivals were still settling into their seats when the
play started. My part wasn't coming up for a while, so I just watched all
the parents craning their necks and smiling. They looked stupid and it
made me mad watching them act this way. Then the door at the back of
the auditorium opened and my mother came in.*

*Her hair was done up and she was wearing her best outfit, a low-cut
red dress and a white coat that she told everyone was real fur, though I
knew it wasn't. Mom stood at the door until she saw me and waved. She
tip-toed, looking for an empty seat, and lurched as if she were about to
lose her balance. When she came up the aisle, the sound of her high
heels hitting the floor caused several people to turn around and look.
Even though she weaved pretty badly, Mom walked the way she always
did, with her head up.*

Near the front, Mom crossed to an empty seat and kept saying, "Excuse me," loud enough that a lot of the kids on stage watched her and got out of sync in saying their lines. When she reached the empty seat, I noticed that there was a man in the seat beside it, probably the only man here that wasn't with anyone, and I thought that somehow my mother had spotted him. I watched real close and saw him checking out her tits as she took off her coat. Mom then sat, smiled at this man, and said something to him and he smiled back and said something. She then pointed me out to him and waved at me again.

Mom and this man kept talking and once she laughed too loud and a couple of people turned and shooshed her. But even while she was talking with him, she kept glancing my way and smiling, though it was a weak smile, a sad smile. I was so busy watching my mother that I didn't hear our cue until the other two shepherds stood and then I got up too. I looked toward my mother, hoping that she was watching, and she was, but it looked like she was smiling and crying at the same time.

I walked across the stage fast and got ahead of the other two shepherds and I listened real close until I heard my cue, "How did you know to come here?" I then turned and said as loud as I could, "A star led us here."

My mother stood and clapped and said, "That's my son." She almost lost her balance but the man sitting beside her steadied her and I saw her tits brushing against his arms as she sat down. Then she looked back at me and smiled. She kept watching me for a long time, and she was crying.

When the play ended, my mother was all smiles as she pushed her way forward. She was alone; the man was not with her. "Isaac, you were wonderful," she said and kissed me on the cheek. I smelled liquor on her breath but I didn't care. "Come on, we're going to take a taxi home," she said. Together, just me and her and no one else, we left the auditorium and I rode in a taxi for the first time in my life with my mother sitting close and talking to me and telling me that she was proud of me. And I was happy, really, really happy. It was the best moment of my life.

The cab pulled up in front of my house and my mother told him to wait. She walked me to the door and unlocked it. "Isaac, I have to go out for just a little while. I won't be too long. Take whatever you want *out of the refrigerator, okay? You'll be safe. And I won't be gone long, I promise."*

I wanted her to come in and for us to keep talking, but I just nodded and said, "Don't be too late, okay."

"I promise you, Isaac, I won't be long."

.   .   .

Drum stirred on the bunk, but kept his eyes closed. This memory left him feeling pretty good, but he wondered why his mother had been crying and some darker memory stirred. Drum then remembered feeling afraid after his mother left him alone that evening. He wasn't afraid because she had gone out; he was used to that. What was he afraid of, then? He had a feeling that something had happened the night before, and with this feeling came an image of someone large and dark. Drum now felt certain that when his mother left him alone that evening, he was afraid that this person would come to the house because he had come to their house on the night before the school play. Then he remembered.

It was getting dark when someone knocked on our door. Mom was in the bedroom and yelled for me to get it. Our porch light had burned out so the man at the door seemed large and dark. He had on a plaid coat and had dark hair, like mine except his was real thin on top. What struck me most about him, though, was that his hands seemed so large. He looked down at me, but didn't smile. "You must be Isaac," he said.

I shrugged.

"I'm your grandfather," he said, and then pushed past me without asking.

"Who is it, Isaac?" Mom called as she came into the living room. When she saw him, she froze. Usually, my mother filled a room in a way that everybody watched. But when she saw this man, who claimed to be my grandfather, Mom seemed to become smaller. "What do you want?" she said, and even her voice sounded small.

"I thought it was time I came to see you," he said.

"I don't want you here, okay," Mom said and wrapped her arms around her upper body. "I want you to go, right now."

"I'll stay as long as I want," he said and took a step toward her. Mom, who never took shit off anybody, stepped back and started rocking with her upper body and looked even smaller as he closed the distance

between them and wrapped his large hand around her forearm. "Come on, now. It's time we patch things up. Be a good girl like you used to. You know I'll help you with money, just like I used to," he said and put his large hand on her breast, squeezing it hard, and pushing her toward the bedroom.

"No, Daddy, please."

I grabbed an ashtray off the coffee table and threw it as hard as I could and hit him on the hip. "Leave her alone," I shouted.

He let go of Mom and looked at me. "You little heathen. You do something like that again and I'll straighten you out good."

Mom had stepped sideways away from him. "You leave my son alone and you get out," she said, sounding more the way she usually did when somebody fucked with her.

"I come to see you and I'm going to. And I don't want you getting smart-mouthed the way you used to."

He tried to grab Mom again and she ducked into the kitchen and he followed. I picked up the ashtray and was going in after him when he came backing out. Then my mother came out holding a butcher knife. "You fucking bastard, you leave me alone. And don't you ever mess with my son."

He stopped backing up and she stopped pressing, but her expression didn't change.

"You're worried about your son? Who are you kidding," he said. "Don't you think Mary's told your mother how you treat that boy? You're not a fit parent and you know it. You're nothing but trash, Reba, and you always have been, hooking up with any tomcat that looked your way."

"And what are you, Daddy? You're so goddamn proud of being a church deacon and then you . . ."

He lunged and grabbed the wrist of the hand holding the knife and then grabbed Mom's other wrist so she couldn't switch hands with the knife.

But Mom yelled, and it was the loudest I'd ever heard her yell, "Rape! Rape! Rape!"

He let her go and moved back across the room. "Shut up! Shut up, for Christ's sake!"

"Get out, now, or I start yelling and won't stop until someone comes

and I'll tell them everything, like I should have done a long time ago."

He stood there until Mom opened her mouth to yell again. "All right, I'll go," he said. At the door he stopped and looked real mean at my mother. "I promise you I'll be back," he said, then left.

Mom paced with the knife for several minutes, then poured herself a drink and cried while she drank it. After that, she kept pouring herself drinks and paced some more, cursing now, and I knew better than to say anything to her. She stayed home that night and we both slept in her bed with the butcher knife on the nightstand and a chair propped against the door.

The next day, she came to my school play. But she didn't come home that night. I was left alone, afraid that my grandfather would come back, and it occurred to me that maybe she was afraid, too, and that was why she didn't come home.

On the morning after the play, she still hadn't come home. I got myself ready and went to school. A lot of things were bothering me and I decided that I would talk to the girl who had been friendly before the play and tell her about all the stuff that had happened, even though Mom always said that what we did was nobody's business. When I got to school she was standing outside of homeroom, talking to a couple of other girls. I went up and stood beside her, but I didn't know what to say, especially with those other girls standing there. "Is there something you want?" she asked. I just shrugged. She frowned. I smiled at her but she didn't stop frowning. "Okay then, I need to go," she said and walked off with those other girls. She looked back once and then I heard her and the other girls giggling.

Later in the morning, I asked the teacher if I could get something from my coat. While I was alone in the cloakroom, I found that girl's coat and peed on it.

Drum stirred, got off his bunk, and pissed in the small steel commode at the back of his cell. He couldn't understand why he hadn't remembered any of this stuff before, or why he was remembering it now. Probably because Keenan had fucked with his mind. Thinking of Keenan, he felt angry, felt more like himself. He buttoned the orange jumpsuit that they forced him to wear while in the death house. "Well, fuck Keenan, because those things probably never happened."

He looked at the clock. It was seven A.M., not that it mattered.

41

armed and dangerous

I

STITH HELD the palm-sized Chief's Special Airweight above his head and squinted down its snub barrel. Gun oil hung in the air and stained his hands. Satisfied, he placed the little .38 beside the fresh cleaned Sig Sauer, and glanced at the window above the kitchen sink. Enough light had come into the sky to silhouette the treetops across the apartment complex's parking lot. An M16A1 assault rifle also lay on the table along with the Remington shotgun that he kept in his car's trunk. Stith picked up the shotgun and unscrewed the cylinder from the end of the pump. When the barrel came loose, he lay the rest of the gun aside, and pushed the rod holding the bore brush through the barrel's length to scrub the lead from the rifling. Of course, Stith's guns had been spotless before he started this cleaning. It was more ritual than necessity, a way of honing his focus on what was at stake and what might be required.

For several weeks now he had been awakening early, sometimes as early as five o'clock. He never felt quite rested. In fact, he always seemed to be restless and in a lousy mood. And spending his days sitting behind a desk wasn't helping. That was partly why he had taken over the Rawson manhunt.

Stith unscrewed the bore brush from the cleaning rod and replaced it with an eyehook that he threaded with a felt-like cleaning patch. He squeezed a little oil on the cloth and worked it through the barrel several times. Finished, he held the barrel toward the light like a hand-held telescope. Inside, it gleamed like dark glass. Satisfied, Stith oiled the pump's slide and firing mechanism. He reassembled the shotgun, then slammed the pump back and forth a couple of times before he pushed red-cased shells through the slot.

Stith had never fired a weapon in the line of duty. He had drawn his gun several times and a few times even charged through doors with weapon in hand—the last time he had done that he still carried a .38 Smith and Wesson, it had been that long ago. Luckily, he had controlled every dicey situation with something other than deadly force. A couple of times after he finessed a close call, he claimed that he held back because he didn't want to do the blizzard of paperwork required after firing in the line of duty. In truth, Inabinet had drilled him again and again about the decision to fire being the most serious choice he would ever make and that it afforded no error either way. Stith knew that if he ever used deadly force, even after he moved from Inabinet's department to SLED, that one way or another he would have to account to Inabinet. In fact, if he ever crossed over the line just a little, he would have had to answer to Inabinet.

Stith remembered one particularly mouthy perp from his first year as a patrolman. The guy's wife had watched as Stith led him out, ignoring the EMT who urged her to go to the hospital for stitches in her lip and to have her right eye checked, it looked that nasty. Stith knew she wouldn't file charges; this wasn't the first time he had been called to this house, and this scene. As they walked to the patrol car, the guy just kept mouthing off about what a tough man he was and that this was a family matter, a matter of honor, and the police should butt out. He tried to jerk his arm away from Stith and puffed out his chest. At the squad car, Stith thought how easy it would be to smash this piece of shit's nose against the roof and then ask the guy if he was man enough to take what he dished out. If Stith had done that, he would have had to answer to Inabinet, and he had never lied to the old man. So Stith put his hand over the perp's head and guided him in almost as gently as if it had been his mother.

But Inabinet wasn't around anymore.

Pressing the Remington to his shoulder, Stith looked down the barrel. He wondered what it would be like to have its bead on Wayne Rawson's chest. And who really cared any longer what Stith might do?

42

faraway

I

THURSDAY STARTED with another perfect autumn morning, though the weatherman said a cold front would arrive tonight. Dressed in gray sweats, Joe once again settled into his patio lounge chair surrounded by butterfly patterns of light. Oblivious to the flickering fall beauty, Joe sipped occasionally from a coffee mug, whose red letters claimed WORLD'S GREATEST HUSBAND, and studied barely legible writings in a worn green notebook. He moved his finger slowly across each line and mouthed the words as he deciphered them. He went over every line a couple of times, yet understanding what the notes meant remained just beyond his grasp.

Joe twisted to pick up his coffee mug with his left hand—his right, the hand that Drum had squeezed, remained too stiff to completely flex, though it didn't hurt as much as last night, so Joe didn't think he needed to see a doctor. Most of his anger from last night had also subsided. He still had not reconciled a loving God with so much senseless suffering, and this left a gaping emptiness that he hoped these notes might somehow fill.

Joe had begun looking through this notebook late last night. He had stayed up late, sitting in the family room and trying to distract himself from his depression and anger by watching television. Mostly, he had stared at the screen while his mind tumbled with a thousand thoughts. Wendy checked on him once, then left him alone. At eleven, when the news came on, Joe sat in his La-z-Boy with a glass of milk and a box of Oreos that he chewed without tasting. Dog-tired, his mind seemed too numb even for the sedative of TV. Then something on the news had completely captured his attention.

A young woman in a fashionable business suit had interviewed Mrs. Gladys Paulus, whose husband of thirty years, Pop Paulus, had been murdered by Drum in order to steal his truck. Mrs. Paulus had a round face with skin the color of dark molasses, thick glasses, and wore a matching blue outfit and hat with a large flower brooch. When the interviewer asked her how she felt about the execution, Mrs. Paulus had said, "I believe that only God should have the power over life and death. If they would just keep that man locked up so he can't hurt anyone else, I'd be at peace with that. Matter of fact, I hope that man, who has caused so many wonderful people to suffer, can make his peace with God."

"Do you really mean that?" the interviewer asked.

"Yes, ma'am," Mrs. Paulus answered. "It's what my faith demands of me. After losing Pop, it was my faith that allowed me to go on. If I'd gotten all clogged up with hate, then I might not be able to still share my family's love and joy. But I can, I truly can."

Joe felt shamed by her faith. He did not want to believe her. He had never had that kind of faith, not even in the spiritual euphoria right after baptism. And if someone killed Wendy, he certainly did not think he could forgive that person. How could anyone forgive someone who had done him or her such harm? Could Mark Kemper or Adeline Cornish? Joe had no idea how to forgive such wrongs, but he believed this was one shortcoming he shared with lots of others.

Feeling as if Mrs. Paulus had personally rebuked him, Joe picked up the remote and, jabbing it toward the screen, hit the off-button. But he could not stop wondering how anyone could be so forgiving. Then, for some strange reason, Joe recalled a man named Faraday, who absolutely had been the worst instructor at seminary. Short, bald, and energetic, Faraday's classes were a huge waste of time. Rather than prepare and teach, the old charlatan would throw out whatever preposterous idea popped into his bald head and then badger you into expressing your opinion and then badger you about your opinion, obviously trying to embarrass you. Even worse, many of Faraday's ridiculous ideas stood at odds with what every good Baptist knew to be the truth. Joe had joked that Faraday was a Lutheran in Baptist clothing. And he had coined the nickname "Faraway," which had stuck.

So why think of Faraway now? Punishment from hell? Vaguely, Joe thought that maybe it had something to do with forgiveness and that Faraway had said something similar to what Mrs. Paulus had said. He tried to stop thinking about Faraway but thoughts of the man just kept pestering him. Maybe if he could remember what Faraway had said, he could finally relax and go to sleep.

Since Joe never knew when he might need something, he was a pack rat, with all his old class materials stored in the attic. Trying to be quiet and not wake Wendy, Joe rummaged in the attic until he found a small cardboard box sealed with dried-out packing tape and labeled "Faraway." He lugged the box to the living room and broke the yellowed tape with his penknife. A worn, dark green notebook lay on top. Beneath it were books Joe considered quasi-religious at best, some even by Jewish writers, whose doctrines a good Baptist had no business reading. There were books by Eric Fromm, Paul Tillich, Martin Buber, and even Albert Camus and Immanuel Kant. Joe had not read any of them because Faraway had not been smart enough to include recommended readings on his tests.

Quickly, Joe closed the box, as if afraid heretical ideas might spill out and pollute his home. He then leaned back and began leafing through the notebook. Most pages contained more doodles than notes. Joe stopped on a page headed "Free Will." At the beginning of each class, Faraway would write something on the board, and Joe always copied it verbatim. This note read: "Proposition—An omnipotent and omniscient God both determines and knows the future. This negates free will because actions that are foreknown and predetermined cannot be chosen. Or does it? Can an omnipotent God choose not to foresee the future if that is His will? This power would mean that free will is a possibility. What does your experience lead you to believe?"

In the margin, Joe had written, "HOKUM—we know God's will by studying His words in the Bible." Lots of looping doodles, arrows, and a couple of funny faces with big noses followed. Usually, Joe wrote down examples and the other things that Faraway said, because professors only test on stuff they tell you. One barely legible note read, "Does a good and loving parent try to control a child's life or does this parent attempt to prepare the child to live his or her life as best he or she can? Is it possible that a good and loving God would want his children to experience all the joys, uncertainties, and heartbreak from the consequences of their choices? Or would a loving God determine exactly what they should choose and what they should experience?" In the margin, Joe had written, "HOKUM—READ THE BIBLE."

Turning the page, Joe read the lessons last note; "If we have free will, this means that whether we fail or succeed, it is not God's will. His will is that we have the opportunity to fail or succeed."

Joe slammed closed the notebook and said, "Hokum."

.   .   .

After so much turmoil last night, Joe hoped he would sleep late this morning, especially given what lay ahead of him tonight. But much earlier than he wished, he seemed suddenly to be awake, just staring at the ceiling and thinking of the pesky Faraday. Once he arose, he couldn't leave the notebook alone.

So Joe sat outside on that blessed morning, squinting at his barely legible handwriting. With each new page there seemed to be more HOKUMs. The intensity of this antagonism surprised Joe. He had never been a smart aleck or a rebel. He wanted people to think of him as a good boy, and to like him. What about Faraday had brought out so much animosity? Sure, Joe had believed him at best an apostate, more likely a heretic for so recklessly challenging bedrock doctrines. And sure, Joe had been idealistic, even a little arrogant with his religious zeal; like he sometimes now saw in youths at his church.

As Joe now read these notes, with two decades' more life experience, he began to see Faraday as a man prodding apprentice ministers to think through their faith. And in a rare flash of insight, Joe understood his rancor for Professor Faraday. Joe had been a deeply insecure youth whose faith told him that he had been chosen to receive the absolute truth and was, therefore, special. Faraday's challenges had kicked at the certainty bolstering the "specialness" of Joe's famished esteem. So Joe had fortified his beliefs by belittling Faraday's dissonant voice—a psychological killing of the messenger.

At last, on a page labeled "MORE HOKUM," Joe found the notes about forgiveness. They were very, very sketchy, less than half a page including doodles. Joe had not paid attention that day. At the top he had written, "Proposition: What does forgiveness most change? The one who is forgiven? Or the one who forgives?" Below this, Joe could only make out two fragmented lines: "Hate is a poison," and "When someone forgives another, it stops hate's poison." That was all Joe's notes said. Nowhere did Faraday tell him how to forgive.

Joe closed the notebook. He should have known that these notes would be a huge waste of time. In a few hours, he would be going to Golgotha, supposedly to comfort a man that Joe very much thought deserved to suffer.

43

memorial

1

KEENAN ARRIVED at Marianne's house at noon. Too restless to remain inside until everyone was ready to leave, he carried a large wreath, delivered that morning, to his car and centered it in the back seat. While waiting by his car, he curbed his tendency to pace by rocking heel to toe. He knew that much of the day would be spent waiting around like this, and in constant vigilance for danger, which would probably worsen his feelings of being tightly wound.

Finally, the others came out of the house. Marianne's mother, Trudi Ross, and her sister, Bonnie Frawley, rode with Marianne in the silver Mazda and en route to the cemetery she would also pick up Will's mother, Adele Paxton. With everyone unable to fit comfortably in the Mazda, Zack asked to ride with Keenan in the Buick. An unmarked police unit followed at a discreet distance.

On the drive to Marianne's, Keenan had turned the Buick's air conditioner to its maximum setting. Now, starting for the cemetery, frosty air billowed from the plastic vents and by the time they reached the exit for the subdivision, Zack had tucked his hands under the armpits of his blue suit. Marianne gunned the Mazda into the heavy flow of traffic that zipped along Broad River Road's four lanes and Keenan followed, then turned off the AC and opened his window a couple of inches.

"Thanks," Zack said and switched his hands from his armpits to under his legs. He looked uneasy wearing a suit, which a recent growth spurt had left an inch short at his wrists. "Can I ask you something?" Zack said.

"Ask anything you want," Keenan said.

Zack looked down, then sighed. "Don't take this wrong, okay, but it's just that Mom keeps talking about us remembering Dad, when I really don't remember him at all. And whenever she says anything about him, you'd think he was a candidate for sainthood. I just wish somebody would tell me the truth."

"What do you think it is that you're not being told?"

Again, Zack looked down, then back over at Keenan. "Okay. I know for a fact that if my father had waited for backup, that Pop Paulus would be alive today."

This surprised Keenan and he opened his mouth, ready with a quick denial, then paused—there was some truth to what Zack had said. Measuring his words carefully, Keenan glanced at Zack and said, "The important thing is that if your father had not found Drum when he did, others would have died. And no one believes your father is responsible for Pop Paulus's death."

"My mom does. Not long after my father died, I heard her on the phone talking to Mrs. Paulus. Mom was crying and kept saying she was sorry that my father had caused Pop's death. She said, 'If he hadn't gone there alone, your husband would still be alive.' So my mom thinks that, yet all she tells me is how great Dad was."

It had never occurred to Keenan that Marianne might feel this way. Not once had she confided any misgivings about Will; but to do so might seem like dishonoring him, and she would never do that. He did recall Marianne once telling him that Mrs. Paulus was the most for-giving person she had ever met.

"I know Mom wants me to pretend he was so great. So I don't say anything. But I'm sick of pretending. People should tell the truth. Everybody knows, anyway. So why not tell the truth? Right?"

In front of them, the Mazda's turn signal blinked and Marianne turned onto a two-lane side road with older houses that had large yards blanketed by tawny pine needles. She then took a quick right into a grav-el driveway that was flanked by a pair of large hydrangeas. Keenan pulled in behind her. Marianne opened her door but before she could get out, a gray-haired woman, her shoulders hunched from osteoporosis, came out of the brick, ranch-style house and pulled the door shut. Clutching a shiny black pocketbook in front of her, she sprightly approached the Mazda and waved at Zack before getting in.

Zack waved back.

As Zack's grandmother climbed into Marianne's car, Keenan looked at the boy and said, again choosing his words carefully, "In judging your father, which it sounds like you're doing, you need to consider the pressure he was under. In a matter of days, another woman might die a horrible death and in his desperation to prevent this he made a mistake. But, Zack, even a bad mistake doesn't mean that he wasn't a good man and a great father. And everyone knows that Drum killed Pop Paulus, not your father."

"You just can't understand what it's like to have your father do something that bad," Zack said and pulled his hands from beneath his legs and folded them across his chest, his mouth puckered down.

"Maybe I do understand," Keenan said. He did not like bringing up his past and especially hated talking about himself. Yet, his experience might have some relevance to things that were bothering Zack.

Keenan waited until he backed out of the driveway and again fell in behind Marianne's Mazda, then said, "When I was the age you are now, my father died in a car accident in which he was at fault. He hit another car and a woman and little girl were also killed. My father had been drinking."

Keenan kept his eyes fixed on the road. Telling this about himself was more difficult than he expected. He swallowed, then said, "The night before my father's funeral, we had the viewing at the funeral home. It was crowded and the air conditioner was broken so the funeral parlor was stuffy and I could hardly breathe. People just kept coming up to me and patting my shoulder and saying nice things about my father. I didn't believe they meant those things because everyone knew that my father had been driving drunk and killed a twenty-two-year-old mother and her pretty little daughter. It was a small town. Everybody knew.

"After a while, I needed a break from all that attention and went into the funeral home's bathroom and sat in one of the stalls. While I was in there, two . . ." Keenan shook his head. "I guess they were friends of the family. Anyway, these two guys came into the bathroom and, hidden in the stall, I overheard everything they said. One of them said, 'What a terrible thing.' 'Yeah,' the other one agreed, 'what a shame.' 'Sorry-assed drunk driver.' 'You know, there's no excuse for something like that.' 'Well, I sure feel sorry for his family.' 'His family, hell. What about the other family.'

"After they left, I went out on the porch and sat in a corner until my mother was ready to go home. Later that night, I went out to my father's workshop. He'd bought this old chair that he and I had started refinishing. I took a hammer and smashed that chair to bits. So you see, Zack, I do know something about shame."

"Yeah, I guess you do," Zack said. He thought about this for a good while before he turned in the seat to face Keenan. "Did your mother make excuses for your father, or did she blame him?"

Keenan thought about this. "I don't recall her ever making an excuse for what he did. As for blaming him, like your mother, she was a proud woman who deeply loved her husband, so I'm sure the senselessness of his death hurt her badly. But also like your mother, I never heard her say one bad word about my father. I think that's a result, not of dishonesty, but of pride and character. Plus, your father didn't do something widely regarded as shameful; most people think he was a hero."

"I guess," Zack said without much enthusiasm. They rode in silence for a while before Zack asked, "What about you? Did you have any problems?"

Keenan nodded. "My main problem was my temper. The week I went back to school, a boy on the bus called my father a drunken killer and I was big, even then, so I beat that boy up pretty badly."

"What did your mother do about your fighting? Did she excuse that?"

Keenan caste a quick glance at Zack and smiled. "Not a chance. The night after the fight, she drove me to the boy's house and made me apologize to his parents for throwing the first punch and for hurting their son so badly. When we got back home, she made me sit at the kitchen table and told me that because I was larger than most other kids, I could probably become a bully if that's what I wanted. Then she warned me that no one respects a bully, said it was contempt that most people felt.

She said, 'Johnny, if you're smart at all you'll use your his intelligence to get what you want. And don't ever forget that a truly strong person always remains in control.' And I did what she asked, though at first for the wrong reasons. Even in high school, I think I was afraid that if I loosened up too much people might see the flaws of my father in me."

"I don't worry about anything like that," Zack said.

"Good. It's not a path you want to start down."

"I guess not. But the way your mom handled your problems, I wish my mother would be more like your mother."

Keenan hesitated, then said, "Did you ever think that it might be as much your fault as hers that she treats you the way she does. If you want her to treat you like you can handle things, you need to stop acting so damn sullen with her. If you want respect, you have to earn it."

"I guess that makes sense."

The Mazda's brake lights came on and it slowed as they reached a vast lawn dotted with marble grave markers. Marianne turned in between curved brick walls with black gothic letters that spelled out "Woodland Cemetery."

"Did you ever forgive your father?" Zack asked, as Keenan turned into the cemetery.

"It stopped mattering," Keenan answered, then lowered his window because the car seemed so damned stuffy.

44

the weight

I

TODAY, IT seemed fitting that Joe wear the black suit he usually only wore for funerals. Though his stomach churned, he managed to keep down a light lunch before leaving for Golgotha at two o'clock. Over and over, he kept telling himself to relax and stay calm.

A dozen yards beyond the turn into Golgotha's parking area was a wooden barricade. A CO checked Joe's name on a list, then a Columbia policeman pulled aside the barrier on the right and pointed down a row lined by more blue barricades. Midway down the row sat three large trucks with satellite dishes on top and a swarm of reporters with microphones and cameras corralled behind the wooden barriers. Joe drove past these reporters to an area reserved for those with official business at Golgotha. Face flushed, Joe ambled to the walkway as reporters shouted and their cameras clicked and whirred, recording his every self-conscious move. He supposed that all this attention didn't matter now. When he came in from his patio this morning, Joe found Mark Kemper had left a message on his answering machine asking why Joe had lied to him about ending his involvement with Drum. Joe didn't return Kemper's call; how could he begin explaining why he was doing this?

At the checkpoint, two escorts came for Joe. Both men wore sergeant's stripes and had generous guts hanging over their thick belts. One, an older white man with a crew cut, wrote Joe's name in a red book, while the other, a somewhat younger black man, slowly ran a metal detection wand around Joe's outstretched form. When done, the black officer said, "This way." Flanking Joe, they stepped out of the checkpoint into the afternoon sun and walked at a good pace past the entrance to Golgotha's main building.

Centered in front of Golgotha's mammoth structure were double security fences that surrounded an oasis of neatly mowed lawn that was about half the size of a football field. The Capital Punishment Facility, or CPF for short, stood in the middle of this area. The CPF, a one-story brick building, reminded Joe of low-end nursing homes that he had visited in poor neighborhoods, except it had no windows. Thirty feet behind the death house was another brick structure, comparable in size to a state park outhouse.

A wide gate in the outer fence slowly clanked open. They walked through this gate, then it closed and the inner gate opened. A gravel road led to the back of the squat building and they stopped there in front of a red metal door. The white CO pressed a button and announced, "It's Burkhalter with the two o'clock visitor."

Though sweating and slightly out of breath, Joe thought coming here much better than going through that awful Tunnel.

Then, a sudden sound, like a diesel truck roaring to life, startled Joe. Turning, he saw that the noise came from the smaller building behind him. Its door stood open and inside Joe saw a man in coveralls making adjustments to a bulky generator. When Joe turned back around, the door of the Capital Punishment Facility stood open and a handsome black man scrutinized him. "This way," the officer told him. Joe entered an atrium that smelled of fresh paint and had three doorless openings. Beyond these doorways, Joe saw only more white walls with no signs or other indications of how to get from one place to another. It was like being in a maze.

Pointing to the door on the right, the officer, whose nameplate read "Lt. A. Hayward," said, "In there." Joe's escorts stayed with them as they went down a short hall to a monotonously white eight-by-ten room. A stainless steel table was attached to the wall, with five metal containers stacked on top, along with a box of latex gloves, and a large jar of petroleum jelly. Stashed beneath the table was a steel trash can with a foot-pedal lid. Otherwise, the room was bare.

"Sir, you probably already know that security at CPF is the strictest of any facility in the state. So you're gonna have to strip to your underwear and hand each garment to one of these officers for inspection," Lieutenant Hayward instructed. "If you have any contraband you need to declare it before we search you or else you may be duly charged. Contraband includes drugs, weapons, razors, medications, string, penknifes, any cylindrical hard objects, or anything with a sharp point. Your keys and wallet will be locked inside one of these boxes and I'll keep the key until you're ready to leave. Now, are you in possession of anything that might be considered contraband?"

"Ah, no," Joe replied, fidgeting under the officer's scrutiny.

"Then please start by emptying the contents of your pockets into this box."

Quickly, Joe dug into his pockets and pulled out keys, change, wallet, comb, and from his shirt pocket a ballpoint pen. "Ah, I'm sorry," he said, holding out the pen. "I forgot about this."

"That's all right sir. But don't give it to me, put it in the box. Good. Now, please remove your clothes and hand them to these officers."

"I'll get them back before I go see Drum, won't I?" Joe asked, horrified at the prospect of facing Drum wearing only his underwear.

Unable to suppress a smile, Hayward said, "Yes sir, we just have to check them first."

Modest about his body, even before flab engulfed it, Joe blushed hotly as he removed his shirt with three men watching. One at a time, Joe handed his clothes over to the COs, who carefully inspected each garment by running their hands along seams, probing inside his shoes, and twisting the heels to check for hidden compartments. When down to his underwear, Hayward said, "You can leave those on." Then Hayward pulled a rubber glove from the box, and as he slipped it on Joe winced at what was coming. But Hayward said, "Please open your mouth so I can check inside."

Meekly, Joe did as he was told. Surprisingly gentle, the officer's latex-covered finger slipped between Joe's teeth and cheeks and under his tongue. When finished, Hayward said, "Now sir, please turn around, pull down your drawers, and lean forward with both hands on the table."

Joe did not want these men to see his privates, so he turned and inched his briefs over his rump a few inches while covering himself with his other hand, like he'd seen in paintings of Adam and Eve being driven from Eden.

"Sir, you need to pull your drawers further down, then lean over and put both hands on the table," Hayward said firmly, as he put on a fresh glove.

Blushing hotly, Joe did as he was told. With his gloved hand, Hayward felt beneath Joe's scrotum. Finished, he stepped to one side and, to Joe's tremendous relief, took off the latex glove and dropped it in the trash can. No need to do the other thing, Joe thought, breathing for the first time in seconds. Then the CO yanked another glove from the box, pulled it on with a snap, and said as he dipped two fingers into the petroleum jelly, "If you hadn't smuggled that letter, we wouldn't have to be checking you quite so close. Now, this may be a little uncomfortable."

Sweat streaming from his forehead, Joe thought the warning grossly understated.

II

While Joe dressed, Lieutenant Hayward explained the rules. "The inmate will be in his cell and you have to stay behind the yellow line.

We prefer you remain seated but that's not required. You may not have physical contact or pass anything to him. If you want him to have something, you give it to us and we'll pass it to him. You're not allowed to smoke or eat while in the holding area, but you can use a plastic cup if you want to take something to drink. As his clergy, there are no time limits on your visit. And most important, if we tell you to do something, you do it without hesitating or asking questions. Is there any part of these instructions that you need explained?"

Joe shook his head no.

Hayward then led Joe through the white, maze-like halls. At every point, at least one surveillance camera was visible, usually more. They passed a control room where two COs monitored a bank of green-tinted screens. Large Plexiglas windows occupied three sides of the booth and, looking through to the other side, Joe saw Drum in a cell; he wore an orange jumpsuit and leaned against the bars, smoking.

Beyond the control booth, double doors opened into a spacious waiting room that was furnished with a tan Naugahyde couch and console television. One of the control booth's three windowed sides looked out on this area. "This is where you'll wait when the inmate has other visitors," Hayward explained, then pointed out a dorm-size refrigerator that contained juice and soda as well as a small table bearing a coffee maker and supplies. In contrast to Golgotha's bowels, this room had fresh paint and a buffed floor. It seemed more like a hospital waiting area than a prison.

On Joe's far right was another set of double doors. A younger officer stood there and motioned to Joe. "He's waiting for you," the officer said.

Past these doors, Joe took a hard right and entered a rectangular area with four roomy holding cells on his left and the control booth to his right. Three feet from the cells, a broad yellow stripe ran the room's length. Two plastic chairs sat in front of the third cell and a television had been pushed against the wall behind them. Next to the bars sat a small metal table, crowded with a plate of stew, aluminum ashtray, red Bible, and deck of Ace playing cards.

Drum stood with his back to Joe, urinating into a stainless steel commode. CPF was stenciled on the back of Drum's orange jumpsuit and he wore white slip-on bath shoes. Beside the commode was a small sink. Attached to the wall on Joe's right was a metal bunk with a thin sheetless mattress and balloon-sized pillow.

Drum finished relieving himself and walked to the front of the cell, then stuck his hand through the bars and told the CO, "Gimme a cigarette." He didn't even seem to notice Joe as he eased into one of the plastic chairs.

The CO pulled a Marlboro from a pack on top of the television and Drum accepted it without comment. Perching the cigarette between his lips, Drum stepped to an outlet-sized apparatus in the corner and, holding down a black button, pushed the cigarette against a glowing coil. Staring at the CO, he exhaled a swirl of smoke, then said, "I'm doing it your way, so give me back my smokes."

"You got another half hour, then we'll allow you one more chance."

"Well at least let fat boy here dole them out."

"He's not allowed to pass anything to you."

"Fuck you," Drum snarled. "I'm gonna chain smoke, so you get your black ass back in here as soon as I finish this one. You got that, *boy*?"

"When the butt's in the ashtray, I'll bring you another." The officer started to leave, but Drum crushed his just-lit cigarette into the ashtray and said, "I need another smoke . . . *boy*."

The CO masked whatever resentment he felt as he passed another cigarette through the bars. But he did leave the holding area before Drum finished lighting it.

More to himself than Joe, Drum said, "Drop one goddamn butt on the floor and they try to jerk you around. Little men trying to feel big." Talking with the cigarette perched in his mouth, Drum went to the back of the cell and washed his hands. "I'd sue 'em, but with the incompetent shysters I'm stuck with, it'd be a waste of time." He took a hard hit on the Marlboro, then turned and looked at Joe. "If I had money I wouldn't be here. But I never got one goddamn break my whole life. Not one." Pacing, Drum muttered, "Hell, they're not going to do it. They're just fucking with me. That's all."

Morosely silent, Drum paced for a couple of minutes. Joe waited with his elbows on his knees and head down. He had yet to say one word; probably a good thing considering how angry he felt every time he looked at Drum. If anyone ever deserved to burn in hell, Drum sure did.

Drum smoked the cigarette to its nub, then pulled the one he had stubbed out from the ashtray and lit it with the butt's embers, muttering, "They think they're so damn smart." He sat on the edge of the bed nearest Joe and took several hard hits while staring at Joe. "I wanted you here earlier." Before Joe could explain, Drum said, "Isgett's taken care of the problem you caused with my mother. Some do-good prison service organization is going to take her a cell phone so we can talk tonight and straighten out everything."

Joe didn't think he had caused any problems with Drum's mother, but didn't say anything.

"So I'm going to give you a chance to make up for your fuckup," Drum informed Joe. "But you're going to have to work fast." Drum leaned closer and pointed at Joe with the hand holding his smoke, "I want you to find the reporter that I talked to yesterday and tell her that you arranged a deal for me to give up Rawson's name in exchange for my sentence being commuted. Tell her I kept my end of the bargain but Stith didn't."

Joe looked at Drum and shook his head. "I can't do that."

"The fuck you can't. You're going to do what I tell you, you got that?"

"I'm here as your minister, not to lie for you."

"If you don't do exactly what I want you to do, then I'll tell them about you smuggling out the letter."

"They already know," Joe said.

Drum tried to stare Joe down, but Joe didn't flinch. Finally, Drum said, "You holy Rollers make me sick, you know that? You're always whining about being made in the Almighty's image, but do you really think God loves a pathetic weakling like you? You're not made in his image, I am. So you need to do what I tell you."

Still looking Drum in the eye, Joe shook his head, and it felt good to stand his ground.

Drum rose and paced once across the cell, then came to the bars and stared down at Joe. Again, Joe did not look away or squirm.

"Fuck you," Drum said. "I want you to get off your fat ass and go tell that black boy I've changed my mind and want some meds. And tell him to get that slop out of here," he said pointing at the plate. "Tell him, I'm not eating any more food cooked by inmates. That diseased bunch of scum spit in it, piss in it, or worse."

Joe got up and started walking away to go find the CO. Drum yelled after him, "And tell that boy to bring me another smoke."

III

A half-hour later, Drum regained possession of his cigarettes. He spent the afternoon lying on his bunk with the ashtray balanced on his stomach and lighting each new cigarette from the embers of the last one to avoid the effort of getting up and using the electric coil. Every ash and butt went into the ashtray. From time to time, he halfheartedly looked at the television, its volume barely audible. Mostly, Drum smoked and stared at the ceiling.

Joe slumped in the plastic chair with his forearms on his knees, available should Drum want to talk, but not really caring if he did because every time Drum spoke it was for some evil purpose.

With nothing better to do, Joe's mind kept wandering back to the notes from Faraday's class. It occurred to Joe that if Drum acted out of free will, and not part of some divine plan, then the horrid things he did were consequences of man's being allowed to choose and act. It seemed better for such evil to come from man's failings rather than being part of God's plan. But if Joe accepted this view, he also had to accept that he had not been chosen by God to be special, and that all his failures and shortcomings were not part of some master plan, but his responsibility. Shaking his head, Joe then thought that there must be a divine hand behind everything that happened because it was impossible that Drum could have chosen to become so vile a monster. It had to be preordained. Or did it?

Joe went around and around thinking about this with no resolution. Time passed slowly and later in the afternoon both men dozed for short periods. Once, on awakening, Joe noticed that Drum had his hand in his pants diddling with himself. Joe shut his eyes and pretended to be asleep, though for the first time in over an hour he felt fully awake. A few minutes later, through half-closed eyes, Joe saw Drum pull his hand from his pants in what looked like frustration, then he rubbed his eyes hard with his shirtsleeve.

Other than this brief diversion, Joe had the same feeling that he had as a child when he visited his grandmother and sat listening to the hall clock ticking. Who would have thought that a deathwatch would be so boring?

.   .   .

Drum stared up at the ceiling, scarcely tasting the cigarettes. Eventually, he failed to pay attention and let the ember die. It seemed too much trouble to go to the coil and light another; just as his throat felt dry but it took too much effort to get up or even to ask for a drink. Sure, he still felt angry and restless, but it seemed that all of last night's and this morning's rage had spent every bit of his energy. This was Keenan's fault! *Just like everyone else, he was only waiting for a chance to screw me. People are no good. It really is screw or be screwed. And what chance do I have with all of them ganged up against me.*

His mind swamped by a fog of apathy and medication, Drum wondered if maybe death would be better than going on like this. He then felt angry with himself for thinking this. It was exactly what they wanted, to turn him into something with no more will than a wet rag. *Yeah, that's exactly what they were trying to do to me. Well, I'll show them. When I need to, I'll show them that they can't beat me.*

Drum wished that something would happen, anything, to shake him out of this funk and get him going again—even if it was the pudgy minister fretting over his soul or doing something else just as annoying. But there was only the waiting.

After lying with eyes shut and attempting unsuccessfully to doze, Drum tried to shake off his lethargy by spitting on his hand and slipping it into his pants and finding his flaccid penis. He thought that pleasuring himself might help him relax, help him feel better, maybe even get him going again, or at least get his mind focused. He wanted to bring up a memory of the little blonde on one of the four nights that he had taken her. An image of her came, but it was the wrong one. Instead of one of the nights when he had desired and enjoyed her, his mind's eye opened to the night she had finally died.

That whole night had been so unsatisfying that he never videotaped even a minute of it—he had not recorded the deaths of any of his victims. On that night, he had started feeling lethargic even before he went downstairs; the longer he had her, the less exciting she became. This had been more or less the case with the others, but was especially true with her—maybe it had something to do with his expectations for her. He was already annoyed with himself for keeping her an extra night; she was in such shape that she might have died while he slept during the day. But he heard her rasping breathing as he started down the steps and could smell her and the moment he dropped low enough to see her, he felt . . . disgusted.

Drum squeezed his eyes tight, hoping this would somehow stop this memory, but it only sharpened the images now leaking from his mind.

The wrinkled sheets were soiled and reeking with her sweat and urine from where she'd lost bladder control, and her hair fell across her face in greasy strands. She didn't even look at me as I came close to the bed, so I yelled and ordered her to look at me. She did by barely moving her eyes, which were dull and puffy and caked with matter. Nothing else about her moved, except her chest, heaving in a way that reminded me of the first cat I ever stuck as a kid, the one under the grape arbor that lay on its side heaving without moving for a few minutes before it died. I leaned closer to the little blonde thinking I would yell again and force some life back into her eyes, but her breath was too rancid with the smell of puke and sickness, so I backed off and stood looking down on her. For a moment, I wished I could go back to before she became such a disappointment, and considered cleaning her up. But I knew that it wouldn't matter, that I could never again feel anything except disappointed with her. Standing there, looking down at her, I realized that without her painted face and lying expressions she was ugly, and I wondered what I ever saw in her. In fact, I felt so much contempt that I no longer wanted to touch her. I wanted her away.

I expected to feel some kind of rekindled excitement as I stirred the strychnine into some baby food, triple strong tonight, though given her condition the normal dose probably would have proved fatal. Instead of arousal, however, I felt irritated, and my irritation got worse when I pushed the spoon into her mouth and the pulp just fell out the side like the drool of the feebleminded. I had not let the others go this far, they still showed some life at the end. "Eat or I kidnap your daughter, tonight!" I yelled. Recognition came into her eyes and she looked at me and I saw hatred. "This is the last time," I told her and pushed the spoon against her cracked lips. She looked at me, then looked at the spoon and greedily swallowed the pulp, then took two more spoonfuls. She had done exactly what I wanted, but I didn't get any satisfaction. I saw no fear, no signs of respect.

She didn't convulse, she barely even quivered. And her eyes did not change after her breathing stopped, so it took me a while to realize that she was dead. I felt completely empty. I wanted to stop everything and lie down and not move. Normally, I would want to clean her and dump her as soon as possible, and knowing that these important things must be done, I would be energized and begin thinking again and planning for the future.

With her, though, I sat for a long time looking at her pale skin wishing that I didn't have to touch it again. I had had such great hopes. But in the end, she was the worst disappointment of all.

Yet, with her gone, I couldn't stand the emptiness and loneliness and felt desperate to find someone else, quickly.

Disgusted at remembering this woman, who dying by degrees had no more life than a wet rag, Drum pulled his hand from his pants and his flaccid penis. Momentarily overcome by grief for his own wasted life, tears welled into his eyes and blurred the bars of his death house cell. He rubbed his eyes dry with his shirtsleeve. It was a terrible thing to have led such a lonely life.

45

war

I

MILWOOD AVENUE cuts through an old-money neighborhood with large homes shaded by stately hardwoods. Seventy-two-year-old Beatrice Roberts lived in a picturesque Victorian with a slate blue roof, trim of the same color, and a white picket fence across the front. Azaleas, camellias, hostas, and variegated spider grass thrived in the shade along the tall, plank-board fences that ran the length of the property's sides and back. Thick beds of rust-colored mums curved with a wraparound porch that was tastefully furnished with a traditional porch swing, white wicker furniture, and baskets of ivy hanging above the white banisters.

Today, all this tidiness and late afternoon serenity stopped at the opened front door, where a uniformed policeman stood. This officer was the crime scene recorder and she took down Stith's name, badge number, and time in. "The techs started a couple minutes ago," she said.

"Where is she?" Stith asked.

"Upstairs. Just follow your nose."

A half-hour earlier, Stith had been walking around the perimeter at the house of Trudi Ross, Marianne's mother, and selecting positions for sharpshooters with night scopes. He didn't have much faith in Keenan's ideas about luring Rawson there, but he had to be prepared just in case. He was more concerned about placing a tactical team around Marianne and Zack at Bradley Miller's place. Miller disliked police, especially SLED, so Stith thought he might cause problems.

Stith had been ready to drive out to Miller's place when Bob Marshall called and said that Stith might want to come have a look. Marshall said the same news station that had gotten the call reporting the location of Jimmy Gilpin's body had received another call from someone claiming to be Gary Wilmet. This time the caller said they should check out the dead lady, and gave Beatrice Roberts's address.

While driving here, Wes Felton radioed and told Stith that SLED chief Carl Jones wanted Stith to come by headquarters and meet with him. Stith didn't have time to keep wiping Jones's nose, so he needed to deal with both Marshall and Jones quickly and then get over to Miller's place.

Stith stepped inside Beatrice Roberts's foyer and immediately smelled human decay, a retching odor even when weak. Dark red lipstick spelled out "WAR" on an oval, wood-framed mirror. It was Rawson's initials, but Stith also thought it a declaration. He took the painter's mask and vapor rub from his pocket, and after smearing the mask slipped it on. Then he put on the rubber gloves that he had also taken from the kit in his car.

Empty potato chip bags and soda cans were scattered on the living room floor. Stith paused to watch a tech wearing a surgical mask use tweezers to lift what looked like the tip of a marijuana roach from an ashtray and bag it. If Rawson was smoking the PCP-and cocaine-laced joints, then this cold-blooded killer might become a raging madman. Stith shook his head and cursed quietly.

At the top of the stairs, a photographer's flash led him to Beatrice Roberts's bedroom. In the middle of a four-poster bed, her nude body lay on its side with her back to the door. Her hip bone looked ready to punch through sagging skin that had turned a sickly reddish-green but not yet begun to blister. A large, black-looking stain covered the rumpled bedspread near her waist. On the dresser mirror, "WAR" had been painted, this time in blood.

The photographer finished and moved elsewhere in the house as another tech began taking measurements. Stith walked around the bed to look at her front. Everything about Beatrice Roberts's house suggested that she had been a proper woman, and Stith thought she probably would have been mortified to think that so many strangers would come in and gape at her uncovered remains.

He knelt beside the bed and saw on her stomach what he knew would be there—the weeping, accelerated decay of stab wounds. "Goddamn it," he said loud enough to cause the tech to turn and ask, "What?"

"Nothing," Stith said and walked out of the room with his fists clenched.

. . .

The sun had dropped until it only shone on the tops of the trees in Beatrice Roberts's backyard, which was also tastefully landscaped and had garden sculptures of a rabbit, squirrel, and tortoise peeking from discreet spots in the thick shrubbery. Stith found Bob Marshall back there, sitting on a picnic table dangling a bottle of soda between his legs and working over his ever-present gum.

"I had to get some fresh air. It stinks in there," Marshall said, but he didn't grin as he usually did, and there was anger in his eyes. It looked as though Marshall had found out about Stith's unsuccessful attempt to get him removed from the Gilpin case.

"You didn't touch anything inside, did you?" Marshall said. "I observe strict crime site procedure and expect you to do the same."

Stith could have pointed out that a good detective would be inside doing his or her own sketch and measure. A good detective wants to be in on all the details, wants a chance to see what others might miss.

Stith suppressed his impulse to put Marshall in his place; too much lay on the line for tangents.

"It looks like she's been dead for less than two days," Stith said. "Rawson must have come here straight from the halfway house. Any idea how he chose her?"

"Yeah," Marshall said. He stood and hitched his pants. "Gatti of Gatti Appliances heard about her murder on the radio and called us. He said Rawson helped deliver a new refrigerator to the old lady last week. The driver left Rawson to set it up while he and Roberts sat back here and did the paperwork. The driver said when he finished he had to go looking for Rawson and found him coming down the stairs. Rawson claimed he just wanted to see how so-called upright people live and that it wasn't a big deal. Then the guy said Rawson got in his face and said if he knew what was good for him, he'd get off his back and wouldn't snitch."

The kitchen had been so haphazardly cluttered with dirty dishes and opened food containers that Stith had not noticed the newness of the refrigerator.

"I need a list of every delivery Rawson went on," Stith said.

"Yeah, I already planned to get that," Marshall said. "But this is *my* case, and just because I called you as a courtesy doesn't mean you can come in here and start telling me what *you* need."

Stith very much needed to know if Rawson had gone on any deliveries near the home of Trudi Ross. But the last thing he wanted was for Marshall, a notorious big mouth, to know anything about the trap. Stith would have Felton call Gatti and get what he needed.

"All right," Stith said, "have it your way. Anything else I should know before I leave you to grope around *your* crime scene?"

Marshall took a swig of the soda and waddled his pear shape closer, slightly crowding Stith. "You know, I don't think you're going to be working this case or any other case much longer; not after the way you messed up with Drum. From what I hear, I don't think you're in a position to call anybody a screwup."

Once again, Stith reminded himself that he was juggling too many important things to let Marshall's pettiness distract him. "If there's nothing else, I'm out of here."

"You tell me, smart guy, is there something else?" Marshall said. "You bet there's something else. You think you can mess with my career and not get burned. People in high places—and I mean high places—are questioning your fitness, did you know that?"

"Fuck people in high places," Stith said and walked away.

"I guess what they say about you not having it anymore is right," Marshall said. "I've heard talk that when Inabinet chose the coward's way out, that it took it all out of you. Looks like there's truth to that, huh?"

Stith stopped walking and flexed his fists a couple of times. He had heard talk like this before. In the week following Inabinet's death, Stith had been in the fax room when he overheard a couple of ranking investigators in his department in the hall, mocking Inabinet. *"Looks like the old man couldn't take it." And the reply, "Yeah, he took the easy way out. I guess he wasn't so tough, after all."* Stith had stayed put until they passed, swallowed his bile, and did nothing. What could he do? Nothing that would change their opinion. You can't bully people into changing what they think.

Now, standing in Beatrice Roberts's sedate backyard, Stith's fists stayed clenched. He had always hated Marshall's smugness. He could have that fat-assed daddy's boy on the ground with two or three cracked ribs in less than a minute, and not even break a sweat.

But while Marshall might be a fool, he wasn't stupid when it came to political maneuvering. If Stith even bumped Marshall, the son of a bitch might fall to the ground, grab his back, go on disability for a while—maybe permanently, he fit that type—and, in so doing, crush Stith's career, all for petty spite.

Too many important things depended on Stith for him to allow that to happen. He started walking and, without turning around and needlessly tempting his restraint, threw Marshall the bird. As he passed through the cluttered kitchen, Stith glanced at Beatrice Roberts's new frost-free refrigerator and wished she had kept her old one for just a little while longer.

It then occurred to Stith that Inabinet would have approved of the way he had kept his priorities clear when taunted by Marshall. For several weeks now, time and time again Stith would be thinking about something and then get snagged by awareness that Inabinet wasn't there anymore. Behind this awareness, Stith knew he was scared of what he might do without Inabinet's steady restraint. Stith regarded himself as a passionate and driven guy, and had always feared that one day his nature might swallow the good cop he wanted to be. Yet, here he was, long after Inabinet's death, continuing to act in ways that would not disappoint the old man. Inabinet's values had become his values. A piece of the old man's goodness lived on inside him.

Hurrying back to a fight that mattered, a fight to stop Wayne Rawson, Stith's head felt clearer than it had in weeks.

46

gathering

I

TIRES CRUNCHED on gravel and a breeze scattered the trailing dust, as Keenan pushed the Buick at a good clip along Bradley Miller's long driveway. Twilight deepened the shadows beyond the edge of the woods. Keenan drove with his headlights on, though it was not yet dark enough for them to do much good. Zack rode in back, Marianne in front with Keenan.

"I feel perfectly safe with these arrangements," Marianne said again. "And remember, John, Bradley has never gotten over the death of his daughter. He's a terribly a sad man. So please, for me, be patient."

Keenan's eyes remained on the gravel road. He didn't care that Bradley Miller had been devastated by his daughter's death. And he didn't care that Miller had channeled much of his anger at law enforcement, especially SLED, for what he regarded as an appalling lack of consideration for victims' families. Nor did Keenan care that Miller's wife had died three years ago and that afterward his resentment hardened into a truculent and militant animosity. At the moment, Keenan didn't care about any of this.

Moments before they left to come here, Wes Felton telephoned and told them that Miller had contacted a friend in the state senate, who on his behalf talked to SLED chief Carl Jones and requested that no

SLED agents be posted anywhere near Miller's property. Jones went along, apparently believing that the intensive manhunt and misdirection about Marianne and Zack's whereabouts should be enough. Felton said Stith was now in Jones's office and he could hear shouting through the closed door. Felton, however, did not think Stith would change Jones's mind, not with the request coming from a ranking senator.

Miller would allow two Jeffcoat County officers on his property, provided they stay well away from the house. He was more amenable to having patrol cars block the end of his driveway, which was over a quarter mile from the house, in order to keep out reporters and the morbidly curious.

"John, please promise me you'll not cause problems with Bradley," Marianne pressed.

"All right," he said, though he wasn't sure he would keep his word.

The driveway curved and Bradley Miller's two-story home came into view. Painted yellow with white trim, the house was shaped like a squat L and had large, multi-pane windows. In the fading dusk, it glowed warmly from atop the crest of a fairway-sized yard that was dotted here and there with Bradford pears, crepe myrtle, and an occasional maple. Near the house, three cars were parked on the grass beside the paved area in front of a detached garage. At the Buick's approach, motion detectors kicked on a floodlight in the garage's eave.

Keenan switched off the engine and forced himself to be patient as Marianne and Zack got out of the car, seeming to take their sweet time. A wide porch extended along two sides of the house with flared steps midway at the corner. Keenan walked beside Marianne as they climbed the steps onto the porch with Zack languidly hanging behind. Keenan rang the bell.

"John, please remember that it doesn't matter," Marianne reminded him in a hushed voice.

Like a dog with his hackles raised, Keenan stood especially straight, nearly a head taller than Marianne, and stared at the door as he told her, "Don't' worry." His face was red and his jaws clenched. He had been tightly wound all day with raw tension and a need for some kind of action.

The door opened and Miller looked out at them. He was a slight, wiry man with deep creases in his face, and wavy, gray hair combed back without a part. He wore gray slacks and a red sweater over a navy polo shirt buttoned to the collar. Liver spots marked the back of his veined hands.

Keenan did not wait for introductions. "I wish you would reconsider your decision to not allow SLED agents on your property," he said. Then his efforts to sound reasonable faltered. "Because there's a goddamned psychopath stalking Marianne and Zack."

Miller's sour expression became more so. He stepped outside and shut the door, apparently so those inside would not hear. "I forbid that kind of language to be used in my home," he said. "If you curse again you'll have to leave. And I'm not sure you belong here, anyway."

Marianne squeezed between them. "All right you two, stop it!" She then faced Miller. "Bradley, if John doesn't stay, I'll leave; and I'll see if any of the others feel the same way." On the drive over Marianne had told Keenan that there was going to be a smaller turnout than Miller had hoped, but that he had only himself to blame. He didn't want anyone here except immediate family and allowed no young children who might disrupt what he referred to as a "'solemn occasion.'" Zack was deemed barely old enough. Miller's nine-year-old granddaughter, Jennifer, was not. Marianne had also once told Keenan that Miller treated her with uncharacteristic kindness, and Keenan suspected this was due to Marianne's closeness in age to Alicia, Miller's murdered daughter.

"John is worried about us, so he's tense," Marianne explained. "Bradley, you of all people should know how upset someone gets when they worry."

Miller pursed his face as he considered. "All right. I'll do this for you. But I will not tolerate any profanity or questioning of my judgment."

"There won't be," Marianne assured him. "Go back inside and I'll be along in a minute."

Miller turned to open the door, then looked back at Keenan. "I get the impression that no one is taking your voodoo predictions about tonight too seriously, anyway."

Marianne put a hand on Keenan's chest and shook her head no. Keenan bit back his caustic reply. The door shut behind Miller. Marianne left her hand on Keenan's chest. Zack stood near the steps, watching.

"John, you have to promise me that you'll let it go," Marianne said.

"I don't think you should stay here."

"I feel perfectly safe here," Marianne said. "Rawson thinks we're elsewhere and we have as many police watching us as we've had most of this week. More with you here. And Martin will be along soon. John, we don't need a tactical unit, not here. And you know why I have to stay," Marianne said, her expression pleading. "When I talked to Alvin earlier, he said that Bradley had already started in on him. I can't leave Alvin and he won't go—I think his own guilt about Alicia's abduction causes him to put up with Bradley's accusations. And besides, John, I have a lot on my mind. Mostly about Will and . . . I want to be with these people. So please let it go? Okay?"

"I want extra protection," Keenan said stubbornly.

"Either promise me or leave," Marianne demanded and removed her hand from Keenan's chest.

For the most part, Keenan agreed with Marianne. Rawson had hidden Jimmy Gilpin's missing car in one bay of Beatrice Roberts's garage. It was still there along with her Cadillac. No other auto thefts had been reported in the Millwood area and most thought Rawson had gone to ground somewhere nearby. Plus, Felton had informed him that within a half-hour the roads leading past Miller's property would be saturated with traffic checks. And, should Rawson somehow slip though all the patrols, he had no way of knowing that Marianne and Zack were here.

"All right, I won't cause any problems," Keenan said, and the wound-tight feeling that had been with him all day returned.

II

A refreshing breeze swirled through the wide porch. Keenan had spent the last half-hour perched on a banister, scanning then scanning again the dark tree line along both sides of the huge lawn. In the west, black clouds had almost snuffed the sunset's dying glow. A storm, should it come, would make the scant security even more difficult.

A few feet away, Zack, wearing jeans and a navy blue windbreaker, slouched in a porch swing, rhythmically pushing himself with planted feet as he played a handheld game. Keenan had urged him to go inside and take part in the remembrances but Zack said he would rather stay out here.

Keenan had asked Marianne to keep the porch lights off and the drapes of the formal living room open, so the porch's only light spilled from the living room's windows. Through these panes he could see everyone gathered here. Glancing inside, he found Marianne on the far side of the room standing at a table arrayed with snacks, and noticed again how nicely her blue dress accentuated her supple curves—all evening, Keenan's attention had been torn between watching Marianne and watching the darkened woods. Marianne talked with Alvin Owens as he placed a few nuts and chips onto a small Styrofoam plate. Owens was a slightly pudgy man with thinning, reddish-brown hair and mustache, and meekly slumped shoulders. Tonight he wore a short-sleeved white shirt with blue slacks, and it seemed to Keenan that he was never far from Marianne.

On the opposite side of the room, the pig-headed Bradley Miller stood in front of an unlit, catty-cornered fireplace talking to Solomon Paulus, Mrs. Paulus' eldest son. Dressed in a gray suit, Solomon looked trim and dapper, with a short beard and wire-rimmed glasses. The only other persons present, Mrs. Paulus and Caroline Carmichael, sat on a peach-colored sofa, and Keenan could only see the backs of their heads.

Since arriving here, Keenan had not gone inside. Marianne probably thought it was because of Bradley Miller—and given Keenan's mood, it was probably best to avoid Miller. Keenan told himself that he was staying out here, where he breathed more easily, primarily to keep watch. His vigil, however, felt like an enormous sham because he was literally standing guard unarmed. In eighteen years as an FBI profiler, he had never once needed a weapon—being armed was irrelevant to what he did. And tonight he had expected to be surrounded by black vested agents carrying dark matte assault rifles. Now, being unarmed caused him to feel useless and naked.

He also felt disappointed because he had given up on his hopes of possibly unseating Stith so that he could watch Drum die. Earlier, Marianne had brought him coffee and told him that Miller was grudgingly allowing Stith, a SLED agent, onto his property only because Stith was *their* witness to the execution. If Keenan undermined this role, Stith might be asked to leave the house. Then Keenan would have to leave for the execution, and no law enforcement, apart from the uniforms outside, would still be there. He had been over it again and again, and there was no way that Rawson could know that Marianne and Zack were here. But he had been cavalier in his assumptions about Will, and would not repeat that mistake, at least not where Marianne and Zack were concerned.

Having made the choice of duty over desire, Keenan resolved to do everything required. Marianne regarded him as extra protection and he had let her believe that. When Stith arrived, Keenan would swallow his pride and ask Stith for a gun. Every time Keenan thought of doing this, he tasted bile.

Zack interrupted Keenan's ruminations by asking, "Do you know a man named Scalaro?"

It took Keenan but a second to place the name. "Yeah, he was briefly a suspect before Drum was identified. Why do you ask?"

Rhythmically pushing himself in the swing, Zack said, "We got a letter from him today to say that his thoughts were with us. He also said that after everything that happened—which I guess was being a suspect—that his marriage broke up and he went back to Philadelphia and was real bitter for a while. But he said that he kept thinking about my father's kindness and that helped restore his faith in people, so he remarried and now he's happy. Mom pointed that part out when she gave me the letter but was too rushed getting ready to explain much. I was just wondering what my father had done?"

Keenan thought for a moment, recalling the taped interview that Will had done in Scalaro's kitchen scarcely an hour before he died, and then he remembered something he had seen on the news soon after Will's death. "When Scalaro became a suspect," Keenan said, "he believed that his neighbors and everyone he knew was shunning him. Your father went to question him and Scalaro gave him the lead that led to Drum. So, your father then went out of his way to shake Scalaro's hand in front of news cameras."

"Oh. That doesn't seem like such a big deal."

"If Will had been wrong and Scalaro turned out to be the killer, then your father would have been publicly humiliated. It was a courageous and humane act."

Zack shrugged. "I guess." Then he looked down at the Game Boy in his lap, and gently pushed the swing back and forth.

Zack's unwillingness to give Will a fair shake exasperated Keenan. "What would it take for you to give your father credit where credit's due?"

Zack kept gently pushing the swing. Before he answered, headlights swung around the curve of the long driveway so fast that both Keenan and Zack stood as they watched. The engine's rumble grew louder as the car accelerated toward the house. Motion sensors tripped the garage's floodlights as the sleek Thunderbird pulled to a stop, blocking the other cars parked there. Stith got out and started toward the house with his usual bull-like walk.

Keenan crossed the porch and went down the steps to meet him. Zack followed, but when he reached the foot of the stairs, Stith pointed at him and said, "You go back up there. We have police business to discuss."

"But I . . ."

"Do what I say," Stith ordered, and without slowing walked onto the dark lawn, then stopped and began surveying the sprawling property. "I don't like this at all," he said, still scanning as Keenan joined him. "What's this Miller think he's doing? Doesn't he give a shit about anyone's safety?" Stith glanced at Keenan. "And what's the big deal if a few cops surround his place? Huh?"

Keenan also scanned the tree line. The edge of a rising three-quarters moon peeked between the spiked treetops. Soon the approaching clouds would cover it, but for now its pale light showed clear enough that Keenan could see a skunk about fifty yards away waddling at the edge of the trees. He also could see how heavily Stith sweated. Everything behind the tree line, however, remained dark and impenetrable.

Stith shook his head and looked around the yard again. "I should tell those guys at the end of the driveway to get up here." He turned and faced Keenan. "And Marianne insists on staying?"

"She believes she's safe here."

"And whose fault is that?" Stith said.

"I don't like the situation any better than you do," Keenan replied.

"Yeah. Right," Stith said and looked toward the house, rubbing his jaw along the scar. He turned back to Keenan and asked, "How sure are you that Rawson will try something tonight?"

"I'm certain of it."

"Well then fuck that old man and fuck Carl Jones and every god-damned one of his political cronies. I know a couple of tactical guys who will cover these woods if I ask them. And if Jones wants my badge over this, he can have it tomorrow." Stith pointed his index finger at Keenan. "Look, I'm going to make a quick appearance inside, then get on the phone and have three or four good men over here. That way I'll feel a lot easier when I have to leave. And Miller won't know a god-damned thing about it, unless you blab."

"I think that sounds like a damn good plan," Keenan said. He could no longer put off asking Stith for a gun. Taking a deep breath, Keenan cleared his throat and said, "By the way, I need a weapon. That way we'll also have someone armed at the house."

Perfectly visible in the moonlight's silver hue, Stith wrinkled his nose and shook his head. "You're some piece of work, you know that? I guess your agency's rule about remaining armed at all times doesn't apply to you, huh?"

"Will you help me with a weapon or not?" Keenan asked. He had expected Stith to be an ass about it; still, it took effort to tolerate his condescending attitude. This became even more difficult when Stith pushed his index finger close to Keenan's chest.

"You know, Keenan, every time I try to make nice with you, you do something that pisses me off," he said, then brushed aside his jacket and pulled a small gun in its holster from his back belt. "It's a five-shot .38 caliber Chief's Special Airweight. It fits well in the small of your back. It doesn't exactly have a hair trigger, but it's close, so be careful and don't shoot yourself in the ass."

His face flushed, Keenan clipped the holster to his belt at the small of his back. "Thank you."

"You know what else?" Stith said, his finger punching the air between them. "I ought to . . ."

"Hey, no need to shove," someone shouted in the darkness. Stith whirled and drew his other gun, the Sig Sauer, scanning, ready to go into a crouch. Sensors again ignited the garage's floodlights, as a uniformed officer came into view roughly pushing a handcuffed man. The man had long hair and a beard, but did not look as tall or bulky as Keenan thought Rawson would be. Then he saw two cameras slung around the man's neck and his giddy hopes crashed.

"I caught this guy sneaking out of the woods," the officer explained.

Stith slipped his gun back into its holster. He checked the guy's press ID, then said he wanted the photographer booked for trespassing and told the officer to take him to the patrol units at the end of the driveway and have them call a squad car to pick him up.

"You can't do that," the man protested. "I have rights. The public has rights."

"Add resisting arrest. That'll hold him until morning," Stith said. "Get him out of here."

The photographer, who intended to steal pictures of wounded people's private moments, continued stammering about his rights as the officer led him away.

Drawn by the commotion, Miller and the others came onto the porch. Miller walked to the bottom step and called out, "Is everything all right?"

"Just a reporter trespassing," Stith said. "He'll spend the night in jail."

"Good. I'm Bradley Miller. You're Martin Stith, our witness, aren't you? I'd like you to join us for a few moments."

"And I'd like a word with you," Stith said, and started toward the porch. He paused for just a moment to look back over his shoulder at Keenan and shake his head.

Angered by Stith's taunts and not trusting himself to remain calm, Keenan prudently walked farther into the yard, away from Stith and Miller and the others gathered on the porch. He did not want to say or do something that might embarrass Marianne and get him ordered off Miller's property.

Across the yard, Keenan saw the Jeffcoat officer walking the trespasser down the driveway. This left only one policeman covering Miller's huge property. To both fill this gap and burn off tension, Keenan started toward the tree line at a hard pace. The breeze had turned cooler and maybe picked up a few notches; its gusts soothed Keenan's flushed face as it whooshed through trees and rattled limbs. About a dozen feet from the underbrush and trees, Keenan turned and began walking parallel to the shadowy woods. He wondered briefly, as he had all day, about what Drum might be doing, and hoped that Drum felt at least as much frustration and tension as he did. Keenan pushed his pace a little harder.

"Hey, wait up," Zack yelled and trotted along side.

"You need to go inside and spend time with the others," Keenan said without slowing. He did not want Zack with him. He wanted to be alone, wanted to clear his head, and it seemed that whenever he talked with Zack it was about things that . . . distracted him.

"I'd rather stay out here with you," Zack said, jogging to keep up. "What was that Stith gave you, a gun?"

"Yeah, it was," Keenan answered.

"Can we slow down?" Zack asked, as a gust flattened his windbreaker against his chest.

The moon had risen above the trees and bathed the yard with silver light; but not for long, as dark clouds closed fast. Keenan glanced at Zack and saw the earnest way he looked at him. This kid had no grandfather, uncle, or other constant male in his life, and Keenan thought that void caused Zack to hungrily latch on to him. Given that Keenan's poor judgment had denied Zack a father, it seemed very wrong for him to become attached to Keenan.

"It's time you started getting to know your father," Keenan said, feeling completely out of patience. "So I want you to go inside and ask your mother about him."

"I'd rather be out here with you," Zack said, huffing and sweating. He paused to catch his breath then added, "You understand things. I can learn more from you, okay?"

"No," Keenan said brusquely and stopped walking. To steal the respect of Will's son seemed the worst thing he could do, worse even than lusting for Will's wife. He could not allow this to happen. Facing Zack, Keenan admitted what he had never admitted to anyone. "I want you to listen very closely, you understand? I liked your father a great deal, and for that reason I recommended him for a leadership position that he was wasn't ready to handle. It was my fault that he was under so much pressure. So any mistakes that pressure caused him to make are my fault. Do you understand? So those things you fault your father for . . . I'm the one." Keenan slapped his chest. "And that includes Pop Paulus. So think about that. And now that you know the truth, maybe you can forgive your father."

Zack stood looking at Keenan, his young brow wrinkled. Keenan waited for Zack to condemn him and tell him how disgusted he was. Yet, Keenan's breathing came a little easier.

They had stopped near the yard's back corner. Keenan had been so focused on Zack that he only now noticed the uniformed officer coming up rapidly from behind. This officer was apparently making double time to cover the gap while his partner took the photographer to the bottom of the driveway.

When the officer came within a few feet, Keenan said gruffly, "You need to slow down or you'll miss something."

"Is that right?" the man answered. Then, in a quick lunge, he grabbed Zack with one arm while moonlight glinted on a large hunting knife as it arced toward Zack's throat.

47

helter skelter

1

THE MAN had one arm wrapped around Zack's chest, the other pressed a broad knife against his throat in such a way that a downward swipe would sever Zack's carotid artery. Large and powerfully built, the man had to be Rawson. There was ample moonlight for Keenan to easily see details that he should have noticed before Rawson reached them, like the beard stubble and tufts of hair jutting below the patrolman's cap, or the jeans and work boots. Poorly attentive, he had been fooled by the patrolman's shirt, cap, and heavy equipment belt. Now, much too late, he even saw the dark stain around the shirt's collar from where Rawson had, no doubt, killed the officer who remained to cover the yard while his partner escorted the photographer off the grounds.

"Do exactly what I say or I slit his throat," Rawson told Keenan.

They stood only three feet apart, but Keenan couldn't risk provoking Rawson. Even if he somehow took Rawson down quickly, one slash of the knife would put Zack beyond help. Better to get Rawson talking and distracted, then wait for the right opportunity. Keenan held up his hands at chest level with the palms toward Rawson. "I'll do anything you say as long as you don't hurt the boy," Keenan said. "Tell me what you want?"

"Shut up."

"If you've come for money, I know where there's a suitcase full of money that I'll trade you if you let the boy go."

"I said shut up. One more word and I slit his throat. Now turn around. And if you try anything, I'll cut his throat and I'll shoot you." Less loudly, he said, "Here, put these on him." Then louder, "Big man, put your hands behind your back and remember I have a razor-sharp knife at the kid's throat."

In a lull between gusts, Keenan heard Zack's quick and hard breathing, then felt soft hands and cool metal on his wrists. After Zack snapped the handcuffs closed, a rougher hand squeezed each cuff tight enough to pinch off circulation. To keep Rawson from feeling the gun tucked against his spine, Keenan held his hands well away from his body. "Use this key to lock them," Rawson told Zack. Prison educated, Rawson knew that unless double-locked with a key, most handcuffs could be worked loose.

"Now big man, walk to the house. And if you try anything you both die, got it?"

Keenan felt a hard push on his shoulder and he started walking as slowly as he dared. He angled so that they would walk past the living room windows on a chance that someone might look out and notice them. There was also a chance that the other officer might be returning up the driveway and see them and keep his wits. His bad luck held as the clouds that had been creeping in from the west finally reached the moon and covered it, cloaking the three of them in darkness.

Drawing on everything he had ever learned, Keenan tried to entice Rawson into talking. "Why did you come here? Drum said that you wanted the Paxtons and they're over on Wisteria Road."

"I'm not Drum's pussy boy," Rawson said.

"But you wrote down that Paxton kid's name and address," Keenan said. He hoped that Zack listened closely and understood his subtle deception. Marianne had gone to great pains to shield Zack from media attention so Rawson should not recognize him. Marianne, however, was frequently on the news and that could be a problem unless he stopped Rawson from going into the house. "So it looked like you were thinking about that kid and something changed your mind, right?" Keenan pressed.

"Even if I did consider that kid," Rawson said, "it was all over the news about Drum's other victims going to Bradley Miller's on Big Pond Road. As soon as I heard that, I knew this was a hundred times better because everybody will know that this was my idea."

Hearing this, Keenan berated himself. Given Rawson's fixation on Manson, he believed he should have better read his mind and anticipated something like this. But there was no time for self-blame now, he needed to keep Rawson talking. "So what are you going to do with us?" he asked.

"Make you famous."

To hell you will, thought Keenan, and he moved his hands closer to the gun. The handcuffs pinched off circulation and his fingers stung. If he could turn his back to Rawson and work out the gun, and if he could find a way to separate Zack from Rawson, and then if he could get close to Rawson . . . it seemed like too many ifs.

They reached the steps, and suddenly faced with going into a crowded room with his hands bound, Keenan balked and began breathing harder, yet still felt as if he could not force air into his lungs.

Rawson shoved his shoulder. "Let's go."

Keenan squeezed in as much breath as he could. He considered telling Rawson that there were several policemen inside. But if he were caught in a lie, he would lose any chance of later deceiving him when lives might be even more on the line. Keenan turned his head until he had Rawson in his peripheral vision. The knife was still pressed against Zack's throat. "We don't need to go inside with all those people, you have us," he said.

Rawson raised his other hand, which held a gun, and pushed the barrel against Keenan's cheek, forcing his face forward. He left the weapon pressed on Keenan's jaw; it felt cool and smelled of gun oil. "Now, we're going inside, and you know what happens if you try anything stupid. In fact, big man, you better hope the door don't squeak."

.   .   .

Easing open the door, Keenan looked down a wide, bright hallway with polished hardwood floors. Rawson jammed the gun barrel hard between his shoulder blades and again warned Keenan not to make any sudden moves. A few feet down the hall, doors stood open on either side. Moving very deliberately, Keenan came abreast of these doorframes. On the left was a darkened family room and on the right a brightly lit but empty kitchen. Twenty feet farther ahead, wide arches opened on both sides of the hall. From looking in through the window he knew that through the arch on the right was a formal dining room; to the left, the living room where Marianne, Stith, and the others were gathered.

"Not a sound," Rawson whispered. "And keep close to the wall." Moving slowly, Keenan's breathing felt shallow and inadequate, and his shirt became sticky with sweat. They passed an oval mirror and in it Keenan saw Rawson crouching behind Zack with his left arm wrapped across Zack's chest, holding the knife near his throat. His other hand pointed the gun at Keenan's back.

Keenan tried to think but his only lucid thought was of the cooler air outside. If only he could go back onto the porch, he knew he would become clearheaded and know what to do.

Nearing the arch, a sliver of the living room came into view and Keenan saw Stith, his arms crossed over his chest, leaning against the wall beside the catty-cornered fireplace with its ornately carved mantel. Stith glanced into the hall, saw Keenan, looked away, then jerked his head back in their direction for a second look. Fanning back his jacket, Stith drew his weapon and Keenan took two quick steps to give him a clear view.

His gun held at eye level and steadied with both hands, Stith hesitated, perhaps because Rawson crouched behind Zack or maybe he saw the knife at Zack's throat. In that instant, Rawson swung his gun on Stith and fired, the shot sounding terribly loud in this enclosed place. The bullet hit Stith in the shoulder, causing him to partially turn as a second bullet hit him in the back. Stith's gun clattered on the floor and, stumbling like a drunk man, his right arm hanging limp, he fell backward against the wall, leaving a bloody streak as he slid downward. Rawson shot him again, this time in the chest. Stith thumped to the floor with his back still against the wall exuding a loud hissing from his chest wound as he breathed.

A few feet beyond the room's center, Marianne sat in the middle of a peach-colored sofa holding hands with Alvin Owens on her right and, on her left, Caroline Carmichael, a plump woman with teased blonde hair and a bit too much makeup. Caroline also held the hand of Mrs. Paulus, who sat in a matching wingback chair, and was closest to where Stith slumped, bleeding badly. Behind Mrs. Paulus stood her son, Solomon. Bradley Miller stood on the opposite side of the sofa, between it and the table containing the snacks; he held open a large white Bible.

Everyone looked stunned. Then Rawson came into view and Marianne saw Zack. Scrambling around the coffee table, she rushed toward him with outstretched arms. Keenan stepped into the room and blocked her way as Rawson pointed the gun at her. She stopped, her hands reaching past Keenan, and implored, "That's my son. Use me instead. Please!"

Keenan looked back over his shoulder at Rawson and said, "You don't need . . . ," but Rawson slammed his foot against Keenan's buttocks, knocking his weight against Marianne. Both stumbled a couple of steps before Keenan fell, landing hard near the chair where Mrs. Paulus sat, pain shooting through his shoulder. Caroline Carmichael began to sob, "Oh, God. Oh God, no." Wincing, Keenan rolled onto his back, hoping his jacket had not slid up and exposed the gun.

Rawson left the gun leveled at Marianne's face. "Sit down," he ordered. Without taking her eyes off Zack, Marianne stepped back until she bumped the coffee table and sat on its edge.

"Everybody do exactly what I say or I slit his throat, understand?" Rawson said and pointed the gun first at Bradley Miller, then Solomon Paulus, then back to Miller, obviously uneasy with two males standing. When no one tried anything, Rawson shifted Zack to his side, as if carrying a baby on his hip, and with the knife pressed recklessly against his jugular dragged him to where Stith lay. Slow bubbles formed in the blood coming from Stith's chest wound. Rawson thrust the gun against Stith's crown.

"Everyone's doing exactly what you want," Keenan called hoarsely from where he lay on the floor. He sucked in as much air as the tightness around his chest would allow and said, "But we're so scared that if you start now . . . you'll freak us out and have trouble controlling us. And besides . . . you can't enjoy seeing him that messed up if he's dead."

Rawson hesitated with the gun pressed against Stith's head. "No one move," he warned, then swooped and picked up Stith's Sig Sauer. As he did, he carelessly drew the knife harder against Zack's throat, causing Zack's nostrils to flare as he panted hard and fast.

"Easy with the knife," Keenan warned.

Straightening, Rawson tucked Stith's gun in his belt and pointed the other gun at Keenan. "You're getting on my nerves."

With the barrel's dark O squinting at him, Keenan forced himself to look at Rawson instead. Tufts of hair stuck below the cap that had been dyed black and hacked shorter than in the composite drawing. Rawson's eyes were widely dilated, and looked wild.

Focused on the immediate crisis, Keenan's feeling of suffocation eased a little, and he realized that as long as he didn't dwell on being trapped in this stifling room he could think. So he asked himself what Rawson most wanted right now, then said, "You'll feel more relaxed when things are secure."

"It's the last time I'm telling you to keep your mouth shut," Rawson said and took a half-step toward Keenan, the gun pointed at him. Keenan nodded and didn't say anything. He also avoided any eye contact that Rawson might perceive as a challenge. Rawson slid the gun into its holster and used his free hand to take another set of handcuffs from a leather pocket on his equipment belt and toss them to Marianne. "You, Mother, cuff the nigger," he said, nodding toward Solomon Paulus. He then leaned over and pulled Stith's gun from his belt. "When you get the nigger cuffed, see if this guy has cuffs" — Rawson pointed the gun at Stith — "and secure the other two men. And if you can't find any cuffs on him, then I'm going to shoot those two, understand? So don't get cute. And you, Blondie" — he pointed the gun at Caroline Carmichael — "while she's doing that you close all the shades and drapes. And I better not see any of the rest of you move an inch."

Once Marianne had secured Solomon Paulus, she knelt beside Stith and found two additional sets of handcuffs in a pouch on his belt. Her hands trembling, Caroline Carmichael unhooked the heavy drapes. While they did this, Mrs. Paulus tore a cloth napkin into strips and, ignoring Rawson's warning to not move, went to Stith. She opened his shirt and gently pushed a rolled strip into each wound to stem the bleeding, though it might be too late; Stith's breathing made a faint gurgling, his pupils were dilated and glazed, and his face ruddy and sweaty.

Zack's pupils were also dilated as he frequently glanced down at the knife pressed to his throat. Briefly, he and Keenan looked at each other. Zack knew Keenan had a gun and looked as if he expected Keenan to give him some kind of sign. While Rawson watched Marianne, Keenan mouthed the word, "wait," hoping Zack would understand and not try anything that might bring him harm.

Once Solomon was cuffed, Rawson pointed the gun and ordered him to get on his knees beside the chair where his mother had sat. Similarly, after Miller and Owens were cuffed, Rawson ordered them to kneel in the space between the couch and table of snacks. Even after all the men were secured, Rawson held the gun at arm's length in front of him, aiming it first at one, then another of his captives, obviously extremely jumpy from attempting such a bold crime. Should anything threaten Rawson's feeling of control, Keenan believed he would immediately reassert himself through violence, and, being so emotionally explosive, once the slaughter began he might lose himself in a bloodbath more frenzied than even he had envisioned. Keenan had to distract Rawson and get close enough to use the gun without in any way making him uneasy. And if he failed to score a hit with his first shot, Rawson's bloodletting would begin.

Shifting slightly, Keenan eased his hands closer to the gun. When Stith handed it to him, he had been so frustrated by Stith's goading that he hardly looked at it. Now, he assumed that even if the gun had a safety, it was probably off because Stith would want it ready to fire if drawn. But he didn't know this for certain. Keenan moved his hands under his jacket and tried to locate the holster's guard. His right hand had gone completely numb. Some sensation remained in his left, but those fingers felt too bloated and too stiff to covertly undo the snap, and he would soon lose all feeling in that hand, too.

Finished with their tasks, Rawson ordered Marianne and Caroline to sit on the couch. Marianne moved to the side near where Owens and Miller knelt and perched on the couch's edge with a good angle to scoot around the coffee table if the opportunity arose.

Mrs. Paulus finished plugging Stith's wounds and tried to lay him down. Blinking rapidly, Stith swatted at her with his good arm and she stopped. This drew Rawson's attention. "Get with the others," he told her. Pulling Zack along, Rawson covered the two steps to where Mrs. Paulus leaned over Stith and put his boot on her shoulder and pushed her to the floor beside where Solomon knelt with his hands cuffed behind him.

"Leave her alone," Solomon yelled.

Rawson again pulled Zack along, seeming careless with the knife, and crossed the four or so feet to where Solomon knelt. As soon as he came close, he brutally kicked Solomon in the groin, causing him to crumple forward and puke. "No uppity nigger's going to tell me what to do," Rawson said and kicked Solomon in the ribs, knocking him onto his side. Then he kicked him again in the chest. Crawling on top of her son, Mrs. Paulus begged, "Stop it, please? Please!"

Fearing that Rawson was perilously close to losing control, Keenan yelled, "The famous ones take their time." He rolled to his side and using his shoulder struggled to his knees.

Rawson turned his head and looked at Keenan with wildly dilated green eyes.

As much from the intuition of experience as from any conscious plan, Keenan told him, "I'm an FBI profiler. I've interviewed Bundy, Dahmer, and Drum. None of them rushed things. We can tell from the crime scene how it went down, and everybody knows that those who do it quickly are chickenshits who lack the courage to do something really big. Scared guys never get a reputation as anything but pukes. You ever hear of Albert Mendlow or Sonny Bredt," Keenan said, making up names. "That's because they're only known in their home areas, and they're considered jokes."

Rawson faced Keenan. "Are you fucking with me?"

"No, I'm not. I've even interviewed that little loudmouth, Manson—a do-nothing guy. But he had a certain style, and that's what made him famous; he never rushed things."

Rawson grabbed Zack's hair and pulled back his head. "Boy, if you move and I'll make a mess of your FBI buddy. Do you understand?"

"Yeah," Zack winced.

When Rawson let go his hair, Zack looked at Keenan and Keenan shook his head no before Rawson stepped between them. Keenan hoped Zack understood and would not try anything. Then Keenan almost came undone. Standing in front of him, Rawson slipped the gun back into his belt and made a display of switching the knife to his right hand. All Keenan's breath seemed squeezed from his lungs as he realized that, while Rawson used the gun for control, he preferred cutting. Until that moment Keenan had managed not to focus on the knife, because the focal point of the worst fear in his nightmare was the knife; and it had grown to phobic dimensions. Barely able to breathe, a feeling of panic swelled.

Rawson squatted and slowly stuck the blade into Keenan's nostril, forcing his head back until Keenan could not stretch any farther. The knife tip felt cold. Vapor fogged and ebbed on the blade with each snorting breath. Holding Keenan this way, Rawson lifted both sides of his jacket. "Where's your gun?"

"I'm . . . profiler," Keenan hissed through clenched teeth. "I don't . . . carry one. Technical support . . . not enforcement."

Rawson let the jacket fall closed. "I guess you know that doing you will make me more famous than even Drum for doing that dumb cop."

"It might," Keenan struggled to say. He felt a wet drop run across his lip. Hissing harder, he said, "I can . . . think of . . . something . . . better."

"What?"

"Give me . . . time. What's your . . . hurry?"

Rawson paused, stretching Keenan's head back with the knife, as Keenan breathed noisily though clenched teeth. At last, Rawson said, "I guess I got time for a smoke. But think fast." He then took the knife away and Keenan drooped and noisily sucked in air, yet still felt as if he were suffocating.

Rawson stood, pointed the knife at Zack, and told him to drag the wingback chair into the doorway. "And if you care about your mother, you won't get cute," he warned. As Zack did this, Rawson again switched the knife to his left hand and pulled Stith's Sig Sauer from where he had stuck it in his belt. When Zack had the chair in the middle of the door, Rawson ordered him to sit on the floor in front of it, then looped a leg over Zack's head and sat with his knees framing Zack's shoulders.

Keenan managed to slow his breathing, though a feeling of panic rolled inside like waves close to spewing over a seawall. He noticed a few drops of blood on his shirt, then continued watching Rawson's every move.

Casually, Rawson draped the hand with the knife across Zack's shoulder, and lay the gun on his lap. Using his free hand, he wriggled a lighter and fat joint from his jeans pocket. "I've been saving this," he said as he lit the joint, inhaling deeply. "I'd share but . . ."

"My son's bleeding," Marianne interrupted and stood. Blood seeped from a thin line on the side of Zack's neck. She stepped forward beyond the coffee table, her hand once again reaching toward Rawson. "Let me put something on it, okay?"

"Shut up," Rawson said, glaring at Marianne though a haze of smoke. "It's just a little scratch. And you should say please when you ask me something. In fact, you should show me a favor or two, because I stopped that big man from taking your kid into the woods, and you know what he would have done back there alone with a kid. So what kind of favors you going to show me for that? Huh?" Marianne didn't say anything. "Answer me," Rawson demanded.

"Please, use me instead of my son and I'll do anything you want, anyway you want."

"You're going to do that anyway," Rawson said, and leered at her.

"No, I won't," she said.

"Don't get uppity with me," he said and turned the blade, forcing Zack's chin upward, the boy's eyes wide. Rawson then leaned forward and with the hand holding the joint fondled Zack's crotch, glaring at Marianne. "Are you going to sit down, or do I make your precious son really bleed."

Marianne, her eyes glistening and her hands forming fists, eased back onto the edge of the couch.

Rawson lowered the knife and leaned back in the chair. There was a red line where the knife had just pressed but no blood, yet. Staring at Marianne, Rawson said, "You look familiar." He took another hit on the joint. His movements seemed jerkier. If the joint contained only marijuana it might dull Rawson, get him to drop his guard a little. But this was probably the "one hit will mess you up" dope that he had taken from Jimmy Gilpin. Hopped up on PCP and cocaine, just a wrong look might spark a frenzied slaughter.

Desperately, Keenan hoped no one else would challenge Rawson. He again tried to will away his tension but the effort only seemed to worsen it, so instead he concentrated on slowing his breathing and surveyed the room. On his left, Solomon coughed up blood, as his mother cradled his head in her lap and wiped his face with a napkin. Keenan looked over his left shoulder. Caroline Carmichael curled up on the near end of the sofa, sobbing softly with her face buried in one of the throw pillows. Turning his head and looking over his other shoulder, he saw Marianne ready on the couch's edge. A couple of feet beyond her, Alvin Owens and then Bradley Miller knelt with their hands cuffed behind them. Stith remained slumped against the wall, his head tilted back. A trickle of blood seeped from the corner of his mouth and Keenan thought he might not be breathing. Then Stith's eyes opened and, though they looked clouded and unfocused, he scanned until he located Rawson.

Their captor sat with his knees jutting beside Zack's shoulders and stared hard at Marianne with eyes that were rapidly becoming glassy. Maybe if he smoked enough, Keenan thought, he might pass out. Or go into a PCP frenzy. Rawson took off the policeman's cap and tossed it behind him, then shook out his poorly dyed black hair. Chopped shorter, the change in his appearance made a fairly effective disguise. He took another hit, then blew smoke into Zack's face. "There, kid, don't say I never gave you anything."

Zack turned his head away and tried to hold his breath. To Zack's credit, he had shown a lot of poise and alertly looked to Keenan for cues, waiting to see how he would use the gun. But there was also fear in his eyes as he looked at Keenan, silently pleading, just like in Keenan's nightmare: the knife; being helplessly bound; pleading eyes; his nightmare come alive. An invisible band tightened even more around Keenan's chest, squeezing air from his lungs and he began to gasp. Outside was cool night air. He could breathe . . . if he could just get . . . outside. But fleeing would bring sure death, and knowing this enabled Keenan to hold on to the barest of restraint.

Holding the joint a few inches in front of his face, Rawson looked at Keenan and asked, "What's happened to you?"

"I need to go," Keenan croaked and brought a foot forward so that he knelt on one knee and one foot

Rawson sat upright and pointed the gun, fully extended, at Keenan, "Stay where you are."

Keenan hardly saw the gun. He could not take his eyes from the knife, and if Rawson pointed the blade at him again, it just might tilt his panic. He began to breathe in short gasps. "Please," Keenan plead-ed, stripped of his dignity. "Just a little air. Please. I can't breathe."

"That's enough of this foolishness," Bradley Miller interrupted and worked his way to his feet. "I don't know what you think you're doing, Keenan, but I've had enough of you."

Rawson turned the gun on Miller. "Shut up, old man, and get back down."

"You must be that Rawson fellow," Miller stubbornly answered. "What you're doing is stupid and pointless. Think about it and you'll see that I'm right."

"I said shut up, old man." Rawson rose to his feet.

"No," Miller said, jutting out his chin. "You're going to listen to me and start acting like you have a teaspoon of sense because you'll never get away with this."

Rawson's eyes were watery and wild and with his butchered hair he looked like a lunatic. Rawson used the hand holding the gun to shove Zack and send him sprawling on the floor a yard in front of where Keenan knelt. "Try anything, kid, and I'll mess up your momma," he hissed. Then, staring at Miller, Rawson tried to thrust the gun into his belt but was so angry he missed on his first try. Once he did get the gun in the belt, he again made a show of switching the knife to his right hand. "Talk back to me again, old man," he said and took a step toward Miller. He then gestured with his free hand as if calling Miller to him. "Come on, old man, say something."

Miller kept quiet and only his Adam's apple moved as he swallowed.

"You don't know anything, you old fucker," Rawson said and waved the knife at Miller. "Nobody's going to send me back to jail. I'm going out like a man. Do you know what I mean? And do you know why? Because old fuckers like you think you run everything." Rawson slashed the air with his knife. "Everybody lay facedown. Except you, old man. Do it," he screamed.

Knowing that it was now or never, Keenan fought his mind-killing fear and struggled to his feet. "Wait."

Cat-like, Rawson went into a fighter's crouch, the knife held low at his side, its tip pointed at Keenan, edging toward him. Panic nearly erased the wisp of an idea that Keenan was trying to turn into a plan. Sweat streamed down his face and he strained to look away from the knife. Beyond Rawson was the doorway leading to fresh air. Inviting . . . if he could get past the knife. Keenan forced himself to focus, and the strain nearly choked off his ability to speak. Hoarse and halting, he said, "I can get . . . your father . . . huh, huh, huh . . . on the phone. You can tell him . . . he was wrong . . . huh, huh . . . and show him . . . you're a . . . helluva man."

"He'll hear about what I've done."

Keenan forced in as much air as he could. "He'll think Drum pulled your chain . . . huh, huh . . . unless you show him. If you can face him."

"I can face him."

"Prove it."

Keenan worked his hands under his jacket. His right hand remained completely numb and his left hand felt bloated beyond use. Doubtful that he could undo the holster's snap, he felt with his wrist above where the handcuffs cut off sensation and located the gun's butt. The handle was turned toward his right. He squeezed his deadened left index finger between the holster and trigger guard, and the pressure caused his pinched nerves to feel as if stinging hornets were jabbing at the finger. Breathing harder from the pain, Keenan pushed his finger in as far as it would go, still not sure if it had gone far enough to get around the trigger. Given the trigger's sensitivity, he dared not risk trying it until he made his play.

The hard concentration quelled some of Keenan's panic. Rawson said something but Keenan had been completely focused on the gun and not paid attention, so he said, "My life. I'll do it in exchange for my life. Just let me go."

Rawson's crouch relaxed a little, probably because he understood and enjoyed seeing cowardice in others. "I said, how could you get my old man on the phone?"

"I interviewed . . . Cottonmouth." Keenan rasped, using the prison nickname for credibility. "They'll put him on . . . the phone for me . . . but only me."

Rawson switched the knife to his left hand and took the Sig Sauer from his belt, pointing it at Keenan. If Rawson shot him now, everyone would think him a coward, a betrayer of those who trusted him. "No," Keenan groaned aloud at this thought.

Rawson interpreted this as begging. "You're scared shitless," he said, and eased out of his crouch to puff out his chest. "Some big, tough FBI agent, huh? Everybody look at your great FBI profiler as he shits his pants." He waved the gun in front of him, drunk with PCP and power. "So who's the tougher man, huh?" Finally, he looked back at Keenan. "All right, we'll get my old man on the phone."

"You have to give me . . . a running chance," Keenan said. "Just a few steps . . . that's all. I'll do it if you put the guns out of reach . . . so you can't . . . shoot me in the back."

"No."

"Please?" Keenan said, sweating heavily. "There's nothing any of us can do . . . not now. You have us. Just give me a running chance. Please. There's a cell phone . . . in my jacket pocket," Keenan added, wanting to lure Rawson closer.

Rawson used the gun hand to rub the back of his neck. "All right. Kid, get up and get the phone out of his pocket."

Keenan considered telling Rawson that he didn't need to use Zack, but that might make him suspicious. Better to wait. Everyone else remained where they were. Zack approached and Keenan nodded to his right, "That pocket." He could step in front of Zack and try to get off a shot, but he was about five feet from Rawson and didn't know how well he could aim with his dead hands; plus Rawson still had two guns and the knife.

Rawson tucked the knife into his belt when Zack handed him the phone. He studied the cell phone, appeared confused, then handed it back to Zack. "You dial." He then looked at Keenan, "What's the number?"

Fighting to hold on to his window of clarity, Keenan said, "You still have the guns." He then added a whiny "Please?"

Rawson leered at Keenan the way Drum had, and hate focused Keenan a bit more. Rawson stepped past where Stith slumped on the floor, maybe dead, and the killer lay the guns on the ornate mantel. As this happened, the doorway was temptingly clear. Keenan forced himself not to think about the cool air so invitingly close, forced himself to concentrate, and pleaded, "Please, the ammunition clips . . . take out the clips, please . . . give me one more step."

Rawson smiled. "All right, big coward. Big, tough G-man. I've really done a number on you. I should let someone go so they can tell the world what a coward you are. You're nothing, you know that?" He snorted derisively, then one at a time popped the clips and lay them beside the guns. It was the best Keenan could hope for.

Rawson came back to stand beside Zack blocking the arch. For the moment, the knife stayed tucked in his belt. Keenan took a half-step closer and said, "There's a card in my inside pocket." He wanted to draw Rawson a little further from the guns and from Zack. Keenan looked at Zack and gave the barest of nods. Zack nodded back. "My inside jacket pocket," Keenan repeated and twisted his shoulder forward.

Rawson came closer, leaving Zack just beyond his arm's reach. Keenan waited until Rawson lifted his jacket and began fishing at arm's length in his pocket, then yelled, "Now." He hesitated long enough for Zack to dive forward and start to crawl away, then lunged behind the outstretched arm, slamming his shoulder into the back of Rawson's shoulder. Rawson stumbled and Keenan kept pushing against him with all his weight, driving him back until he began to trip over Stith's outstretched legs. With Rawson off balance, Keenan stopped pushing and tugged on the gun but it snagged on his belt. He jerked harder and gun and holster came free as Rawson lunged at him. Turning his back and absorbing Rawson's returning charge, Keenan pushed his bloated finger inside the trigger guard and the gun fired. Rawson howled and Keenan fired again as Rawson chopped at his hands, knocking the gun free.

Then Rawson threw a hard shoulder into Keenan's back, causing them both to sprawl on the floor. Scrambling off Keenan, Rawson dove for the still holstered gun, which lay near Keenan's feet. Keenan kicked, missing the gun but knocking Rawson's hand away. He kicked again and this time the gun went sliding across the room. Keenan kept stomping his feet into his enemy's knees, ankles, anything to keep him down. But Rawson rolled away, climbed to his feet, and hobbled toward the mantel, bleeding from a wound high on his thigh.

He reached across Stith—who still slumped against the wall with blood now spurting weakly from a new wound in his upper leg caused by Keenan's second shot. Rawson steadied himself by putting one hand on the mantel as his other hand grabbed the Sig Sauer and clip. Bradley Miller screamed, "You've gotten us all killed." Then Stith used what little reserve he had left and stomped his foot against Rawson's knee, causing him to stumble and, leaning off balance, fall over Stith and land in front of the fireplace, though he managed to hold on to the gun and clip. Stith then slumped over and lay on his side.

Keenan struggled to a sitting position in time to see Rawson push himself up and lean back against the fireplace's woodwork, less than a foot from where Stith lay. Helplessly, Keenan watched him slam the clip into the gun. There was a pop, like a paper bag bursting, and wood splintered about two inches from Rawson's ear, causing him to look up as Marianne fired a second shot. This time, Rawson grabbed his shoulder. Marianne closed quickly on him. Keenan could not tell her that she only had one shot left without also telling Rawson. Keenan rolled to his side but by the time he leveraged himself to his knees, ready to throw himself onto Rawson, Marianne was already past him, and only about five feet separated her and Rawson.

"You win," Rawson said, raising his hands to head level, but still holding the gun pointed upward.

"No," Keenan shouted, as Rawson swung the gun level and another shot sounded. For what seemed like a very long time, Rawson and Marianne remained squared off, each with their gun pointed at the other, both completely motionless. Keenan did not know who had fired until he heard the hammer click on the empty chamber of Marianne's gun.

Rawson looked amused.

A trickle of blood then oozed from a dark spot below his widow's peak. He raised his hand as if to wipe his face, stopped, looked at his hand, confused, then Rawson's eyes emptied and he fell onto his side.

48

revelations

I

LIKE A squat saint without hope, Joe slumped forward, head in hands. He had been in the waiting room for a long time. Drum's attorney, Sammy Isgett, had had a final visit. After that, Warden Edwards came and intended to stay with Drum until eight o'clock, when the telephone call between Drum and his mother was to take place.

Joe rubbed his face with both hands and raised his reddened eyes to look at the clock—it was quarter of eight—and he thought again about how life can be funny. Whenever anyone asked Joe why he became a minister, he always said it was because he wanted to comfort people. Maybe thinking he wanted to help others was really a hood ornament for his own neediness, because the one man everyone now expected him to comfort, Joe thought deserved to suffer. Chalk up one more failure. This failure, though, was not of ability, but of the heart.

Given how strongly Joe already felt, he had not needed more reason to despise Drum. But he had gotten it, anyway. Bradley Miller, the father of Drum's youngest victim, had been interviewed earlier in the day and they showed it on the evening news. To put it mildly, Miller's sentiments were opposite those of Mrs. Paulus. He said he had only agreed to be interviewed because he wanted everyone to understand the exact nature of the monster scheduled to be executed tonight. Miller had successfully sued South Carolina to see the tape that Drum made with his daughter. Joe thought of his own daughter, Faith, and what a crushing thing that must have been to watch.

They had interviewed Miller as he stood on the front steps of his house. "I'll not tell you about the worst of it," Miller had said, sounding combative. "I'll never tell anyone. But when my son-in-law went on television holding my granddaughter and begged for mercy, that man . . . Drum . . . taped it and showed it to Alicia. Then he told her that if she didn't do everything he wanted, that . . ."—Miller's mouth quivered, then he regained his composure—". . . that when Jennifer was older he would kidnap and do the same things to her. And all the while that beast was doing horrible things to Alicia, he kept telling her that what she was doing was not good enough to save her daughter. My daughter probably died thinking that she had failed her child." Miller turned away and the camera zoomed tightly on his teary face as he went into the house and shut the door.

Jutting the remote at arm's length toward the screen, Joe turned off the television. He knew as well as anyone how failure eats away from the inside. To defile that young girl had not been enough for Drum; he wanted to strip her of everything, of her dignity and hope and stomp on all that was good and beautiful about her. At that moment, if someone had offered him the chance, Joe would have gladly gone into the execution chamber and pulled the switch himself.

II

At about eight-thirty, Warden Edwards entered the waiting area. Frowning and brusque, he sat beside Joe and leaned toward him. "We have a problem," Edwards said. "Two Alston Wilkes volunteers have been sitting outside that goddamn woman's house for forty-five minutes and she's not there. They said they talked with her early this afternoon and she knew to be there at eight sharp to take the call. We're trying to convince the inmate that she must have been confused about the time, but I'll bet you a Rolex against a rat's ass that she didn't forget, she just doesn't want to talk to him. Now, the inmate's starting to get agitated and there's not a helluva lot more I can do."

Edwards leaned back into the couch, took a couple of breaths and looked up at the ceiling. "Mr. Cameron, do you remember a man named Butch Chalgren?"

"Not really," Joe answered.

Edwards looked at Joe and his voice sounded more tired. "The press said Butch met his death calmly, said he only needed some assistance because his legs gave out. Mr. Cameron, Butch was a wiry little guy who fought us from the time we went in to shave him. For almost an hour he fought, biting and twisting like a snake. And that was with five or six men trying to hold him down. When it was over, three of my men needed medical treatment, and Butch got pretty banged up and that caused all sorts of rumors. A man pumped up on adrenaline doesn't wear out like a normal man, and the state says they have the right to meet their death clearheaded, so we can't drug them without their consent. Now, the witnesses thought Butch looked calm because by the time we got him into the chamber, he didn't have any fight left. Hell, we had to carry him in with his feet dragging on the floor. Most go numb at that point anyway, and just putting one foot in front of the other is about all they can handle. So we help them; and the witnesses see what they want to see, which is a little courage and dignity at the end. Most men want it that way too.

Edwards leaned toward Joe. "I'm telling you this, Mr. Cameron, so you'll understand the situation. If it gets nasty, you're going to be standing about three feet away and, whether you like it or not, you'll be part of it. And if it gets nasty, you'll dream about it a lot longer. Take my word for it, you will. So your job is to see that it doesn't get nasty. Like I said yesterday, there's no one else. If I'm anywhere near him, he gets more agitated. Same with my officers. So other than you, this guy is as alone as it gets. And I don't want that son of a bitch banging up my men. Do you understand?"

"Yeah," Joe replied weakly.

"Good. We're going to give you more latitude than we normally might. We want you to take care of him. If he wants something within reason, you get it and give it to him. Men in his situation usually want to latch on to somebody, and you're it, Mr. Cameron. Now we're counting on you to go back there and do your job."

III

Drum leaned against the back wall smoking a cigarette like some pock-marked James Dean. "Did you hear about the fuckup?" he asked when he saw Joe.

"The Warden told me. He said the volunteers will stay there until midnight in case she comes home."

"Yeah, sure. What time is it?"

There was a clock above the Plexiglas of the control booth that was clearly visible from where Drum stood, but he seemed to avoid looking at it. Joe turned, checked the time, and said, "Twenty of nine."

"I bet no one ever went to her house and they're just jerking me around. If those fuckups were serious about helping, they'd have asked her to come here." Drum paced the short distance across his cell. "You know all they care about is that their show go smoothly. That's the only reason they pretend to treat me nice. Well, fuck them if they think I'm going to make them look good."

Drum walked up to the bars and looked down at Joe. "I bet you don't know why they stopped having public executions. I've read all about it. When they had them, people would come from three counties away to watch. They'd bring picnics and booze and get drunk and there'd be street entertainers. Then, when the time came, they'd hold their little boys and little girls up on their shoulders so they could get a good look. Can you believe that? It just shows that people are no good. Did you know it was Holy Rollers like you that put an end to public executions? But you didn't do it for humane reasons. No, what bothered your kind was that when people watched some stupid fuck quiver and kick at the end of a rope, it got them all hard and wet and hot. That's a known fact. The church didn't give a damn about some poor guy getting mur-dered—because that's what it is, murder, I don't care who does it. No, you holier-than-thou-hypocrites didn't like so-called good people getting all turned on from watching a murder. You people are sick, you really are," Drum said and took a hit off the cigarette, then another slower hit.

Several seconds passed before he said, "They say you only feel the first jolt and your brain's completely fried in three seconds. But how the fuck can anybody know what two thousand volts really feels like. What if you suffer the whole five seconds? One thousand and one, one thousand and two, one thousand and three, one thousand and four, one thousand and five—that's a long fucking time.

"And did you know that the sadistic bastards zap you with a second surge of one thousand volts for eight seconds—they don't need a sec-ond jolt, they just do it for spite. I've heard that before it's over your innards are so cooked that organs split and you're burned black where the current goes in your head. So if they think I'm going to make nice while they do that to me, they're stupider than they look. They're going to regret fucking with me."

Drum began pacing. Joe thought that if they seriously believed he could do something to calm this man, they were stupider than they looked. But he guessed he should try. Licking his lips, Joe asked, "Is there anything that you'd like to talk about?"

"What time is it?"

Joe turned again and looked at the clock. "Eight-forty-five."

"Man, this waiting's going to take forever."

IV

Morose and silent, Drum sat on his bed, leaning against the wall and chain-smoking. At nine-thirteen Clayton Edwards, stoop shouldered, entered the holding area. "I'm sorry," he told Drum. "There's still no one at your mother's place."

"You're lying." Drum stood and pushed his face between the bars. "You assholes never tried to get in touch with her. You just wanted to screw me one last time."

"We've done everything we can. The problem is your mother's not home. She must have gotten confused about the time. There's nothing else we can do, unless you've changed your mind and want some medication now."

"Goddamned right I want medicine, lots of medicine."

"You can have as much as the doctor has ordered. Is there anything else?"

Mouth slightly quivering, Drum shook his head no.

A few minutes later the attending CO brought Drum a small plastic cup of orange juice and held it through the bars. "Here's your meds." When Drum just stared at him from his bunk, the CO said, "You either gotta drink it now or I have to take it back."

Listlessly, Drum sat up, reached for the juice, and downed it. "When can I get my next one?"

"I think that's it. But I'll check with the doctor when he gets here and see what he says."

"Yeah, *boy*, you do that." Then Drum stood, crossed to the fixed coil, and pushed a cigarette into its orange glow. Returning to his bunk, he began methodically smoking his Marlboro.

Surreptitiously, Joe studied Drum's pale, pockmarked, face. He looked too bland to be a monster. There was no obvious mark of Cain. How could anyone understand such a perverse being? How could flesh become so twisted, so malignantly transformed? What does such evil feel?

"I'm cold."

"Huh," Joe said, startled from his reverie.

Drum stared at him with half-shut eyes. "I said I'm cold."

"I'll get you something."

At the control room, they gave Joe a green blanket flecked with silver fire-retardant strands. Joe passed the blanket to Drum, who lethargically wrapped it around his shoulders, then leaned against the wall.

Rather than retreat into his cistern of silence, Drum surprised Joe by quietly saying, "When I was little, my mother would let me get in bed with her on cold nights and snuggle up against her. She always felt warm and soft. Sometimes she'd hold me real tight. That's what I missed most when they took me from her."

Drum's eyes remained unfocused. "I loved her. She was beautiful, too. So, I could never understand why she let men use her the way she did. She didn't need to. But when a man was around, she changed. The stupid thing about it was how she always said those men didn't mean a thing to her. But every night, off she'd go again. You know, I been feeding myself since I was three or four, getting baloney or whatever shit was in the refrigerator because she was off chasing after some asshole. And if a man was in the house, I had to stay out of the way—it didn't matter who he was, if it was a man, I was in the way." Drum turned his face away from Joe. "I wonder what man she's with tonight." He seemed to have trouble swallowing and ordered, "Get me some water."

Rather than point out that a blue plastic cup sat on the sink, Joe filled an identical cup from the drinking fountain in the waiting area. He handed it to Drum, who took a sip and passed it back to Joe.

"I'm still cold. Another fucking cold night." Drum pulled the blanket tighter. "I had my share of cold nights in Korea. Sometimes it got so cold that your shoestrings would freeze and snap if you tried to undo them before they thawed out. I moved back here to get away from the cold.

"But you know, I think the night I shivered worst was down at the Saluda River. It was about the same time of year that it is now. I guess I was eleven then." Drum stopped talking. Images of a moonlit autumn night flitted through his mind and goose bumps formed on his arms, causing him to clutch the blanket tighter. Drum rested his head against the wall and shut his eyes. "Over the summer, we had moved to Jeffcoat Landing from Charleston so my mom could sorta live with her new boyfriend, Bobby. Man, I haven't thought about that prick in years. He was the worst loser she ever hooked up with. At first, I thought he was kinda cool because he had tattoos and hair that came down almost to his belt, and he was always talking about what things had been like in the joint. The only good thing about him, though, was that he was gone a lot. I think he was a truck driver or something like that. Or maybe he was married to some other bitch, I'm not sure. All I know is that when he was there, I was in the way. And I hated him as much as I'd hated my old man."

Drum breathed heavily a couple of times and shook his head without opening his eyes. "There was this one night that Bobby left because him and Mom had a fight after some guy come to the house to see me, or something like that. Mom started drinking heavy and cussing and throwing things. When she got that way, all I could do was listen because if I said anything she'd get mad at me and wouldn't have anything to do with me. I don't know how late it was when she went to bed. I had to help her get undressed and since it was so cold I undressed and got in bed with her. I still remember how warm she felt and how good her skin felt on mine. I even remember liking the smell of booze on her breath and wishing that I could stay with her, just like we were."

Drum pulled the blanket tighter around him. "We must have dozed off because all of a sudden Bobby was in the room, pulling off the covers. The liquor on his breath was worse than my mom's. He screamed, `You fucking warped bitch. What the hell you doing with your own kid.' Then he grabbed my mom by her hair and dragged her toward the foot of the bed, so I started hitting him, trying to make him stop, but he put one hand around my throat and held me at arm's length. I hated being helpless like that so I spit on his hand, and the way he stared at me . . . I thought for sure he was going to kill me. Instead, he said, 'All right, you stupid fuck, I'll show you what it's all about,' and he shoved my Mom down on her back and pushed me down on top of her. Then he took down his pants and . . . ."

Drum hissed in air and stopped talking. Colorless tears, like melting icicles, trickled down his cheeks. Speaking more slowly, he said, "I asked Mom to make him stop, and she said `Bobby, no' and he said 'Shut up, whore,' and she did. She didn't fight him or anything; she just got real stiff. It was awful and yet . . . I liked being on my mom like that.

"When it was over, Bobby threw me off the bed. And do you know what she said then? 'Bobby, don't be mad at me.' He started cussing her and wasn't paying any attention to me, so I got out of the room. I put some clothes on and left the house. We lived beside the Saluda Woods, so I cut through the woods to the river, and, even though it was cold, I went in the water and stayed there for a long time. I don't know how long. I just remember that the water was a lot warmer than the air, so when I finally got out, I was freezing. I went up to this gully where I sometimes played; it had big rocks at the bottom that formed a little cave. I stayed in that cave until sunup even though I shivered so bad I couldn't stop my teeth from clicking, but I wasn't going back to the house until Bobby left. I don't remember being angry, or hurt, or anything except cold. And wanting to kill Bobby.

"When it started to get light I went to the edge of the woods and watched until I saw Bobby leave. Then I went into the house and Mom was in the kitchen drinking coffee and smoking a cigarette. She looked pretty bruised up. But do you know what she said? 'Get ready for school.' That's all she said, 'Get ready for school.' Then she went back to her bedroom and shut the door.

"Damned if I was going to school. I didn't want anyone to see me. I hated them all, anyway. So I changed into dry clothes and a sweater, got some baloney, bread, a kitchen knife and some other stuff, and went back into the woods. This old guy next door was always threatening to sic his dog on me if I didn't stay off his property, so I sicced me on his dog.

"I didn't come home until the sun was going down. Mom was at the kitchen table, smoking a cigarette and drinking booze from a jelly glass. She didn't ask me where I'd been. She just told me that we needed to go to the bus station before Bobby came home because her sister wanted me to come stay with her for a while. Just a little while, she said.

"She packed me some clothes in a paper bag and drove me to the bus station. Neither of us said anything the whole trip. At the station, she let me play pinball while we waited. Just before I got on the bus, she leaned down real close, and I could smell the liquor on her breath and it made me think of the night before. Then she told me to never tell our secrets to anyone, no matter what. Made me promise. And that's the last time I ever saw or talked to my mother.

"Goddamn her!" Drum said. His eyes still shut, he turned his face toward the back wall.

"I'm sorry," someone said, his voice breaking. "What happened to you was terrible."

Drum opened his eyes and turned his head to stare at Joe, a sudden fear and rage growing inside. Overcome by the intensity of his memories, he had not been aware that he was speaking, and that this man had heard everything, that this man knew his shame. Drum swiped at his tears with the sleeve of his jumpsuit, then stood and squeezed his fists around the bars, looking down at Joe. "You tricked me into making up lies," he said. "If you ever tell anyone these lies, I swear I'll kill you."

Joe sat upright and meet Drum's stare. "I'm your pastor. Your confidences are sacred. On penalty of my immortal soul, I will never tell anyone. Never."

Once again, Drum tried to stare down this nothing man, but Joe held firm. After twenty or thirty seconds, Drum turned away, lit a cigarette, then paced for a minute before coming back to the front of the cell and glaring down at Joe. "Get me a pen, some paper, and two envelopes. Then get the hell out of here. I need to write a couple of letters. And I want you to make sure they get delivered."

When Joe returned with the writing supplies, Drum said, "That stuff I told you, you know I made it up because I was mad about the phone call. I didn't think even you were dumb enough to believe it. Now get the fuck out of my sight."

V

Joe again sat in the waiting room and thought about what Drum had just told him. It was a story torn from the Book of Cain, a story of how the Beast grew strong by feeding on pain and weakness. And seeing this endless cycle of tragedy begetting tragedy, Joe found himself wondering what had damaged Rebekah Drum? He had a pretty good guess of what had taken her innocence and turned her promiscuous and besotted, and this made him want to cry for everyone.

Alone, Joe struggled with this terrible sadness.

Perhaps twenty-five minutes passed before Lieutenant Jenkins crisply walked through the door from the holding area. Sweat beaded on Jenkins's dark face, but his voice remained as matter-of-fact as ever. "You need to go back and sit with him, no matter what," he said to Joe. "He used a cigarette to burn himself a couple of times on the back of his hand. Said it made him feel better. If we take his smokes away, we might have a fight. So we're gonna let him smoke and you're gonna watch him. But don't tell him you're watching him or else he'll do something for spite. One more thing. He wrote two letters and you're gonna play mailman again—this time with official approval."

.   .   .   `

Drum lay on his bunk, staring at the ceiling. His right hand rested on his chest with a cigarette between his fingers; his left lay on his stomach and had a pair of red welts just above the knuckles. Two envelopes were on the metal stand. Joe picked them up. One was addressed to the television correspondent, Amanda Slade, the other to the FBI agent, Keenan. "Do you still want me to take these?" he asked.

"Yeah," Drum said, his voice flat. He didn't look at Joe or move other than to take hits off the cigarette.

Joe put the letters in his inside jacket pocket. "If you've no objections," he said, "I'm going to read from Psalms for a while."

Drum said nothing, and Joe began reading some of his favorite passages. He was still reading at 11:45, when Jenkins and three COs entered the holding area and secured Drum in restraints. Not knowing what else to do, Joe read as they shaved Drum's head, first with electric clippers, then a safety razor. While they were doing this, Drum's eyes darted about and he seemed to have trouble swallowing. Next, they shaved his right leg from knee to ankle. So far, Drum was not fighting them.

49

AFTERMATH

I

POLICE, FORENSIC techs, and EMTs moved in and out of the porch's light at Bradley Miller's house. The wind had picked up even more, whirling through the woods in an almost continuous roar and tousling the hair of Marianne, Zack, and Keenan as they stood on the porch. Marianne had put on a dark suede jacket and her arm was around Zack's waist. Rather than resist his mother's comfort, Zack placed his arm around her waist. Keenan stood beside Marianne, silently watching EMTs carry Stith from the house and slide the stretcher into an ambulance.

They had worked on Stith for a good while before moving him. Tubes ran down his throat and up his nose, and an IV hung from a short rod attached to the stretcher. Stith's face looked ashen and flaccid. He had a punctured lung, but the blood loss was even more critical. If Mrs. Paulus had not stemmed the bleeding there would be no need for haste. As it was, the odds remained against him, but at least, stubborn and tough, he had a fighting chance.

Earlier, another ambulance had left with Solomon Paulus, who had at least one fractured rib and severe testicular bruising. Mrs. Paulus had climbed into the ambulance with her son.

A third ambulance would not depart until the bodies had been photographed, marked, and measured. The body of Jeffcoat County policeman Billy McGrady would accompany that of Wayne Rawson to the Jeffcoat morgue. They had found McGrady's body at the edge of the woods in back of the house, his throat cut. Marianne told Keenan that McGrady was one of the officers who found Will after his murder. She also said that he had two daughters, ages six and nine.

They had also discovered a motorcycle ditched in the woods off an old logging road on Miller's property. The motorcycle belonged to Beatrice Roberts's grandson, who was away in the navy. Topographical maps were found in the motorcycle's boot that had "E. Roberts" penciled in the corner—Eaton Roberts was Beatrice's deceased husband. Judging by the beer and soda cans and sandwich wrappers, Rawson had waited in the woods for several hours.

Keenan and Marianne had each given brief accounts of what happened and would give more detailed statements after seeing Stith off. Moments earlier, the ranking officer had put a hand on Keenan's shoulder and said, "Let me know if there's anything I can do." And from the way all the officers watched Marianne, Keenan almost expected them to doff their hats and bow.

A paramedic had checked Keenan. Both wrists were bruised and if he squeezed his right hand an electric burst stung the side all the way down into his little finger. His nose had scabbed and swollen a little. Livid bruises on his back and side remained tender to the touch. Otherwise, he was unhurt, except that he could not go back into the house, not yet. And, surprisingly, he felt nothing; it was as if he was merely an observer, removed and distant from all that had happened.

Alvin Owens led Bradley Miller onto the porch and they watched the ambulance pull away. Miller had a blanket wrapped round his shoulders and moved with feeble steps. Alvin said he would take Bradley home with him for a couple of days. Before the ambulance was out of sight, Alvin put his arm around Miller's shoulder and guided him back inside. Marianne had always told Keenan that Alvin was a good and nurturing man.

Marianne planned to go to the hospital and await word on Stith. Wes Felton had offered to drive her there, where her mother and sister were already waiting. Caroline Carmichael, whose home was in Tennessee, would go with Marianne and then spend the night at Marianne's house. Felton had arranged police protection for the Paxtons through tomorrow.

The ambulance's flashing lights disappeared around the driveway's curve and that broke the trance. "I guess I'll go finish my statement so that we can leave," Marianne said. "Why don't you come with us? You really shouldn't be alone tonight."

Keenan shook his head. Though he remained cut off from his emotions, there was something he had to do, something that, despite everything that had happened, he still craved. "Marianne . . . I'm going to take Stith's place at Drum's execution."

"No, John. You've done enough." She put her hand on his shoulder. "Drum's execution doesn't matter. It never did, not really. I should have put him out of my mind years ago. Please don't do this."

"I think having a witness there does matter. And I feel . . . as though something is incomplete between Drum and myself. I want to see it though to the end. I need to do this . . . for myself."

Marianne put her hand to his cheek and said, "I won't argue with you. Or deny you anything that you want, ever. But are you sure?"

"Absolutely," Keenan answered. He then took out his cell phone and handed it to Marianne. "I'll call you when it's over."

Marianne studied Keenan for a moment, then nodded. "All right. I'll call the prison and get you approved. John, please call me as soon as it's over because I won't rest until I know you're okay."

"Don't worry, I'll be fine," Keenan said, pretending, as much for himself as for Marianne, that his confidence in his toughness had not been shaken.

II

Heavy rain began to fall as Keenan drove to Golgotha. Wipers beating furiously, Keenan hunched over the wheel to better track the blurred headlights. He left the driver's-side window open about an inch, even as rain blew in with the fresh air—he could not bear being completely shut in. At one point, his hands trembled so badly that he had to pull over. He told himself that this was simply a delayed reaction and that it would soon pass.

For some strange reason, while pulled to the side of the road trying to calm himself, Keenan thought of how monks had once flailed their flesh with barbed thongs, seeking to punish and drive out their human weakness. And he had a sudden intuitive understanding of their misery and of what they sought. Atonement for the undeserving came only through suffering. That was righteous.

By sheer force of will, Keenan stopped his hands from trembling. Still breathing heavily, he pulled back into traffic and cranked the air conditioner to its maximum setting.

He had to make the execution. He had to bear witness for Will. He had to be at this final reckoning. Tonight, both he and Drum must atone for their mistakes.

50

cold comfort

I

THE RAIN had slowed to a drizzle when Keenan reached Golgotha's parking area. Crowded and chaotic beneath bright lights, it reminded him of a carnival midway. A small group opposed to the death penalty lit candles and sang hymns while rowdies there to toast the execution jeered and whooped. Loudest of all were the hungry reporters yelling enticements like carneys hawking their games of chance, promising Keenan fame in exchange for an exclusive on the attack at Bradley Miller's place. Keenan walked to the covered walkway without even a flicker of a glance their way.

The checkpoint had been moved to the parking-lot side of the walkway and was manned by four CO's, all with sergeant's stripes. A tall man in an overcoat told the beefy CO who squinted at Keenan's ID that Keenan was a late approval and not on the list. This man introduced himself as Deputy Warden Crawford and told Keenan he would take him to the Administrative Suite where the other witnesses waited. Keenan nodded and followed without speaking. He didn't care if the tight control with which he held himself came across as unfriendliness or arrogance, or whatever people might think of him. It mattered only that in Drum's final moments, as he sought a face he knew, he would find Keenan and see the mocking contempt in his eyes.

Golgotha's grounds were as brightly lit as the parking area. Rainwater glittered like prisms on the razor wire and turned the building's stones dark and grainy. Tall and grim in their long raincoats, Keenan and the

Deputy Warden might easily have been mistaken as executioners as they crossed the grounds and entered the massive building.

The administrative suite was nicely appointed with two couches, a secretary's desk, and a half dozen walnut and glass doors with names and titles stenciled in black-bordered gold. A table with coffee and pastries sat against one wall. Four men and one woman were gathered around one of the couches, all of them reporters selected by lot. A couple of the reporters nodded a greeting and one of them, a lean man in his forties with a shock of dark hair, hawk-beak nose, and eyes that seemed set too close together, started toward him. Keenan thrust his palm out and shook his head no. The reporter hesitated, perhaps weighing if he should test the hardness of Keenan's glare.

"I'm going to wait outside," Keenan told the Deputy Warden. The suite felt humid and airless, anyway.

Moments later, Keenan stood under the small alcove leaning against one of the glass doors as he waited for the van to pick them up. He checked his watch. It was 12:30. By now, Drum would have showered and put on green fatigues, with the right pants leg split to the knee. He might still be pacing in his cell or maybe they had already asked him to go to the bathroom, whether he needed to or not; after which, a thick rubber band would be wrapped around his penis and a wad of cotton stuffed into his rectum. Everything done by protocol, everything precisely timed.

II

As witness for the victim's family, Keenan entered first. He hesitated at the door; the room, a long rectangle, looked small and the seven folding chairs seemed pushed too close together. A glass partition separated the witness room from the execution chamber and gave the room a bit more of an open feel. Keenan took a deep breath and entered. He sat in the second chair from the left, the seat most directly in front of the electric chair. The five other witnesses filed in behind him, the only sounds being the scuffing of shoes and rustle of clothing—they were an unusually quiet lot. The Deputy Warden overseeing the witnesses, the same man who had escorted Keenan inside, entered last. He walked to where Keenan sat, bent, and whispered, "The witness for the condemned man will come through this side door and sit in the seat on your left. If you think it might be awkward sitting next to the condemned man's witness, I'm sure the guy beside you would change seats."

"I prefer this seat," Keenan said, looking straight ahead. He could care less who sat beside him, but he felt palpable relief as the Deputy Warden stopped crowding him and moved away. He forced down two breaths, not as deeply as he would like, then looked into the chamber. On the back wall, a black-rimmed clock read 12:50. By now, Drum would be in restraints and surrounded by large capable men. The Warden had probably finished reading the death warrant, and might talk to Drum as his men applied conducting gel to his head and leg.

Keenan drew in another breath, but had to force it down. The room felt so damn warm. Keenan thought his breathing loud and obvious because no one talked and the only sounds came from overly cautious movements. He tried to breathe more quietly, but the effort increased his tension. He knew the more he focused on his discomfort the worse it would get, so he distracted himself by studying the execution chamber.

Sturdy and regal, like well-crafted mountain furniture, the electric chair sat on a low dais. The dark grain of the thick seat and arms matched that of the finest oak furniture. The chair's back rose high enough that not even Keenan's head would reach the top. Pliant straps were attached to the chair's arms, legs, headrest, at chest level, and there was a wide lap restraint to prevent the convulsing man's hips from thrusting upward.

Suspended from the ceiling, a white metal pipe ended about three feet above the chair. Dangling from it was a finger-width black wire with a rounded metal cap at the end. Beneath the chair, another black wire lay coiled loosely around a blunt terminal.

Keenan looked around at the rest of the chamber. Attached to the far wall on his left was the mandatory red telephone. Once Warden Edwards completed his other duties, he would stand beside this phone. Positioned there, he would be facing a broad one-way mirror, behind which waited the three official executioners, all volunteers drawn from a pool of Department of Corrections employees. Edwards would give them two signals: on the first, each executioner threw an arming switch; at the second signal, they pressed an activating button. Unlike firing squads, whose marksmen say they can tell by the gun's recoil whether their charge is real or a dud, a one-second delay from activation to delivery prevented these executioners from ever knowing who delivered the fatal charge.

Keenan checked the clock—only 12:53. The room had become unbearably hot. He glanced again at the chair's regal shape and was reminded of the chair his father had bought at an antique shop shortly before his death, that he and Keenan planned to strip and restore. The chair was a Federalist reproduction and they didn't care if restoring it lowered its value, they wanted to learn woodworking together, and they had started the slow process of stripping it inch by inch on the evening before his father died.

Keenan shook off this intrusive memory of his father, annoyed by it and now breathing harder.

"Are you all right," the man sitting on his right whispered. It was the dark-haired, hawk-nosed reporter who had started to approach him while waiting in the administrative suite.

"I'm fine," Keenan said, without taking his eyes from the chamber.

"Look, when this is over, I'd like to hear all about the Rawson manhunt and murder," the man said.

Keenan turned to stare down this irritating man, but they were too close, he felt smothered by the man's nearness and averted his eyes back to the chamber. "When I'm ready, I'll make a statement."

"The public has a right to know all that happened. And from what I hear, you could become a hero with the right coverage."

Still staring straight ahead, Keenan said, "If you bother me again, I'm going to ask the Deputy Warden to move you."

"Maybe later," the reporter said, smiling.

Keenan checked the clock, 12:54. It might be another two or three minutes before they brought in Drum. Keenan was having difficulty sitting still and it seemed that all these people were using up the breathable air.

By 12:55, sweat trickled down Keenan's forehead and he could not stop thinking about the cool night air that waited just outside the door. An impulse to flee seized him and his breathing broke into snorting gasps.

"Are you okay," the irritating man beside him asked. "Your breathing . . . it sounds as though you're having trouble."

"It's warm in here," Keenan said, hoarsely. "That's all."

Shrugging, the man said, "Not much longer."

"Yeah," Keenan said and gripped his pants to prevent his hands from trembling the way they had on the drive here. His chest felt as if an invisible cinch was squeezing out all his air.

At last, Warden Edwards came through a doorless entrance at the back of the chamber. Precise and formal, Lt. Jenkins followed Edwards, and then came a knot of officers with Drum shuffling in the middle. Separated by the glass partition, they moved in eerie silence. The two largest COs held Drum's upper arms. At the entrance, Drum visibly balked. The muscles in the officers' necks tightened as they closed and forced Drum to take his next step. Stiff legged and trembling, Drum again walked on his own.

Beneath the bright lights, Drum already seemed an apparition; his pockmarked face drooped and was as pale as his shaved head. Gone was the sneer. Only Drum's eyes remained animated, darting about, his pupils absorbing most of the iris.

Trailing Drum, with one hand on the condemned man's shoulder and reading from a red Bible, came Joe Cameron. His eyes also looked large behind his thick lenses, and the Bible trembled.

A new anxiety seized Keenan. Cameron was weak. What if he couldn't handle witnessing an execution? What if he bolted from the room? What if that triggered Keenan to do the same?

They reached the electric chair and Drum again balked. This time the officers' coercion was more obvious as they turned him and pushed him into the oak seat. In a coordinated flurry, straps were cinched and leg irons and waist chain removed for the last time, until only Drum's head had not been strapped. The officers moved back and everyone left the execution chamber except for Edwards, Jenkins, Cameron, and the condemned. It was 12:59.

Jerkily, Drum looked around until he saw Keenan. For eight years Keenan had wanted this moment, a moment of final triumph and gloating. But he was already so tense, and looking at Drum caused his chest to constrict even more tightly. Keenan looked away.

Jenkins stood on one side of the chair, Cameron on the other. Warden Edwards walked over to the red phone and threw a switch on the wall beside it. The voice of Cameron, surprisingly strong, suddenly issued from speakers in the witness room: "In thee of Lord I put my trust. Deliver me in thy righteousness." Then he stopped. Drum now looked at Cameron, who placed a hand on Drum's arm. Even when Warden Edwards walked solemnly to the chair and asked Drum if he had any final words, Drum looked only at Cameron. Even as his mouth opened, quivered, and nothing came out, he looked at Cameron. Finally, barely audible, he said, "I'm sorry."

Cameron squeezed Drum's arm one last time before Jenkins escorted him from the chamber. A moment later, the minister awkwardly waddled through the door on Keenan's left and took the seat beside him. Nervously, Cameron smiled at Keenan. Keenan, his teeth clenched, saw Cameron's weak smile turn into concern as he scanned Keenan's face. Then Cameron jerked his gaze back to the chamber where Drum still watched him with eyes whose irises had completely disappeared.

Warden Edwards again stood by the telephone while Lieutenant Jenkins, with practiced efficiency, placed a leather strap with an attached black satin hood around Drum's forehead. As Jenkins pulled the strap tight, Drum's head jerked back against the oak slats. Now, Drum's only visible movements were the heaving of his chest and the shiny hood pulsing in and out with each rapid breath.

Using small buckles on the sides of the head restraint, Jenkins secured the metal cap to Drum's head. This done, he went to stand beside Edwards near the red telephone.

Trapped in this small room and unable to breathe, Keenan's knuckles whitened and his fingers cramped as he gripped his pants legs tighter. Edwards looked at the mirror and raised his hand. Keenan's chest constricted, forcing out a small moan. His heart thumped near the bursting level. If he didn't get out of here, he knew he would die. Doing this had been a mistake; he wasn't strong enough, and his fleeing would shame all those wounded people that he was here representing. Hubris again—his mortal sin, hubris.

Keenan was one heartbeat from bolting, when a soft moist hand squeezed his clenched fist. Looking down, he saw Cameron's pudgy hand gripping his. Keenan let go his pants and fastened his hand around Cameron's, squeezing so hard the minister winced just as Edwards lowered his arm.

For one breathless second nothing happened. Then two thousand volts found ground and Drum pitched forward. A blue-white shimmer surrounded Drum as his body strained against every strap, quivering in a wholly unnatural way. A burnt, acrid smell reached the witness room. Keenan concentrated on holding on to Cameron's hand, knowing it was the only anchor preserving his worthless dignity.

At last, Drum's body stopped shaking and sagged against the straps. A steamy haze floated above the chair. Nothing broke the stillness.

The second surge jolted the body back into its unhallowed death dance. Oddly, these eight seconds did not seem as long as the first five. Then it was over.

A smoky mist hung above the sagging body. No one moved. Finally, a CO and a tall lean man with a stethoscope in his right hand came through the doorless entrance. Alone, the man approached the body. With the rubber tips in his ears, he placed the stethoscope's bell against Drum's chest and jerked his hand back—he had forgotten that the body was hot. Holding the stethoscope further up the tubing, he again placed it against the chest and listened for what seemed an excessively long time. At last, he looked at Warden Edwards and said, "He's dead."

Edwards walked over to face the witnesses and said, "Let the record note that Isaac Abraham Drum was pronounced dead at 1:08 A.M. Execution order 47-302 has been carried out. On behalf of the State of South Carolina, I would like to thank each of you for your willingness to participate in this duty."

With that said, Edwards nodded, and, from behind him, Keenan heard the door open and someone said, "This way, please."

With a way out available, the band on Keenan's chest relaxed and he inhaled deeply. He released Cameron's hand, which had turned bluish red from being squeezed so hard. He risked a quick look at Cameron and saw the man's cheeks wet with tears. Still teetering and unable to handle intimate contact, Keenan looked at the lifeless form sagging in the chair. He felt nothing. It was just a body, now. When it cooled enough to be handled, it would be placed on a gurney and, after cooling some more, sent to be sliced and sawed in a mandatory autopsy. Soon after the autopsy, the state would bury the body in an unmarked grave in the pauper's section of Elmwood Cemetery. If only the consequences of Drum's hate could be buried with him. But that task was left to the living.

III

A drenching rain fell outside the Capital Punishment Facility. At the door, a CO opened a lockbox and Cameron took out his wallet, keys, belt, and a few other things. Once he had put all his personal items back in place, Cameron hurried down the steps and into a waiting van. Close behind him, Keenan made his dash. Wipers stroking rapidly, the van eased along the gravel road and through the wide gates to the administration building. Several employees with umbrellas bustled from the glass doors and helped the witnesses inside.

In the administration suite, no one showed much interest in the replenished coffee and snacks. Only Joe sat; most shuffled restlessly or, like Keenan, leaned against a wall. A couple of the reporters talked quietly.

After a short wait, Warden Edwards hurried in and threw his sopping-wet coat across the back of his secretary's chair. "I hope I haven't delayed you too long," Edwards said, as he unlocked his office. Briefly Edwards disappeared inside and came out carrying a thick manila folder. "There are four copies of the death certificate. Each of you need to make sure that you sign all four in the area marked 'witnesses.' I'm going to lay them out and ask you to move by one at a time. When you finish, you may use one of the telephones in the surrounding offices. A counselor is available if anyone wants to talk to him, and no one will ever know unless you tell them. In a couple of days, I'll call each of you with the same offer. And over the next few weeks, if you have trouble sleeping or anything like that, the Department of Corrections will arrange for counseling. Any questions?" Edwards asked, surveying each face, and seeming to pause a bit longer as he looked at Joe.

"Again, on behalf of the State of South Carolina and the Department of Corrections I want to thank each of you for your willingness to assume this responsibility. Mr. Keenan, as witness for the victim's family, I'd like you to sign on the first line, and then you may use the phone in my office if you want to make any calls. All right, ladies and gentleman, if I can get your signatures we can all go about our business. And please, make them legible."

.   .   .

Keenan sat at Edwards's large desk, the telephone pulled close beside the blotter. He dialed the number for his cell phone and Marianne answered on the second ring. Immediately, she asked, "John, are you all right?"

He still felt nothing, no great release, no elation, no feeling of having been cleansed. He did not even feel anything for Drum one way or the other. It was as if he were empty.

"I'm fine," he told Marianne. "How's Stith?"

"He's still in critical condition. But he's probably too pigheaded not to pull through."

"I think you're right," Keenan reassured her. "How about Zack? How's he doing?"

"He's trying to take care of me," she said. "I honestly think he's handling it better than I am. At least for now. First thing tomorrow I'll call our counselor and get us an appointment."

"And how are you doing?" Keenan asked.

"It's strange. I guess I expected the execution to bring about some huge catharsis, but I don't feel anything right now. Except relief, and tremendous gratitude for what you did. As far as *he* goes, I just want to forget him and get on with my life." Marianne paused. "John . . . Zack and I have been talking ever since we left Bradley Miller's, and . . . he told me what you said about feeling responsible for Will's death."

Keenan rubbed his forehead and his face flushed with shame.

"John, I've always thought that you had something to do with Will's promotion, and I've always been grateful for your faith in him. You gave him a chance to do what he had worked hard to earn. And he solved the case. My husband was a hero because you believed in him."

A terrible sadness made it difficult for Keenan to speak. What Marianne said did not seem right. She didn't understand, not completely. Keenan needed to confess everything. He swallowed and told her the worst. "I knew Will was not handling the pressure very well . . ." —Keenan breathed in deeply—"and I did nothing."

"What could you have done? Have him removed and humiliate him? I could never have forgiven you if you'd done that. But you stood by him, and he proved you right. John, even if you had spoken up and crushed Will's pride things might still have turned out the same. Take my word for it, the 'what ifs' will drive you crazy."

Keenan's eyes felt watery. He did not deserve such forgiveness. When he didn't speak, Marianne said, "Zack feels the way I do. John, don't do this to yourself, please?"

"All right," Keenan said hoarsely. "And thank you." He felt utter devotion to Marianne, much like the disciples must have felt when their sins were forgiven. He did not deserve such grace, but Marianne had given it anyway.

"Why don't you come over and wait with us?" Marianne offered.

"I need to walk for a while. But I'll call you later today and, if it's all right, come by this evening."

"I'd like that a lot," she told him.

Keenan hung up the phone and sat for several seconds, grateful and overwhelmed. His emotions threatened to bring tears, but he held on. The grace of Marianne's forgiveness said more about her than him. Her decency did not erase his wrong.

Moving slowly, Keenan went to the door and opened it. Outside the Warden's office, Joe Cameron sat hunched at the secretary's desk talking quietly into the telephone. "Yes, I'm sure I'm all right . . . No, I really am . . . No, don't wait up, I might be a while . . . Sure . . . See you in the morning . . . I love you too."

This man, for whom Keenan had felt such contempt, had also shown him undeserved decency. There were things he needed to say to Cameron. Keenan stepped from the Warden's office just as one of the other doors opened and the reporter who had sat beside Keenan came out. "Glad you guys are still here," the man said. "I, ah . . . I don't usually feel this way, but I don't particularly want to be alone right now."

"I know what you mean," Cameron said.

"And if there's anything either of you want to get on the record I'd like to hear it. And," he quickly added, holding up his hands in response to Keenan's glare, "if you don't, that's fine too. You fellows mind if we walk out together?"

. . .

The rain had again slowed to a drizzle when they exited the walkway into the parking area, which had the dark glare of rain-slicked streets. Most of the onlookers had gone. The reporters remained, and shouted hoarse questions as the three men came out of the walkway. Joe bent forward as if bucking a strong wind, Keenan walked with total indifference, and the hawk-nosed reporter veered over to share his experience with his peers.

Standing beside Joe's Caravan, they were finally alone and Keenan said, "I want to thank you for . . . helping me during the execution. I'm . . . very grateful."

"It helped me too. I'm still so keyed up. I, ah, don't really want to be alone right now, but I don't want to be around people who weren't there and might ask questions, because I don't want to talk about it. Does that make sense?"

Keenan nodded. "I understand how you feel." Keenan had done what he needed and wanted to be away, wanted to walk and think. Yet it was obvious that Cameron wanted company, a natural human response to trauma. And it seemed ungrateful for Keenan to turn his back on this man's simple need. "Joe, there's a park on the other side of the prison. I'm going there to walk for a while. Would you care to join me?"

"I'd like that," said Joe. "It's been a helluva week."

IV

Night and mist had turned the Saluda into a black River Styx. Drizzle dimmed the streetlights and darkened the wide asphalt path as Joe and Keenan walked, each absorbed in his own thoughts. Both were bareheaded, and the chilly dampness caused Keenan to button his overcoat. To accommodate Joe, Keenan kept the pace at little more than a stroll and surprisingly this pace felt all right.

In contrast to the easy pace, Keenan remained in turmoil, not about Drum but as a result of the extraordinary kindness of Marianne and Joe. And what he now saw with great clarity was his own persistent failure to treat others decently. He had been deceitful and conniving with Marianne, ready to sully Stith's character, and he had very much wanted to hurt Trent Coover. And what of Mary Bishop, whom he had manipulated into betraying family secrets. The only person he had not treated in some deceitful manner was Zack. Was that because he wanted nothing from the boy? Or because he had already done him the greatest harm?

All week long, Keenan had chosen to deceive, bully, insult, and manipulate. He had told himself that such corruption was necessary in order to stop Drum and make sure that justice was done. Keenan had also blamed Drum for the hate he felt. But if Drum could make Keenan hate him, then he had some control over what Keenan felt, and even over what he did. Never, thought Keenan. Never! Drum did not control one thing about me. So my hatred of him comes out of my judgments and is, therefore, my doing. I've always judged harshly, that's just the way I am.

Suddenly, Keenan felt terribly lonely and tried to remember if he had ever truly been close to anyone. Of course he had, his mother. Needing to feel some kind of intimate connection, Keenan tried to recall times when they had felt particularly close, but other memories came.

Keenan's earliest memory was of his father digging the foundation for a cinder block work shed. His father was always working on some project, always trying to improve things. Keenan was maybe six or seven at the time and asked to help. His father, a large man who operated heavy equipment for a living, put his rough hands around Keenan's smaller ones and showed him how to use the spade. Then he stood back and Keenan dug furiously, but to little effect. His father did not mind if it took longer to finish, but smiled and patiently watched.

Other memories. The pride in his father's face after Keenan's junior high football games. His father showing him how to use a wood plane. The night Keenan realized that he was teaching his father the new math, and how proud they both were. Laughing in his father's workshop as they stripped the high-backed chair on their last night together.

For all his adult life, whenever Keenan thought of his father he had remembered him only as the drunk who slaughtered a young mother and her child. The drunk whose infamy forced Keenan to carry himself with defiant pride throughout adolescence. The drunk who, rather than Keenan show lack of character by badmouthing the dead, he never mentioned, even privately.

Now, as memories flooded Keenan, there was not one recollection of his father being drunk or even drinking. The accident had happened because his father had a few drinks with the boys and then tried to drive home—a stupid choice with disastrous consequences. For a hurting adolescent, joining the anger at his father and putting distance between them had been easier than grieving—nothing blocks pain like anger. And he had severed himself so completely from his father that Keenan attributed all of his better qualities solely to his mother's influence. Certainly, his pride, self-containment, and uncompromising sense of responsibility came from her. But he now remembered that his father was intensely curious, paid attention to details, and constantly strove to do things better.

His father had not been a monster, but a flawed man, and a basically good man.

Keenan's long-held grief threatened to break loose when Joe again saved him by suddenly exclaiming, "Oh my goodness, I almost forgot. I have a letter for you. A couple of hours before he died, Drum wrote letters to you and to a reporter and he asked me to give them to you."

Fishing in his jacket pocket, Joe pulled out both envelopes and squinted in the dim light to decipher the names. He handed one to Keenan.

Keenan tore open the envelope and used a penlight attached to his key ring to read the letter. When he finished, he looked at Joe and said, "I think you better give me the other letter."

"Ah, ah, you know I can't do that."

"You better," Keenan said and held out his hand.

"I can't." Joe squinted at Keenan, confused. "You know I can't."

"Then I better explain the facts of life," Keenan said gruffly. "First, I'm betting that tonight Drum told you something that he had never told anyone, something to do with his childhood that he thought was horrible and shameful. Am I right?"

"I . . . ah, I can't reveal a pastoral confidence."

"I'm not asking for the damn details. I just want you to confirm that he revealed something he thought shameful."

Joe shook his head, looked down, and repeated, "I can't betray a confidence. I gave my word."

For a hard second, Keenan stared at him, then said, "So you gave your word? Well, you haven't betrayed your word, but read this." He handed Joe the note and penlight.

As he read, Joe mouthed the words. When he read it a second time, his mouth hung open. "That's not true. It's a lie," he said, his eyes wide and afraid behind his thick glasses as he looked at Keenan.

The letter read: "All my crimes can be traced to being sexually molested by the man who delivered this note, Joe Cameron, when he was pretending to be my Big Brother. Isaac Drum."

"If I'd been working with him tonight," Keenan said, "I might have gotten at the same things you did, and, as a result, he would have tried something like this with me."

"Why?" Why would he do that?" Joe asked, his mouth quivering.

"Revenge for you knowing what he was most ashamed of. Insurance by discrediting anything you might reveal. The pettiness and cruelty of his nature. Turning you into a surrogate for anger he couldn't express anywhere else—lots of reasons. The bottom line is that he wanted to hurt you as much as he could. So you better give me the other letter because I'm sure it says the same thing."

"But I promised."

"Joe, you did your job. But destroying your life wasn't part of the bargain. If you give this to a reporter, he or she will have to make it public. Even when the allegation is dismissed as a crock, the damage to you and your family will have been done, and there will always be some who want to believe you're a pervert. You could never work with kids again. You said you have a daughter; she'll have to defend her relationship with you. And your wife will have to defend both you and your daughter. Look, Joe, I know this letter is a lie. I owe you. Please, let me help you."

Slowly, Keenan held out his hand. Joe started to move, hesitated, then thrust the other letter into Keenan's open palm.

Ten feet up the walkway, a muddy path split the weeds to the Saluda. With faltering grace, Keenan negotiated his way to the river's dark edge. He placed both letters together and methodically tore them into strips, then ripped each strip into small pieces and let them fall onto the water. When finished, he watched until the last fragments of Isaac Drum's malice disappeared into the darkness.

Coming back up the path, Keenan slipped near the top and Joe grasped his hand to help him climb the last couple of feet. Then side by side, John Keenan and Joseph Cameron walked back to their waiting lives.